Sabrina wat
of combat a
the African natives were upon him, amazed that he
was the survivor . . . the victor of the "fight-to-the-
death" battle against their mightiest warriors. Their
shouts echoed through the clearing, shattering the
night.

Sabrina's eyes widened with fear as she watched
Michael stalk across the clearing toward her, his
powerful naked body glistening with sweat, appearing golden in the light of the raging bonfire. His
skin was covered with dirt and blood. Stopping in
front of the high throne upon which the natives had
set her, he glared up at her.

She tried to shrink back away from him. He
grasped her legs and yanked her down into his
muscular arms. His handsome face was bruised
. . . his eyes half crazed. Nothing she could do or
say would stop him now. He had risked his life to
possess her—and now he would claim his prize.

Sabrina's heart beat fiercely as he turned and
carried her off into the darkness of the jungle. . . .

*A handsome American flyer and a dashing En-
glish officer . . . both capture the lovely Sabrina's
heart, but before she can choose between them,
other men will use her—and abuse her—ruthlessly
forcing the innocent young beauty into making . . .*
Passion's Sweet Sacrifice

Also by Melissa Hepburne from
Pinnacle Books:

PASSION'S PROUD CAPTIVE

WRITE FOR OUR FREE CATALOG

If there is a Pinnacle Book you want—and
you cannot find it locally—it is available from
us simply by sending the title and price plus
50¢ per order and 10¢ per copy to cover mail-
ing and handling costs to:

Pinnacle Book Services
P. O. Box 690
New York, N.Y. 10019

Please allow 4 weeks for delivery. New York
State and California residents add applicable
sales tax.

————Check here if you want to receive our
catalog regularly.

PASSION'S SWEET SACRIFICE

by Melissa Hepburne

PINNACLE BOOKS • LOS ANGELES

To my parents,
Lenore and Jack,
with love.

This is a work of fiction. All the characters and
events portrayed in this book are fictional, and any
resemblance to real people or incidents is purely
coincidental.

PASSION'S SWEET SACRIFICE

*Copyright © 1979 by Melissa Hepburne and
H. Broude*

All rights reserved, including the right to reproduce
this book or portions thereof in any form.

An original Pinnacle Books edition, published for the
first time anywhere.

First printing, May 1979

ISBN: 0-523-40471-9

Cover illustration by Bill Maughan

Printed in the United States of America

PINNACLE BOOKS, INC.
2029 Century Park East
Los Angeles, California 90067

Prologue

The French lieutenant bound her wrists behind her back with a scarf, then led her over to the spot in front of the courtyard wall. The morning sun beat down on her. The drummers began a steady drumroll. "Do you weesh ze blindfold?" the lieutenant asked her.

Sabrina shook her head no, then raised her chin high. She would face her fate with dignity, she declared to herself. But it was hard, so very hard. She felt terribly afraid and alone.

As the uniformed French soldiers of the firing squad filed into a row many yards in front of her, she fought hard to hold back her tears. This was so unjust! Here she was barely twenty-one years old, an American citizen born and raised—about to be executed as a German spy. With the undeserved reputation of being the most famous, most desirable whore in all Europe. And all she had done was try to save the life of the man she loved.

The quartermaster came onto the field bearing the dolly-cart of loaded rifles that were to be used in her execution. As the weapons were passed out, Sabrina turned her thoughts back to the time when this had all started. It seemed like ages ago, but it was really only three short years ago, in 1914, just before the start of this horrible World War.

She had been an innocent, terribly naive child of eighteen. God, what an eternity of living she had crowded into her life since then! She had become the most celebrated cabaret dancer in France—a legend in her own time. She had found—and lost—the bold, strong, handsome man who had been the love of her life. But though fate had turned him against her, she loved him still, even now, no matter what he might think of her.

The drumroll became louder.

Oh God, she thought, what a pity he'd never learn the truth about her! That was what hurt most. She remembered how it all began, that strange, horrible day so many months ago . . .

PART I

A Legend in Her Own Time

Chapter 1

Sabrina ran desperately through the field of wild flowers, panting and gasping for breath. She looked sharply over her shoulder and her eyes went wide in terror. He was still coming after her!

She watched the hulking, brutish German baron running toward her, wearing his black, formal diplomatic attire, with the powder-blue waistcoat and the scarlet sash that cut diagonally across his chest. He was completely bald and had a thick brown walrus mustache.

Sabrina turned forward again and continued running. She crested the knoll, then began rushing down the other side, trampling the wild yellow geraniums and white daisies, not caring about anything but the need to escape. *How could this be happening*? she wondered in panic. Things like this don't happen in Washington, D.C. in this day and age!

The long skirt of her empire-style golden taffeta dress swirled up around her knees as she ran. The ends of the brown satin ribbon tied just beneath her bustline trailed in the breeze. Sabrina's fair skin was becoming flushed from exhaustion, and her wavy, strawberry-blond hair—so "strawberry" as to

4

be radiantly pink—was mussed and falling into her face.

"Stop running, you bitch!" Baron von Himmel shouted after her, enraged. "I vill make you pay for this!"

Sabrina ran even more furiously now, though she was so exhausted she knew she couldn't keep running much longer. Oh, she thought tormentedly, if only she hadn't come out into the secluded garden field today! But how was she to know Von Himmel would be motoring along the road with his aides, on the way to visit her father, Justin St. Claire, about State Department business?

She knew Von Himmel had been lusting after her ever since he first saw her at the diplomatic ball her father had hosted last year. Several times he had asked her out socially, though he was in his forties and she was only eighteen. At first, Sabrina turned him down *politely,* even though the bullish-looking man was repulsive to her. But then, catching her alone in the garden one day, he forcibly tried to plant a wet, resounding kiss on her lips. She slapped him and called him a pig, and ran from him. Since then, she had turned her nose up and ignored him whenever they met at any of her father's diplomatic functions.

"Stop running, *verdammen Sie!*" shouted Von Himmel.

Looking at him over her shoulder now, Sabrina saw that he was panting and red-faced, and slowing down. For a joyous moment, she thought she would escape him after all. But then she saw with horror that at his command his two aides were closing in on her from both sides of the field.

The baron was old, but his Prussian aides were

young and lithe and strong. Sabrina ran on in frantic desperation, but soon they had her, converging on her from opposite directions. She swiveled, and began screaming and scratching and kicking in wild fury as they grabbed her by her long hair and her arms. They lifted her off her feet and carried her to Von Himmel. They set her down in front of him, as he stood doubled over at the waist, his hands on his knees, gasping red-facedly for breath.

"You beast!" Sabrina shouted at him. "You Prussian pig! You better let me go. When my father finds out about this he'll—"

"He vill do nothing," said Von Himmel, looking up at her from beneath his bushy brows. He was still doubled over, panting to catch his breath. His beady-eyed stare became venomous. "You should not haf run from me, Fräulein," he scolded. "In Deutschland ve do not put up mit insolence from our vimmen."

"I'm not your woman!" she said, raising her head defiantly.

"You do not understand your situation," he said panting. "I explain it to you once more." As he spoke he stared at her lovely face: at her large, fiery, emerald-green eyes, her delicate upturned nose, her full rich lips. "I haf vanted you a long time, *Liebchen*. Now I can vait no longer. My government is transferring me to a new post in der tropics. Tahiti. I do not vish to be alone there. You vill come mit me as my wife, to please and satisfy me."

"You're crazy!" she shouted, struggling to break free from the two aides. "I'll never marry you. I despise you!"

Now Von Himmel stood up to his full, towering

6

height, and gazed at her scornfully. "You naive young girl," he answered. "You are a spoiled American child. You haf never known hardship. Life is a gay whirl for you. It is time you learned you do not always haf things der way you want them." He looked at his aides. "There is a way to *make* her marry me. Her father will have no choice but to consent after I . . ." He grinned wolfishly and rubbed his hands together. "Take off her clothes," he said.

Sabrina gasped as the aides began pulling off her taffeta dress, raising the hem up to her hips, exposing the smooth whiteness of her thighs. "Stop it," Sabrina screamed. "Let me go!" She twisted and turned and struggled frantically. One aide went down to the ground and held her ankles. Von Himmel's eyes were staring down in rapt absorption at Sabrina's long, shapely legs and her white underwear.

Sabrina cried out as her golden dress was jerked up over her breasts, then pulled over her head and taken off. She had on only a flimsy pink chemise now. The aide threw the dress to Von Himmel, who held it up close to his face, grinning with evil lewdness at Sabrina. He sniffed the dress, then rubbed it against his face. Then he tossed it back to the aide, and said, "Bind her."

Gasps of panic escaped Sabrina's lips as her arms were pinioned behind her and tied at the wrists and elbows with the taffeta dress. One of the aides ripped off her pink chemise. She screamed. Von Himmel came up to her, grasped the hem of her white underwear and pulled the garment down about her ankles. Sabrina moaned and tried to struggle, but when Von Himmel ordered his aides

7

to stand away from her, she stopped struggling immediately. She had to. Von Himmel had pulled her underwear around her ankles in such a way that if she made any movement at all, she would trip and fall to the ground.

She had to avoid that at all costs! She looked at the leering men surrounding her and knew there was nothing they would like better than to have her on the ground, helplessly writhing and twisting, unable to rise.

Sabrina couldn't help moaning with each breath she took, her face contorted in torment, her naked breasts rising and falling with her rapid breathing. She was forced to stand bare in the midst of the circle of men. The way her arms were tied behind her at the wrists and also at the elbows forced her shoulders back, making her firm, large breasts thrust brazenly forward.

Von Himmel was staring fixedly at the tuft of wispy hair at her naked sex. "You do not like my eyes upon you this way, eh, Fräulein?" he taunted, his face breaking out in beads of sweat. "Der eyes of a . . . what was it you called me? . . . a Prussian pig."

"Please," she said, breathing in shallow gasps, her eyelids half closed. "Let me go. Don't . . ." She let the words trail off, fearful that if she said them it might give him ideas.

"Don't what?" said Von Himmel mockingly. "Don't touch you? Is that what you vish to say?" He came up extremely close, and stood directly in front of her. She tensed. She wanted desperately to move back, but knew that if she made any movement while her ankles were held so tightly together, she would fall to the ground. She could only stand

8

there and watch tormentedly as his large, fat hand moved to her breast and grasped the underside of it.

She cried out. Von Himmel squeezed her breast, jiggling it up and down. "How do you like having a 'pig' like me touch you in such a way?" he taunted, leering at her. When she said nothing, showing her horror and revulsion in her eyes, he bent down and took the nipple in his mouth, between his teeth. He flicked it about with his tongue. "Aahhhnnnooo!" Sabrina groaned. He began sucking at her breasts hard, first one, then the other. His hand touched her between her thighs, and she jolted rigid, her eyes wide.

After a minute, he stepped away from her and began pulling off his clothing. "No!" screamed Sabrina, watching the formal diplomatic attire fall to the ground in a heap.

"*Ja!*" he answered gleefully, coming up to her again, naked. He was a very sturdily and plumply built man, though not at all fat. His skin was pink and hairless. His swollen, rigid male shaft touched against Sabrina, making her jerk.

"Please don't . . ." she said, shaking her head, pleading in a desperate whisper.

Suddenly Von Himmel put his hands around her and clutched her buttocks, drawing her tightly against him. He kissed her hard on the lips, and rubbed his naked torso bruisingly against her. He pinched her buttocks and began rubbing the underside of his shaft up and down against her stomach. When his hand moved around to the front of her and a finger slipped in between the petals of her femininity, Sabrina jerked spastically—and then bit him hard on his lips.

"*Ach!*" he screamed, jerking back. "Amerikan- ische bitch!" He shoved her in the breast, knocking her backward. She fell to the field, feeling the moistness of the flowers and grass beneath her. "Make her ready for me," Von Himmel ordered his aides.

Sabrina's underwear was removed from her an- kles, then her legs were spread wide apart and held that way. She screamed in blushing, agonizing tor- ment. She had never been seen unclothed by any man before, and now here she was being spread open and vulgarly displayed like this, abused in such a humiliating, degrading way!

Von Himmel got down on his knees inside her spread thighs. One hand went to her breasts and rubbed repeatedly down over them with great pressure. His other hand went to the mound of her womanhood and pressed inside. "*Stop it, oh stop it!*" Sabrina screamed, beginning to wail hysteri- cally as the wild physical sensations shot through her. "Please don't . . . uhhh! *Uhhh!*"

"Call me a pig, vill you," Von Himmel said in a throaty, angry voice, suspending himself above her, supporting his upper torso with his straightened sturdy arms. "You think you are too good for a baron of der kaiser's reich?" The tip of his shaft pressed against the lip of her womanhood now, though not penetrating. He looked down at her, grinning at the way she seemed to be frozen rigid with terror.

Then, without warning, he thrust savagely into her, breaking through, making her scream in agony. He began thrusting with a wild fervor, his grin un- abashedly gleeful, the sweat from his plump face and body dripping down onto her skin.

10

Sabrina moaned and cried against the pain and degradation, sobbing uncontrollably, whipsawing her body, arching her back in a vain effort to throw him off. Her head was snapping from side to side. She heard a high-pitched, tortured moan—"uh! . . . uh! . . . uh!"—and realized it was coming from her own mouth as each brutal thrust drove the sound out of her.

It seemed as if the torment would never end, but finally Von Himmel grunted a low animal sound, and ceased thrusting. She felt the hotness of him deep inside her, defiling her in the most intimate, horrible way.

Slowly he stood up. He looked down at her, smiling cruelly, seeming very pleased with himself. He started to get dressed. The two aides were still holding Sabrina's ankles apart, staring down at her lustfully. One of them turned to Von Himmel and said, "Baron, may we . . . ?"

"*Schweinhund!*" exclaimed Von Himmel, fiercely slapping him across the face. "You dare insult me mit such a suggestion? This is der woman I am about to wed!" He gestured at Sabrina as she lay on her back, spent, abused, without a shred of dignity remaining. He looked her in the eyes. "She does not believe it, but our little affair here has sealed her fate. Before the week is through, when I leave for my new post in der tropics, she will accompany me—as my *wife*."

To her horror, Sabrina found that it was true. When they finally released her and she went running hysterically back home, sobbing to her father about the brutal rape, he flew into a righteously indignant rage, cursing and stomping about the

11

room, swearing that Hun bastard Von Himmel would pay for this dearly.

St. Claire called the capital police and reported the incident, demanding Von Himmel's arrest, implying that if the police would call him once the German was apprehended, he would come down to the prison and beat him to death. Sabrina felt bitter satisfaction in knowing she would be properly avenged.

But then, something strange happened. The next afternoon, while Sabrina was still withering under the effects of the brutal assault, she was called down to the study for a meeting with her father. Her nanny, Lucille, came to her room to give her the message.

"What is it about, Lucille?" Sabrina asked warily. Her father very seldom had time for her during the day, especially when he was working on business affairs in his study.

"I don' know, honey," said the old black woman, "but if I's you, I'd git my tail down there right quick." Her expression became cautionary, as if she wanted to put Sabrina on her guard, but dared not say anything that would make her father angry with her; St. Claire was quick to accuse servants of disloyalty. "Chile," Lucille said warningly, "he ain't alone in there." She looked at Sabrina meaningfully, shrugged, and said nothing further.

When Sabrina entered the study, she saw the stranger. He was a mousy-looking man, who wore wire-frame glasses and had a black, satchel-type briefcase on his lap. He was sitting primly on the sofa, next to the bookcase partition that divided the room in half.

Her father did not bother to introduce the man.

He just sat behind his big, oaken desk, looking grim. "Sabrina," he began, ". . . sit down, please. I'd like to speak to you." He gestured her to a chair near his desk. His gesture and his posture were formal. He was always so serious and reserved with her. Ever since her mother died a year ago, there had been no love at all shown toward her in this house.

"Now," he said somberly, putting his chin in his hand, "about this Von Himmel affair. I have discussed the matter with various concerned parties, and the conclusion I've reached is that . . . well, perhaps there might be some equitable solution to the problem *other* than arrest and prosecution."

"What?" she cried, leaping to her feet in disbelief. "But he raped me!"

"Now let's not overreact here."

"He *raped* me!" she shouted furiously.

"Sit down!" he commanded, pointing her back into her chair with an unwavering finger. When she complied, he brushed back his impeccably slicked-down hair, cleared his throat, and said, "The fact of the matter is, there are other circumstances involved, which we must take into account."

He looked at her to see her response, pausing for her to ask: what circumstances? But Sabrina just glared at him in angry fury, saying nothing.

"For instance," he went on, "the baron happens to be a consular official. He has diplomatic immunity. You've been the daughter of a career diplomat long enough to know what that means. When someone has diplomatic immunity, they can't be arrested."

"But they can be disgraced!" she insisted. "They

13

can be kicked out of the country, and their career ruined!"

"True. But we don't want to be hasty about taking that alternative."

"But . . . but . . ." she was sputtering in disbelief, "he *raped* me!" She said it expecting that this alone would be enough to impel her father into action, especially considering his attitude yesterday. But he now acted as if it were some sort of minor offense, to be ignored. "What is it with you?" she shouted in frustration, rising to her feet. "How can you treat it so lightly? I'm your daughter! And this man brutally and vilely—"

"Yes, yes, but the fact is, my hands are tied." He stood up and began pacing about the spacious, mahogany-paneled study. "The police did arrest him. And I have spoken with . . . uh . . . his excellency, the baron. He denies the rape ever occurred. He says it's a disgrace and an insult that I accuse him of such a thing, that I actually called the police about it."

St. Claire looked angry, but—amazingly—his anger seemed directed at Sabrina rather than Von Himmel. "Now he's threatening to protest the incident to my superiors at the State Department. Frankly, this alleged rape has gotten quite out of hand."

Sabrina nearly exploded at the term "alleged," which made it seem as if the rape had never happened, as if she had invented the entire affair.

"Sabrina," her father continued, "Von Himmel is a baron; I'm a career diplomat. If I pursue the complaint against him, nothing will happen to him. He's too powerful and highly placed. But a lot will happen to me for causing an international scandal.

My career will be ruined. Fortunately, however, I've talked to his excellency and found that he's a very reasonable man."

He looked at Sabrina testingly, to see her reaction to his words. "The baron made what I consider a very equitable and fair offer to resolve this unfortunate situation to the satisfaction of . . . uh . . . all concerned."

"What offer?" she said icily, seething with rage. Oh, she should never have expected anything from her father! The coward! Of course he wouldn't put his career on the line just because she'd been raped. Oh no, not over a little thing like that!

"Well," said her father, clasping his hands together as if to preface an important, happy announcement. "He's offered to marry you. And I . . . uh . . . I accepted his gracious offer."

"*You what!*"

"Now sit down, Sabrina. It's—"

"Oh, you bastard! You awful, awful man! And you think I'll stand still for it? Never!"

"You will do as I tell you."

"*Never!* You hear me?"

"Think of the bright side of it," he said, watching her as she stomped about the room, passing back and forth in front of the bookshelf partition. "He's a nobleman. You'll be a nobleman's wife. And not only that, but he's being transferred to a post on Tahiti. Why, you'll be surrounded by lush rain forests on an exotic tropical island. With handsome natives all about."

"What else do you get out of this?" she demanded angrily, swiveling to face him. Her father never did anything that wasn't strongly in his own best interests.

"Sabrina!" he scolded sharply, his face becoming severe at the insult.

"What he gets, Fräulein," said Von Himmel, stepping out from behind the bookshelf partition where he had been standing all along, "is my commendation to his superiors on der excellent job he is doing. In addition to my agreement to not lodge a protest against him for insulting an official of der kaiser's government."

Sabrina was staring at Von Himmel, stunned speechless by his presence there.

"Um . . . yes," said her father in embarrassment at being discovered in his duplicity. "As a matter of fact, the baron did graciously offer to commend me to the secretary of state. But that's a minor point, we won't discuss that now."

Sabrina couldn't stand it. Here he was, Von Himmel, in her father's own study. And her father was siding with him! She picked up the inkstand from her father's desk and flung it at the German.

"Sabrina!" shouted her father, enraged at her for risking ruining the agreement he had worked out.

Von Himmel did not duck out of the way. The inkstand hit his chest and bounced off onto the hardwood floor, leaving a thick splotch of black India ink on his blue waistcoat and scarlet sash. "She vill haf to be taught obedience, Herr St. Claire," he said in a cold, hard-as-nails voice. His thick walrus mustache twitched in his otherwise rigidly controlled face.

"As her husband," said her father, "you will . . . uh . . . have that right."

"I'll never marry him!" Sabrina shouted. "You're mad! You think you can make me marry this animal? *Never!*" She started to run for the door.

16

"You will!" declared her father, blocking her way. "I am your father and you'll do as I say! You're only eighteen, a minor, you have no say in the matter. And you'll certainly not ruin my career over this!"

Sabrina backed away from him, shaking her head in panicked disbelief. He actually expected her to marry this man who had raped her, and let him abduct her off to some godforsaken tropical island, thousands of miles from civilization? She'd die first!

She started to run past her father's side, and it was then that she discovered—too late—the identity of the mousy-looking man with the black satchel, and the reason for his being here. He was a doctor. As she ran past her father, Von Himmel grabbed her and held her still. The mousy-looking man pulled a liquid-filled syringe from his black bag and came up to Sabrina. The sight of the needle made her go wild. She began kicking and scratching frenziedly.

"I thought you might become upset," her father said, "so I took the liberty of having a physician ready to sedate you. For your own good."

She screamed as the hypodermic pressed against her arm. Instantly a cloud of wooziness descended upon her. The room, the furniture, her father—everything began spinning around in a dizzying whirlpool. She tried to speak, but no words came. The last sight she saw before falling into a void of deep blackness was the leering, triumphant face of Von Himmel.

They kept her "sedated" throughout the entire day and night, and even during the hurried wedding ceremony that took place the next afternoon.

Aside from Sabrina herself, the only people in attendance were Von Himmel, her father, the doctor, and a seedy, disreputable-looking minister. There was also a photographer, who served as a witness.

Sabrina kept popping in and out of woozy consciousness. Vaguely she noticed she was wearing a lacy white wedding gown, gloves, and a sheer wedding veil. As if in a dream, she was standing before the altar of a deserted church, being held up by her father on one side and Von Himmel on the other. Her mind was numb, blanketed in a thick fog that made her drowsy and dizzy.

The seedy-looking minister was asking her, "And do you, Sabrina St. Claire, take this man to be your lawful wedded husband?"

She could barely speak. Her tongue felt thick in her numb mouth. "No," she mumbled desperately, barely getting the word past her lips. "I don't . . . I won't be married to him!"

The minister continued on, unperturbed, as if she had said "I do." He turned to Von Himmel and said, "You may place the ring on her finger."

"No!" Sabrina cried, the word coming out in a hoarse, frantic whisper. She tried to pull away from the grip her father and Von Himmel had on her, but it was impossible. Her head was spinning. Her legs felt like rubber. She watched in horror as Von Himmel removed her glove and forced the gold-band diamond-mounted ring onto her finger. A flash of sulfur-powder light flared up in front of Sabrina's eyes as a photograph was taken. She could barely move. There was a bouncing black dot before her eyes, an afterimage of the flash.

"I now pronounce you man and wife," declared the minister.

"Noooo!" shrieked Sabrina, finding her voice at last, struggling hysterically.

"Doctor!" called her father. The mousy-looking man took another syringe from his black bag, and hurried forward. Sabrina felt a sharp pinprick, then darkness descended upon her again and she collapsed into the arms of Baron von Himmel—her new husband.

Chapter 2

When she regained consciousness the next morning, she found that she was lying on a bunk in what appeared to be a ship's cabin. She was still wearing her lacy, white gown and gloves, though her veil was gone. She sat up slowly, feeling very weak and dizzy, her entire body aching. For a moment she remained motionless, letting the effects of the drug wear off, slowly returning to her senses.

She looked at her surroundings. The cabin was large, but shabby and squalid-looking. Its walls were painted in flaking, dirty whitewash. The floorboards creaked, and beneath the floorboards she felt a rumbling vibration, like that of a warming-up engine. It was dim in the cabin. What light there was in the room was coming in from a single porthole in the wall.

She went to the porthole and flung it open. It was chilly outside, and extremely foggy. She was on a ship, all right, she could now see. The ship was berthed in a harbor, held fast to a wooden wharf by docking lines. Near the front of the ship a boarding ramp was connected to the wharf. Sabrina could not see past the stem and stern of the ship due to the thick gray fog. She took several deep breaths of the fresh cold morning air. Her head seemed to clear a bit.

Suddenly she heard two loud blasts from the ship's foghorn, and knew it meant the ship was preparing to put out into the open sea. The realization made her sick to her stomach. She stuck her head out of the porthole and looked up and down the deck. No one was visible. She tried to see if she could escape through the porthole, but it was too small. Her head and neck fit through, but her torso was too wide.

She went to the door of the cabin now, certain it was locked. She tried it anyway, only to prove herself right. It was firmly locked. She put her ear to the wooden door and heard, on the other side of it, gruff voices speaking in German. She pulled her head back. Suddenly two more foghorn blasts sounded from the steam whistle. I have to get out of here! she thought frantically, seized with desperation. But what can I do?

She rushed to the porthole and again peered out, sticking her head as far out as she could. The fog had thinned some in the last few minutes, and now as she looked past the bow of the ship, she saw another vessel off in the distance, also tied to the wharf. It was a French freighter. As she watched, a twin-wing airplane was being hoisted by crane into the hatch of the forward hold.

The ship was bound for France, Sabrina knew. She remembered reading in the newspapers about the new trade agreement that had the United States supplying military equipment to France, to help prepare her for the coming war that was expected against Germany.

Aside from the crew, there was only one other

man on the wharf watching the transport of the plane. He was tall and dark-haired and dressed in an American flier's uniform. From the distance, Sabrina could not see what he looked like or hear what he was saying, but it was clear from his angry gestures and the way he was shouting that he was cussing out the freighter's crew. His attention was riveted on the way they were letting down the biplane.

That's probably his plane, Sabrina thought. He must be one of the fliers being sent to France to help teach the French how to use American planes.

The plane was finally lowered to the deck of the ship, but it was done too jarringly to suit the American. He shouted a loud string of obscenities, grabbed a crowbar from a crate near him, and flung it at the crew on the ship. The French sailors scurried out of the way, shaking their fists at him and cursing back in French. The American airman stalked away angrily. He was coming down the wharf in Sabrina's direction.

Sabrina tensed. She pricked up her ears to hear if there were Germans above on the uppermost deck. She heard no sound of talking or moving about.

The flier was almost directly opposite her on the wharf now, about to pass by. She could see him very clearly. He was extremely handsome, in the rugged sort of way that for some reason excited her. He looked like a street-tough ruffian, with a strong face and glowering blue eyes. He had a powerful square jaw and a cleft chin. Unkempt black hair hung down over his forehead, beneath his visored military cap.

He seemed to Sabrina to be about thirty or so years old. He wore a gray serge, buttoned-to-the-collar, aviator's uniform with royal blue piping up the legs and sleeves. He walked with a fierce animalistic gait, leaning aggressively forward. The insignia on his stiff high collar showed that he was a Major in the newly formed army air corps—the most dangerous branch of the military.

"Psst!" Sabrina whispered from the porthole. He did not hear her, and continued stalking past. "Wait!" she said in a louder, more desperate tone, still trying to keep her voice quiet. "Please! Stop! Please, you!"

Major Dallas Hunter stopped and looked at her, squinting one eye in an expression of intrigued surprise. He turned to face her fully, and put his hands on his hips. A tight grin broke out over his features. "What the hell . . . ?" he said. His voice was deep and manly.

"Please," Sabrina answered in a hushed urgent voice, "you've got to help me. They're holding me a prisoner here."

"Who is?"

"The Germans! They drugged me and dragged me on board, and now they're going to take me off to Tahiti. Against my will!"

He stared at her skeptically, still grinning. "Sure they are, honey. You just sleep it off a little longer and you'll be fine." He turned to go.

"Wait! Please! Do I have to beg you? Please, you've got to help me!"

He turned to her again, and his expression became more serious. "This isn't some kind of joke?" he asked. His eye still narrowed in that glowering, skeptical look.

"It's the truth! I swear it! They've kidnapped me and drugged me and they're going to—"

"Yeah, yeah, take you off to Tahiti." He was still doubtful, but now he glanced up toward the topmost deck, to make sure no one was watching or overhearing their conversation. "All right," he said, looking back at her. "You sit tight. I'll go get the harbor master."

"There isn't time!" she exploded. "Can't you see they're about to cast off? The engines are already warming up." She knew this from the churning, humming sound, and from the vibrations in the floor of her cabin.

"Well, what do you want me to do?" he asked belligerently.

Some hero you turn out to be! she thought frustratedly. But what she said was: "Can you come aboard? And let me out of here? The cabin door's locked, you see. If you could just open it . . . ?"

He stared at her gloweringly for another moment, trying to decide whether to believe her or not. He looked clearly suspicious. He turned his eyes toward the stern of the ship, where the boarding ramp was connected to the wharf.

Just then there was the sound of three more loud foghorn blasts, indicating that the ship was about to put out to sea at any moment. Sabrina heard German voices from the deck above her and quickly pulled her head back in. When she cautiously looked out again a moment later, the single boarding ramp was being disconnected from shore. She watched in horror as the ramp was pulled aboard the ship. She turned back to Hunter, her eyes desperate and pleading.

Hunter scowled and gritted his teeth. He looked at her sharply, as if about to make a decision. For the first time his expression became determined and resolute. His eyes scanned the ship, and Sabrina could tell he was counting the number of her porthole, so he'd know which cabin she was in. Then, as she watched with bated breath, he sprang into action.

He ran down to one of the rope docking lines holding the ship fast to the wharf. He shucked off his jacket, fixed the docking line in his line of sight, then leaped off the wharf. He plummeted a few feet down toward the sea, but his aim was true and he managed to grasp the line with both hands, abruptly stopping his descent.

Dangling over the sea, he started moving hand over hand toward the ship. He wore a white, sleeveless undershirt, and Sabrina could see his powerful muscles rippling and bulging as he hand-walked along the rope. When he reached the ship, he raised himself up until he could peer over the side. A second later, he jackknifed his body over the side of the ship.

Sabrina rushed to the cabin door and put her ear to it. The two guards outside her door were joking and talking in German. She waited nervously, tense with anticipation. Would he be able to reach her door? How many Germans were there on the ship who would try to stop him?

After what seemed an eternity, she heard what she was waiting for: "*Halt!*" shouted one of the guards outside her door. "*Dies Zone ist verboten!*"

"Sorry, pal," said Hunter's voice, "I don't *sprechen Sie.*"

"Get back!" commanded the other guard threateningly in English. He then shouted something at Hunter in German.

The flier's voice was very close now. "I'd really

like to oblige, Fritz, but you see I've got a date waiting for me."

Sabrina heard sudden sharp, smacking sounds, and knew that fists were flying. The sound of the scuffling was loud and violent. There were shouts in German and then a crash as someone or something hit hard against the cabin door. The commotion continued.

An instant later, Sabrina heard a click near the handle, and smiled with joy. She was going to be set free! But when the door opened, instead of seeing just Hunter, she saw two bodies locked together in combat come crashing into the room. Hunter and the brawny German he was fighting were swinging at each other furiously. The second guard, Sabrina saw, was lying in the corridor outside her cabin, bloody and groaning.

A third German, alerted by the shouts, now came running down the corridor toward the cabin. Sabrina grabbed a ceramic water pitcher from the table and held it high. The instant the German entered the cabin, she smashed it down on his head, shattering it. The man dropped to the floor without a sound.

Hunter hit the German he was fighting with a powerful right hook. Then he grasped the back of the man's head, forced his face forward, and smashed him hard with a quickly upraised knee. The German crashed back against the wall and rebounded onto the floor.

Hunter looked at Sabrina, his blue eyes bright with fierce excitement. "Let's get the hell out of here," he said. He grabbed her hand and they rushed out.

They ran down the passageway, then up the

metal stairs onto the deck. A German sailor stood guard near the hatchway exit, armed with a Mauser pistol. He swiveled around as they appeared on deck. Before he could fire, Hunter lunged at him, assailing him with a flurry of blows. Hunter grabbed the gun from his foe's hand, pulled him by the back of the collar to the side of the ship, and flung him overboard.

Other Germans were now converging on them from all sides. "Hold it!" Hunter yelled at them, waving the Mauser from side to side. His expression was murderous. None of the enemy advanced toward them, but each was watching for an opening, waiting to jump the American.

"Can you swim?" Hunter asked Sabrina. She was at his side, cowering close to him, her hands on his upper arm.

"Yes," she said fearfully, watching the Germans, who were now surrounding them in a semicircle, as she and Hunter backed up against the side of the ship.

Hunter glanced briefly at her white gown with the long flowing skirt and train. "Get rid of that dress," he ordered. "Or you'll drown in it."

She hesitated, looking shocked. Remove her gown? Here? In front of this handsome stranger, and all these Germans?

"Now!" Hunter commanded. He waved the gun menacingly at the Germans, as several of them stepped forward testingly.

Sabrina began to fumble with the cloth latches in back, trying to undo them. Her white gloves made it difficult. She was about to remove the gloves when Hunter glanced at her impatiently, saw what

27

she was doing, and decided there wasn't enough time for Sabrina to do it her way.

He grasped the front of the gown and violently ripped it forward. Sabrina gasped and covered herself with her hands. Then she realized that this was no time for modesty. She began stepping out of her torn gown. She wore only a short white chemise underneath it.

Just as she finished, she saw a flash of movement on the upper deck, near the ship's bridge. Looking up, she recognized Von Himmel and the ship's captain; they had just come into view.

"What is der meaning of this?" Von Himmel demanded angrily. He was staring directly down at Hunter. "You dare to kidnap my *Liebchen*? You come onto a sovereign ship of der German reich, and steal her away under force of arms?"

"Who the hell is he?" Hunter asked Sabrina.

"He's the one who . . . who kidnapped me!"

"*Ach*," said Von Himmel, breaking into a cruel smile that was meant to seem amused. "She told you dot story?" He laughed loudly. "Und you believed her?" He laughed again, as if at a big joke. "My *Liebchen*, Sabrina, she tells dot to everyone! I hate to say it, but she is a spoiled child, my dollink Sabrina. A thrill-seeker. She loves causing excitement—at other people's expense. She does this all der time. It is how she gets her . . . how do you Amerikaners say it? . . . how she gets her thrills."

Hunter stole a quick, uncertain glance at Sabrina.

"It's not true!" she declared.

A German sailor rushed forward to tackle Hunter during the brief moment he looked at Sabrina. Hunter smashed the barrel of his gun across the man's brow, slicing a deep, bloody gash in his forehead, dropping him to the deck screaming and holding his head.

Von Himmel's expression became deadly serious now. "You listen to me, Amerikaner," he said in a growl. "You were deceived by her lies. I vill take dot into account. If you put down der gun and end this foolishness now, I vill let you go unharmed. If you do not, I vill see dot you pay . . . dearly. *Verstehen Sie*? Understand?"

"You ready?" Hunter asked Sabrina in a low voice.

She was clasping the white gown in front of her, wearing only her chemise now, and her gloves. She shivered in the cold air. "Yes," she said, nodding, feeling very frightened. She looked over her shoulder at the sea below. It seemed a great distance down.

Hunter sensed her fear. He winked at her, trying to reassure her. Then he motioned her up onto the railing, and joined her when she climbed. They stood teetering on the narrow ledge as the German sailors closed in on them.

"Now!" yelled Hunter. He took her hand and the two of them leaped into the sea, hitting it with a great splash. The water was freezing cold. Sabrina lost her breath. She bobbed up to the surface and took deep drafts of air, and began swimming hard toward the wharf. Hunter swam alongside her, watching to make sure she was all right.

To Sabrina's surprise, the Germans did not leap into the water after them. Instead, on Von Himmel's instructions, they began extending the boarding ramp back to the wharf. Hunter saw this too, but instead of swimming faster, so he could reach the wharf before the Germans, he held back, swimming only as fast as Sabrina could manage.

By the time they neared the stone steps carved into the wharf, the Germans were waiting for them. Sabrina's heart sank. No escape was possible. She was too exhausted to swim any further, even if there were anyplace else to swim to. She had to get on dry land now or she would drown.

Hunter was furious—not at her but at the situation. He was obviously a fighter, and hated the idea of surrendering. But he saw the way Sabrina was gasping for breath after the long swim along the wharf wall, to reach the stone steps, and he knew there was no choice. He helped her climb up the wet steps, raising her up ahead of himself. Sabrina stepped onto the wharf into the waiting arms of the Germans.

Hunter came up after her. He saw the way she was being held by one of the Germans, her back pulled against the man's chest, his arm tightly encircling her waist. Her chemise clung to her body, sopping wet, practically transparent. When Hunter saw the German's other hand start to encircle her bustline, he lunged at him. All the other Germans on the wharf descended on Hunter at once, beating him mercilessly.

"Stop it!" Sabrina screamed. "You're killing him!" But her pleas went unheeded.

Finally the Germans tired of their sport and stepped back. Hunter slumped forward, bloody and bruised, barely able to stand. Two Germans remained behind him, holding his arms pinned. Through his blurry sight he was aware of a towering figure coming in front of him and standing looking at him, hands on hips. It was Von Himmel, immaculate in a white traveling suit of tropical material, his bald head uncovered.

Through sheer force of will, Hunter made himself stand up straight, despite the pain, to face Von Himmel. Sabrina winced, seeing the agony he was putting himself through.

"So!" said Von Himmel. "You did not believe me, Amerikaner? You thought maybe I vas lying, when I said you would pay if you persisted in defying me?"

Hunter said nothing. His expression was defiant and unflinching.

"Und maybe you think dot I was not telling der truth ven I say my Sabrina she is a thrill-seeker—" He turned to her. "Aren't you, dollink?" He pinched her cheek.

"You animal!" she cursed, pulling her head back, her eyes fiery.

"Ah, my little *Liebchen*," Von Himmel said to Hunter. "She is so playful. Und you, you poor fool, you probably believed her—*nein?*—ven she say I am some mean ogre who kidnapped her off der streets. But look, Amerikaner, look here."

He suddenly grabbed Sabrina's left hand and peeled off the wet white glove, then held the hand out toward Hunter. "Does this look like der hand of a Fraulein who is being kidnapped? Or does it look like the hand of . . ." He shouted now: "My *wife!* *Meine hausfrau!*"

Hunter stared at the diamond and gold wedding ring on her finger. His expression was disbelieving at first, but slowly it turned bitter. When he raised his eyes to her face, there was a look of powerful resentment, as if he felt he had been tricked and deceived.

"They forced me!" she insisted. "They drugged me and—"

"Ha, ha, ha!" laughed Von Himmel boisterously. "There she goes again. What a prankster she is, my dollink wife." He sighed deeply and looked at Hunter again, his expression turning deadly. "But unfortunately, you believed her, Amerikaner. Und worse, you defied me. Dot is der unforgivable sin. Now you must pay der price." He nodded to the Germans who were holding Hunter's arms pinned behind him.

Sabrina saw one of the Germans jerk Hunter's left arm into a strange position, but she did not know what was happening—until she heard a distinct sound, and suddenly saw a look of incredible pain seize Hunter's features.

The pain from his just-broken arm was clearly so intense, Sabrina could not believe it was possible for him to resist screaming in agony. But he did resist. The only concession he made was to bite his lower lip to stifle the outcry, bloodying himself still further. He was determined not to give Von Himmel the satisfaction of hearing him scream. He succeeded—at enormous cost.

"Let him go," Von Himmel said to the Germans. The two men holding Hunter released him. Hunter's left arm dangled limply at his side at an unnatural angle. He held it close to his body with his right arm, to ease the pain. Then, suddenly, he swiveled around and kicked the German who had broken his arm, catching the man full in the groin, doubling him over in screaming agony.

The other Germans immediately converged toward Hunter again, but Von Himmel ordered them to stop. Sabrina knew why. The harbor master and police were only yards away now, rushing toward them along the wharf.

"What the hell is going on here?" asked the harbor master as he approached. He was a bulldog of a man.

"Our Amerikaner friend," said Von Himmel, "has met mit an unfortunate accident."

The harbor master turned to Hunter. "I saw what happened, buddy. You want to press charges?"

Hunter was looking at Sabrina, his expression hard. He was fighting the agony from his broken arm. "Check your passenger roster," he said to the harbor master in a thick voice. "Is this girl his wife?"

"She's his wife all right. It's been verified by the registrar."

"I don't want to press charges," Hunter said disgustedly. "Like the man says: I met with an accident. It's my own fault—for being a damn gullible fool."

"He's kidnapping me!" Sabrina cried. She looked at Hunter with pleading eyes, begging him to believe her. She turned to the harbor master. "Can't you do anything? I'm being held prisoner! He drugged me! I didn't marry him freely! You can't just let him take me away like this!"

"Ha, ha, ha," laughed Von Himmel. "There she goes again mit der jokes. But of course you know der truth, Herr harbor master, *nein*? Her father vouched for der integrity of our marriage I believe? You have that in your records?"

The harbor master gritted his teeth and nodded. He obviously didn't like the German, and wished he could help Sabrina. But so long as she was legally the man's wife, there was nothing he could do.

"Take her back aboard," Von Himmel ordered the German sailors curtly. "Ve haf a long journey ahead. Und nothing vill stop us now."

As Sabrina was pulled and tugged toward the boarding ramp, struggling fiercely, she turned her eyes back to Dallas Hunter, in a last plea for help. Hunter had turned, though, and was stomping away from her down the wharf, holding his broken arm close to his body—without even an instant's backward glance at her.

Moments later the ship was miles out at sea, steaming toward Tahiti. Sabrina stood on the deck wrapped in a thick wool blanket, sadly watching the shoreline of America disappearing in the distance.

Chapter 3

Living on Tahiti for Sabrina was like living on another planet. The islands, the people, her day-to-day life—all were unlike anything she had ever known before. The island itself was a tropical paradise, surrounded by the crashing blue sea and jagged coral reefs. The rain forests were lush and fragrant. Aside from Sabrina and Von Himmel and his German aides, there were almost no white people on the island.

The natives were beautiful, simple, dark-skinned people of Polynesian caste, very lithe and happy and graceful. Though Sabrina did not speak their language, after a while she learned to communicate with them to a small degree through sign language and facial expressions—mostly smiles to show that she was friendly.

It was difficult to smile, though, for her days were filled with misery. Most of the time Von Himmel confined her to the big white mansion that he had made his headquarters. His staff of German hoodlums made sure Sabrina did not leave the grounds except when Von Himmel gave his permission. And at first, Von Himmel seldom gave his permission.

He was furious at her for continuing to fight him

whenever he tried to make love to her. She never gave in to him, always scratching and biting and resisting with all her might. Twice he had her tied down to the bed so he could have his way with her in peace.

After the first few weeks, though, Von Himmel decided that having her constantly around the house was a poor idea. He disliked being subjected to her sullen, hateful stares. "*Ach du lieber!*" he finally exploded one evening, after she had glared at him hatefully without letup. "Go, then! Roam der island if you wish it. See if dot pleases you better. It won't, I warn you! There is nothing of any interest on this godforsaken island. I curse der fates that ever sent me here!"

Though being allowed to visit the natives and walk about the island made Sabrina happier, she still was sick at heart. No matter how lovely her exotic surroundings were, she was still a captive. And she was very lonely.

Often she found herself daydreaming about the bold, handsome flier who had tried to rescue her back in America. If only they had met under different circumstances! If only there were some way she could see him again. Sabrina always sighed wistfully when she thought of this, figuring that such a fantasy could never become reality.

To take her mind off the misery of her life, she began to learn the graceful, sensual dances which the natives performed at their tribal ceremonies. Since she had much time to practice them and nothing else to do, she became so good that soon the natives began asking her to dance with them at their celebrations. Sabrina felt nervous about doing so, but once she saw how pleased the Tahitians were at the way she danced, she became more confident.

She enjoyed the shaking and shimmying movements. They helped work off some of the frustration and hatred that ate away at her. The natives treated her like an adopted little sister, and were delighted at the way she took an interest in their dances and tribal customs.

She danced the native dances . . . she walked about the island . . . she endured Von Himmel's brutal attacks. The days wore on . . .

Then one evening, while she was dancing around a giant bonfire during a tribal ceremony, she met a drunken French ship captain who was visiting the tribe. His name was LeFleur, and he was fascinated by Sabrina. It wasn't only the uniqueness of a beautiful, coral-haired, white girl performing native dances that piqued his interest. It was also the sight of the elaborate golden ring on her finger, highlighting the large diamond.

When LeFleur asked her about it, Sabrina did not tell him it was a wedding ring; and he could not guess it, since she had moved it to her right hand. She told him it was a family trinket and that if he would help her return to her wealthy family in America, she would give it to him.

LeFleur was interested—intense greed was in his bloodshot eyes. But certain problems had to be worked out. For one thing, he was bound for France, not America. And for another, Sabrina could see from the lecherous, hungry way he gazed at her that she would not be safe from him during the escape voyage from Tahiti.

Sabrina did not mind ending up in France. Any-

where was preferable to being held captive here by
Von Himmel. But she did not want to have to endure any physical abuse from this Captain Le-
Fleur. As they talked in front of the bonfire,
though, she had an inspiration:

"I have relatives in France," she said to him. "If
you take me back with you, and I arrive *unharmed*,
I'll see that you're rewarded with another family
trinket, worth twice as much as this ring. And,
here, to show you my good faith, I'll give you this
ring now. Here, go ahead, take it. Its value is nothing, really, to a family as wealthy as mine."

LeFleur was highly suspicious, and he also vaguely
understood that there was some sort of relationship
between Sabrina and the powerful German baron
on the far side of the island. But his greed got the
better of him. He accepted the offer.

Late that night Sabrina was smuggled aboard
LeFleur's ship in a crate labeled COCONUTS. An
hour later, they were on the high seas, sailing away
from the sordid life Sabrina had lived on Tahiti.
When they finally arrived in the French port of
Marseilles, Sabrina quietly slipped overboard just
before docking, swam to the pier, then ran away
before LeFleur could catch her.

*Now here she was, in one of the wickedest, most
dangerous cities in the world . . . and she was
penniless, hungry, alone. With no friends and no
one to turn to. She had spent the last night hiding
in an alley, shivering with cold. Now it was morning. But what could she do? Where could she
go? . . .*

She sat under a service porch in the alley, hugging herself to ease the chill. Suddenly she felt a
hand grasp her from behind, and jerk her roughly

to her feet. Oh no! she thought. Some derelict had found her!

But when she turned, she saw two French gendarmes staring at her. They wore black uniforms with silver buttons, and had round black hats with flat tops and short visors. The one who had jerked her to her feet had a mustache. He began scolding Sabrina in French.

"I . . . I don't understand," she said.

"Ah!" he said to his partner, his face brightening, "an Engleesh!" His expression became harsh as he said to Sabrina: "You are a vagrant. Vagrancy eez against ze law. We take you to ze jail now. We have good time weeth you in ze jail. I *love* ze Engleesh." He began pawing at her breasts through the thin fabric of her blouse.

"Stop it!" she exclaimed, fending off his hands. She wanted to strike him, but did not dare. He was a policeman. Hitting him would surely lead to even worse trouble.

"Come," he said to her, continuing to make passes at her breasts as she continued to push his hands away. "We go to ze prison now."

"Please don't take me in," she pleaded. "I'm not really a vagrant." She could not let them take her to jail. Von Himmel would surely ask the gendarmes' help in finding her as soon as he arrived in France searching for her. And he would arrive soon, that was certain. It would not take him long to find out it was the French captain who helped her escape.

"You say you are not a vagrant," said the gendarme. "But you appear as a vagrant. You sleep in ze alleyway as a vagrant. But maybe you are only a whore instead, eh?"

"No!" she declared.

"Zen you are a vagrant and we must take you in."
He paused. "Unless you can show zat you have
money. Do you have money?"

Reluctantly, she shook her head.

"Do you have a job maybe?"

"I . . . well, I . . ."

"Just as I thought! No money. No job. You are a
vagrant and we must take you in." His face brightened. "We have much fun weeth you in jail. You
see."

"Wait, Pierre," said the second gendarme, who
until now had not spoken. "Remember what ze
magistrate say. Eef we take in another vagrant
weethout first giving warning, we be in *beaucoup*
trouble. He say we must respect ze law and give
warning first."

"Oh, zat eez nonsense!" said the first gendarme
disgustedly. "He will never know we do not give ze
warning."

"I'll tell him!" Sabrina declared, spying a ray of
hope. "If you bring me up before a magistrate, I'll
tell him you refused to give me a warning first!"

She could see that her strategy was effective, but
also that it might have made the situation even
worse for her in the long run. The gendarme stared
at her with cold fury. "You will have your warning
zen," he said. "Consider yourself warned. Eef we
find you weethout employment by six o'clock tonight, we take you in." He sneered at her nastily.
"And I tell you, eet will go much harder for you, now
zat you make eet harder for me." He released her.
"See you at six, *cherie*. I look forward to eet." He
grinned cruelly and left the alley, his partner at his
side.

Sabrina spent the entire day looking for work. She

tried everywhere. Marseilles, though, was in the middle of an unemployment pinch due to the glut of foreign workers who came into the city to work in shipping. And since she could not speak French, she could not even find work as a waitress or girl Friday in any of the shops. As evening approached, she became frightened and desperate.

At a few minutes before six, she was on a dingy street near the waterfront when she saw the two gendarmes coming toward her, their expressions gleeful. Sabrina ran down the street away from them. They continued walking after her, taking their time.

As she neared the end of the street, where it came to an abrupt halt at the waterfront, she looked frantically to the left and to the right. Then she saw it: a seedy-looking bar with a sign in the window, beneath a theater-type marquee. DANCER WANTED the sign said in three different languages.

The gendarmes were nearly upon her. She turned and rushed into the bar. It was dimly lit inside. There were only a few patrons at this early hour, and a fat, white-shirted proprietor behind the bar. Everyone stared at her. "What is it you want?" said the proprietor in an unfriendly voice.

Sabrina knew she was letting herself in for trouble. But there was no choice. "I—I want to work for you," she stammered. "As . . . as your dancer."

Chapter 4

Sabrina sat before the lightbulb—encircled dressing-room mirror, listening fearfully to the rowdy, drunken voices coming from the bar. It was nine o'clock. The voices were laughing and shouting in English, French, and German, clamoring for her to come out.

In the background she could hear the loud, scratchy music of the gramophone. The thought of going out there in front of the mob of drunken men made her skin crawl.

She jerked around sharply when the fat proprietor came into her dingy, cramped dressing room. He was greasy-faced, and his white shirt was missing a button near his waist, exposing his belly. "So?" he said in a throaty French accent. "You are ready?"

Sabrina looked at him fearfully, her pale green eyes very wide. "I . . . I really don't want to do this. If I could just change my mi—"

"You do not *want*?" he said with astonished rage. "Who gives ze *damn* what you want! You are my new 'exotic dancer,' and I now have ze house full of customers yelling for you to entertain zem. I tell you, *cherie*, you weel not disappoint *my* customers!

Come! You come now, you dance!" He grasped her wrist.

"Please, you don't understand!" she said, drawing back, her eyes beseeching. "I've never danced in public. I only answered your sign in the window because the gendarmes wanted to put me in jail as a vagrant, and—"

"Enough! Enough!" He began tugging her roughly forward. "You are my new dancer, now you dance."

"Please! I—"

He raised a beefy hand as if to strike her. She cringed in fright and quickly became silent. He pulled her out through the doorway, down a narrow hall, then into the main room of the dark bar. The bar was small, low-ceilinged, and seedy-looking, crowded to overflowing with rowdy, drunken, uniformed men sitting at round tables. Being located in the old waterfront port of Marseilles, the bar played host to transient sailors and soldiers of every nationality.

The noise from the laughing, shouting, cursing men was deafening, and the room was so thick with cigarette smoke Sabrina began to cough. The air was warm and muggy, filled with the offensive odor of alcohol, tobacco, and sweat. Her breathing quickened with fear as she was pulled toward the raised round podium in the center of the room.

The instant the bar patrons noticed her, they erupted into raucous shouting and applauding. These were well-traveled men, but still they were not used to seeing such beauty as Sabrina possessed. They stared at her long, radiantly pink hair and at her lovely face.

43

Their eyes traveled down her firm, ripe body that was in the full bloom of womanhood. She was wearing a brightly colored, floral-pattern sari (which the proprietor had given her) wrapped around her. Her exquisite shoulders and slim, lissome arms were bare. The clapping and wolf whistles became louder.

"*Bienvenu, messieurs,*" announced the proprietor as he climbed up onto the round podium, tugging Sabrina up with him. "Welcome to La Grande Bouteille. Tonight I have ze great pleasure to present to you a new entertainment for your—" He smirked. "—'*cultured*' delectation."

The audience broke up in laughter at the phrase.

"Knowing what sophisticates all of you are," he said, causing even more raucous laughter, "I have imported for you tonight a *jeune fille* of rare beauty from ze exotic tropics. Such a life she has led." He invented an outrageous story: "Raised from infancy by savages, she eez ze only white woman to become ruler of zeez island peoples, using her mysterious sensual charms—"

The room erupted in more wild laughter, knee-slapping, and tabletop banging. Sabrina watched the drunken, creased-faced, carousing men fearfully. She tried to cower back, but the proprietor's grip on her wrist was too tight.

He was acting wounded by the laughter that greeted his introduction. He waved a hand before him in mock seriousness. "*Non, non,* do not laugh, messieurs! Every word I say eez absolutely ze truth. I swear eet on my dear mamma's grave."

More raucous laughter and deliriously contorted smirks. Sabrina was becoming more and more frightened as she looked out at the wildly drunken

44

men who were staring at her with lewd, hungry eyes.

"Now, messieurs! *Alors!* Now I present to you from ze exotic, erotic tropics—"

Sabrina wished she hadn't told the proprietor she was from the tropics. She had been desperate to prove she knew "exotic" dances, though, to get the job—and had blurted it out without thinking.

"—Ze one, ze only . . ." The proprietor stepped down from the podium and gestured grandly at Sabrina with a sweep of his hand: "Princess Breena!"

Wild applause and wolf whistles greeted her as she looked out wide-eyed at the horde of fiercely staring, violently grinning men in the dark, smoky room. Her legs were pressed together tightly, her arms crossed protectively in front of her. A bright orange spotlight burst into life, bathing her in a blinding fog of golden luminescence. She had to squint to see out through it.

The proprietor had rushed to the gramophone, and now a scratchy record of Indian snake-charming music began playing loudly. In his ignorance, the proprietor thought this was the same as tropical music.

Sabrina could not move. She was petrified with nervous fear, staring out at the crowd, trembling, her lips slightly parted. In response to her failure to perform, the remarks from the audience started becoming nasty.

"C'mon!" someone shouted. "Boo! Boo!" chimed in others. Soon there were scornful catcalls in a variety of foreign tongues. "Hey, André," shouted a drunken Italian, "some kinda princess you bring us, huh?"

Sabrina wanted to jump down from the podium

45

and flee, but as she stared out at the crowd she saw the two gendarmes who had tried to arrest her earlier. They were gazing at her with feverishly expectant expressions.

They *wanted* her to leave the stage, she realized. She would be out of a job then. They could arrest her as a vagrant, and have a chance at abusing her while she was held captive behind steel bars. No, she knew she could not jump down and flee, giving them the excuse they needed to arrest her.

The catcalls and jeers became fiercer. She saw the proprietor stalking toward her from across the room, a murderous look on his face. Terror gripped her, and slowly, frowning in helplessness, she began dancing, moving her arms and hips in the graceful rhythmic motions she had learned in Tahiti . . . arching her back, tossing her head backward . . . pirouetting in small graceful circles.

She saw with relief that the proprietor halted in his menacing advance, but—surprisingly—the nasty jeers from the audience did not die away. Instead they continued just as loudly as before, and now the audience began stomping their feet angrily too.

What is it? she wondered. *What was wrong?* Then, as she squinted through the bright orange glare of the spotlight, she saw a burly Frenchman stand up, put his hands to his mouth, and shout in English "Take eet off!"

An English sailor followed, yelling, "C'mon, sister, off with the bloomin' rags already!" Several foreign voices joined the chorus.

Sabrina stared at the audience, shocked. They expected her to strip? She'd never agreed to do that! Where had they gotten such an idea? She looked over at the proprietor, who was shaking his hands menacingly at her, his face urgently demanding, and suddenly she realized the truth: He had advertised her on his outside marquee as a strip-dancer, to bring in more business. How dare he! she thought. But more important: what could she do now?

The audience was becoming vicious. The proprietor was rushing toward her furiously. Desperately she scanned the audience for some sign of help. Everywhere she turned the situation seemed hopeless. But then, staring through the glare of the spotlight, she was startled to see a familiar face at a table very near her, in front of her.

The face was strong and masculinely handsome, with a powerful square jaw and a cleft chin. Unkempt black hair hung down over the man's forehead. It was Dallas Hunter, the aviator who had tried to save her from being abducted to Tahiti so many weeks ago.

He was wearing his gray serge uniform. His left arm was in a cast supported by a sling around his neck, protruding from his only half-buttoned tunic. The cast was the reward he'd received for trying to save her.

She looked at him with pleading, desperate eyes as the proprietor reached the podium and climbed angrily up onto it. Instead of making any move to help her, though, Hunter just narrowed an eye at her in a glowering look, and raised his whiskey glass in a mocking toast to her helpless situation.

Oh, no! she thought agonizingly. He still thought she had tricked him, and now he was bitter!

Her eyes were forced away from Hunter as the greasy French proprietor grasped her hair at the back of her head and jerked her face toward his own.

"What you think?" he screamed at her, his face only an inch away. "You can cheat my guests? You think zay pay good money to see you dance weeth ze clothes hiding your body?" The audience shouted their approval of his scolding words. "Zay can go to ze haberdasher eef zay weesh to see clothes!" the proprietor roared.

Sabrina started to protest in panic—"I *never* told you I'd take off my"—but her words turned into a scream as the proprietor grasped her colorful sari at the top of her bustline and ripped it down to her waist. She grasped his wrist to try to stop him from ripping it further. but he slapped her hands away and then jerked the garment savagely, tearing it completely off her.

She cried out and covered herself with her hands. She was wearing only a strapless, short chemise now, and underwear beneath it. She tried to pull away from the proprietor, but his fist was tightly clenching a handful of her hair at the back of her head.

"More better, *oui?*" he shouted to his customers. The audience broke up in wild applause and shouts. The proprietor smiled down at them, pleased. He twirled her shredded sari in the air over his head, around and around, then flung it out into the crowd. A dozen men scrambled for it hysterically, ripping it apart in their eagerness to possess it.

One of the men who had lunged for the garment was the mustachioed gendarme who had tried to arrest Sabrina. He came up from the scuffle now glaring at Sabrina furiously, having failed to secure any part of the garment. She could see in his face that now he wanted more fiercely than ever for her to flee from the podium, so he could arrest her . . . so he could have another chance at getting his hands on her young body.

The proprietor forced Sabrina's eyes back toward his own face, as he glared at her viciously. "You do what ze men want now, you hear? You please my guests. You make zem happy so zay buy *beaucoup* drinks, so zay spend *beaucoup* francs." He released his grip on her, and stepped down from the podium.

Sabrina turned to Dallas Hunter once more, pleadingly, as the audience clamored loudly for her to strip herself naked. But the rugged aviator just took a swig of his whiskey and stared back at her gloweringly, with that perpetual one-eye-narrowed look of his.

Sabrina was on the verge of tears. The proprietor was screaming curses at her from the sidelines. The audience was throwing pretzels and lit cigar butts.

Burning humiliation swept over her as she stood half naked on the elevated platform . . . vulgarly on display before all these drooling, lecherous beasts, and before the newcomers who were constantly entering the bar. Even now a new group of men came into the bar. A young, blond, English officer—not with the others—moved off toward the back of the room. The main group remained clustered together near the door, watching Sabrina intently. She was too distracted to notice them.

Desperately she made a decision. She would leap off the stage, rush past her dressing room to grab her dress, then flee out the back door of the bar.

The gendarmes might catch her, but she had to take the chance.

She tensed her muscles to jump down and begin her escape when suddenly someone leaped onto the podium with her, from the side, and grasped her shoulders. Sabrina turned her head to look at him, horrified. Her worst fears were realized. It was Von Himmel. He was the leader of the group that had just entered the bar and stood by the doorway. The others in the group—five roughneck German sailors— remained at the door.

Von Himmel's grip on Sabrina's shoulders tight- ened and he began shaking her violently, cursing her in German laced with bits of English. His face was red with anger, and spittle kept spraying onto his thick walrus mustache. He was so furious at her for having run away from him, and making him hunt through half of Marseilles in search of her, that even his bald head was red.

The audience did not know what to make of the giant, powerfully built German until, in his rage to pull her off the podium and take her back with him, he grasped the top of her chemise just as Sa- brina jerked back away from him. The garment ripped, exposing her firm, full breasts. Now the au- dience knew how to react: they burst into a wild clapping ovation.

Sabrina screamed and grasped the top of the chemise to stop Von Himmel from pulling it far- ther, from ripping it completely off her. Her other hand and arm went to her nakedly exposed breasts and pressed against them, trying to cover them.

Von Himmel looked at the audience now as if noticing them for the first time. A mean look came into his eyes as he watched the way Sabrina was cringing in humiliation before them, almost on the verge of tears . . . and at the way the audience was becoming excited at the sight of her defilement.

"*Meine Fräu ist gut, ja?*" he sneered at the audience, sensing a way to punish Sabrina for running away from him.

"*Ja, ja!*" shouted the audience.

"*Oui!*"

"You bloody well know it, Fritz!"

Sabrina was staring at the mean-looking German, her eyes beseeching, her body half bent forward. "Don't do anything to me," she begged.

In answer, he released the bunched-up top of her chemise he had been clutching. But then he grasped both her wrists tightly, stepped behind her, and held her arms over her head, out to the sides.

She screamed in anguish and struggled wildly, but could not free her wrists from his ironlike grip. He held her so she faced the audience, her arms stretched out, her shapely young breasts nakedly exposed to the men's scorching gazes. Her nipples became rosy and erect. Her chemise hung loosely at her waist. Her skin was flushed and she felt pinpricks of sensation all over. Intense shame and degradation washed over her.

As she stared out at her tormentors, she saw the blond Englishman who had entered the bar a moment ago, stalking purposefully toward the podium. His handsome young face—he seemed no older than twenty-one or -two—was set in grim determination, his lips tightly compressed. He threaded his way through the crowd and was about to approach Von Himmel on the podium, when he passed the table

51

where Dallas Hunter was sitting. Hunter stopped him, grasping the man's arm.

The English soldier turned to Hunter sharply. Hunter shook his head slowly, and said in a gruff masculine voice, "Don't be a damned romantic, kid. She's not worth it. I know from experience."

The Englishman jerked his arm free. "Stow it, mate! Yanks like you can stay back shivering in your boots, but Michael Yorkshire won't stand by while a lady is in need of aid." He continued on and jumped up onto the podium.

The German ruffians by the door glanced at Von Himmel, but when he did not give the sign, they made no move to accost Michael Yorkshire.

The young Englishman was directly in front of Sabrina now. As he glanced at her briefly from so close up, with his righteously indignant brown eyes, she couldn't help grimacing with mortification: here she was, half naked before him!

Michael's eyes turned to Von Himmel. "All right, Jerry, you've had your fun. Now let the lady go and get out."

The big German released one of Sabrina's wrists, pushed her to his side, and then did a surprising thing: he bowed from the waist in a gracious, formal bow. When he came up from the bow, his right hand was clenched into a fist, and he slammed it into the unsuspecting Englishman's jaw with such force that it sent him flying backward clear off the podium.

He landed on Hunter's tabletop several feet away, out cold. Hunter glanced down at him and shook his head. "Hero," he said. He unfastened the man's collar so he could breathe easier.

Now that the distraction was over, Von Himmel

again turned his attention to Sabrina. He pinned her arms behind her and pulled her so her back was against his chest. His coarse hand came over her shoulder from behind and rubbed down across her collarbone, then traveled to her breast. She writhed and squirmed, but it was impossible to break free.

Von Himmel cupped her breast from the bottom and jiggled it up and down in the crook of his thumb and forefinger, as if brandishing it on display to the audience. The drunken men went wild with lust. A groan escaped Sabrina's lips and her eyes shut tightly.

Her eyes opened in shocked sensation an instant later, though, as Von Himmel's hand moved to her other breast and pinched her sensitive nipple. Her open eyes had no direction and they fell upon Hunter. His expression was bitterly angry, with the bitterness appearing to be directed at himself.

Von Himmel pulled up the hem of Sabrina's chemise, exposing her underwear. His fingertips went to her belly just above the top of the garment, rubbing along the top edge, from side to side.

Sabrina tensed in fearful anticipation. A feverishly intense silence fell over the audience. "No," Sabrina whispered pleadingly. "Please . . . ?"

Von Himmel *plunged* his hand into her underwear and *clutched* her roughly. Sabrina screamed and could not stop. She squirmed about insanely, beads of perspiration breaking out all over her. The audience dissolved into a horde of drooling, lust-crazed beasts.

Suddenly Sabrina heard a single, loudly shouted obscenity, and looked to see Dallas Hunter leaping to his feet in angry fury. Again it seemed that his anger was directed at himself, for the stupidity of the action he was about to take. He looked as if he had endured all he possibly could, and now he could stand it no longer, no matter *how* senseless he knew it was to intervene.

The table in front of him had overturned as he shot to his feet, and crashed over to the floor. He kicked at it viciously now, splintering the wooden top. The Englishman who had been lying unconscious on the table now began moving about groggily on the dirty floor, jolted partially back to his senses by the sudden drop.

As all eyes in the bar watched him, Hunter stomped up to the podium and leaped up on it. He glared at Von Himmel in silence for a long moment. The room became hushed. "Let her go, you stupid son of a bitch," Hunter said finally, in a low gruff voice.

Chapter 5

Von Himmel at first looked stunned, but then he grinned at Hunter with a false look of great friendliness. "Ve meet again, eh, Amerikaner?" He pushed Sabrina to the side, still holding her with one hand, and bowed from the waist in another formal bow.

The instant he started coming up from his bow, Hunter swung at him *hard* with his cast-enclosed arm, catching the man's jaw in a sharp uppercut with the granite-hard plaster cast. Sabrina heard a crackling sound she thought to be from Von Himmel's jaw, and saw the German stagger backward, his mouth gushing with blood. He stumbled about the podium as if in a daze, not falling down, not releasing her.

The five burly German sailors charged toward Hunter now, their expressions murderous. He swiveled sharply and in a swift follow-through raised his boot high, kicking the nearest one in the throat, leaving him gagging and choking and clutching his windpipe.

Before the other four could reach him, Hunter surprised them by leaping forward from the podium, right into their midst. He brought one down under him as he landed, smashing the man's head against the wooden floorboards as he came down on top of him. He shot up to his feet again instantly, knowing that if the Germans caught him on the ground, he would have no chance at all.

He seemed to have no chance at all anyway, though, Sabrina thought, for the odds were enormously against him. As she watched, one of the Germans smashed him in the face with his fist, and grabbed the front of his jacket as he fell backward, ripping the coat open. Another German hit him in the stomach while he was withering under the force of the first blow.

Sabrina thought he must surely crumble to his knees now, but instead he came up from a doubled-over crouch, lashing out with his fist, kicking in all directions, using his plaster cast as a short-range club.

Soon the insurmountable odds took their toll, however, and he was being mercilessly beaten by the four Germans who remained on their feet. Yet *still* he was fighting back, with the viciousness of a madman, refusing to go down as long as there was a shred of strength left in him. Before long, his face was bloody. Sabrina felt certain he could not remain on his feet even a few seconds longer.

But then, just as she thought he would fall, and that there would be nothing left to stop the Germans from spiriting her away with Von Himmel, back to the island where a horrendous punishment awaited her . . . another figure came flying through the air suddenly, arms and legs extended like wings.

"Hold on, Yank, I'm coming!" shouted Michael Yorkshire as he careened into the middle of the battle, having launched himself from a tabletop.

He brought down two Germans at once, easing the pressure on Hunter. Hunter began fighting with renewed vigor now, more fiercely than ever. Michael lashed out frenziedly also, kicking, punching, jabbing, butting with his head.

Even with the two of them together, though, they were still no match for the brawny German hooligans who outnumbered them, and soon it became clear that they had no chance at all of winning the battle. Their only hope was to grab Sabrina and shelter her between them as they attempted to charge out the doorway. They looked at each other and seemed to concur.

Hunter leaped up on the podium just as Von Himmel was regaining his senses. The German ceased staggering about and opened his mouth to shout to his men. Hunter caught him full in the face with a swing of his plaster cast, making him shriek, dropping him to the podium floor like a deadweight of bricks.

Hunter grasped Sabrina's hand from Von Himmel's slackened grip. He gazed into her eyes with searing intensity for the briefest second. Then he jumped from the podium, taking Sabrina with him, his torn-open jacket flapping at his sides.

Michael freed himself from his antagonists and took up a position on Sabrina's other side.

"Now!" shouted Hunter.

They charged toward the door, sheltering Sabrina between them. Two of the Germans managed to get in front of the door to block their exit, while the other two advanced toward them. Hunter and Michael closed ranks in front of Sabrina and pulled her with them as they rushed forward at full speed, their heads lowered. They burst through the Germans, sending one flying off to the side, trampling the other.

Then suddenly they were outside, and Sabrina felt the chill of the cold night air on her naked upper body and legs. They ran down the dark, wet street, the sound of shouting German voices close behind them, echoing against the buildings on both sides.

They turned a corner, and Hunter pulled Sabrina hard against him into a tiny alcove in the side of the building. Michael rushed in also, flattening himself against the opposite side. Sabrina's breasts were pressing tightly against Hunter's muscular, hairy chest, as the sound of their pursuers became louder. Her nipples became taut and a prickling sensation quivered through them. She felt intense guilt that her body was responding in this way. She looked up shamefully at Hunter's handsome bruised face.

His eyes were narrowed in concentration as he listened to the sound of the approaching Germans. They were within a few yards of them now, and then suddenly they were rushing right past the alcove in full view. Sabrina pressed herself even tighter against Hunter's chest. Then the Germans were past. Sabrina listened to the sound of their retreating boots.

After continuing for a moment more, however, the bootfalls ceased. It was clear that the Germans realized they'd been tricked and were about to reverse direction.

"Let's go!" Hunter said, rushing out from the alcove, pulling Sabrina with him. Michael brought up the rear.

"There! There! *Schnell!*" came a German shout.

Hunter led Sabrina and Michael back around the corner from which they had just come, and started them running down a narrow cobblestone street.

The three of them were soon gasping raspingly, panting for breath as they rushed out of one dark alleyway and into another, across streets, around corners, over fences. They had gained distance on their pursuers due to Hunter's maneuver, but the clickety-clacking sound of the Germans' boots on the wet pavement still followed relentlessly behind them.

Sabrina was freezing due to her near nakedness. Her bare feet felt almost frostbitten as they kept striking the cold streets and splashing through small puddles. Her breath came out like fog, condensing in the chill night air.

Hunter kept glancing at her as they ran, watching the way she was attempting in vain to hide her breasts from view by pressing her arm over them. She knew he realized she was freezing, but he didn't seem to care to do anything about it. Finally when Sabrina caught him noticing the goosebumps covering her taut skin, Hunter said, between gasps for breath, "You look cold."

"I am cold!" she declared pantingly, angry that he had not offered her his coat. "And I'm half undressed too, in case you haven't noticed."

"I noticed," he said, the shadow of a grin creeping across his hard features.

He refused to take the hint. Sabrina was grateful to him for rescuing her, but still—damn the man! How could he be so *insensitive*? "Why don't you give me your coat to put over myself?" she said finally, spelling it out for him.

"Give you my coat? You must be joking. It's freezing out here."

Her mouth dropped open in astonishment at such a response, and she was about to give him a piece of her mind, when she heard Michael's strong, English-accented voice behind her. "Here you go, pet," he said, slipping his coarse wool tunic shirt-jacket over her shoulders.

She glanced back at him to say thank you, and was surprised by the sight of how muscular his hairless, light-skinned chest was. The tunic had made him look slimmer, disguising the fact that he had such a handsome physique.

"You're a true gentleman, sir," she said to him. Then she turned back to Hunter with a disdainful, nose-in-the-air look, to show that she thought *he* was a true something quite different.

Hunter snorted in cynical amusement.

They ran on in silence. Sabrina's legs were so weary, she knew she could not keep running much longer. After a while, Hunter said to her, "You have a place to stay?"

"Not anymore," she said, feeling a stab of anguish at the thought. "The owner was going to let me stay in the upstairs loft above the bar, as part of my wages. Now, though . . ." The words faded.

"You'll stay with me tonight," Hunter said commandingly. "I have a one-bedroom apartment near here."

"I certainly will not!" she said indignantly, knowing she was being foolish, but responding with stubborn pride to the arrogant way he assumed he could order her about—into his bedroom no less!

"She certainly won't!" echoed Michael with equal indignation. "I say, Yank, where do you get off

60

with that rot?" He pulled up even with them and said to Sabrina, "My cousin has a room near here. It's not large, mind, but she'll be more than happy to share it with you I'm sure. Louisa is *terribly* hospitable."

"I thank you again, sir," Sabrina said. "I seem to be quite indebted to you this evening."

Hunter rolled his eyes heavenward in a smug "spare me" gesture. When they rounded the next corner, he came to a stop and motioned the others to do likewise. Sabrina sank against the brick wall, panting for breath, on the verge of dropping from exhaustion. She almost wanted to cry in frustration when she heard the ominous sound of running boots in the distance. *The Germans were still after them!*

"Listen, Limey," Hunter gasped to Michael. "We can't outrun them, we'll have to do something else. Here's the plan." He inhaled deeply several times, trying to catch his breath, then continued. "One of us leads them on a wild goose chase, while the other takes the girl off to safety. Then we meet up again afterward, at the Lautrec Street Bridge; that's just north of here."

"Right," gasped Michael. "I volunteer to lead the heinie blighters on an artful little dodge."

"Of course you do," said Hunter. "You're a real hero." He slapped him on the shoulder in a gesture that seemed to Sabrina to have more than a hint of smug sarcasm.

The clickety-clacking of the boots was drawing nearer.

"Well," said Michael, with an earnest, purposeful expression, "I'm off then." He glanced at Sabrina and she could see the glimmer of affection for her

61

in his sensitive brown eyes. Then he ran across the street and down the length of the block, his lean, naked back glimmering with sweat in the moonlight.

Hunter took Sabrina's hand, and they began moving down the street, turning in the opposite direction from Michael when they reached the corner.

Sabrina heard Michael's voice from across the street, yelling "Come on now, they'll never catch us! The buggers have too much weinerschnitzel in their guts to do any real running!" Then she heard angry German voices and running feet. The sound grew fainter as the Germans rushed off after Michael.

Hunter let Sabrina slow her pace now, as they continued down the street. When they reached the corner and Hunter started to turn, Sabrina tugged at his hand, and said, "Wait! You said we'd meet him at the Lautrec Street Bridge *north* of here. That direction is south."

"It's the direction where my apartment is," Hunter said, his eye narrowed. "And where there's going to be blazing fire in the fireplace within minutes."

She pulled away from him in astonishment, her eyes going wide, her mouth opening slightly. "Why, you never intended to meet him at the Lautrec Street Bridge at all!" she declared accusingly.

"It'd be a damned hard thing to do, considering that there *isn't* any bridge on Lautrec Street. Not north *or* south."

"You . . . you . . . Why you—you *cad*!" she blurted out finally. "Oh you vile, deceitful person!" Her face was blushing hotly with fury. "You sent that brave boy off by himself, not just to lead those animals astray, but so . . . so . . . *so you could have me all alone with you here, and I'd have no place else to stay!*"

"That's true," said Hunter thoughtfully. He removed a pouch of tobacco from his pants pocket and began rolling a cigarette with his one good hand.

"But that's awful! Just so you could . . . just . . . Why, if they catch him, they'll tear him to pieces!"

"They'll do no more than bloody his nose and maybe break a bone here and there." When he saw that she was about to become even more enraged, he came up close to her and said with a darkly serious expression, "Listen, babe. He volunteered to lead the Huns away because he thinks it's 'romantic' to be a hero. Let him learn the truth early. It might save his life in this coming war."

"Oh, and you never do anything heroic, is that right?" she said tauntingly, infuriated by his self-righteous conceit.

"That's right."

"When you risked your life tonight attacking Von Himmel to rescue me, *that* wasn't heroic, I suppose?"

"No, it was just plain stupid. If I'd had any sense I'd have left you to the animal." He lit his cigarette, dragged deeply, then blew the smoke out bitterly. The cigarette paper became stained red from his bleeding lower lip. "Look," he said, with impatient weariness, "I'm tired. It's been one hell of a night. I'm going back to my apartment now. You're either coming or you're not."

The arrogant, unrepentant way he said this fired Sabrina's indignant rage anew. "I wouldn't stay

63

with you if the kaiser's whole army were after me!"
she declared. "I wouldn't stay on the same hotel
floor as you, or even in the same hotel! Much less
in your . . . your apartment!"

She waited to see him cower under her scornful
rebuke, but instead he just shrugged, and said,
"Suit yourself." Then he turned and started off.

She watched him disappear around the corner,
and heard his footsteps fading into the night. She
continued staring after him, not fully believing that
he had really left her alone like this.

What have I done?! she thought, when it dawned
on her. She had a strong urge to call out to him, to
make him come back—but she stifled it. I won't
give him the satisfaction, she said to herself, knowing even as she thought this that she was once
again being too pigheaded for her own good. Her
forehead furled into a helpless frown.

She turned and looked around, noticing her surroundings fully for the first time. The narrow street
she was in was flanked by high, dirty-walled buildings. Garbage littered the thin, cracking sidewalks.
Every moonshadow, nook, and cranny seemed
darkly menacing.

Looking down at herself, she saw the torn chemise that was bunched up around her waist. The
tight soldier's coat, which was half open, came
down to just above her knees. To an observer it
would look as if she were tantalizingly naked beneath the coat. And here it was, an ungodly hour of
the night.

The acute danger of her situation suddenly became clear to her.

She became frightened. She thought of walking

cautiously up Lautrec Street in search of the young Englishman. She might meet the German sailors, though, instead. They were probably still hunting for her. Without her two protectors, she was absolutely helpless. The Germans would slowly surround her and then—

A sudden sound—CRASH!—interrupted her thoughts. She screamed in terror, and swiveled around to see where the sound had come from, her heart racing. She saw a scruffy black cat scurrying away from the garbage can it had just tipped over. It was the falling can that had made the sound.

Sabrina shuddered. She had to get out of here. Her heartbeat was pounding loudly in her ears, along with the sound of her fearful breathing. Her nose and ears and feet were nearly frozen with cold. She eyed the corner around which Hunter had disappeared.

Even if she did lower herself so humiliatingly as to rush after him, would she even be able to *find* him still? Or had he disappeared forever by now, lost to the turns and twists of these foreign waterfront avenues?

A tormented moan broke from her lips as she made a decision. She ran widly toward the corner, praying desperately that she was not too late to track him down, to beg him to let her stay with him. She rushed around the corner and bumped right into his chest. She fell backward on her behind, stunned. He was leaning nonchalantly against the side of the building, puffing on the cigarette that hung from the corner of his mouth. "You ready yet?" he asked, one eye narrowed.

Oh, she could have killed him! But instead, she

picked herself up from the wet pavement, lowered her eyes, and heard herself say in a small voice: "Yes."

He flicked away his cigarette, put his arm possessively around her waist, and started walking her forward with him. She tried to pull away, but he wouldn't let her.

She looked at his rugged glowering profile and tousled black hair, and at the way the trousers of his uniform fit so snugly around his firm behind. She realized that—for the next few days at least—she would be in constant physical proximity with this man, and almost helplessly at his mercy.

The thought filled her with dread . . . and with a shocking thrill of excitement.

Chapter 6

Hunter's room was on the second floor of a small old apartment building. It was spacious but almost empty of furnishings. Worn and faded maroon carpeting covered the floor. There was a large four-poster bed, an armchair, a dresser, and a few other odds and ends, all old and shoddy-looking.

Hunter moved past Sabrina, as she stood just inside the closed door, and went to the fireplace. He knelt down and began lighting a fire. Sabrina pulled the English soldier's military jacket tighter about herself; it was very cold in the room. It was dim, too, with the only illumination coming from a single lamp in a corner.

Sabrina stood very tensely and nervously as she watched him light the fire. When he finished, and the logs were blazing in the small hearth, he went over to the washstand and turned on the single faucet. With difficulty he managed to shuck off his military jacket. Then he unfastened his trouser belt, and as Sabrina watched, wide-eyed, he stepped out of his trousers and his shorts.

She turned her eyes away quickly. She looked skittishly about the room, anxious to find something to look at other than his naked manly body. From the corner of her eyes, though, she could see him wet a cloth and begin washing the blood away from his various wounds and bruises.

He didn't ask for help, but she could see what a hard time he was having as he tried to reach certain parts of his body with his one free hand. She watched him secretly, as he tried to wash a bleeding gash at the right side of his lower back. He strained, but could not quite reach it.

"Here, let me," she said nervously, coming forward. It was the least she could do, she thought to herself guiltily; he had gotten these wounds rescuing her.

He looked at her but said nothing. She took the cloth from his hand, wet it in cold water from the faucet, then began cleansing the open gash. He jerked slightly and grimaced as the wet cloth touched his wound, stinging him. Then he gritted his teeth and made himself hold still.

"I . . . I want to thank you for rescuing me tonight," she said, not looking at him.

He didn't answer. He was watching her, though, very intently. Sabrina wet the cloth again, and this time moved it to his face, to wash his cut lower lip and puffy left eye. There were many cuts and bruises on his gaunt cheeks and his forehead. She kept her eyes on the wounds she was washing. She felt his eyes upon her as he stared at her with burning intensity. The relentlessness of his gaze made her skin feel prickly, and a wave of heat swept over her. She tried hard not to notice, but as she stood near him she couldn't help but be aware of the way his male shaft was growing long and rigid.

She wet the cloth again and was about to wash a wound on his shoulder, when suddenly his hand went to the back of her neck and he grasped her hair in his fist. She raised her eyes sharply to glare at him. He stared back. Then, without warning, he pulled her face close to him, and his lips pressed searingly against hers. His mouth opened, forcing hers open too. His lips and tongue were wet, firm, and aggressive.

She tried to cry out but the sound died in her throat, coming out only as a soft moan. She knew she should struggle to push herself away from him, but her body would not respond to her commands. She remained motionless, her mind reeling, feeling the hot wet sensation of his mouth tightly against hers.

His hand moved to her back and he pulled her close against him, his naked skin touching her. The hardness and the heat of his body startled her. She was pressed up against him from her knees to her breasts. She felt the mat of hair on his muscular chest, and the way his hard, swollen manhood prodded against her through the thin remnants of her clothing.

When his hand moved around to the front of her, she tensed. She felt his hand pushing inside the coarse material of the military jacket she still wore, and alighting on her naked breast. She jerked back sharply, instinctively. He did not come after her. He simply stood facing her, straight and tall, his manhood incredibly rigid and angled up. "Come back here," he said in a low, commanding voice.

She shook her head vigorously.

"I said, come back."

The sight of his hard muscular body and handsome bruised face made her feel weak in the knees. Power and raw masculinity radiated from him like an irresistible force, drawing her near.

Without realizing that she was doing it, she stepped forward, coming close to him, though not touching his body. She looked at him with big, frightened eyes as he put his hand inside the flap of her jacket and caressed her breast. She gasped. He began kneading and fondling her breasts, and rubbing his palm over her sensitive nipples. A shocking sensation of wild pleasure surged through her. Her nipples became pert and erect against the palm of his hand.

He pushed the jacket back from her shoulders and let it fall off onto the worn carpet. His hand went to her torn chemise, which was bunched up around her waist, and in a swift, sharp movement he ripped it off. Then he ripped away her underpants.

Sabrina's hands went up to hide her nakedness, one hand over her breasts, the other over her sex. Hunter grinned dryly. He pushed her hands away, until they were helplessly out at her sides. Then he stepped back to behold her. His eyes traveled up and down her body, searingly, as she stood naked before him, blushing with shame and excitement.

"You're not just lovely," he said in a low, raw voice, narrowing an eye in appreciation. "What you have is rarer than that, babe: true beauty."

He took her arm and moved her over to the bed, and up onto the soft, quilted comforter. She lay on her side, covering herself with her hands.

"Onto your back," he said. When she did not respond, he put his hand to her shoulder and forced her roughly backward, pushing her hands away from her body. She watched his ruggedly handsome, bruised face lower to her breast, her heart pounding wildly. When his mouth encircled her nipple, she gasped sharply, making a loud sound. He began sucking at her nipple, licking it wetly, flicking it with his tongue.

Sabrina's breathing was rapid and loud now. Her head moved from side to side on the comforter. The pleasure that tingled through her breast was unbearable. His mouth moved to her other breast and continued its assault, lighting fires of blazing sensation. His tongue moved all over her nipples and breasts, wetting them, licking them. Without fully realizing she was doing it, Sabrina moved her hands to his head and began running her fingers through his thick thatch of sweaty, tousled black hair.

When his mouth moved over her stomach, below her navel, she began panting loudly for breath, her mouth remaining wide open. She felt the wetness of his lips and tongue touch her at the very kernel of her being, and she jolted rigid, her eyes going wide. She pulled her hands back from his head and for several seconds clawed the air with them.

Wicked flashes of pleasure shot through her loins as she felt him down there, probing her, licking her into a seizure of wild rapture. She moaned and whimpered and writhed about. Then he came up even with her on the bed and she felt the tip of his sex pressing against her womanhood. He looked at her tauntingly. She glanced along the space between their bodies and saw the hard jutting shaft touching against her. She felt a surge of anticipation flash hotly through her. Then, as she watched, the shaft pressed into her and disappeared, accompanied by the most shocking thrill of sensation she had ever experienced.

She cried out in a long, endless groan of pleasure.

Hunter began thrusting in and out of her rhythmically, continuously, sending waves of searing ecstasy surging through her lower body. She felt the heat and fullness of his rigid, swollen shaft as he penetrated deep inside her, time after time, relentlessly.

The sensation was practically unbearable. She flung her arms out to the sides and her nails clutched at the mattress. She tossed her head back sharply, still breathing in gasps. Then she moved her arms to him and put them across his back, feeling the hotness of his skin on her palms. She had never *wanted* a man before, not in this way. But now there was no lying to herself. She knew she wanted this brutal, glowering, animalistic flier, this Dallas Hunter—and she wanted him in this, the most violent, passionate, way.

Pleasure surged through her, and then erupted ecstatically in her loins, burst after burst of vicious, violent pleasure that made her cry out. Her arms locked around his neck, her legs locked tightly about his hips, and she held on for dear life as he moved frenziedly about on top of her. Soon his body began shuddering and quaking. Then after a moment, he lay still atop her, he too breathing in rasping gasps. Somewhat distractedly, she felt the plaster of his cast pressing against her breasts.

He rolled off her. Then he did something that surprised Sabrina: he rose on his elbow and kissed her gently on the lips. He looked at her with a gaze that held strong emotion. She stared back, wide-eyed, stunned. Then he lay back and closed his eyes. She continued looking at him, not quite believing she had seen that look of his. After what seemed a long vigil just watching him, she succumbed to the utter exhaustion she felt, and fell asleep.

In the morning she awoke and looked at him beside her, still sleeping. She got up, showered in the bathroom stall, then put on his dark blue flannel bathrobe that she found in the closet. It was way too long for her, coming down to the floor in folds, so that she had to be careful to avoid tripping when she walked. She tied it around her with the sash. When Hunter awakened, she began making him breakfast from the meager fixings in the pantry. She glanced over at him as he stood before the mirror shaving, lathering his beard with white foam from the brush, then attacking it with the straight razor.

She had found cheese, sausage, and crusty French bread in the pantry, which she cut into slices and arranged on a plate. She set it before him on the table, along with the orange juice she had discovered out on the windowsill where he had placed it the day before, so the night's coldness would chill it.

When he came to the table, after dressing, and saw the food she had prepared for him, he looked at her strangely. She stood with her hands clasped in front of her, unable to conceal the pride she felt at having done this for him.

His expression became bitterly amused. "So it starts already," he said.

"What do you mean?" she asked, puzzled.

"The domestic routine. Putting the ring through the man's nose. Getting ready to tie him down."

"How dare you think that?" she said sharply.

"Forget it," he said. He sat down at the table,

took several slices of cheese, bread, and sausage onto his plate and began eating.

Sabrina remained standing by the table, furious. He glanced up at her, said nothing, and returned to his food. After a moment, he said, "Come on, babe. Don't be so defensive. Sit down. Eat."

"Why are you acting like such a bastard?" she asked.

"Because I like my life the way it is!" he declared with a hint of anger. "I like flying, I like adventure, and I like being single." He put down his fork and pointed a finger at her to emphasize his words: "Listen," he said, "there's nothing that could ever take me away from the fast and dangerous *unattached* life I'm living now. If you ever start thinking you can do it, watch out. You're in for a letdown."

"You're the one who made me come here last night!" she protested angrily. "If not for you, I could have gone to that Englishman's cousin's home! And now you're acting like *I'm* the one who lured *you* here. As though I have some grand designs on you. Well, let me tell you, mister, I wouldn't want you if you were the last man on earth! *God*, are you conceited to think I would!"

"That's fine," he said, standing up from the table. "That's the way I want it. Just so we understand each other." He turned away and left the apartment.

They lived together during the next two weeks, and Hunter never mentioned the subject again. For Sabrina, the days spent with him were the happiest of her life. She had never been with anyone who really cared for her, the way Hunter soon seemed to come to care for her. He was reluctant to show his feelings openly, but she could tell that he was beginning to feel more and more strongly toward her. She could see it in the way he gazed at her and from the things he began doing that were contrary to his nature.

One sign of this was that he had been offered a secret mission called "Red Tango" in the north of France, and had turned it down in order to stay here in Marseilles with Sabrina—so he could return home to her every evening after his flight-training duties were done. They spent a lot of time touching and making love. They went for walks in the evening along the waterfront, gazing at the moon's reflection in the sea. She cooked for him often, making amazing meals from the simple ingredients he brought home from the butchers, bakers, and produce stores.

The only problem with their relationship was that Sabrina soon realized something major was troubling Hunter, and that he refused to talk about it. She could tell from the increasingly cold way he began looking at her as the days progressed that whatever the problem was, it threatened to ruin their relationship.

Finally it came into the open one evening, when he began acting coldly toward her after they had made love, acting as if he did not really care about her at all. When Sabrina asked in a hurt voice why he was behaving this way, the answer burst from him in a wounded, involuntary snarl: "Because I don't trust you!"

"Don't trust me?" she said stunned. "But . . . why?"

"Because I don't like being played for a sucker."

"Dallas, what are you talking about!?"

"You neglected to tell me something that time I tried to rescue you from the dockside. Or have you forgotten? I sure as hell haven't. It's been bothering me ever since."

"You mean that I was . . . married?" she said painfully, lowering her eyes.

"That's right. A small thing like that. You were married, babe, to the man you told me was kidnapping you."

"But he *was* kidnapping me! He was taking me away against my will! And I didn't marry him by choice, Dallas. I was forced to do it, while I was drugged!" She saw from the way he was looking at her that he wanted very much to believe her, but part of him was wary and cautious, not wanting to be tricked twice.

"Listen," he said, showing what was really on his mind. "What that Kraut said about your being a thrill-seeker, a girl who likes creating excitement at other people's expense. Tell me about that."

"It was an outright lie! You don't *believe* that?"

He didn't answer, just looked at her scrutinizingly.

Now Sabrina understood what the real problem was. "You're afraid I'm just leading you on," she said. "You think I might be just looking for excitement and that's why I'm staying with you now."

He still didn't answer, but she could see from his look that she was right. This was what had been troubling him all along. She went to him and put her arms around his neck. "Dallas, I love you. That's why I'm staying here with you. You're the . . . you're the best thing that's ever happened to me," she said in a quiet voice, knowing in her heart that it was true.

76

She could see that he wanted to believe her, but that he could not let himself give up his doubts. "Tell you what," he said. "So long as you're still here for me to come home to in the evenings, I'll know you're telling the truth. If I ever come home and find that you're gone and that you don't come back . . ." He shrugged. ". . . Well, nothing lost, nothing gained. I'll figure you were just playing me along, for thrills, and that you got tired of it. I'll chalk it up to experience, babe."

"That will never happen!" she protested. "Don't talk this way. You scare me."

"That's what I want to hear." He grinned, and closed his arms around her. He kissed her forcefully.

When she looked into his eyes, though, she could see there was still a specter of doubt. Well, she thought, that will just take time. After a few more days, or weeks, he'll see how wrong he is about me. Then he'll believe me, she thought, believe how deeply I care for him . . .

Several days later, just after Hunter left for the air base in the morning, there was a knock at the door. What is it? she wondered. Did he forget his keys again? When she opened the door, smiling, she saw two stubble-bearded German sailors standing directly in front of her, staring down at her. Behind them stood Von Himmel, who was glaring at Sabrina in red-faced fury. "Ve haf you again at last," he said in a low growl.

She screamed as the sailors grabbed the front of the blue bathrobe. A hand went around her mouth, stifling all sound. Other hands grasped her arms and legs, and she felt herself lifted off her feet. She was carried bodily out of the room, down the stairs, to a waiting tin lizzie automobile, whose engine was running.

She was forced into the back seat, sandwiched between Von Himmel and a triangular-faced colonel in full uniform, who was already in the car. The sailors hurried into the front seat next to the driver, and the car sped off.

Von Himmel raised his fist to strike Sabrina. She yelped and put up her arms defensively. But before the red-faced Von Himmel could hit her, the German colonel exclaimed sharply, "Von Himmel! You forget your orders so quickly? She is to be delivered *unmolested*."

Von Himmel lowered his hand slowly, a look of burning fury and frustration in his eyes.

Sabrina turned to the severe-faced colonel. "Delivered?" she asked. "Delivered to whom?" The colonel ignored her completely. "Where are you taking me?" she asked. No one answered. The colonel stared out the window impassively. Von Himmel glared at her with fierce hatefulness.

They had left the city traffic behind, and were driving down a long country road now. After a while they turned into a driveway that took them to a closed, very tall, ironwork gate. A sign proclaimed that the compound within was a consular office of the German Embassy. A German soldier appeared from the guardhouse, saluted the colonel, and asked to see the driver's papers. Then he opened the gates and the car passed into the compound.

After a short drive down a winding road, they stopped finally in front of a formidable gray building. Von Himmel and the colonel marched into the building, followed by Sabrina, who was flanked by the two sailors, each holding her by the arm.

As they ascended a stairway inside the building, Sabrina kept wondering who it was she was being delivered to. At first she had thought Von Himmel was behind her capture, and that he intended to take her back with him to Tahiti. Now, though, it seemed as if some superior authority had taken command of the situation—for some reason Sabrina could not begin to guess—and that Von Himmel no longer controlled her fate.

Whoever this mysterious superior was, Sabrina thought, he must be very powerful to command such impressive quarters and such a strong guard.

At the top of the stairs a lieutenant saluted the colonel.

"I leave her with you now," the colonel told the lieutenant. "I have delivered her as instructed."

"*Danke,* Herr Colonel. Der general will be most pleased." The lieutenant turned to Von Himmel and said, "You may leave too."

"*Me?* But she is my wife! I have a right to stay. No, I won't leave, certainly not!"

"You would disobey General Wolfschmidt's direct orders?" said the lieutenant icily, staring him down.

Von Himmel's face went beet red with rage and began trembling. He glared at the lieutenant, who held his stare unwaveringly. Then he looked at Sabrina, his eyes filled with rage, turned sharply on his heel and left.

The lieutenant led Sabrina by the arm to the closed doorway of the inner office, and knocked on the door.

"*Kommen Sie,*" said a sharp, staccato voice from within.

The door was opened and Sabrina was led inside. The room was large, high-ceilinged, and well-appointed. At the tall French windows stood a deceptively slim, ramrod-straight man facing away from them, gazing out the window. His hands were clasped behind his back, his black-booted legs braced apart. The lieutenant saluted the general's back, turned and left the room, shutting the door behind him. Sabrina was left alone, staring at the general's back.

When he finally turned to face her, she was surprised. He seemed so young to be a general. He had gaunt, sharply chiseled features beneath close-cropped brown hair. His eyes were pinpoints of steel-gray intensity. He would have seemed quite handsome, in a severe sort of way, if not for one thing; the cruel set of his thin-lipped mouth. A monocle was in his left eye. He wore civilian clothing rather than a uniform.

"Ah, good," he said in a staccato, thickly accented German voice. "Your photograph did not lie. You truly are this lovely."

"What photograph?" she asked, bewildered.

"The one your idiot husband showed me. It was taken at your wedding." He paused. "The fool," he said, shaking his head, a contemptuous grin on his lips. "That oaf Von Himmel showed me your photo out of pride. He is proud you are so beautiful. He did not consider that I would take you away from him, because of your beauty. To have you serve my own ends."

"Serve what ends?" she said, becoming very upset. "What are you talking about?"

"Frau von Himmel," he said in a clipped, staccato voice, "you are about to become my most important spy."

She stared at him in disbelief. He was looking her up and down, slowly and purposefully. Before she could say anything, he came forward and in a swift movement pulled open her bathrobe.

There was an instant during which he stared at her nakedness, before she could react. Then she swung wildly at him to slap him. He blocked her swing with a quickly raised arm. He did not strike her back for attempting to slap him. He seemed scornful of her effort, which had failed so miserably against his skillful, expertly executed arm-block.

He walked to his desk and leaned back against the edge of it, holding his chin in the crook of his thumb and forefinger. He regarded Sabrina critically as she jerked the sides of her robe closer around her, and tightened the belt at her waist. "That *Dummkopf* Von Himmel has a woman with beauty such as yours, and he does not know what to do with you," he said scoffingly. "I know what to do with you, however."

His eyes became cold and calculating as he spoke. "I did not achieve my rank by lack of foresight, Fraulein. I have foresight, and because of it I am building a spy ring now, in preparation for the inevitable war. I want you as my principal spy in France. Why? you are wondering. Because I know the French high command. I know that a woman of your beauty will be irresistible to them. Here is my plan: I will put you in a position where you will come to the attention of the highest-ranking military and government officials. You will loosen their

81

lips through intimate means, and relay their secrets back to me."

"This is ridiculous!" she exclaimed, flustered and angry at the way she was being mistreated. "You can't force me to do anything against my will. I'm an American citizen! You have no right to . . . to . . . Why, you had me *kidnapped* from where I was staying! That's illegal. I'll report you to the gendarmes!"

"Will you now?" said General Wolfschmidt smugly. He snorted contemptuously at her indignation, walked over to a door in the wall and flung it open.

In the small room now revealed to her, Sabrina was shocked to see Michael Yorkshire, the English officer who had helped rescue her from Von Himmel that night in the bar. His wrists were manacled above his head to chains embedded in the wall. He was seated on a long bench. He was bare-chested, and Sabrina could see the countless bruises on his muscular, hairless chest and on his arms. A German soldier stood next to him.

It took a moment for her to overcome her shock at seeing him here. The first thing she said was, "You've been beating him!"

Wolfschmidt shrugged noncommittally.

She looked back at Michael. Though he seemed very groggy from his beating, he forced a grin as he gazed back at her. So this is what happened to him that night, she thought bitterly. He *didn't* escape from the Germans he was leading on a wild-goose chase, away from her and Hunter. They caught him! And he's been a prisoner ever since.

She went toward him, but the guard moved quickly in front of her, blocking her. Without thinking, reacting automatically to the sight of the Englishman, who had been so kind to her, chained this way, she pushed the guard in the chest and tried to move around him.

The guard became enraged at her effrontery—embarrassing him in front of such a high-ranking officer. He raised his black-gloved hand sharply to strike her.

"You hurt her, heinie, and I'll kill you!" declared Michael, through cracked, bruised lips.

The guard turned to face him, enraged even more at the fact that even the *prisoner* was now defying him. He slugged Michael hard across the face, bloodying his mouth. He started to strike him again.

"No!" screamed Sabrina, attacking him, scratching, biting, flailing about wildly.

The guard's hands went to her throat and he was about to choke her, when Wolfschmidt barked: "Corporal! Release her!"

The guard immediately pulled his hands down to his side and snapped to attention.

Sabrina rushed over to Michael. They stared at each other in silence. What was there to say? He tried bravely to grin again, but the bruise on his face made it hard. "Here," said Sabrina, pulling the sleeve of her bathrobe over her hand, then using it to dab gently at Michael's cut, bleeding lip.

Michael grimaced sharply, but said nothing.

"Are you . . . are you all right?" Sabrina asked, knowing it was a stupid question, not knowing what else to say.

Wolfschmidt spoke up in his staccato German voice, before Michael could answer. "I don't have time for this," he declared. "I wanted to show you the reason you will spy for me. Now I have shown you. You will do as I say now, of course?"

"The hell she will, you bastard!" exclaimed Michael. "You keep your filthy schemes to yourself. Leave her out of them!"

Wolfschmidt nodded at the guard, who struck Michael again, hard, snapping Michael's head to the side with the force of the blow. Sabrina screamed.

Michael slowly turned his head back to Wolfschmidt to glare at him. He was hurt, but his foolish courage was not diminished. "Hit me all you want, you coward. But you jolly well better keep away from her, you hear me! Or I'll break free from here somehow—I swear it!—and I'll tear you to pieces."

The guard hit Michael again, hard, in the stomach. And when Sabrina tried to stop him from hitting him again, he grabbed her arm and twisted it high up behind her, hurting her, doubling her over forward.

"Leave her alone, damn you!" Michael gasped, his voice an agonized whisper due to being hit in the stomach.

I have to get out of this room, Sabrina thought to herself desperately. For the Englishman's own good! Hunter was right: this man is too much of a foolhardy "hero." He doesn't know when to keep quiet! Sabrina realized that if she remained here in the room with him, he would continue antagonizing Wolfschmidt, sticking up for her—with the result that he would continue to be beaten even more savagely.

Wolfschmidt entered the small room and came up to Sabrina, as she stood bent over at the waist. "I will not wait longer for your reply, Fräulein." As his icy eyes looked piercingly into hers, he un-latched the flap from the leather holster on his belt, pulled out a black metal pistol, and aimed it at Michael's head.

"Wait!" Sabrina cried. "Don't! I . . . I'll—"

"Now blast it, pet!" declared Michael, "Don't get mixed up in this spy business! You're too . . . lovely, darling, really. And too sweet and innocent. I can see that, even though I don't really know you. Don't sacrifice yourself on my account."

Wolfschmidt snapped back the hammer of the pistol, cocking it.

"Make him let me go," Sabrina pleaded to Wolfschmidt, referring to the guard who was twisting her arm back. When Wolfschmidt nodded, and the man released her, Sabrina walked quickly out of the small room, without another word to Michael. If she and the general remained here, Michael would talk himself into being shot; there was no doubt about it. Wolfschmidt followed her out. She looked back into the room and had a last, brief glance at Michael's handsome, sensitive face, commanding her not to give in, before the door was slammed shut.

Wolfschmidt looked at her impatiently. "Well?" he demanded.

She was repulsed and terrified at the thought of becoming a spy for him, for the Germany of the fanatic Kaiser Wilhelm. But what else could she do? It was her fault Michael was chained here as their prisoner, at their mercy. He'd been captured leading the Germans away from her.

"*Will you do as I say?*" demanded Wolfschmidt, becoming furious with impatience.

"Yes!" she answered. She held his stare for a moment, then turned her eyes down.

He went to his desk and began rummaging through a drawer in search of something. "Do not deceive yourself that you can tell me yes now, but then go to French Intelligence and betray me later. They will not be able to rescue your Englishman. He will be dead long before they ever enter this compound."

"I wasn't thinking of doing that," Sabrina said quietly, lying. She had been thinking of doing exactly that. But she knew now that the idea would not work. Wolfschmidt's threat to kill Michael before he could be rescued was not an idle one.

The general found what he was searching for: a large, sealed manila envelope, bulging with its contents. He put it on the desk in front of him.

"Now here is the plan," he said stern-facedly. "To be useful to me you must come to the attention of the highest-ranking ministers and officers. I will arrange it. I want you to make a career of your exotic dancing—the kind you were doing in the *La Grande Bouteille* bar before Von Himmel stopped you. I will arrange for you to become one of the most famous acts in the land, in demand at the most celebrated night spots in all France. I will *personally* take command of your career. I will see that you are sought after by the Ritz. The Moulin Rouge."

Sabrina was flabbergasted. "But that's absurd!" she protested. "Me? Performing at the Moulin Rouge? Why it's . . . it's impossible!" She almost felt like laughing at him.

Wolfschmidt became absolutely still. His thin lips turned down in a sneer. "Nothing is impossible to Heinrich Wolfschmidt," he said, pronouncing each word sharply and distinctly. There was such a single-minded, ruthless intensity about him, Sabrina found herself almost believing him. "You have heard of the Marquand Club?" he asked.

Sabrina nodded. The club was world-famous as a favorite hunting ground for talent agents seeking new attractions for the most famous clubs.

"You will begin performing there tomorrow night. I have already arranged it."

Sabrina was surprised—and impressed. The general had to be extremely skillful to get an engagement at the Marquand Club for a simple exotic dancer like herself. She regarded him with wary respect. It was clear he had planned this meeting with her well in advance and that he had known how she would respond to seeing Michael chained with a pistol aimed at his temple. He had *known* she would agree to spy for him.

Don't underestimate this man, Sabrina warned herself. He has to be extremely talented and ruthless to achieve such a high rank at such a young age. Still, the idea that she, Sabrina, could be in demand by clubs like the Moulin Rouge . . . why, it was ridiculous.

"Once you begin dancing at France's most famous clubs," he continued, "you will be deluged by social invitations from ministers, generals, government officials. They will woo you and court you. They will invite you to the grandest theaters, the finest restaurants. You will accept their offers. You will become 'friendly' with them, and when they divulge military secrets, you will relay them to me."

"And if I do this," she said, "you'll let the Englishman go?"

Wolfschmidt ignored her question. He opened

the manila envelope before him and emptied the contents onto his desk. "The lieutenant who escorted you into this room—Gunther—he will be your contact. Here are your instructions for meeting him and delivering information." He handed her a sheet of typed paper. She took it.

"Here are five thousand francs," he said, handing her a packet of bills. "Buy clothing, jewelry, whatever you need. From now on you must keep up an image. You are to be a famous celebrity. You must live like one."

"I don't believe this," she said, half dazed that such a thing could really be happening to her.

"And here is the key to your new apartment. It is on the Rue Madeleine. It is already well furnished, and stocked with a few odds and ends of clothing, mink stoles, material of that nature. You will—"

"Now wait a minute!" Sabrina interrupted, flustered. Too much was happening too fast. "Before you go any further, I want to get one thing straight: you'll let the Englishman go free, if I do this for you?"

"Do you think I am a fool, Fräulein?" he said angrily. "Of course I won't let him go! He will be held as security, to make certain you continue doing as you are told. Here is what I will promise you: he will remain unharmed. And I also promise this," he said ominously. "If you refuse to spy for me as I tell you, I will kill him. This instant."

Sabrina wanted more, but she knew she would have to settle for just this promise to leave Michael unharmed. At least for the moment. Later she could try to find some way of setting him free.

"What else do you wish to know?" Wolfschmidt asked impatiently.

"You just want me to dance as I was dancing before? In a colored sari?"

"Would you agree to dance any other way?"

"You mean with less clothing? I certainly will not!"

"Then obviously I will have to settle for you dancing in your sari." He said this with a look of sarcastic malice that made Sabrina feel very distrustful. He pressed a button on his desk, though, before she could pursue the matter. Lieutenant Gunther appeared in the outer doorway.

Wolfschmidt said to Sabrina: "You will leave me now, Frau von Him— I beg your pardon. *Princess Breena.* That is the name you use in your act I believe? From this day on, it is your only identity— that and 'X-79,' your agent designation in our organization. Sabrina St. Claire von Himmel no longer exists."

He stood up and leaned forward over the desk toward her, his knuckles pressed against the top. "Gunther will escort you now to your new residence. Do not return to the apartment of your American flier. Ever. You are to avoid him completely. No one is to know of your mission as my spy."

She started to protest, but he turned his back on her sharply, and began looking out the window. Lieutenant Gunther took her arm and escorted her out the doorway. She looked back for a last glimpse of the room where Michael was being held. The door to Wolfschmidt's office was closed in her face, though, and then she was being hurried downstairs, to a waiting German staff car.

Chapter 7

She had to get back to Hunter. She needed to explain to him what happened and get his advice on what she should do next. She also needed, desperately, to be hugged, to be comforted. Her meeting with Wolfschmidt had left her shaken and disoriented.

The instant Lieutenant Gunther deposited her at the door of her fancy new second-story apartment, after making sure she opened it and stepped inside, Sabrina rushed to the window that looked down on the street. She saw the staff car waiting at the curb, its motor still running. After a moment, Gunther reappeared on the sidewalk and entered the car. The car sped off.

Sabrina hurried downstairs and out through the lobby. She was still wearing the trench coat Gunther had given her to cover her bathrobe. As soon as she was outside the building, she began looking down the street for a taxi to hail.

She stopped cold, however, when she saw a heavyset, beefy-faced man standing on the corner, pretending to be reading the evening *Le Figaro*. The paper was held up partway in front of his face, and his hat was pulled down low. His eyes were watching Sabrina. Despite the civilian clothes he wore—a baggy suit that fit him poorly—Sabrina knew he was one of Wolfschmidt's men, there to keep an eye on her. A car was parked near him, probably for his use in case Sabrina entered a taxi.

Instead of hailing a taxi, Sabrina went to a news kiosk and bought a paper, to make it seem she had a good reason for coming outside. Then she returned to her apartment, cursing under her breath and feeling fiercely upset and frustrated.

She watched the heavyset man through the window of her apartment, waiting for him to go away. He refused to leave his post. Finally, just after sundown, the man did leave his corner. But to Sabrina's dismay, he was replaced by two more of Wolfschmidt's henchmen, both just as obvious as the first. Sabrina paced about the apartment furiously, not knowing what to do.

Late at night, she decided upon a plan. The apartment building had only a single exit—the one in the lobby. The windows of her room faced the street where Wolfschmidt's men could watch them. She was sure the Germans had chosen this apartment for her for these very reasons. There was one thing they had not counted on, though, Sabrina knew: her desperateness.

A fire was going in her fireplace now. She took a wool blanket from the bed, folded it up, and threw it onto the fire. This banked the flames enough to allow her to reach in under the mantle and, with a thick stocking protecting her hand, to pull the flue shut.

The blanket began burning swiftly and the fire roared back to life. Now, though, there was no place for the smoke to escape except back into the room. The smoke began billowing forth more quickly than she expected and she began coughing hackingly before she could make it to the door. She flung open her door and stepped out into the hall. Within seconds the hall was filled with billowing black smoke, making it seem as if the fire were raging throughout the building.

"Fire!" Sabrina shouted, running up and down the hall.

People, most of them wearing nightcaps and gowns, stuck their heads out of their doors quizically.

"Fire!" Sabrina yelled to them.

An old woman, alarmed at the smoke, began yelling *"Feu! Feu!* Fire! Fire!" Others took up the chant. Instantly the hall became crowded with yelling, running people, who surged down the stairway in a frenzied rush to get out of the building.

"Feu!" they yelled as they descended the stairway, alerting those on the bottom floor to the danger. Soon these residents too were rushing toward the single exit in the lobby.

Sabrina pushed into the center of the crowd, and felt herself carried along by the stream of moving bodies out into the night. She felt the chill of the night breeze upon her face, and she could breathe clean, crisp air again. She remained hidden from view behind several people as she moved quickly around the corner, then down the street. A sizable crowd of onlookers had gathered on the sidewalk now.

Sabrina had had a brief instant to look back at the Germans before rushing around the corner. She saw them scanning the crowd with frustrated, horrified looks on their faces, desperately seeking her out.

She hailed a taxi as soon as she was several blocks away, and took it to Hunter's apartment. Hunter did not answer, though, when she banged on his door. Where could he *be*? she wondered in a panic. It was past midnight! He *had* to be here!

She pounded on the door more loudly, until finally a groggy, clean-cut young man from the room across the way came into the hall. "Hey there, lady, whatcha doin'?" he asked in English, irritated. There were several American fliers in this building, Sabrina knew, from Hunter's squadron. Hunter had told her about this young man from across the hall, who was his friend. His name was Eddie Rickenbacker.

"I'm looking for Major Hunter," Sabrina said to him. "Please, I have to find him. Do you know where he is?"

"Gone, that's where. Left for a shot at Red Tango up north. Left only a couple hours ago, too—too bad you missed him. Hey, ain't I seen you around here before?"

"Listen," Sabrina said urgently, "I have to contact him."

"Ain't no way, lady," Eddie Rickenbacker said, trying to be friendly, but perturbed at being awakened at this hour. "I'd like to help you out, but everything about Red Tango is top secret, exceptin' its name." He scratched his hole-ridden undershirt and yawned sleepily. "Come back on the fifteenth of next month. Dallas'll be around again then."

She was looking at the closed door of Hunter's apartment, not quite believing he was really gone. "But . . . *why* did he go?" she said despairingly, mostly to herself.

"He said something about how he thought he

had a good reason for sticking around here, but then he found out he didn't have that good reason after all, whatever it was. Said he'd just been led on, been taken in. Messed with for the sake of some thrill-seeker looking for a little excitement."

"Oh, no!" she cried.

He looked concerned. "Whatsa matter, lady? You all right? You want to come in and sit down for a minute, I'll get you some water?"

Sabrina turned and ran down the hall, her eyes filling with tears. The sleep-groggy American looked after her in bewilderment, scratching his cheek.

The next evening at seven, she stood in the backstage area of the Marquand Club, waiting nervously for the master of cermonies to introduce her. She peered out through the red velvet curtain as the dinner-jacketed Frenchman began his introduction. "And now, laideez and gentlemen, our newest attraction, ze mysterious young woman whose background no one knows . . ."

Sabrina looked out at the well-dressed men and women of the audience in their evening clothes, and at the attractively appointed cabaret room. This club was definitely a prestigious one, and she was impressed by it. But still, it was a far cry from here to the Moulin Rouge. Had Wolfschmidt really been serious when he said he'd arrange for her to become famous enough to play the Moulin Rouge?

No, Sabrina thought, he must have been fooling himself. Such a thing was impossible. Even the very idea that a simple exotic dancer like herself could achieve such fame was ridiculous. And yet . . . he had seemed like such a ruthlessly efficient man. How could he have made such a major error in judgment?

Her curiosity was cut short as the master of ceremonies finished his introduction: " . . . the one and only Princess Breena!" The curtain parted, and Sabrina stepped forward onto center stage. Then, totally surprising her, the man added: " . . . and her Satanic Slaves!"

What's that? she thought, frowning in puzzlement. Suddenly two burly strongmen came from the wings and joined her, taking up positions on either side. "Who are you?" she asked, alarmed, as the two men bowed to the audience. The sound of the applause greeting her introduction was loud, drowning out her question.

The strongmen wore shiny purple satin vests, and purple satin pants with billowing legs, which highlighted Sabrina's own purple-and-orange sari. They had hairy chests and strongly muscled arms. Though Sabrina continued to stare at them in surprise, they did not look at her at all. They acted as if nothing unusual were happening, as if they were part of her act.

The musicians in the pit began playing. The audience was watching expectantly. There was nothing Sabrina could do but begin dancing. She started performing the graceful dances she had learned in Tahiti, swirling and twisting and moving about the stage.

The strongmen began dancing also, on either side of her. Their dancing consisted of nothing more than twirling around in circles, and occasionally going down on one knee. It was crude and amateurish and did not in any way enhance her act. Was this how Wolfschmidt intended to get her booked into the Moulin Rouge? she thought cynically. Were these apelike clowns supposed to somehow make her act more exciting? What folly! Obviously, she had overestimated the young German general.

But then, just as she thought this, the dancers twirled over to her. One grabbed her around the waist and held her tightly from behind. The other danced twirlingly around her in a circle. Then in a swift gymnastic movement he leaped into the air and came down in front of Sabrina—and ripped the front of her sari down and completely off of her.

Sabrina screamed. The audience, however, thought this was part of the act. The dancer continued twirling about stylishly, executing more complicated moves than he had done earlier. The one who was behind her began moving from side to side, shimmying, as if he too were part of the act.

The dancer who had torn her sari now leaped back in front of her once more, and this time tore away the brief camisole and underwear Sabrina had been wearing, leaving her completely nude.

The audience cheered wildly, thinking that this too was part of the act. The Marquand Club had a reputation for "arty" avant-garde acts, and the audience assumed this was only one of the more extreme examples. Sabrina was twisting and writhing wildly in the grip of the strongmen behind her, but her movements, and those of the men, seemed in time to the loud music, furthering the impression that the three were a single act.

The male dancers began something new now: pantomiming a scene. One of them produced a long pink silk scarf and began whipping it back and forth through the air, its end coming close to Sabrina but not touching her. He was pantomiming that he was whipping her.

Sabrina's look of anguish and humiliation seemed to the audience to be part of the pantomime, as were her efforts to struggle free and to hide her nakedness with her hands. All of it fit into the scene the dancers had established. Sabrina seemed to be playing the role of a woman being stripped and abused. The audience loved it. Their applause rang throughout the cabaret.

Sabrina felt the grip of the man holding her from behind loosening. She could tell he was about to release her, and she prepared to flee from the stage. The dancer put his hand to the back of her head, though, and forced her to look off to the side of the stage, at a particular table. There Sabrina saw Wolfschmidt, attired in civilian clothing, the monocle in his eye. He was staring at her with a ruthless, intimidating look of warning.

The message was clear. The dancer was pointing out to her that Wolfschmidt was watching to see if she did as she was ordered. She had to continue dancing when he released her, or the threat to kill Michael would be carried out.

The music reached a loud crescendo of horns and drums. The dancer released Sabrina. For a moment, she stood frozen, uncertain. She looked at Wolfschmidt, who was still staring at her with those cold, watchful eyes. The dancers began pirouetting around the stage. There were only minutes left to the act. Soon the music would end, the performance would be over. *What could she do*?

Sabrina began dancing. She bent her head back and made graceful movements with her extended arms, while prancing lightly like a gazelle across the front of the stage—all the while completely naked, her breasts jiggling with her movements. Shame and embarrassment overwhelmed her, but she fought down the fierce desire to run and hide. She thought of the brave Englishman who was chained somewhere in the German Embassy. She had to do this now . . . there was no choice.

She danced for several minutes more, the "slaves" continuing to pantomime as if they were whipping her with the pink scarf. Finally the music reached its climax and then, mercifully, the performance was over. The musclemen each took one of Sabrina's hands, and came before the footlights with her so that the three of them were facing the audience. They bowed deeply in acknowledgment of the avid cheers and applause they were receiving. Many members of the audience—mostly men, but several of the women as well—had risen to their feet. None of them seemed to even suspect that Sabrina was a victim rather than a participant. The applause was thunderous.

When the curtain closed, hiding the three of them from view, Sabrina turned to the two dancers and glared at them hatefully. She wanted to strike them with all her might. The men looked at her expression, and broke out in snide, contemptuous laughter. Their eyes began traveling over her naked body.

Sabrina ran away from them, fighting back tears. She went to the dressing room that had been provided for her and locked the door behind her. She pulled on a robe, sat down at the makeup table, and lowered her head to her arms, her eyes watering.

Was this what she would be expected to endure

every night? she wondered. Would she have to perform like this regularly, to have those muscular goons strip her naked before leering crowds, night after night? Yes! Yes, if she wanted to save the Englishman's life! The thought made her shudder in an agony of helplessness.

A knock came at her dressing-room door. She did not answer it. Then came another rap, more insistent than the first. She heard a jumble of boisterous voices in the hall outside.

"Who is it?" she yelled through the door. "What do you want?"

Several French voices answered her, and a few English ones. "Mademoiselle, who is your agent?" called one.

"What?" she said, stunned by the question.

"Your agent, your agent," said another voice. "Who eez eet?"

Various others began shouting all at once, asking her questions through the door. Curious about what was happening, she opened the door and looked out. There, standing in the hall, were seven or eight men, each anxious to talk to her, each trying to jostle and elbow the others out of the way. Several men were holding out printed forms and pens for her to sign with. Others began jabbering at her all at once.

Sabrina frowned in concentration, trying to make out what they were saying. Most of them were talent scouts, she soon realized. The others were reporters.

"We want you for our club!" shouted one. "No, *non*, you come weeth us, our club eez better!" "Sign here, milady, let my English contacts represent you. We'll do right by you; cor, blimey, you bet we will." "Some background, madame, for ze *illustre*! *S'il vous plâit!*"

She slammed the door on the shouting, jostling men, and leaned her back against it. She almost wanted to laugh, even through her tears.

So Wolfschmidt had been smarter than she thought after all. He had arranged for her to appear at this club, where she would be observed by talent scouts and reporters. And he had arranged for her "act" to be so outrageously steamy that—coupled with her beauty—it would surely excite the reporters, and make the talent scouts realize the profit potential of having her perform in their own clubs. By tomorrow morning, she knew, news of her performance would be all over France.

So, she thought . . . Wolfschmidt had won after all.

Sabrina knew that other girls her age would be thrilled beyond belief at the prospect of the future which now lay before her: performing at the most celebrated clubs, being courted by Europe's most powerful and dynamic men. Sabrina felt horrible at the thought of it.

Oh, if only there were some way she could contact Dallas! But no, she knew there was no way. Not unil he returned from his mission on the fifteenth.

The flattering, demanding, insistent voices were still outside her door, clamoring for her to come out. She sank into a chair and shut her eyes, feeling very tired, with a weariness that reached deep into her soul.

Chapter 8

The next month was unlike anything Sabrina could ever have imagined, even in her wildest fantasies. She had to constantly remind herself that she was still naive, young Sabrina St. Claire—not someone named Princess Breena, a sultry seductress who was the toast of France and who used men as playthings. If she did not eternally bear it in mind, she knew, she would be in danger of losing her perspective.

The very first night after her initial performance, it began to happen: she returned to her dressing room after her dance, and there, sitting on the bureau, was a giant bouquet of red roses. With it was a note praising her beauty and begging to be allowed to take her to dinner. The note was signed by one of the most famous stage actors in all Europe.

Sabrina turned him down. She felt wretched about being forced to perform naked on the stage, and since she did not have to go out with this man (he wasn't of strategic importance to Wolfschmidt) she didn't.

The next night, though, there were several bouquets of flowers from various suitors, along with boxes of bonbons, gifts of jewelry, and all manner of elaborate cards requesting the pleasure of her company at social gatherings. When she moved from the Marquand Club to the Ritz, after the second week, she soon had her suitors personally beating a path to her stage-room door, not merely dropping off notes and flowers.

It was Wolfschmidt who decided which of her distinguished suitors she would go out with . . . and what information she would try to get from them.

Soon Sabrina was being escorted to the fanciest cafes, theaters, and private clubs on the continent. She became accustomed to being waited on hand and foot by maître d's anxious to please her and her distinguished escorts . . . to seeing crystal chandeliers and plush surroundings . . . to dining on the finest china and with the most exquisite silverware. She was taken to the opera, the races, the theater—all manner of high-society entertainments. And she was invariably treated like royalty, because her newfound fame always preceded her.

Sabrina had not known such a glittering, swirling, exquisite world as the European social whirl even existed. And now she was thrust right into its center.

Since she had to dress elegantly to be accepted in the exclusive places she was now being taken, Wolfschmidt provided her with a complete wardrobe of beautiful, extravagantly expensive and stylish clothing. For the first time in her life Sabrina knew what it felt like to have real silk next to her skin, and the feel of the finest fabrics in the very latest fashions. Instead of wearing her radiant hair in long, curly tresses down her back, she now began to have it arranged in the most stylish way by the most renowned coiffeurs.

The thing that fascinated and excited her most though, no matter how hard she tried not to be affected by it, was the type of men she was being courted by; the ones who escorted her to these various affairs and entertainments. Back in Washington she had been permitted by her father to go out on "dates," but the males who invited her out had always been boys of her own age or a year or two older. And they had always acted like boys of that age. The men who were courting her now, though, were *men*—real men, interesting men, with suaveness and sophistication, and often with an aura of the immense power and fame that surrounded them.

Whether it was a younger man, like the dashing French cavalry officer she had dined with two nights ago, or an older man, like the Belgian grand duke who had squired her last weekend, her escorts invariably had one thing in common: they always commanded the attention of others wherever they went. Sabrina was constantly noticing all eyes turning toward them as she and her escort entered public or private places, she on the arm of the dynamic, usually famous man. What a heady sensation!

Sabrina knew she was in danger of becoming so swept up in the glamour of her new life that she might abandon herself to it completely, forgetting her true values and why she was doing what she was doing. There were two things that saved her from this, though: the nude dancing she was forced to perform, which she detested . . . and the fact that her suitors always tried to make love to her before the evening was through.

They acted as if they expected it. As if they *deserved* it. After all, wasn't she an exotic dancer? Certainly she couldn't be too very prudish.

Despite the fact that Wolfschmidt had ordered her to make love to the men she dated, since "pillow talk" was always the most revealing, Sabrina refused to do so. Instead, she let the men lure her back to their apartments, and then she lied to Wolfschmidt afterward, saying that she did sleep with them.

It did not matter to Sabrina that her escorts were always bitter and resentful when she refused to make love to them. The hell with them! They only wanted her for her body anyway. All she really cared about was whether she had gathered enough information from them to be able to make up authentic-sounding lies about the secrets Wolfschmidt wanted her to learn. She never told Wolfschmidt the real information she gathered. She only used it to make up tempting lies.

The problem came during nights like the last, when one of her escorts refused to take no for an answer. She had been scheduled to dine with Rasputin, the Russian "Mad Monk," confidant to Czar Nicholas himself. But five minutes after he came to pick her up, he physically leaped upon her, trying to force her to submit. She had run from her own apartment, her evening gown practically in shreds.

She thought of last night's encounter with Rasputin now, this morning, as she walked out through the luxurious lobby of her apartment building, on the way to visit Dallas Hunter. Today was the day he was supposed to be back from his mission. She desperately needed to see him. She feared her situation was suddenly about to take a turn for the worse. Wolfschmidt knew by now that she had failed to learn the information he demanded her to get from Rasputin. She had not even learned enough to make up an intelligent-sounding lie.

How angrily would Wolfschmidt react she wondered, as she stepped out the doorway into the bright morning sunlight.

She did not have to wonder long. A black automobile pulled away from the corner where it had been parked, sped down the street, and came to a screeching halt at the curb directly in front of her. Lieutenant Gunther, seated in the back, flung open the rear door. "Get in," he said coldly, jerking his head toward the empty seat next to him.

She stared at him fearfully, trying to decide whether or not to run.

"Der Englisher vas beaten half to death this morning as a result of your actions. If you do not come mit me *right now*, he vill be killed immediately."

Sabrina looked longingly up the street, in the direction she had intended to take to reach Hunter's apartment. Then she entered the car, and it sped off with a roar.

Wolfschmidt was taking files out of a cabinet when she was led into his office, and placing them in a wooden crate. He let her stand before him for a minute before looking up at her, the monocle in his eye. He turned to face her, slowly, his face reddening with fury. "You failed in your mission," he said in a steely, staccato voice. "You did not find out if Russia will defend Serbia in case of an invasion."

"I . . . I tried to get the information! He just wouldn't loosen up."

"You did all in your power to loosen him up?" he asked coldly.

"I—yes."

"You made love to him?"

"Yes, I did. But he still wouldn't—"

"Liar!" he shouted, slapping her across the face with the back of his hand.

The slap stung Sabrina sharply. She looked at the general's reddening, raging face, and realized for the first time that she was truly in danger. He was absolutely furious.

"You lie to me!" he exclaimed. "You have lied all along! You never slept with the men you went out with, did you? You thought to play me for a fool. To foil my plan of forming a tight, efficient spy ring in the midst of the French Republic, with you as the key figure."

"How do you know I didn't sleep with him?" she charged back, though without the conviction she tried to fake.

"You ran from your room last night, just after Rasputin arrived. Gunther was there, outside in the street. He saw you!"

"But I—I—" She tried to stammer out a plausible excuse, but none would come to her lips. The sight of the ferocious look on the general's face nearly paralyzed her into speechlessness.

"Do not try to explain," he said, waving away any excuses with a sharp gesture of his hand. "I need no more lies."

She stood watching him helplessly, her hand raised to her stinging cheek.

The general clasped his hands behind his back, raised his chin arrogantly, and looked down his nose at her. "A card has been sent to Rasputin," he said, "signed with your name. It apologizes for your rudeness of last night. It requests the chance to enjoy his company this evening. You will go to the engagement with him tonight and . . ." His eyes suddenly became inflamed, his voice rose to a raging shout: ". . . *You will get that information! You will get it even if you must lay under the Russian pig until you're flattened like paper!*"

Sabrina surprised even herself with her response. "I won't!" she declared, raising her chin defiantly. A moment of electric silence ensued, as their eyes locked. Sabrina had not intended to react this way. It was her natural stubbornness coming out though, as it always did at absolutely the worst times.

"I won't go to bed with that horrible man for you or anyone else," she declared, too enraged by his insulting demands to think clearly about what she was saying. "I'm not some kind of *whore*, whom you can order to lay with anyone you choose!"

"No?" said Wolfschmidt, his face growing redder. "No?" He pulled up the flap of his holster and withdrew the black pistol. "Fine, then," he said. He went to the door at the rear of the room and flung it open. Through the doorway, Sabrina saw Michael inside, his wrists manacled in front of him. Wolfschmidt pointed the pistol at him and fired.

He got off two shots in rapid succession before Sabrina rushed at him hysterically, screaming, "Nooooo!" pushing his arm to the side. The bullets had hit the wall on either side of Michael, and ricocheted zingingly about the small room.

"You wish to reconsider your decision?" Wolfschmidt said to her. "Here, you take your time. You think about it. As a guest of our hospitality." He motioned with a jerk of his head to Lieutenant

107

Gunther, who was already rushing forward. Gunther clasped his hands on Sabrina's shoulders from behind, pivoted her toward the open doorway, and shoved her forcefully into the small room. Sabrina fell down to her hands and knees, roughly scraping her skin.

Gunther was about to slam the door shut, when Michael stood up and said to him, "Uh, beg pardon, Fritz . . ." He raised his manacled wrists and made a beckoning motion with an index finger.

Gunther looked at him curiously, then came forward. Michael suddenly raised his fists up sharply, smashing the man in the jaw. Gunther's head jerked back with the blow, but then he leveled his gaze again at Michael, murderously, pulled his pistol from his holster, and smashed Michael across the cheek, leaving a streak of red blood.

Michael staggered back and tried to remain standing, but Gunther hit him again, dropping him down to the floor. "*Schweinhund!*" he roared. He turned and left, slamming the door.

Sabrina crawled over to where Michael lay, and looked at him with deep concern. "That was foolish," she said to him, gently brushing back his sandy blond hair, to get it out of his face.

"I know," he grunted. He was grimacing from the pain, but at the same time half smiling for some crazy reason of his own.

They really *had* beaten him half to death earlier, Sabrina saw, just as Gunther had said. One indication of the severity of the beating was the black eyepatch Michael now wore over his left eye. He's been half blinded, she thought to herself guiltily, all because I refused to go to bed with Rasputin.

"Why did you hit him like that?" she asked. "You

have your wrists chained together. And he has a gun. You had no chance at all."

"I know," he said, with a halfhearted laugh, then wincing against the pain. "I'll tell you, though, pet, I couldn't help it. I see someone throw you to the floor like that, and something inside me just explodes. I don't think too clearly at times like that. I just act."

"Here, let me help you." she said, seeing that he was trying to sit up. She tried to support his back as he moved over to the wall and leaned against it.

He was wearing a gray German fatigue uniform, without insignia. They probably had nothing else to dress him in. She saw him watching her intently, and she lowered her eyes, feeling embarrassed. "Do they . . . keep you here in this room?" she asked, feeling foolish at the question, but not knowing what else to say to him.

"No. In the basement. They only bring me up here when I have guests. Meaning you."

She still did not know what to say to him. She felt frustrated and awkward. What could you say to a man who is suffering greatly as a result of rescuing you? And whom you have seen only two times in your entire life? "Um . . . are you—"

"Listen, pet," he interrupted sharply, "you don't have to make small talk. I'm glad you're here, because I want to tell you something. Here's what I want to tell you." He pointed his finger at her and tapped it scoldingly on Sabrina's nose. "Don't come back here again! You shouldn't be here even now!"

She was stunned. "You think I'm here by choice?" she said defensively. "I'm here because—"

"I know the bloody hell why you're here; you don't have to tell me. You're here because you're still mixed up with these heinie blighters. You're doing what they told you to do last time, and what I told you *not* to do. You're spying for them."

"I'm just—"

"Spying for them, that's what you're just doing. And I want it to stop. You hear me?"

She met his eyes for a moment, her expression defiant in reaction to his aggressiveness. But then she had to turn her eyes away. What could she say? She couldn't stop spying for General Wolfschmidt, because if she did they would kill Michael instantly.

He put his hand to her chin and turned her face up again, making her look at him. "Listen, luv," he said in a softer voice, "I am grateful for what you're trying to do, now don't think I'm not. But the thing is, you see . . . well, I can't let a wonderful girl like you risk her neck over a rotter like me."

He seemed embarrassed at having revealed how he felt about her in the way he just referred to her. "If you don't break off with these Huns now, why, pretty soon they'll be telling you to actually *lay* with some of the blighters, to get more information from them. But don't you do it!" he commanded righteously. "You're far too good for something like that."

Sabrina's eyes glowed with emotion. Here he was, she thought, this brave Englishman, saying he'd rather die than have her dishonored in order to save him. He truly cared for her, even though he hardly knew her. Sabrina felt deeply touched. Except for Dallas, hardly anyone else in her life had ever really cared for her, or worried over her feelings.

She looked at him, and could tell from his

110

strangely naive expression that he did not realize it was too late to worry about preserving her "honor." He thought of her as a pristine virgin. She considered setting him straight, but something inside her made her stop. She couldn't quite bring herself to tell him the truth. But she had to tell him *something*, to explain her position.

"If I don't keep spying for them," she said, "they'll kill you."

He half smiled at her, as if she had said something amusing. "Bree, can't you see? They're going to kill me *anyway* . . . ?"

"No!" she exclaimed, shocked, not wanting to believe it.

"Of course they are! You really think they can let me go? And then try to explain to my government why they held a British subject prisoner in their embassy, when there isn't even a war on?" He shook his head, then smiled at her gently, sadly. "Don't worry about me, pet. Won't do any good. The one to worry about is you. We can't let them drag you down like this."

Sabrina had not wanted to believe it, but now she knew it was true. She could not save him by continuing to spy for Wolfschmidt. Not even if she consented to make love with everyone Wolfschmidt told her to. But then, what could she do to save him?

She had an idea. "I can go to the French Counterintelligence office," she said tentatively, not really sure of the idea. "Wolfschmidt said he'd kill you if I did, but if he's going to kill you *anyway* . . . ?"

"You might as well try it." He looked thoughtful. "Yes, it could work. If the French believed you, they could mount a raid on this embassy, to free me."

"They will believe me!" she declared. "They have to!"

He was looking off to the side, concentrating hard. Sabrina had a chance to study his handsome profile without his noticing. She looked at his strong, youthful features and his firm lips. Her skin began feeling very prickly suddenly, and it occurred to her that this was the first time she had been alone with Michael. He certainly had an exciting sensuality about him, she thought. And a powerfully magnetic charm that attracted her.

"We'll do it," he declared, suddenly turning to face her, catching her looking at him. Sabrina blinked in surprise.

He put his hands on her shoulders and his expression became serious. "But there's one thing I want to hear from you, pet: you won't spy for them anymore. Even if this idea about the French Counterintelligence rescue doesn't work."

"I won't," she said.

"You'd better not. Because if I think you're doing it, I'll make a rush at my guard the first bloomin' chance I get, to try to make my own escape."

"But he'll kill you!"

"Probably. And that'll solve the problem of making you stop this spying business to try to save me."

"I . . . I won't spy anymore," she said. "I promise. But I'll have to tell them that I will, to get out of here."

There was a moment of silence. Sabrina stood up to leave. Michael stood up also, slowly. They faced each other, and a look of tenderness passed between them. Sabrina had a sudden urge. She reached out and gently touched the back of his wrist. No more than that.

Michael suddenly extended his manacled arms and embraced her. He drew her as tightly against him as he could. His face was now hard, his expression smoldering with intensity. He kissed her passionately, a long, searing kiss that made Sabrina's head swim. A thrill of fiery excitement flashed through her. She felt as if she were melting inside. Time seemed to stand still.

When he relaxed his arms, so that she could pull her head back, Sabrina looked at him with surprise. There was a surprised look on Michael's face, too, as if he had not expected to do such a thing. But there was also a confident look of unapologetic affirmation. He had done it and he was glad.

"I . . . well, I . . . I should go," Sabrina finally managed to say, flustered. "I'll see you again soon. This plan will work. I . . . it . . ." Her words failed as she looked at his strong, serious face.

Michael raised his manacled wrists over her head, releasing her from the circle of his arms. Sabrina looked at him a second more, almost in bewilderment, not quite believing this had actually happened. Then she went to the door and knocked on it hard, calling loudly that she wanted to be let out.

When the door opened, she told Lieutenant Gunther that she would do as General Wolfschmidt asked. Gunther let her out and closed the door after her. She was trembling from Michael's sudden, unexpected passion—and her own response!

General Wolfschmidt was at the other end of the room still taking folders from his file cabinet and packing them into open crates. He stood near a jet-black, steel safe whose door, curiously, was ajar rather than closed and locked. "So," he said to Sabrina, regarding her sternly, "You will keep your engagement with the Russian tonight. Yes?"

"Yes," she said. "I'll keep it."

"And you will learn from him whether Russia will defend Serbia if that country is attacked."

"I'll try."

"You will *succeed*!" he declared. It was an absolute command, allowing no alternatives. "You will use your body to achieve my ends. Whatever is asked of you, you will do." His eyes lowered down from her face to stare at her bosom with intense absorption. His eyes narrowed. A twitch came to the corner of his thin-lipped mouth.

Sabrina drew her breath in sharply when she saw the bulge begin to rise up in his trousers. She realized now, for the first time, that he lusted after her. She had suspected it last time, from the way he gazed at her—but for some reason she decided she would not have trouble with him in that particular area.

Now, though, she saw perspiration break out on his upper lip as his eyes lowered to stare at her skirt. His jaw began trembling, and the lustfulness burned clearly in his eyes. It was when he took a step toward her that Sabrina held up her hand and said, "That's not part of our agreement."

He looked up, glaring into her eyes, furious.

"You touch me . . . and the deal is off." She said this in a nervous voice that she was trying desperately to make sound steady and self-assured.

She knew she was gambling now, and that the stakes were incredibly high. But she thought she knew this man's one weak spot: his ruthless, single-

114

minded devotion to his goal. His goal was to develop a major espionage network in France, with Sabrina as one of its key figures. She was gambling that he would not risk failing in his goal, no matter how violently he craved her body.

She tensed fearfully as he came toward her, stopping directly in front of her, their bodies almost touching. Sabrina felt shaken. Maybe she had misjudged him, she thought in panic. Maybe he would rape her right this instant, and kill Michael—and to hell with the goal and the game-plan.

But then she knew she had won her audacious gamble. "Get her out," he said in a low voice filled with cold fury. His face was sweating and trembling with rage, an inch away from hers.

Lieutenant Gunther grasped her arm and pulled her to the side, then marched her quickly through the doorway. Wolfschmidt stared after her with violent rage.

As the German staff car sped through the streets several moments later, on the way back to her apartment, Sabrina turned her thoughts to Hunter, and to the French Counterintelligence command. Which should I go to first, she wondered, after Gunther drops me off and leaves?

She wanted and desperately needed to see Hunter, to seek his advice and help. But if she went to the French first they might be able to rescue Michael immediately, before tonight, thereby sparing her from having to meet with that wretched, vile monk, Rasputin.

No, she thought, as the car pulled to the curb in front of her apartment building, there was really no question about it. She would have to go to Counterintelligence first. She opened the car door

115

and stepped out. "Good-bye," she said frigidly to Gunther, slamming the door.

"I am afraid not, Fräulein," said Gunther, opening the door again and stepping out to join her. "Ve vill vait for the Russian together."

And to Sabrina's dismay, they did just that. Gunther made himself at home in her apartment and did not leave her for even an instant. Then it was evening, and Sabrina jerked nervously in horror as the loud, heavy knock came to her apartment door.

She recognized the knock. Rasputin was here.

Chapter 9

He was one of the most bizarre, grotesque men Sabrina had ever seen. He stood in the doorway, tall and skinny, with his long black beard, and his black eyes burning into her with hypnotic intensity. "Good of you to honor me with an encore visit," he said in a deep, rumbling voice. His gaze was so menacing it made chills go up and down Sabrina's spine.

"C—come in, please," she said, holding the door for him.

Rasputin entered the room and stood just inside the doorway, his tall body hunched forward, his hands rubbing each other absently in front of him. The long, black monk's robe he wore made him appear very sinister. His eyes glanced around the room in a nervous, jerky manner. Then he looked at her sharply.

Sabrina stepped back involuntarily. "Shall we . . . go." she said quickly, thinking that she had to get out, away from the apartment. Last night he had begun pawing and attacking her within minutes of coming in the door. If he began a similar assault now, Sabrina knew, the fact that Lieutenant Gunther was hiding in the bedroom closet would not matter in the least. Gunther would certainly not intervene to protect her.

The hulking, black-robed monk stared at her with his hypnotic eyes as she grabbed her evening cape with the fur collar and pulled it around herself, clasping it in front with a golden neck chain. Rasputin made no move to help her with the cape.

When she was ready, she faced him, apprehensively.

"My coach awaits," he said, grimly, bowing, yet looking up at her with a cold, menacing expression. She quickly went out the door.

It was chilly outside and the stars were just beginning to show in the darkening sky. Rasputin had an open horse-drawn coach rather than an automobile. Sabrina bundled herself up in her wrap and climbed in.

As the horse clip-clopped along the Paris boulevards, with the wind blowing against Sabrina's face, she began questioning the monk immediately. Her only hope of salvation lay in finding out the information she needed very early, before the evening progressed to the inevitable bedroom scene. If she didn't learn the required details before, she might actually have to go to bed with the despicable monster, for she *had* to pry the secrets out of him. Otherwise, Wolfschmidt would kill Michael before she could go to French Counterintelligence to arrange a rescue.

"What a beautiful horse," she said, nodding at the sorrel drawing the coach. "But of course, if your country does defend Serbia in case of an invasion, your forces will have the finest steeds of any in the war."

Rasputin said nothing.

"Your cossacks would certainly join the battle against the Prussian invaders?" she prodded.

"Our cossacks are murderous!" he declared, gazing at her fiercely. "True barbarians! Bloodthirsty holy avengers." But he would not comment upon her question. He took her hands and held them between his own long-fingered, bony-jointed ones.

Sabrina wanted to cringe, to jerk her hands away. Instead, she tried to ignore his cold, scaly touch, and continued probing for the vital information. "But would these 'holy avengers' be used against the Germans?"

"No more politics!" he exclaimed, his eyes blazing, frightening her. "All day I hear politics. Now I want something else. Now we speak of . . . love."

His eyes were burning into hers hypnotically. His face moved close to hers. She blinked and backed away. He continued caressing her hands, staring into her eyes. It unnerved Sabrina, and for a few seconds she was seized by a fit of shuddering that went all through her.

"Here we are, Your Holiness," said the driver after a while, pulling to a stop in front of a run-down, one-story establishment. Sabrina looked at the building with wary curiosity. It wasn't at all the sort of place she was used to being taken to. Instead of being brightly lit, gaily extravagant, and fronted by expensive coaches and well-dressed men and women, it looked dark, shabby, and ominous.

Sabrina had heard of the mad monk's perverse appetites—he was notorious throughout Europe for his sexual deviances. "What is this place?" she asked nervously, as she was being helped down.

"A little-known spot of sophisticated diversion. Patronized by only the most discerning."

His hand was on her back as he guided her inside. The interior of the cafe had a dingy look, but there were no patrons seated at the wooden tables. Rasputin nodded knowingly to the waitress who greeted them, and immediately she led the way to what appeared to be a hatcheck stand. Inside the stand a narrow stairway was disclosed, down which Rasputin guided Sabrina. At the bottom, a door was opened for them.

Immediately Sabrina's senses were assailed by the sweet, musky smell of incense. She heard loud chanting in what appeared to be a foreign tongue: *"Omni . . . obdi . . . zembuday . . ."*

"I don't like this," she said, trying to draw back, frightened.

Rasputin's hand on her back continued pushing her forward. "You will be fascinated," he said. "Only the select few witness the ceremony."

The small room was illuminated by candles burning at each table, each covered with a red glass chimney. Sabrina and Rasputin were seated on wooden straight-backed chairs at a round, uncovered wooden table. The men nearby stared openly at them as they took their seats. There were no women in the place. Rasputin seemed not to notice the stares. They burned into Sabrina's skin, as she tried to ignore them.

A waitress wearing a black, low-cut, catlike outfit, with a black eye mask and black hose, came to them and took their orders for drinks. When Sabrina turned her eyes away from the sinister-looking room and inhabitants, to look at Rasputin, she saw that he was staring at her again.

"If . . . if a war were to start," she said nervously, trying clumsily to get into her topic, "would—"

"Silence!" exclaimed the monk suddenly, raising his bony hand. Sabrina jerked back. "The ceremony is about to begin."

She looked to where Rasputin's eyes were now focused, at the side of the room. A frail looking blond-haired girl was brought out from a side door, and taken to the stage at the front of the room. She was wearing a black cape. Two bare-chested, bulky men, both of them bald, were at her side. One of them produced a black leather strap.

The chanting in the room grew louder. "*Omni . . . obdi . . . zembuday . . .*"

"What's happening?" Sabrina whispered urgently to Rasputin. The monk ignored her. He joined in the chanting, in his deep grim voice.

The hands of the girl on stage were bound at the wrists with the leather strap, then the strap was tied to a metal ring dangling at the end of a chain. One of the bald men pulled at the other end of the chain, which was draped over a ceiling beam, and the girl's bound wrists were raised into the air, higher and higher, until she was standing on her tip-toes, then dangling an inch above the ground. The chain was secured.

Sabrina felt a chill of terror sweep through her as she watched Rasputin and the others in the room, all of them focusing their eyes in erotic intensity at the straining girl. The chanting grew louder and more feverish, making Sabrina want to put her hands over her ears. The faces of the men in the room became beaded with sweat. The air grew muggy.

121

"Please," Sabrina said to Rasputin. "I'd like to leave now."

But he grasped her wrist tightly, not turning even to look at her, his eyes directed straight ahead.

The girl's black cloak was removed. Sabrina gasped upon seeing that she was naked from the waist down beneath the cloak. From the neck to the waist she wore a black silk blouse speckled with silver beads.

Suddenly a black leather whip appeared, and one of the bald men raised it high, then *slashed* it down across the blond girl's bare buttocks. The girl jerked and screamed. The audience's breathing quickened. The chanting grew louder still.

The whip slashed down across her buttocks once more. She screamed again, and this time Sabrina did also. Everyone turned to look at her.

She was on her feet now, struggling to free her wrist from the monk's bony grasp, shouting "Let me go, let me go! Let me out of here, you lunatic!"

Rasputin's fierce eyes were on her, and for a second Sabrina had the bloodcurdling premonition that he had brought her here so that *she* could be the next to be whipped on the stage. This act was too frighteningly similar to her own—except that here the whip was real rather than symbolic. "Let me go!" she screamed frantically, clawing at the back of his hand holding her wrist.

The monk looked down at his hand, which was being scratched bloody, then back up at Sabrina. He stood up and led her out of the room, still holding tightly to her wrist.

She stopped clawing at him, now that they were leaving. Once they were outside in the chill night air, the monk released her, pulled a handkerchief from his robe pocket, and wrapped it around his bloody hand. The blood escaped through the material, staining it red.

"I . . . I'm sorry," Sabrina said half sheepishly. "But you see, I thought . . ." She let the words trail off.

"My mistake," said Rasputin. "I assumed you were more enlightened." His expression was one of anger. They climbed into his carriage and it started down the street. Sabrina began asking questions again, trying to lead into the discussion of the czar's intentions. Rasputin responded to her in monosyllables. For the most part he was silent, and his displeasure with her was clear.

The streets they rode along were unfamiliar. Sabrina knew they were coming closer and closer to the monk's quarters. The coach finally stopped outside the palatial hotel where he was staying, and he turned to face her, his eyebrow raised questioningly. "You will join me for a drink in my room?"

She closed her eyes tightly in anguish. Oh, if only she had stayed in that evil, red-lit room! Watching the girl be whipped! Better that a thousand times than to have to face this—now!

She threw her head back, her eyes still shut tightly, lips parted. She nodded slightly.

His room was extravagantly furnished, as befit a visiting dignitary of his station. Sabrina kept her wrap on. Rasputin filled two wine glasses with a clear vodka—the only liquor he kept—and handed one to her. "In Berlin you will be drinking schnapps," she said offhandedly, in a desperate-but-hopeless last effort to wheedle the information from him.

123

"Yes," he said, downing his drink. "When our cossacks strike at the Germans they will drink German schnapps, over the bodies of the Hun dogs. Our soldiers strain at the bits even now, waiting for a provocation. If Serbia is invaded, then we feast on Steinhäger and—" *pah!* he spat "—their putrid schnitzel."

Sabrina's eyes went wide. She almost couldn't believe he had said that. He'd given her the information she needed. She watched him as he poured a second drink, and downed it in a single, head-tilted-back motion.

She glanced anxiously at the door. She could leave now. She didn't have to stay any longer. She didn't have to go to bed with him. Relief and joy flooded over her.

Rasputin suddenly moved between her and the door, having seen her look in that direction. "What are you doing?" she said nervously. Then, without warning, he came to her and grabbed her shoulder wrap, ripping it off. Then he swiveled her around roughly so she was facing the bedroom door.

"Let me go!" she screamed, trying to strike him. He began pushing her forcefully toward the bedroom. Sabrina struggled to resist, but his strength was too great, and she found herself rushing headlong into the chamber, then crashing down on the massive bed, the long, gangly body of the monk coming down on top of her.

She struggled to beat him off, but his full weight was pressed upon her. He grasped her wrists and then, as she watched fearfully, he reached into a pocket of his robe and withdrew a black leather thong similar to the one used to bind the girl at the club. He overpowered Sabrina, and bound her wrists together tightly with the leather thong. When she started to kick, he bound her ankles together with another thong.

"You can't do this!" Sabrina screamed in panic and fear. "You'll be arrested! I'll report you and—"

"No arrest!" Rasputin declared fiercely. "I am an emissary of the czar!"

She began crying out for help. Rasputin took a cloth and stuffed it into her mouth, his bony fingers preventing her from pushing it out with her tongue. Then he wrapped a gag around her mouth, holding the cloth in place, muffling her screams.

She watched in horror as Rasputin tied one end of a hemp rope to her leather-bound wrists, then passed the other end of the rope through a hook in the ceiling, which he reached by standing on a chair. The loose end of the rope now dangled down in front of a giant, full-length mirror affixed to the wall.

As Rasputin tugged on the rope, hand over hand, Sabrina was pulled forward across the bed, then across part of the floor, until she was on the floor in front of the mirror. As he continued tugging on the rope, Sabrina felt herself being raised up until her arms were taut above her head and she was standing on her tiptoes, then dangling inches above the thick carpet. She peered in the full-length mirror and saw the monk grinning at her with a feverish intensity. She watched him lash the rope to a closet doorknob, as she continued to dangle from the hook in the ceiling.

Then she watched in the mirror as he went behind her and put his hands to her waist. She felt them encircle her waist and begin tugging at her skirt, ripping away at the front buttons which held the waistband fastened. She twisted and squirmed, the mirror reflecting the stark terror in her eyes.

Rasputin tore open the seam of her skirt and let the garment fall about her legs in a clump at the floor. Then he ripped viciously at her chemise until it hung in shreds around her ankles. Only her underpants remained. She felt his hands clutch at the hem, and in a single swift motion he ripped that garment away.

Now she was naked from the waist down, blushing in humiliation as the Russian ogled her. It was when he reached into a closet that Sabrina began to squirm even more wildly, in panic. She had a premonition about what he was reaching for . . . it was the same premonition she had had earlier at the club. And now she saw that she had been right all along, as his hand came back into view, clutching a raw-leather whip.

Sabrina screamed into her gag and writhed about in hysterics. This man was a lunatic! What sort of religious fanaticism was he using to excuse such wicked perversions, she wondered, as suddenly—thwww*wack*!—the whip sang through the air and slashed down across her naked buttocks, stinging her with searing pain. She watched helplessly in his mirror as the whiplash was raised once more over the maniacally bright eyes and grave face of Rasputin . . . then: th*wack*! Th*wack*! Th*wack*!

She was on the verge of fainting from the agony, when finally he unfastened the rope and let her sink to the floor, sobbing. He picked her up and carried her to the bed, then untied her arms and legs, and retied them so that she was spread-eagled, her limbs tied to the corners of the bed.

"*Omni . . . obdi . . . zembuday,*" he chanted,

as he stripped himself naked. Sabrina watched his throbbing hardness in terror as he moved closer to her, then came down on top of her. She screamed in agony and horror as he entered her. Her wild writhing and squirming was in vain, though, for the straps that bound her to the bed were lashed tightly.

Finally he was finished with her and he rolled off. He lay by her side, silently. After a while, Sabrina strained her head to the side to look, and saw through her tears that his eyes were closed and he was sleeping.

She strained and worked frantically at pulling her left wrist free from its bonds, which were not as tight as the strap on her other arm. Finally she succeeded. She untied her other wrist, and freed herself completely. She was gasping and sobbing as she quickly dressed in the remnants of her clothing.

Then she stared down at the sleeping, black-bearded figure with such violent hatred that she was certain she would grab one of the metal bookends from the shelf and *smash* it down across his sinister forehead, again and again, until no spark of life remained in his evil soul. He *deserved* to die, the horrid animal!

But no, she did not have it in her to murder him, though she wished that she did. She grabbed her handbag and left the apartment, stumbling down the hall, sobbing hysterically.

She did not know how she finally arrived at Hunter's apartment. She vaguely remembered stumbling out into the street and hailing a taxi, while Lieutenant Gunther came up to her from across the street where he had stationed himself, demanding to know where she was going, insisting that she come with him instead.

She vaguely remembered screaming at him while waving her hands crazily in the air, "You want to know if Russia will defend Serbia? They will! They will, yes, they will!" And then as the astonished lieutenant rushed away frantically, to avoid being seen with her now that she was making such a commotion, she entered the taxi and ordered it away.

She was still hysterical when she finally found herself outside Hunter's door, banging on it weakly with her fist, her cheek pressed against it as she leaned her full weight forward. She was sobbing uncontrollably, praying that Hunter was back as he was supposed to be, praying that he was home.

She heard footsteps on the other side of the door, and the doorknob turned. When the door came open, she fell forward, directly against Hunter's chest. She felt his strong arms go around her to support her.

"Oh, Dallas!" she cried, sobbing against his chest.

He held her for a moment, supporting her weight, but then pushed her back so he could look at her face. His expression was distant and quizzical. But then as he gazed down the length of her body, at her torn garments, the hardness in his eyes softened. "What happened?" he demanded. "Who did this to you?"

She could not answer. All she could do was cling to him desperately, crying, "Oh, Dallas! Oh, Dallas!," wetting his white, sleeveless undershirt.

The horror of the past hours with Rasputin finally caught up with her, and with that all the pain and agony of the life she'd been forced to live the past few months. The humiliation of being stripped onstage nightly by Wolfschmidt's henchmen . . . of having to play up to men she despised in order to get secret information . . . these thoughts flooded her emotions all at once, making it impossible for her to stop crying.

Hunter put a hand behind her knees, and lifted her into his arms. He carried her to the bed. The cover was already pulled back; he had been sleeping when she knocked. He set her down gently and turned to shut the door. But Sabrina grasped at his arm. "Don't leave me," she pleaded.

He looked at her for a moment with more tenderness than she had ever seen in him before. Then he lay on his side on the bed and hugged her to him, holding her tightly as her body shuddered and she cried against his chest.

"It's all right," he said in a low voice. "I'll make them pay, whoever did this to you."

She felt his strong arms hugging her, and his hand stroking her hair. It seemed like an eternity since she had last seen him and been held by him like this.

She wanted to tell him what had happened in the intervening weeks, ever since she had been abducted from his apartment. She wanted to tell him about Michael, and the urgent need to do something quickly. But none of the words came to her lips now.

She felt a warmth and a sense of security flow through her, for the first time in as long as she could remember . . . and all she could do was lie in the circle of his arms, feeling the anxiety ebb as she drifted off into a sea of sleep. He's back, she thought dimly, as she drifted off. It'll be all right now . . .

Chapter 10

In the morning, she awakened to the pleasant aroma of brewing coffee and the crackling sound of bacon grilling. She opened her eyes and looked across the room at Hunter, at the stove, turning strips of bacon in the pan.

He glanced at her. "How do you feel?" he asked.

"Better." She smiled weakly. The horror of last night seemed to have dissipated during her sleep. Her body still ached, especially her behind, which she was sure bore scars from the insane Russian's whip. But all in all she felt much better and more buoyant.

She got up to go to the table, and discovered she was naked. "Ahh!" she gasped, pulling a blanket from the bed in front of her. "Who . . . ?"

"Who do you think?" said Hunter. He turned his eyes back to the frying pan, and began removing the slabs of crisp bacon onto slices of toasted bread. "You weren't looking comfortable the way you were dressed. I took off your clothes, and then I washed away some of the . . . blood from your backside." He suddenly flung the spatula violently toward the sink, where it clattered against the back and bounced to the floor. "And when I find out who did that to you, I'm going to tear him to pieces."

Sabrina looked around the room. "Where are my clothes?"

"I burned them."

"Burned them?"

"What was left of them, anyway. They wouldn't have been much good to you."

"But what'll I *wear*? I have to go out later."

He looked at her with appreciative eyes. "That blanket looks great. Try that."

She wrapped the blanket tighter around her, and went to the table to sit down. Hunter put the plate with the bacon and toast on it in front of her, and poured a cup of strong black coffee. Then he sat down across from her at the small table, folded his arms before him on the tabletop, and just looked at her.

"All right," he said. "Now what the hell happened? After the way you left me, I never expected to see you again." There was a hint of bitterness in his voice. "Especially not like *this*."

"The way I left you?" she exclaimed. "I *didn't* leave you! I was taken away! By force!" She began telling him the whole story, while ignoring her breakfast, which grew cold on the plate. She watched Hunter's expression turn from skeptical to grudgingly accepting as he listened silently, sipping at his coffee.

She spoke in a rapid, excited voice, anxious to tell him all of it, to get it all out. Finally, when she finished, she took a deep breath and settled back in her chair.

Hunter was shaking his head, a surprising look of amusement on his face.

"What's so funny?" she demanded irritably.

Hunter had just listened to her telling him how she had been abducted by the Germans, forced to dance naked, made into one of France's most popular attractions . . . forced to become a spy, and finally assaulted by a mad Russian monk. He shook his head now, and looked up at her, unable to stifle a huge grin. "I leave you alone for just a *minute*," he said, "and look what happens."

Sabrina gaped at the fact that he could find anything even the least bit humorous in her situation.

Hunter then stood up, came around toward her, and pulled her up to her feet. "At least now I know you didn't walk out on me," he said seriously. "You didn't leave me of your own free will." He gazed into her eyes with intense emotion.

Sabrina understood now why he had been grinning: he was relieved. He had really believed, until just now, that she had deliberately deserted him. Though she was happy that he now believed her, part of her was upset that he had even doubted her in the first place. Her expression became sullen, and she said in a small, scolding voice, "You shouldn't even have *thought* that I'd run—"

But he interrupted her by pressing his lips hard against hers, kissing her deeply, passionately. The sensation nearly made her melt inside. She had forgotten how it could be with a man like Hunter.

When he started to pull down the front of her blanket, though, she exclaimed "No!" and grasped his wrist.

"Why not?"

"Because . . . because there's a very urgent problem here! That's why not. Weren't you listening to me at all?"

"I was listening. I heard you say that dumbbell 'hero' Limey got himself captured, and now he needs rescuing."

"*You* got him captured," she declared accusingly, backing away from him to gain some distance. It was hard to think when his body was so close to hers, exciting her. "You were the one who told him to lead the Germans off on that wild-goose chase, all by himself."

"Yeah, yeah," said Hunter, bored with the subject. "I got him into it, and I suppose I'll have to get him out of it. Give me 'til the twentieth of the month; I have to make arrangements. But in the meantime . . ." He started coming forward again.

"Oh, no you don't," she said warningly, raising her palm in front of her, backing away. "You think that settles it, but that doesn't settle it at all. You can't rescue him! You're only one man. My plan to go to the French, though, is—"

"—About as stupid a plan as I've ever heard. Come on, be sensible. War is going to break out any day now. You say your German general was packing up his files. You know why? Because he's moving his headquarters! If he's caught on French soil when war is declared, he'll be in jail within minutes.

"The French aren't going to risk sending any men to wherever Wolfschmidt locates his new headquarters," Hunter continued. "They're going to have their hands full fending off a full-scale German invasion! You think they're going to worry about rescuing one crazy Englishman who got himself captured trying to defend a lady's honor? Be serious."

"You be serious," she shot back, bending half forward in a rage now. "How dare you belittle that brave man, just because he—because—" She was sputtering and at a loss for words she was so angry. "You just don't want the French to rescue him because you're jealous!"

"Jealous?" he declared, laughing.

"That's right! That's right! You know how deeply grateful I am to both of you for rescuing me that night. And you don't want Michael to be back in the picture, maybe giving you competition for me! You want to have me all to yourself, without any competition. That's why you sent him off on that lead-them-away mission in the first place, remember? So you could have me all to yourself!"

He put his hands on his hips, and his face became grave. "I've had enough of this," he said, his voice low. "Your idea on how to rescue him is crazy, and my idea—good or bad—is all we've got left. So you just stay out of it, and let me do it my way, on the twentieth."

"Oooohhh!" she cried, flustered and angry. The arrogance of the man! The conceit! To think that he, single-handedly, could succeed in rescuing Michael, when he says the entire French Counterintelligence service can't? It was too much! She threw her hands into the air in frustration, and started for the door.

He grabbed her arm. "Where do you think you're going?"

"To French Counterintelligence!"

"In a blanket?"

She looked down at herself. She had forgotten. But what else was there to wear?

"You're not going anywhere," he said. "You're staying here with me."

"I'm not!"

She tried to force his hand away from her arm, but only succeeded in making Hunter grab her other arm also, and pull her near him, so he could look directly into her eyes as he said: "Sabrina, now listen to me." His face was full of concern for her. "I'm not volunteering to try a dangerous rescue just to save the life of that idiot hero of yours. I'm doing it to maybe save yours as well."

She frowned in perplexity. "What do you mean?" Was this some kind of trick to make her stay with him?

"Don't you see? You're a German spy, babe. An unwilling one or not, that doesn't matter. What matters is that you gathered military information from allied sources, and passed it on to a hostile foreign power."

"But not the real information!" she protested. "Almost everything I told them was a lie!"

"You think they'll believe that?" He shook his head grimly. "You go to the French and tell them what you just told me, and then ask them to please go rescue your hero . . . and you know what's going to happen, babe? You're going to find yourself behind iron bars."

She looked at him uncertainly. Then she tossed her head back, raising her chin defiantly. "You're just trying to scare me."

"And I hope I'm succeeding. Otherwise, you're going to get yourself into such hot water I won't be able to get you out of it."

Sabrina did not know what to do. He could be saying all this to trick her into staying with him; he was certainly capable of it. But what if he was right? She frowned in perplexity. Well, she decided stubbornly, even if he were right, she would have to go ahead with her plan anyway. She couldn't let Michael be killed. She had to try to rescue him.

She backed away from Hunter. "I have to try," she said. She started toward the door and opened it.

Hunter shot out his arm and slammed it shut. "You're not going anywhere, Sabrina. I won't let you."

"Oh, you . . . you bastard!" she shouted, almost on the verge of tears. "Who are you to order me about?" She had an idea: she stomped off toward the bathroom, went inside and slammed the door, making it look as if she had to be alone now, to cry, away from him.

Yes, she saw, it was just as she had remembered: the small window above the shower stall was large enough for a slim woman to fit through. But she certainly could not leave wearing only a blanket. She looked in the laundry hamper and found a pair of trousers and a blue chamois workshirt. She quickly put them on.

She turned on the shower, so Hunter would think she was bathing. Then she put the wicker laundry hamper into the shower, and while it and she got soaked, she climbed up on it, then maneuvered through the small window. She heard Hunter talking to her through the door, telling her his plan was for her own good, but she did not answer.

She moved along the wide ledge, keeping her back to the brick wall, looking down at the street and the bustling rush-hour horse and automobile traffic two stories below. She entered the first window she saw open, without bothering to look to see who might be home. It was a living-room window,

136

and she climbed through it into the living room of a French family that was seated around the table eating breakfast.

They had all been babbling to one another in French—the stolid, squat Frenchman and his thin wife and two loud children. And they all stopped in unison as Sabrina came through the window in her soaking-wet clothing. They stared at her. The husband's spoon was arrested halfway to his lips, his head still bent forward over his plate.

"Excuse me," Sabrina said. She walked briskly through the room and out the front door, leaving the family to wonder whether she had really been there or if they had seen a wet, stringy-haired hallucination.

When she was finally on the street, she ran along the sidewalk until she saw a cab; then she waved it down and entered, even though she had no money. Let the French Counterintelligence pay for the cab, she thought wryly, as the vehicle pulled away from the curb. It was the least they could do for her if they were going to be so unfriendly as to put her in jail . . .

The Office of Counterintelligence occupied an entire floor of the French Ministry of Defense. It was a busy, bustling bureaucracy, with people passing in the halls hurriedly, speaking loudly to one another, consulting documents and sheafs of papers they carried.

Sabrina stood in the middle of a spacious foyer, uncertain of which office to go to, or whom to speak to. After standing around in bewilderment for a moment, she stopped a short, timid-looking clerk who was limping past her, using a cane to take the weight off an evidently game leg. "Excuse me," she said, "can you tell me whom I should talk to? I have this problem . . ."

"And what sort of problem eez eet?" he asked.

When she explained to him that she had been forced to spy for the Germans, but that now she wanted to tell all she knew to the French, the hapless clerk seemed flabbergasted. He stared at her with his mouth open. Finally he guided her against a wall and said urgently, "Do not move. Do not go away. Do not move even an inch! I go to summon my superior." Then he rushed off, casting astonished glances at her over his shoulder.

A moment later, an army officer appeared, looking around the foyer searchingly. He had a pencil-thin mustache and wore a uniform with a flat, visored cap. When his eyes lighted on Sabrina, he seemed relieved. He came up to her quickly, took her arm, and said, "You weel come weeth me." He led her off to a nearby room, instructed her to enter, then followed her in and shut the door.

"Sit," he ordered in a domineering manner. There was only one chair in the small room. Sabrina sat down. The officer sat on the edge of the wooden table facing her, his expression severe. The room was tiny, with no windows and unattractive green walls. A light bulb dangled from the ceiling, surrounded by a conical metal hood. It cast a circle of light down upon Sabrina. "Now," said the officer, folding his arms across his chest, "you tell me your story."

He listened with a look of mounting anger, and when Sabrina finished, he slammed his fist down on the tabletop. "What you have done, madame, eet eez *treason!*" He glared at her. "You engage in espionage against the French Republic, and now you expect us to help you rescue your captured lover? What gall you Americans have!"

"He's not my lover!" Sabrina protested. "He's—"

"*Non, non,*" said the Frenchman, waving his hand from side to side vigorously. "Whatever ze man is to you eez beside ze point. Ze point eez thees: why should we not throw you een prison and let that be ze end of it?"

Sabrina held his eyes. She had come prepared for this question. She had a single ace up her sleeve, and now she played it: "Because I will work for you as a double agent, spying against the Germans. If you help me rescue Michael." She knew she was betraying her promise to Michael not to spy anymore. But the main thing now was to save his life.

The Frenchman stroked his pencil-thin mustache, looking at her with distaste—but also with growing interest.

"The Germans will think I'm still on their side," Sabrina said. "They'll give me information that will be of interest to you. Just knowing what secrets they want me to find out will help you. It'll tell you what they don't already know."

The Frenchman continued stroking his mustache, apparently lost in deep, frowning concentration.

"Besides," Sabrina insisted, "it's not as though I'm an enemy of the state or anything. I almost never gave them the real information I learned. I changed it so it was inaccurate."

The Frenchman stood up. He said nothing, but merely stared down at her. Sabrina looked up, but his head was silhouetted against the cone of the bright light bulb, making it impossible for her to see his face. "Wait here," he said finally. "I must confer."

He left the room. A draft of air came in when he shut the door, making the single light bulb sway slightly. Sabrina sat breathing the still, muggy air for what seemed a very long time, watching the shadows from the swaying bulb dance across the floor.

She noticed she was perspiring nervously. Maybe Hunter had been right, she thought. Maybe they would throw her in prison and not bother rescuing Michael. She began idly playing with a loose button on the front of her makeshift garb, wishing the Frenchman would return.

Finally the door opened and he was back. He sat down on the table across from her, leaned forward, and said, "Mademoiselle, we accept your offer."

A wave of relief washed over Sabrina.

"You realize ze dangers, of course, eef you are found out? Herr Wolfschmidt eez not known for restraint in dealing weeth those who cross him."

"I know the danger," Sabrina said, thinking that she certainly knew them better than the Frenchman did. She remembered the black eyepatch Michael now wore, as the result of a savage beating carried out under Wolfschmidt's orders. If Wolfschmidt discovered she was a counterspy . . . the thought made her shudder.

The Frenchman offered a cigarette to Sabrina, and lit one for himself when she declined. Then he began telling her how she would go about working for the French as a double agent. Afterward, he turned to the topic of Michael's rescue, and how it would be arranged.

"Wolfschmidt eez no longer at ze German Embassy," he said. "He has moved his headquarters to an island off ze coast of North Africa. You must arrange to go to heem there."

"But . . . how?"

"Tell your contact, thees Lieutenant Gunther, zat you must see ze general personally, on an urgent matter. Since you are so valuable as a spy, he would not be able to refuse you." He said this bitterly, glancing at Sabrina sharply, indicating that her value was purchased at the price of French secrets.

"Now," he said significantly, emphasizing the point with a raised finger. "When you arrive een Wolfschmidt's office, you must—and zeez is very important!—you must make certain he does not leave ze office for at least half an hour."

Sabrina looked bewildered.

"These eez absolutely vital," he continued. "Because during thees half hour ze rescue weel take place."

He leaned forward. "I tell you a secret: we have an undercover agent within Herr Wolfschmidt's headquarters. As soon as you enter Wolfschmidt's office, our agent will present a forged authorization to ze jailers. Eet will tell zem to release ze Englishman into heez custody, and will bear Wolfschmidt's forged signature. Once ze Englishman eez freed, he weel be brought to ze outskirts of ze base, where we will have people waiting to spirit him and our agent away to safety."

He blew out a stream of cigarette smoke and looked at Sabrina meaningfully. "You see why Wolfschmidt must not leave ze office during ze rescue?"

Sabrina nodded. "He's the only one who would know the release authorization is a forgery. If he sees Michael being released, he'll stop it. And have your agent arrested."

"Arrested, hell!" declared the Frenchman irately, rising to his feet. "He'd have heem shot!"

"How will I keep him in his office for a whole half hour?" Sabrina asked.

"Tell heem Lieutenant Gunther eez a spy," he said off-handedly. "Tell heem you learned this from Rasputin. In fact," he continued, becoming enthused, "you can even tell heem zat you heard Gunther was going to try some major deceit right there in Wolfschmidt's headquarters. Zat way, maybe they'll assume it was Gunther who arranged ze rescue, when zay discover eet, and zay won't look any further for accomplices."

He regarded Sabrina scrutinizingly. "You can do thees, yes? Keep Wolfschmidt in ze office for half an hour, away from ze other areas of ze headquarters?"

"I . . . I think I can."

"*Non!*" he said sharply, gesturing with his lit cigarette. The tobacco smelled strangely fragrant, with the scent of pine needles. "Think eez not good enough. We cannot risk our agent in such an operation unless you can tell me, with certainty, zat Wolfschmidt will *not* leave heez office until half an hour after you enter."

"All right," Sabrina said. "I . . . I'll make sure of it." She remembered how attentive Wolfschmidt was every time she had something of military importance to tell him. Holding his attention for half an hour shouldn't be hard—not when she would be telling him about a spy within his own organization.

"Good," said the Frenchman, motioning for Sabrina to stand up. "We begin ze plan at once. Your password eez 'Justice wins out.' Only our agent knows eet; you can recognize heem if he says eet to you." His arm was on Sabrina's back and he was leading her to the door.

"You are a brave girl," he said. "Thees eez a dangerous mission you embark on. Be careful or you and your Englishman weel be dead before ze month eez over. *Au revoir!*"

He led her out the door, then turned sharply on his heel and walked off down the hallway. Sabrina looked after him, smelling the wisps of sweet, pine-scented tobacco smoke that wafted back over his shoulder.

Several days later, she was being escorted into the waiting room of Wolfschmidt's outer office on a small island off the coast of North Africa. She was so apprehensive, her stomach felt cramped.

She knew the rescue attempt had already begun. It had begun the instant she stepped foot into this waiting room. She stared at the closed door to Wolfschmidt's inner office, through which the adjutant had just gone to announce her arrival. Would the rescue succeed, she wondered, as she watched the door nervously. Or would it fail?—and with it, her chances of ever leaving this island alive.

Chapter 11

The door opened and the adjutant came out of the office. A moment later, General Wolfschmidt himself came forward. He stood in the doorway, regarding Sabrina with silent scrutiny.

His hair was cropped even shorter than before, in the Prussian manner, and now for the first time she saw him in his full-dress military uniform. He wore a severely tailored brown tunic, double-breasted with two rows of gold buttons. It had a high, stiff collar, adorned with an iron cross at the front. Golden epaulets were on each shoulder, bearing the twin stars of his rank. His tight trouser legs were tucked into his high, black-leather cavalry boots.

He looked very handsome in a cold, menacing way. His posture was ramrod straight, showing off his lean stength. He stared at Sabrina with a stern look on his gaunt, high-cheekboned face. Looking back at him, Sabrina felt that he was like a taut steel band, ready to slash murderously in any direction without warning.

"You have disrupted my organization and caused me to go to great pains to bring you here, X-79," he said to her sharply. "You had best have an excellent reason for doing so."

"I do," she said, looking him squarely in the eyes.

He stared at her for a moment, silently, without moving. Then he jerked his head toward his office, motioning her in. She went past him into the room. He followed her in and closed the door.

"Wait a moment," he said, picking up a sheaf of papers from his desk and taking them over to a jet-black safe. The safe was positioned near a pleated curtain that served as a room partition.

As he leafed through the papers, Sabrina thought to herself: so far everything is going according to plan. She thought back to how she had gone to Lieutenant Gunther after leaving the French Counterintelligence office several days ago, and how she had insisted that she be allowed to see Wolfschmidt personally. She kept insisting, over Gunther's refusals, until finally the word had come back from Wolfschmidt himself: let the girl come.

Sabrina's voyage to the island had started out on a German merchant liner, but during the last leg of the trip, she had been transferred to a small military gunboat. This was because war had finally broken out in Europe. Austria-Hungary had declared war against Serbia. Russia, England, and France had declared war against Austria-Hungary . . . and Germany, who had started it all by backing Austria-Hungary's barbaric demands, had declared war on the three allied nations.

"Now," said Wolfschmidt sharply, putting the papers into the black safe, but leaving its door ajar rather than closing it. "I would like to know why you insisted on seeing me personally. Why couldn't you tell your information, whatever it may be, to your contact?"

"Because my contact," she said slowly, preparing

for the lie she would spin out over the next thirty minutes, "is a spy for the French."

"Lieutenant Gunther?" queried Wolfschmidt, astonished.

Sabrina nodded, keeping her eyes riveted to his. "I heard the information firsthand from—"

"Don't bother telling me," Wolfschmidt said disgustedly, holding up his hands. "If this is what you have traveled all these miles to tell me, then bringing you here was a waste of my time and resources." He snapped open the office door. "You may return to your assigned post, X-79. Transportation will be provided."

"Wh . . . what?" Sabrina gasped, astonished.

"Quickly, if you please, Fräulein. I have pressing matters to attend to: an engagement downstairs in five minutes."

Sabrina was shocked. "But . . . but . . ." She glanced at the door he was holding open for her. "But *wait*," she said pleadingly, looking at his cold, impassive face. "This is important! Why, it's—"

"It is *Scheiss!*" he said contemptuously. "I've known Gunther longer than any of my other agents—except for Herr Deep Mole, who is in a secret undercover position in the heart of the French forces. Both have been with me since I was a lowly colonel in the *Nachricht Gewalt*. As far as Gunther being a spy—"

"He is!" she interjected desperately. "I have information that—"

"Silence!"

Sabrina stopped speaking, frowning deeply.

"As far as his being a spy," Wolfschmidt continued, "I have known for weeks that the French were trying to plant that story, to make me doubt one of my most valuable operatives. You simply fell for the information without realizing it to be false." He looked at his watch irritably. It was noon. "Now if there is nothing else," he said crisply, "I have an appointment downstairs. So if you'll please leave."

Sabrina was dumbfounded and at a total loss. This was happening too quickly. She had been here only three or four minutes, and already she was being ordered out! She had to think fast. She racked her brain, but no ideas came to her. One thing was certain: she could not let herself be evicted from the room.

She found herself marching to the open door and closing it, then pressing her back against it. She looked at Wolfschmidt's surprised—but also coldly calculating—expression. He was waiting for her next move, to see how she would explain her action.

"Please," she begged, "you have to listen to me. I came all the way out here just to talk to you."

"About Gunther being a spy?" he sneered disdainfully. "You should have saved yourself the journey."

"About Gunther and . . . and more! There are other matters to talk about. Urgent matters!"

Wolfschmidt sighed disgustedly. "I'm afraid your 'urgent matters' will have to wait. It's time for my appointment." His hand went to the handle of the door.

"I have news of the Russian movements on the Eastern Front!" she declared desperately.

"Later!" he shouted, his expression furious. "Enough of this insolence!" He turned the door handle, intending to open the door forcefully and shove Sabrina aside in the process.

Her mind raced feverishly to find some way to keep him there. Her heart pounded with the terrible knowledge that he was about to discover the rescue attempt in progress. Sabrina reacted automatically resorting to the first thing that swept into her panicked mind: she flung her arms around the German's neck and kissed him fully on the lips.

The kiss endured a few seconds before she realized what she was actually doing. Then she drew her head back and looked at him, her own eyes shocked, her mouth half open in surprise.

Wolfschmidt's eyes were cool and appraising. There was a hint of wicked glee in the cruel grin that came to his lips. His hand remained on the doorknob, but his motion had been arrested. He made no move to pull the door open now. He looked at her with malicious curiosity.

"And what is this?" he said.

Her face was only inches from his, her arms still around his neck. "I . . ." She bit her lower lip; it was hard making the words come out. "I want you," she heard herself saying. "I came all the way out here because I . . . I want you to . . . take me."

He grinned cruelly. "*Now?* It has to be this very instant?"

Sabrina said nothing.

Wolfschmidt became suspicious. "This is a bit of a change, isn't it?" he said distrustfully. "You did not seem possessed of such desire during our earlier encounters. Just the opposite!"

"It was hard holding myself back. But now, I can't any longer. Please, you must . . . take me."

She saw the unspoken word on his lips, and she responded. "Yes, *now!* Now, now, now!" She put her lips to his mouth again and kissed him hard, openmouthed, thinking of nothing but the fact that she *had* to stop him from leaving the room, no matter what it took.

His hand was still on the doorknob. He was undecided about whether to leave.

Sabrina knew he wanted her. She remembered her last visit, when he had gazed at her longingly. Suddenly she ripped open the front of her dress. Then, overcoming her powerful reluctance, she pulled her chemise top down, baring her firm white breasts. She could not bear to look him in the eye now. She quickly pressed herself up tightly against him. As she did so, a strange thing happened. She noticed a warm tingling sensation flowing up from her sex, and realized that she was becoming extremely excited.

The realization shocked her. She quickly tried to pull away, but he wouldn't let her. Sabrina felt a surge of self-disgust at the way her body was responding. This was a barbarous, savage man, she scolded herself. But still, above all, she knew, he was a *man*—an intelligent, exciting man of power, whose cruelly grinning, wickedly handsome face was only inches from her own.

Wolfschmidt's hand left the doorknob now and moved between their two bodies. It alighted on Sabrina's breast, fondling and kneading it. She had a violent desire to wrench herself away from him, but she forced herself to fight the desire. "Is this what you want?" Wolfschmidt asked, pawing her breasts with rough, stroking movements.

She tried to say the word *yes*, but no sound came. She nodded dumbly, her expression tormented. His other hand pressed between her legs, through her skirt. The abruptness of it made her gasp, her eyes going wide. "And is this what you want?"

God, was there nothing she could do? His eyes were on her, still bearing a trace of suspiciousness.

"Yes," she said. "That's what I . . ." She couldn't say it.

He began rubbing his hand up and down her loins through the skirt, forcing from her a suddenly gasped "Ohhh!"

Wolfschmidt's grin was cruelly gleeful now. He was definitely enjoying it. He stepped away from her and leaned back against his desk, folding his arms across his chest. "Take off your clothes," he commanded.

Sabrina shut her eyes in torment. But then she quickly opened them again, so her revulsion would not become obvious. If she failed to disguise the fact that she didn't really want to make love to the general, he would know something was wrong. It would become apparent she was doing this only to keep him from leaving the room.

Slowly she let her torn-open blouse slip off her shoulders. She unfastened her skirt and let it slide to the floor. She raised her leg onto a chair, to begin unbuckling her shoe, when Wolfschmidt said, "Never mind that"—and then in a swift motion he grasped the chemise where it was bunched up around her waist and jerked it hard, ripping the garment away from her body.

Sabrina stifled a scream. She frantically sought to cover herself with her arms. She was wearing only her underpants, her garter belt, and hose.

"What is the matter?" Wolfschmidt asked. "You

150

are embarrassed? I thought you wished me to love you?"

"It's the . . . the suddenness," she explained. "You surprised me."

"Good," he said, flinging away the torn chemise. "And now that you are no longer surprised, please stop hiding yourself from my eyes." He stared at her demandingly.

Sabrina lowered her hands and held them slightly away from her sides. She could not keep from frowning in helpless anguish as her shapely young breasts came under the German's searing gaze. Wolfschmidt came up to her and grinned tauntingly, his face close to hers. He put his hands on her breasts and pinched her nipples.

Sabrina's breath caught sharply. A wild rush of sensation came to her breasts. She started to move her hands to his wrists, to pull his hands away, but she stopped herself in mid-motion. She gazed up helplessly into his taunting eyes. After a minute, he removed his hands, his grin becoming all the more pronounced as he noticed that he had left her nipples hard and rosy and straining pertly forward.

Sabrina glanced at the clock over his shoulder: it was twelve-fifteen. Only fifteen minutes more to go.

"Take off your underdrawers," Wolfschmidt commanded.

She hesitated. "Please," she breathed, "if you could give me just a minute. I'm not used to—"

His hand flashed in a swift motion down to her waist. She felt a jerk and heard the ripping sound as the garment came away in his hands. She was wearing nothing but her black garter belt and dark hose now, framing her naked loins. Again her hands went down to cover herself, but Wolfschmidt grasped her wrists and placed her hands firmly on his shoulders. She did not dare move them away.

"Now kiss me," he ordered. She hesitated, looking at him with fearful helplessness. His voice became harsh. "You say you wish me to love you," he accused, "but you will not kiss me?"

She moved her mouth to his and kissed him on the lips. When his lips opened, hers parted also.

Suddenly Wolfschmidt pushed her violently backward until she slammed against the door, where she was pinned by his hand at her throat. His other hand began roaming unhindered over her naked body, pressing and pinching and probing. It moved over her skin roughly, rubbing everywhere, lighting small fires of sensation wherever it touched. Sabrina began moaning deep in her throat. The sound was muffled by Wolfschmidt's thin lips which now pressed against her mouth.

Though she tried hard to fight down the sensations, it was impossible to stop her body from responding to his touch. His caresses were not gentle; they were brutal. But his relentless rubbing and pinching was fanning the flames of passion within her, making it impossible not to respond to the wicked sensations. Her mouth was pressed against him all the while, kissing him deeply. The violence of the pleasure surging through her made her feel as if she were burning up with fever.

Wolfschmidt backed away from her and began undressing. Then suddenly he was naked before her, and she was watching his lithe, lean body coming toward her, his thick, long staff straining proudly upward, spearheading his advance. The evil grin on the German's face was positively gleeful now, and it made Sabrina feel very strange. It was almost as if he *knew* she could not refuse him, as if he *knew* she could not permit him to leave the room.

There was no time to pursue the thought further, though, for in an instant he was pressing himself against her, rubbing against her naked breasts and loins.

His hands went to her flanks and she felt his powerful, deceptively slim-looking arms raising her up several inches off the ground, pressing her back against the wooden door. Then he mashed his body against hers, thrusting hard with his hips—and suddenly *he was inside her*.

She cried out sharply, unable to stifle the sound. Her hands started to descend upon his shoulders, but she did not want to touch him voluntarily. It was important to her that she not do so. Her hands waved about frantically in the air for a moment. Finally she raised her hands up over her head, the backs of her wrists pressing against the door.

Wolfschmidt was thrusting violently into her as he held her pinned back against the door. His strong, tight-skinned face, with the sculpted high cheekbones, was against her breasts, his mouth sucking hard at a nipple. Wild fires of sensation surged through her loins, and a tingling electric feeling came to her breasts. Each thrust of his hips against hers banged her up against the door and drove a sharp moan from deep in her throat.

Her eyes caught sight of the clock on the wall. It was twelve-thirty exactly. Her hands came down on his shoulders and she tried frantically to push him away. Wolfschmidt kept thrusting into her, though, relentlessly, with full, long strokes. Finally he drove into her and remained, his body trembling. Sabrina heard him moan with pleasure. She dug her fingernails tightly into his shoulders, her face contorted in horrified disgust.

Wolfschmidt did not lower her gently to the ground, but instead simply released her and moved quickly away, so that she came down hard, her knees almost buckling. Then, whether deliberately or not, Sabrina did not know which, he hooked her ankle with his foot as he walked away, tripping her and making her stumble unceremoniously to the ground.

He gazed down at her with a taunting grin. "That is what you wanted, Fräulein, yes? You asked for it, and you received it. Do I hear no *shönen Dank* for my cooperation? No thank yous?"

Sabrina cupped her hands over her breasts and curled her legs up, cowering against the wall. She felt soiled and degraded. The only saving grace was in knowing that by now Michael was in the hands of the French, being spirited off the island.

Despite her torment, Sabrina felt a warm glow of satisfaction. I succeeded, she thought. I stopped him from leaving the room, and now Michael is free. She also felt good realizing that Wolfschmidt would be made to suffer. He would have to endure the humiliation of having his entire command know that a prisoner had been rescued right out from under his very nose. So much for his beloved reputation of being brilliantly efficient!

As she was thinking this, Wolfschmidt said casually, "It is good to know that 'justice wins out,' is it not, Fräulein?"

"*What did you say?*" she exclaimed in horror.

"About justice winning out?" he asked innocently, repeating the code phrase that only the French undercover agent was supposed to know. He grinned sneeringly as he finished pulling on his uniform. "What could be more 'just' than my finally despoiling your lovely body, after you so indignantly refused my attentions before? And to have you *begging* me for it," he gloated. "*Ach du lieber*, it was worth a thousand times the preparation I put into the scheme."

He turned his eyes away from Sabrina's horrified expression, and looked across the room toward the hanging curtain partition. "Is that not right, Herr Deep Mole?" he called out.

Sabrina watched in shock as the curtains parted and a man with a pencil-thin mustache stepped forward. He casually lit a cigarette and blew the distinctively sweet, pine-scented smoke toward Sabrina. "*Jawohl, mein general,*" he said. He was wearing a German military uniform now. The last time Sabrina saw him, in the French Counterintelligence office, he had worn a French one.

The two men suddenly broke into uproarious laughter at the success of their nasty little scheme. Sabrina cringed back with humiliation, wishing she could shrink away into the woodwork. She understood it all now. She had been tricked.

No rescue had taken place, or even been planned. Michael was still in Wolfschmidt's captivity. Wolfschmidt had obviously overheard her when she told Michael she intended to go to the French; he ordered his undercover agent in French headquarters to intercept her. Then the agent had told her to keep Wolfschmidt in the office for half an hour, under the pretense that a rescue would be underway. And all for only one reason: so Wolfschmidt could see her groveling at his feet, *begging* him to make love to her.

Suddenly as Sabrina watched them laughing at her with such obscene delight, she began to see red. A violent, insane anger raged through her. How dare they treat her like such gutter trash?! Looking around, her eyes alighted upon the black Luger pistol on Wolfschmidt's desk top. Sabrina scrambled up off the floor and rushed to it. Before either of them could stop her she had the weapon in her hands and was pointing it at Wolfschmidt's chest.

The laughter froze on the men's faces. Herr Deep Mole circled off to the side, to try to approach Sabrina from behind. Wolfschmidt held up a hand to stop him. *"Nein,"* he said. His eyes were on the girl, cold as steel, unwavering. Then, showing one of the qualities that had allowed him to rise to such high rank, he began advancing on her.

"Stay back!" she shouted, her voice as shaky as the pistol in her outstretched hands.

Wolfschmidt continued coming straight on, showing raw courage and fearlessness to the point of foolhardiness. His face was tightly drawn.

"Stay back!" she shouted. The gun was waving wildly due to her nervousness. When he continued coming forward, she shut her eyes tightly and pulled the trigger. The ear-splitting *crack* of the shot filled the room. The gun jerked in her hands. She opened her eyes to see that the bullet had passed through the side of Wolfschmidt's arm, leaving his sleeve bloody.

Wolfschmidt tore the gun out of her hands. Sabrina looked at his furious, raging face and thought he would strike her with the weapon. She held up her hands to fend off the blow, her face contorted in fearful expectation. She stood naked but for the black garter belt and hose, her arms raised protectively in front of her.

But Wolfschmidt just glared at her, his face trembling with rage. The door to his office had crashed open at the sound of the shot, and two guards now rushed in, rifles in hand.

"Get her out of my sight," he said in a tightly controlled voice, speaking through gritted teeth. "Throw her down in the basement with the Englishman. I'll decide what her punishment will be later."

The guards grabbed her brutally and dragged her out of the room.

Chapter 12

Sabrina was given fatigue dungarees, which she put on quickly: a gray, long-sleeved shirt and a pair of trousers, both of loose-fitting, coarse material. Then she was taken downstairs to the basement.

A metal cage built of steel bars was situated in the center of the large, high-ceilinged basement, and there, inside it, she saw Michael. He wore the same gray fatigue pants Sabrina had on, but instead of a shirt he was bare-chested. The black patch still covered his left eye, held in place by a cord that circled his forehead.

Michael seemed flabbergasted at seeing her, and could not hide the stunned, disbelieving look on his face as Sabrina was shoved into the cage by one of the guards. He continued staring at her as the iron-barred door of the cage slammed shut, and the guards departed the basement, closing the wooden basement door after them.

Sabrina stared back at him, not knowing what to say. Finally Michael spoke. "What the bloody hell are you doing here? You're the last person I'd expect to turn up in this place. I mean, after the conversation we had last visit."

"Don't be angry with me," she said in a small

voice. "I couldn't bear it if you were angry with me now."

He turned away from her animatedly and walked to the bars. He turned back to face her, gesturing with his raised arm. "I'm not bloody well *angry* with you, luv, I'm just . . . I'm just . . ."

"Angry," she concluded for him.

"Well, what the bloody hell are you doing here?" he demanded. But then, seeing the on-the-verge-of-tears look that came to her face, he relented. He lost his steaming rage and his features softened. He looked pained, as if it hurt him to realize he had just hurt her by his anger.

"I'm sorry, Bree," he said, coming to her, putting his hands on her arms. "It's just that . . . well, I thought we had it *settled*. You weren't to risk your neck anymore to save me. You were going to contact the French and let them handle it. But now—" He gestured in helpless frustration at the bars of the surrounding cage. "—here you are, a prisoner just like me."

"I did go to the French," Sabrina said. "But the man I saw, you see, he was . . . it's complicated. He turned out to be one of Wolfschmidt's spies, and—"

"It's all right," Michael said, seeing how distraught she was. "You don't have to talk about it now." He put his hand to her cheek, then lay her head on his shoulder. He put his arms around her and held her protectively.

Sabrina felt comforted and relieved, having his strong arms around her this way. For a brief moment she was able to forget her fearfulness about the "punishment" Wolfschmidt had promised to inflict on her later.

"They didn't mistreat you, did they?" Michael said hesitantly. "If they did, if they laid even a finger on you—"

"No," she said quickly, drawing her head back and looking at his concerned expression. She knew she could not tell him the truth.

"They better not have, the blighters." His anger turned to a half-sheepish look as he added, "Anyone can see that you're a lady, as pure as they come. Some girls, you know, they've been in the rough and tumble of it. They know their way around. You, though—anyone can see you're more delicate than that. More pure and innocent."

"Michael, why do you think of me that way?"

"It's as clear as the day, pet. In the way you look, the way you act. You're just an innocent young girl. A babe in the woods." He gazed at her with respect and affection.

Sabrina did not know how to respond. She felt uneasy about him having such an idealized, naive image of her. He thought of her as some sort of lily-white, untainted goddess on a pedestal—which she certainly was not, though through no fault of her own.

But on the other hand, she felt good about the way he thought of her. It was nice having a strong, handsome man believe in her basic purity. Because deep in her soul, Sabrina *did* feel that she still had her basic purity in spite of the sordid things that had been done to her these past months.

Suddenly, looking at him, Sabrina felt a great warmth for Michael. She wanted him to keep his illusions about her; she wanted it desperately. As long as he thought of her that way, it almost made it seem as if none of the horrible, sordid things had really happened to her at all. She was still the same virtuous, innocent young girl she had always been; she could see it reflected in the way he gazed at her.

What a strange, wonderful man he was, Sabrina thought, looking at his blond hair . . . his handsome, strong face with the black eyepatch . . . his muscular, slim physique. How could anyone be so potently masculine and at the same time so sensitive and naive? She snuggled close against him and took refuge in the circle of his arms, trying not to think about Wolfschmidt's promised punishment.

It was several hours later when two brusque, unsmiling soldiers came into the basement and marched up to the cage. Sabrina watched them with mounting fear as the taller one inserted a large key in the cage door, unlocking it. Michael went up to the door to meet the soldiers.

"*Nein!*" said the taller of the two, waving him away with a pistol. "*Das Fräulein first.*" He indicated for Sabrina to come forward. "*Now!*" he yelled, when she hesitated. "*Mach schnell!*"

"Leave her alone," Michael said in a low voice, "or I'll wrap that pistol around your head."

The guard did not understand what Michael was saying, but Michael's tone was clear enough. The guard became enraged, and aimed the pistol at Michael's face.

"*No!*" Sabrina screamed, rushing forward. "Please, Michael," she said to him, "let's just do as he says. All right?" She looked at the pistol. "Please?"

Michael grudgingly stepped aside.

Sabrina walked out of the cage. The shorter German motioned for her to put her hands behind her back, and when she did so, he clasped a pair of iron handcuffs on her wrists. The feel of the cold metal pinning her arms behind her made her shiver with terror. Michael was ordered forward, and his wrists were also handcuffed behind him. Then the two of them were marched out of the basement, up several flights of stone stairs, and into a brightly lit mess hall.

The mess hall held several long wooden tables and benches. Wolfschmidt was seated at one of the tables, somberly drinking coffee from a mug. The left sleeve of his uniform had been slit and pinned up, and his wounded arm was bandaged. Other officers—about ten of them—were seated or standing around the tables, talking to one another in German. The big room was spacious enough to provide a resounding echo to the voices, and to Sabrina's footsteps as she was marched forward, right up to Wolfschmidt.

The German voices died away. All eyes turned to Sabrina. Wolfschmidt set down his steaming cup of coffee and looked up at her. His thin lips seemed exceptionally cruel.

"You will be pleased to know, Fräulein," he said, "that I have decided not to punish you after all. Instead, I merely ask your cooperation in an educational endeavor. I told my men that you have become expert at using your femininity to aid you in your services as a spy for Deutschland. What we would like from you now is a demonstration of your technique."

"What do you mean?" Sabrina asked warily, trying to ignore the queasy feeling in the pit of her stomach which told her she knew exactly what he meant. She was aware of the stares of the German officers around her.

"You know what I mean by 'technique,'" Wolfschmidt said, sneering contemptuously. "Simply show us the way you gained information from your assignments." He paused. "Surely you did more than just *ask* them to give you their military secrets?"

Several of the German officers laughed.

"You filthy, lying scum," Michael cursed from behind Sabrina. "Only a maggot Hun could suggest a girl like her would ever—"

Sabrina heard a sharp sound and knew Michael had been hit by the German guarding him.

"Your chivalrous friend seems skeptical," Wolfschmidt said to Sabrina. "Perhaps we can allay his doubts by having him aid you in your demonstration?

"Please," she said helplessly. "Don't . . . ?"

Wolfschmidt rose to his feet. "But it is such a fine idea! That's why I had your friend brought up here with you. I recall the conversation you had with him in my embassy back in France. He seemed naive and disbelieving even then. It is time for him to gain an education."

"What the bloody hell are you talking about?" Michael demanded. "What sort of tommyrot is this?"

Wolfschmidt turned to his officers. "This man," he said, pointing to Michael, "will play the role of an allied minister. The Fräulein will play her usual role of spy. Her mission is to loosen the minister's tongue. And how does she do this, you ask?" He turned to Sabrina. "Go on. Show the gentlemen."

Sabrina shook her head in helpless torment, her eyes pleading.

"Show them!" growled Wolfschmidt, spinning her around to face Michael, shoving her against him. Michael tried to step back, but the Germans held him steady. Wolfschmidt pulled on the back of Sabrina's hair, forcing her head to tilt back. Then he pressed her face forward, trying to make her lips touch Michael's.

"You stinking bastard!" Michael roared. He began cursing at Wolfschmidt, as a thick wad of cloth was stuffed into his mouth by his guard, silencing him. A piece of tape was placed over his mouth.

Wolfschmidt grinned evilly as he pressed Sabrina's body up tighter against Michael. "Not having the desired effect, I see?" he said. "No military secrets are forthcoming from the minister? Here, perhaps this will loosen his tongue a bit." He put his arms around Sabrina from behind and ripped her shirt front open.

Sabrina cried out sharply. Wolfschmidt put his hands to the collar of her shirt and pulled it backward and down. The shirt came off Sabrina's shoulders and slid down her arms, bunching up at her manacled wrists behind her.

Gasps escaped from the surrounding circle of German officers. Wolfschmidt pushed Sabrina hard from behind, so that her naked breasts pressed against Michael's muscular, hairless chest. Michael tried to back away. It took the efforts of three Germans to hold him still.

Wolfschmidt was smiling coldly, enjoying himself. "Still no information from the minister? Perhaps if we step up our attack. Like so." His arm went around Sabrina's throat from behind, in a choke hold, and he forced her to move from side to side so that her breasts rubbed tantalizingly against Michael's chest. Sabrina's nipples became hard, and a tingling excitement surged through them. Wolfschmidt forced her head back so she was staring up at Michael's face. His expression was tortured.

"I'm sorry," she said pleadingly to Michael, feeling the erotic tingling as her erect nipples brushed against his chest. The Germans laughed at her remark. Michael's hard face broke out in sweat.

"*Still* no information?" marveled Wolfschmidt. "What else do you have in your bag of tricks, X-79? Ah, there's always *this*, isn't there?"

His booted foot came forward and caught her in the back of her knees, making her collapse to the wooden floor, in front of Michael. Wolfschmidt nodded, and one of the nearby Germans unfastened the buttons of Michael's trousers. The baggy trousers fell down in a heap about his ankles. He was wearing no underclothes.

Sabrina's face was held only inches away from Michael's waist, and she struggled to keep it back as Wolfschmidt began pressing it forward. "No," she cried, "please!"

Right before her eyes she watched Michael's long, smooth shaft grow hard and thick. Michael was struggling fiercely against the Germans who were holding him.

Sabrina struggled too, but could not resist the strong hands pushing her head forward. She scowled in helpless agony as Michael's smooth, hard maleness came closer and closer to her, straining upward at a rigid angle.

"No," she groaned, as the tip of his shaft touched between her lips. She sensed the vibrations that shook Michael's body from the small area of her contact with him.

"Enough," said Wolfschmidt, releasing her. Sabrina jerked her head back and began gasping for breath, her eyes closed tightly. "Obviously your technique did not work, X-79. So you will have to try another." He issued a command to the men holding Michael. "Onto the table with him. X-79 will now demonstrate her prowess in obtaining information from even the most closemouthed sources."

Michael was raised struggling and kicking onto a long wooden table, and was held down on it on his back. Then Sabrina saw two men coming toward her, their faces obscene with lecherous excitement.

She struggled wildly as they raised her up in the air, and as a third grasped her loose gray trousers at the waist, front and back, and tugged them down over her hips, without bothering to first unbutton them. Other hands joined in the trouser pull, and there was a fleeting moment when hands were all over her lower torso, touching her everywhere. Then the trousers were off, and she was completely naked.

She was gasping and moaning as they raised her up over Michael and pulled her legs apart in the air. Then they lowered her down slowly on top of him. Michael's head had been moving wildly from side to side, but now, as their loins made first contact, his head ceased moving and became still. He looked directly at her.

"No!" Sabrina screamed in protest against the look, which in her imagination seemed like one of shameful accusation.

She was now completely on top of him, her legs

166

straddling his hips. The rigid manliness of him, fully inside her, made her catch her breath. For a moment she thought she would faint. She had been secretly excited by him ever since that first time she saw him bare-chested, after he gave her his tunic as they fled away from the bar. Now here she was on top of him, gazing down at his hard, flat stomach and his muscular chest and arms. *And he was deep inside her.* Waves of melting pleasure flowed all through her.

Wolfschmidt circled around the table until he was in front of Sabrina. Then he motioned the men holding her to release her. They did so quickly. Sabrina was surprised. She was free to move! She started to rise up off Michael, but then she saw Wolfschmidt draw his pistol and point it at the top of Michael's head. He was standing behind Michael, so the Enlgishman could not see that a gun was aimed at him.

"Now, X-79," sneered Wolfschmidt tauntingly, "do you have any other tricks you would like to demonstrate for our enlightenment?" He grinned maliciously. His meaning was clear. Sabrina could either do as he wanted, or he would shoot Michael. Sabrina looked down at Michael, trying to apologize to him with her eyes, with her expression that begged forgiveness. Then, slowly, she began raising herself up and down on top of him.

The sweat streamed down Michael's face in a torrent. Sabrina felt her loins burning with violent pleasure. She wished he would peak quickly now, so this would be over and done with. But he did not peak. His maleness remained rigid and swollen. *Why doesn't he peak?* she wondered agonizingly, after what seemed an eternity of moving up and down atop him, shaming herself in unbearable degradation.

Then she realized the answer: he was resisting her . . . deliberately holding back, refusing to "sully" her. She tried to beg him with her eyes, but to no avail. The sweating German faces were glaring at her lustfully. There was the sound of loud, rasping breathing.

She had to hurry the situation to its end! She could not bear this any longer! Suddenly she began bouncing up and down on Michael with a vigorous zeal, moving about frantically. She saw from his face that she was getting to him; he could not hold out much longer. But *she* could not hold out much longer either. Flames of ecstasy licked at her insides, ravaging her. Her loins were ablaze with excruciating pleasure. *God, please let it happen to him*, she prayed, looking at Michael. *Let it end!*

She moved about fiercely, until she felt it coming. . . . Her eyes suddenly went very wide, and then the ecstasy exploded in her loins in a white-hot burst of volcanic pleasure, erupting inside her, making her scream with pleasure, though she tried not to. She collapsed forward on top of him, her breasts pressing against his sweat-soaked chest.

Now Michael could stand it no longer either, and his body tensed and shuddered violently. He shuddered for a long moment, and then finally it was over.

The Germans broke into vulgar applause. Wolfschmidt lost all interest immediately. "A fine performance," he said, though there was weariness in his voice rather than enthusiasm. He reholstered his pistol. "Dress them and take them back to their cell. She's learned her lesson about shooting an officer of the German high command." He turned on his heel and left the room.

Once they were dressed and back in their iron cage, alone in the basement, Sabrina could not bear to face Michael. She sank down, facing a corner, her head lowered. She kept hugging her arms tightly around herself.

Michael was pacing furiously about the cage, breathing through gritted teeth. Sabrina felt certain he reviled her now. She felt more shameful than she had ever felt in her life.

The pacing stopped. She heard his footsteps coming toward her. She tensed. His hand came down on her shoulder, and she was afraid he would swivel her around violently to face his anger.

He did turn her to face him, but he did so gently. Sabrina's eyes were cast downward. Michael put his hand to her chin and raised her face. He squatted down next to her, and as she looked up at him, she heard him say something that surprised her. "Can you ever forgive me?" he said softly, pain in his voice.

"Forgive *you*?" she said, stunned.

"I should have fought them to the death before letting them do that to you."

"Oh, but no!" she protested, seeing the self-hatred on his sensitive face. "It wasn't your fault. It was *me*, I should have—"

"No," he said, "there was nothing you could have done. You're so good, how could I ever think anything bad of you?" He stopped talking. For a long moment they stared at each other, their faces very close. Looking at his rugged yet sensitive face, Sabrina felt a wave of deep affection flow between them. Michael came forward and his lips touched hers in a firm but gentle kiss. His hand went to her cheek and stroked it softly.

A sob broke from Sabrina's throat. She lowered her head against his chest, crying shudderingly. The pain and aloneness she had been feeling poured out of her as he held her tightly, rocking her back and forth. "It's all right, Bree darling," he was saying. "At least we have each other."

Chapter 13

Early the next morning, Michael surprised Sabrina by saying in a low, cautious voice: "Now don't get unnerved, but I have to tell you something. We're going to try to escape today."

"Escape?" she echoed, stunned. She had been permitted to leave the cage earlier to go to the shower, and had been astonished at all the armed men she passed as she was escorted down the halls. Escape seemed impossible.

Michael saw the look of protest on her face, and said, "We have to try it. Look, you don't think they're going to leave you alone now, do you? A beautiful girl like you, here in a cage where you're completely at their mercy?" He shook his head grimly. "I think that 'demonstration' last night was so Wolfschmidt could show you off to his men, to tantalize them. I think he plans to use you as a reward, to be given to those who do the best work."

"Oh, no!"

"We can't risk it. We've got to get you out of here."

Sabrina knew he was right when the guard came into the basement several minutes later, carrying a pair of handcuffs. He motioned Michael toward the side of the cage, indicating he wanted to handcuff him to one of the iron bars. "*Der Oberlieutenant*, he come down soon," said the guard with an unmistakably lecherous grin. "You must be chained out of der vay. It is not *you* he come to visit." The guard laughed a tinny-sounding laugh and winked at Michael, as if Michael were a fellow conspirator by virtue of the fact that he was male.

Michael refused to move toward the side of the cage as ordered. Sabrina quailed fearfully. A strange buzzing sound began coming from outside the building, very faintly, as the guard again motioned Michael toward the side of the cage. "*Mach schnell*," he ordered, becoming impatient. When Michael still did not come forward, the guard pulled his pistol from his holster, his expression turning fierce. He clearly wanted to hurry and get Michael chained to the bar; the oberlieutenant was due at any moment.

The buzzing, droning sound outside the building became louder, making the guard glance up toward the ceiling, perking up his ears. Then he looked back at Michael, and cocked his pistol.

Michael came forward now, and put his wrists close together. Instead of sticking them out through the bars, though, he held them just an inch inside the cage. The guard snorted disgustedly and reached into the cage with his left hand, to clasp the cuffs on Michael. He held the gun leveled in his other hand.

Suddenly Michael grasped the hand holding the cuffs and jerked it hard into the cage, while his fist flew out through the bars, smashing into the guard's jaw.

The guard grunted in pain. He fired his pistol. By pulling the guard's arm through the bars,

172

though, Michael had pivoted him sideways, offsetting his aim. The bullet whistled off to the side. Michael grasped desperately for the arm holding the gun as the guard struggled wildly to keep the arm free. "*Hilfe!*" the guard screamed over his shoulder, calling for aid. "*Ich brauche helfen!*"

Sabrina rushed forward and circled from one side of Michael to the other, trying to be of help. There was nothing she could do though. "Get back!" Michael yelled at her, as the German squeezed off another shot, this one whistling an inch past Michael's ear. The sound of running footsteps came from the stairway beyond the basement door, in response to the guard's screams.

The guard began firing more shots wildly. Michael continued yanking his arm all the way through the bars, forcing his shoulder to jam against the cage. The buzzing sound from overhead became so loud now that it began shaking the building.

Suddenly two other soldiers burst through the basement door, their weapons drawn. One of them—the oberlieutenant Sabrina was to have been ravaged by—aimed at Michael without even bothering to stop running forward. Michael jerked the guard directly in front of himself as the oberlieutenant fired. The guard screamed, the bullet striking him in the chest.

Michael grasped the gun from the guard's lifeless, unresisting hand as the man slumped to the ground. He fired at the oberlieutenant, hitting him in the face, sending him somersaulting over backward.

The second soldier began firing, and the sound was almost drowned out by the deafening roar that was now recognizable as an aircraft passing very low over the building. Michael grabbed Sabrina's arm and shoved her to his rear. "Behind me, get behind me!" he yelled, crouching down, returning the German's fire. Then his gun clicked empty. The German continued firing, one bullet ricocheting off an iron bar, another sideswiping Michael bloodily in his left flank.

Suddenly there was a loud whistling sound, becoming shriller and shriller. Then the ground seemed to heave upward as a thunderous explosion came from beyond the walls of the building above. A shower of concrete dust rained down from the ceiling. Michael, Sabrina, and the German were knocked to the ground by the concussion.

The German looked up at the cracking ceiling in stark terror. There was another whistling sound, followed by a second concussive, earthshaking blast. More white concrete powdered down from the groaning ceiling, which looked as though it would collapse at any moment. The soldier ran out of the basement in terror.

Michael was covering Sabrina's head and body, sheltering her. He cowered lower over her, squinting hard against the rain of concrete. "The base is bloody well being attacked!" he shouted to Sabrina, above the roar of the plane and the concussive blast of the bombs. Through the open basement door they heard the screaming voices of the Germans as they rushed about in a panic to get outside the building, certain it was going to be bombed and destroyed. "Who could bloody well be *attacking* us?" Michael wondered.

A sudden notion flashed into Sabrina's mind,

making her mouth drop half open in disbelief. "What day is today?" she asked.

"*What?*"

"What day is it?" she repeated, shouting above the clamor and thunder.

He looked at her dumbfounded. "What the bloomin' hell does it matter what day it bloody well is? Have you gone stark raving mad?"

"Is it the twentieth?" she persisted.

"Yes!" he shouted, covering her head against a new shower of concrete that rained down upon them.

"It's him!" Sabrina declared joyously. "He's come to rescue you after all, just as he said he would!"

Michael didn't know what she was talking about. "Who?" he shouted. "And whoever he is, does he call *this* a rescue? He's jolly well going to get us crushed to death!"

High up in the blue sky dotted with tufts of cotton clouds, far above the building in which Michael and Sabrina were imprisoned, Dallas Hunter banked his Sopwith biplane into the wind and began circling for a descent. He pointed with an exaggerated motion of his arm down to an access road situated across a field from the building.

Several yards away from him in the sky, Eddie Rickenbacker nodded to acknowledge Hunter's landing site, and to indicate that he'd strafe the area to keep the Germans away from Hunter's plane once it was down. He then gave Hunter a thumbs-up sign of encouragement as Hunter nosed down his plane and prepared to land.

Meanwhile, in the basement, Michael was frantically searching through the pockets of the dead guard lying outside the cage, his arms extended through the iron bars. Finally he found the key to the cage door. When he inserted it into the lock, though, the key wouldn't turn. A stray bullet had hit the lock, jamming it. "Damn!" Michael cursed fiercely, trying to force the lock. It took a long time, but finally the key turned. Michael kicked the door with all his might. It burst open, clanging against the wall of bars, rebounding halfway back. "Come on then!" Michael said, taking Sabrina's hand and pulling her forward.

They ran headlong toward the basement doorway. They reached it just in time to hear running footsteps coming down toward them from the stairs beyond.

Michael pulled to an abrupt halt, looked feverishly around him until his gaze found the Luger pistol the oberlieutenant had dropped. He grabbed it and jerked Sabrina behind him. Then he braced himself with his legs apart, knees half bent, the Luger held in both hands. His arms were extended straight before him, pointing toward the doorway.

A tall man, wearing a white scarf and a brown leather jacket with a fur collar, burst through the doorway, flung himself upon the ground, rolled over twice and came up in a crouch with a gun in his hands. He aimed at the first figure he saw, without taking even a fraction of a second to notice anything about the figure except that it held a Luger.

Michael jerked the muzzle of his Luger down toward the man's chest.

"No!" Sabrina screamed, shoving hard against him as he squeezed off a shot, making him miss.

"What the hell!" exclaimed Michael.

"Sabrina!" declared Hunter. Then, squinting, he

recognized Michael too, despite the black eyepatch and the German fatigue clothes he wore. He lowered his gun and stood up.

Michael frowned hard. He recognized Hunter now, but still, when he lowered his gun it was very reluctantly. He watched Sabrina rush toward Hunter, flinging her arms around him and exulting. "Oh Dallas! You did come!"

Hunter grinned tautly at Sabrina, putting an arm around her.

Michael went up to the two of them, grabbed Sabrina's hand, and without a word pulled her with him as he rushed out the basement door. He hurried up the steps, continuing the escape that had been interrupted. Sabrina felt stunned, having been forcibly pulled away from Hunter. She did not say anything, though, as the three of them ran up the stairs in single file.

At the top of the stairway landing, Hunter caught up to Michael and swiveled him around to face him. "Where the hell do you think you're going?" he demanded.

"Out of here!" Michael shot back. Their stares locked in angry confrontation.

"Don't you think you should find out *where* you're going, before you rush out into the thick of the battle?" When Michael said nothing, just seethed angrily, Hunter told him and Sabrina where his plane was located, across the field. Then he said, "Follow me," and rushed out the doorway.

All at once, Sabrina found herself running at full speed across a field of tall grass, through a scattering of German soldiers on either side of them. The soldiers were not paying attention to them, however, for they were busy fleeing in all directions from the assault of Eddie Rickenbacker's Sopwith biplane, which kept flying low, chasing them with machine guns blazing.

As the three of them rushed through the field toward Hunter's plane, puffs of smoke rose everywhere around them, and clumps of dirt churned up to the left and right, sometimes showering them with clods and mists of dirt. The Germans had noticed them now, and some of them turned to fire. Michael shot one who loomed up in front of him. Hunter shot two more, dropping them in their tracks screaming.

Sabrina's lungs ached and burned, and her legs felt weak. She stumbled in a pothole and fell, scratching her elbows and cheek. She tried to rise up quickly, but fell back down, pain shooting through her ankle. Hunter instantly stopped running and stood braced in one spot, swiveling his gun from left to right, defending their position while Michael leaned down and scooped Sabrina up into his arms. "Right!" he shouted to Hunter. They resumed running.

Michael's side was covered with blood from where the German's bullet had sliced through his flesh. As they ran, Sabrina's shirt became stained red from his bleeding.

The plane seemed to grow larger and larger as they ran toward it. Then finally they were there. Hunter leaped onto the bottom wing and helped Michael deposit Sabrina in the open rear cockpit. Then he climbed into the forward cockpit and switched on the ignition. "Turn her over!" he shouted to Michael.

"The blades?" Michael asked, looking uncertainly at the propeller.

"Yeah, the blades!" shouted Hunter. "You think I'm telling you to turn over the whole damn airplane?"

Michael went to the propeller and gave it a forceful turn, putting his back into the effort. Nothing happened.

"Again!" shouted Hunter.

Michael repeated the procedure. A bullet zinged into the ground an inch from his boot heel. The engine sputtered into life, and the propeller began revolving like a whirlwind, nearly knocking Michael down. Hunter gunned it, making it roar. Michael rushed to the rear cockpit just as the approaching Germans were getting close enough to aim carefully. He leaped up into the cockpit, landing half on top of Sabrina. "Get off!" she shouted.

"Stay down," Michael ordered, continuing to half cover her, sheltering her from the gunfire. He began firing his pistol at the Germans, emptying it. The engine roared thunderously, and the plane jolted forward. Michael righted himself in the seat, permitting Sabrina to sit up in time to see that Hunter had turned the plane so that they were heading not away from the pursuing Germans, but directly toward them.

Michael saw it too. *"Are you crazy?"* he shouted at Hunter. Hunter ignored him. The Germans scattered out of their way in screaming panic. Then suddenly they were airborne. Sabrina looked down past the side of the fuselage to see the ground racing by under them several feet below. Their acceleration and the steepness of their ascent increased. Then they were speeding thunderously into the freedom of the vast blue sky, heading at a crazy angle toward the blazing sun.

They were miles up now, gazing down at the magnificent panorama of the blue-green sea, and the tiny dot that was the island, which they were leaving behind. Sabrina had to squint her eyes against the forcefulness of the freezing wind. It whistled loudly in her ears and pressed forcefully against her skin, giving her goose bumps.

Michael said something to her, but she could not hear a word of it above the roar of the engine and the whistling of the wind. She nodded, though, and smiled. She felt wonderful! She was free! What a wildly liberating sensation, she thought, being high up in this bird of wood and wires and struts, looking down at the green treetops of the African continent they were now approaching.

The white silk package attached to the compartment wall in front of her was partially sliced apart, for she had cut strips out of it to use as bandages around Michael's side. She had thought nothing of slicing into it with the knife she found in the utility kit. She did not realize it was an emergency parachute. She had never even heard of a parachute.

Eddie Rickenbacker was flying along at their side, grinning at Sabrina, looking like a happy country boy out on a lark.

For the first time in a long time, Sabrina felt that fate was beginning to smile on her. It was then that she saw the three small black specks on the horizon, coming toward them from the east. She felt a sinking feeling as the sinister-looking specks grew larger, turning into rapidly approaching airplanes.

Hunter and Rickenbacker saw the attackers too. They nodded to one another, gave the thumbs-up sign, and then Rickenbacker veered off to the side to engage two of the aircraft. Hunter dove sharply, banked in the opposite direction, and began making wild, evasive maneuvers.

It was no use, though. The British Sopwith that Hunter was flying—since he was now assigned to the British Expeditionary Force—was built for two people, not three. Despite Hunter's skill as an ace pilot, the extra weight greatly reduced his maneuverability. And he needed every bit of maneuverability he could get, for the German plane that now began pursuing and firing at Hunter was piloted by none other than Manfred von Richthofen—the dreaded Red Baron. The bright red Fokker with the black crosses on the wings was unmistakable.

"Damn!" shouted Hunter, his voice lost to the wind. "I've been wanting a shot at this bastard for months. And now, to meet him like *this*!" He began diving and rolling and looping the plane, blasting away with his machine gun every chance he had to get a clear shot. He was at too great a disadvantage, though, due to the extra weight.

The Red Baron got behind him, and before Hunter could shake him off, there was a shattering blast of machine gun fire, accompanied by a sound that struck terror into Sabrina's heart: the sound of bullets smashing into the body of the aircraft, splintering and shattering everywhere they hit.

"The tail!" shouted Michael. The tail stabilizer section was completely shattered. The plane began wobbling and quaking violently. Hunter tried to maintain control, and for a brief moment he did manage to hold the craft steady. But then the stabilizer section, already half off, caught the wind at a bad angle and flew off the aircraft.

The plane lurched, then dived down at dizzying

speed, making a shrieking whistling sound as it plunged toward the earth. Sabrina screamed and grasped Michael tightly about the chest as the green treetops of the African jungle below rushed up at them.

Her mind reeled. The ear-splitting noise and ripping-sharp winds battered her, hammered at her. A stretch of open green field in the midst of the trees came into view as Hunter fought desperately to level out of the plunge, to attempt a crash landing.

The next instant Sabrina felt the wrenching jolt as the plane leveled and veered into the grassland field, screeching and skidding through low brush and bushes, smashing headlong through the landscape.

She saw the impenetrable wall of trees and lush jungle rushing toward them as they plowed through the field, and she wondered crazily if they would crash into the trees and explode in a ball of yellow flame . . . or if the aircraft would splinter apart first, from the screeching headlong skid, killing them before they ever reached the trees.

A sudden crashing jolt tossed her into the air, and she blacked out.

PART II

Rapture in the Jungle

Chapter 14

Sabrina regained consciousness slowly, feeling the coolness of the thick grass beneath her and the pleasant breeze wafting over her. She did not open her eyes; she was still half dazed. Then she noticed the feel of wetness all over her face, and the memory of the crash came back to her. She snapped her eyes open fearfully. Was the wetness blood?

Instead of blood, though, she saw a young, gangly legged gazelle bending over her, licking her face. Her startled scream sent the young animal galloping off gracefully.

Sabrina sat up and looked around. She was in a lush green field of tall, thick grass. Several yards in front of her, the field ended abruptly in a wall of trees and dense undergrowth, as the jungle began. The sun was low, close to the treetops, showing that it was late afternoon, near sundown. A pleasant, slightly chilly breeze rippled across the field, making the tall grass bend and wave.

She shook her head to clear it. Her mind seemed temporarily fogged. She looked at the airplane only a few yards away, and saw that it was sharply tilted, with the left side of the wings high up, the right side touching the ground. One wheel had broken off from the lower wing during the crash landing. It was this that had tossed her out of the plane, and that had stopped the plane before it crashed into the trees.

Hunter was hanging half out of the cockpit, slumped over the side, unmoving. Michael was not visible at all.

She stood up intending to rush to the plane, and instantly felt searing pain shoot up from her ankle. She had forgotten how she had turned her foot during the escape. Limping and hopping, she made her way through the grass toward the crippled plane.

Michael was crumpled in the bottom of the rear cockpit she saw. She felt great relief at seeing that he was breathing, his chest rising and falling. She went to Hunter very gingerly, feeling a stab of fearfulness at his immobility. She could not tell if he was breathing or not. His face was badly bruised and bloody from a cut eyebrow.

"Dallas?" she said tentatively. She touched his face when he did not answer.

"Hmmm!" he mumbled sharply, twitching under her touch. She jerked her hand back. He opened his eyes, closed them and squinted tightly, then opened them again. He gazed at her. "You're looking good, babe," he mumbled thickly, grinning, still slightly dazed.

He raised himself, grimacing at a bolt of pain that stuck him in the chest.

"Are you all right?" Sabrina asked worriedly.

He gritted his teeth and said nothing. He stood up in the cockpit, despite the pain, and climbed out onto the wing. He went to Michael and looked at him carefully. "Hey," he said, trying to rouse him. He slapped him lightly a few times.

"Don't do that," Sabrina protested, concerned.

"Come on, Limey, rise and shine," said Hunter, continuing to slap him lightly.

Michael awakened with a start. "I say, what?" Dallas grabbed a canteen from the utility compartment and handed it to him, opened. Michael took several swallows, then handed it to Sabrina, wiping his mouth on his sleeve. She drank the warm water gratefully.

Now Michael came out of the plane too, and the three of them began moving about, checking themselves to see what kind of shape they were in. Each of them was bruised and battered, and the two men were bloody—but no one seemed to have any broken bones or ribs.

While Sabrina checked the bandage she had put on Michael's wounded side, Hunter began circling the airplane, scrutinizing every inch of it. He climbed up on the wing, pushed back the engine cowling and looked inside. After tinkering around a bit, he climbed back into the cockpit.

"What are you doing?" Sabrina asked.

He did not answer. Instead he turned the ignition switch. The engine made a clicking sound. "Rotate the blades," he said to Michael. He frowned in concentration, checking his instruments, while Michael put his back into giving the propeller a good spin. Nothing happened. "Again," Hunter said. This time the engine sputtered into life, the propeller caught and whirled about in a windy blur. Hunter raced the engine, grinning. "We're back in business," he declared.

Michael looked over the cockeyed tilt of the wings, the broken wheel, the shot-up tail section and the gaping hole where the stabilizer had been. He looked up at Hunter in astonishment. "You bet-

186

ter have those bruises on your head looked at, Yank. You're in worse shape than you think."

Hunter killed the engine and jumped down from the cockpit. "They haven't shot me out of this war yet," he declared, circling the plane with mounting excitement. "The engine's still sound," he said, slapping it. "The wings are unbroken. That right wheel is gone for good, that's for sure, but hell, who needs it?" He looked out at the field, spreading his legs, putting his hands on his hips. "This tall grass is bad for wheels anyway. We'll get rid of the other one and put skids under both wings and the tail. Then we'll fashion ourselves a new stabilizer—have to custom make it out of the available materials. But we'll make it. We'll have her airborne again."

"Is there enough fuel to get us back to whatever base you took off from?" Sabrina asked.

"No."

"Ah," said Michael hostilely. "But no matter, eh, Yank? You plan to use your Yankee ingenuity to squeeze petrol right out of the trees."

Hunter looked at him with a hard expression. "There's enough to get us back to civilization. To the British forces north of here."

Sabrina began to shiver. Night was descending rapidly and the air was growing cold. "How long do you think before we can leave here?" she asked.

"Two weeks. Maybe three. Depends on how much trouble we have making a stabilizer and putting on the skids." He saw the worried look in her green eyes and guessed what she was thinking. "Don't worry about the Krauts. We're too deep inland for their Afrika Korps to find us. Besides, it wouldn't be worth their effort to hunt us down."

Michael was looking at the way Sabrina was

hugging herself to still her shivering. He turned to Hunter. "Why don't you give her your coat, mate?"

Hunter grinned tautly at Michael. "Still the boy scout, huh kid?"

Sabrina saw the way their stares locked with bitter intensity. Nothing had changed, she thought; they were still at odds with each other, and she was the cause of it. She rushed between them, seeing that violence could erupt at any minute. "Stop it, you two!" she declared. "Let's just—settle down. It's going to be pitch-dark soon. We should get ready for it, shouldn't we? Well, shouldn't we?"

Hunter continued to stare stonily at Michael, who returned his stare. Then he took off his flier's jacket and put it around Sabrina's shoulders. Sabrina sensed that he had been about to do it all along.

Darkness was descending very rapidly. Hunter removed the two parachutes from their compartments in the plane and laid the silken sheets out on the ground, the torn one on top of the other. After a while, the three of them lay down on the sheets and closed their eyes.

Sabrina could not fall asleep. She was too keyed up. She kept wondering how she would manage to keep the two men away from each other's throats during the time it took to make the repairs on the plane. She sat up and looked around. The night had come upon them so quickly in this strange land that it unnerved her. It was very dark out and the stars were incredibly bright. The air was scented with the fragrance of moist greenery.

She sat looking around at the jungle very near them. A million strange sounds were coming from within: the chirping of crickets and squeals of small creatures . . . the scurrying movements of tree-living animals . . . the sound of the strong wind that whistled through the branches of the trees. There were also sounds of animals that seemed very foreign and frightening to her. She pulled Hunter's flight jacket tighter around her.

Suddenly she was aware of a flash of movement several yards in front of her, and looking more intently she saw a lion stalking toward them. "Dallas!" she whispered loudly. "Michael!"

They sat up and looked toward where she was pointing. "Quick," said Hunter, "into the plane." He didn't wait for Sabrina to stand, but instead put his arms under her and raised her up quickly, and then deposited her into the forward cockpit. He quickly climbed in with her. The lion was almost upon them now. Michael dived into the rear cockpit.

The lion sniffed all around the plane for a moment. Sabrina pressed fearfully against Hunter's chest, his arms around her. After a moment, the animal sauntered away, as if deciding that the strange machine and its inhabitants were not worthy of his interest.

None of the three of them intended to return to the ground to sleep now. Michael, however, was not satisfied with their respective accommodations. "Come on back here with me, Yank," he said, his voice irritable.

"Like hell I will," said Hunter.

"Like hell you *won't*, blast you! Get back here or I'll come and get you."

"Stop it, Michael," said Sabrina. "It's all right."

Michael said nothing. She could hear his angry breathing.

"Nothing's going to . . . happen," she said,

trying to soothe him. "Let's all just get some sleep now, all right?" Michael still said nothing. "It's just because we're here like this already, and . . . and tomorrow we can worry about different arrangements." The truth was that she needed to be near a strong male body now, and she did not want Hunter to leave her. She felt more secure and protected with him here next to her, than she would if she were alone. "It's all right," she repeated once more.

Michael still said nothing, but his angry breathing eased a bit. She thought everything was going to be peaceful until Hunter said, for no other reason than to taunt the Englishman, "Yeah, Michael, it's all right. It's just dandy, in fact."

"*That* does it," declared Michael irately. He climbed angrily out of the rear cockpit and came to the forward one. "Out of there, Yank. If anyone's going to stay up here with her, it's going to be someone I know I can trust. Meaning *me*. As for you—" He jerked his thumb over his shoulder. "Out!"

Sabrina sensed Hunter tensing, preparing to start swinging on the Englishman.

"Oh, damn it!" she exclaimed in frustration. "You two are such *children*. Here, *I'll* be the one to sleep in the rear cockpit. And you two can do whatever you like." So saying, she clambered over the top of the plane, into the rear compartment. She huddled down in the bottom of it, her knees up to her chest, her arms closed around them.

No further words were spoken. She heard Michael climbing onto the highest part of the tilted wings and stretching out. Then there were no sounds other than the chirping, rustling, hooting sounds of the jungle. A bone-deep weariness overcame Sabrina, and she fell into a deep void of black, silent sleep.

When she awakened in the morning, Michael was gone. He was not on the wing where he had lain, or in the forward cockpit, where Hunter was still sleeping. She looked all around, then climbed down onto the ground, stepping gingerly on her hurt ankle. She heard a sound and turned toward the forest. There, coming forward out from the wall of trees, she saw him, grinning at her, carrying an armful of round, purple fruit. The canteen was slung over his shoulder, its outer cloth case dripping wet.

"Anyone for breakfast?" he said, when he came up close. He handed her a small fruit. "Looks like a plum, but tastes like a sweet grapefruit." He smiled at her as she bit into it. "Hope you like it," he said. "It may be breakfast for the next two weeks."

As it turned out, though, the tangy fruit was not at all their only staple during the days to come. The jungle proved to be a treasure chest of strange and delightful fruits, nuts, and vegetables, as well as game of all sorts. A wide, rushing stream was discovered nearby too, with the coolest, freshest-tasting water Sabrina had ever drunk.

In fact, the jungle provided for them so abundantly that during the next few days Sabrina found her fears and anxieties leaving her, being replaced at first by contentment . . . and then by actual enjoyment and happiness.

Hunter and Michael noticed the change in her as she became more gay and joyous with each passing day. They both thought it very strange, and neither of them understood it. Sabrina understood it, though. The reason for her change of mood was very simple: she was delighted with the way the situation had turned out.

And how could she be otherwise? she asked herself. Her life before the plane crash had been horrid and unbearably tormenting. But now it was pleasant and relaxed. No demands were put on her. She spent her days in the sunshine as the men worked on repairing the airplane. Aside from the worry about the men's antagonism toward one another, there really were no problems at all. Sabrina had not felt so carefree in months.

She loved walking through the jungle. She no longer felt terrified of it. There were strange, but graceful animals to watch and beautiful lush greenery to admire. There were even wildly colorful flowers among the hanging vines and up-arching tree roots. She loved doing womanly chores, too, and laughed in delight at the surprised looks on the men's faces when they saw how she had "decorated" their tree house.

The house consisted of nothing more than some sturdy branches the men had hacked off and vine-tied together, to form a level platform at the top of a thick tree. This was to protect them from predatory animals that roamed the jungle floor at night. One day when Hunter and Michael were off working on the plane, Sabrina strung up the two parachutes to make tentlike, billowing-in-the-breeze "walls." Then she gathered dead leaves and tufts of grass, and spread them over the floor of branches to make a soft, cushiony rug. She collected pretty flowers and multicolored rocks and strung them up to adorn the new walls of her tree house. As a finishing touch, she made a bowl out of a coconutlike husk and filled it with nuts, and then put it out for the men to snack on.

When Hunter and Michael returned after a hard day of working on the plane, they were flabbergasted. They had left a crude floor of branches in the morning, and were now returning to an attractive, comfortable home in the evening. Sabrina clapped her hands and laughed with joyousness at their astonished expressions.

Now Sabrina was preparing a new surprise for them. I'm tired of looking like a bag of rags, she thought to herself as she sliced into the excess silk yardage at the base of her parachute walls. These German fatigue clothes have become dirty and wrinkled enough. It's time for a new addition to my wardrobe.

When she had enough cloth for the pattern she wanted, she put down the utility knife and picked up her porcupine needle and the "thread" she had fashioned from the fibers of tree bark. Then, sitting on the floor and humming to herself, she began sewing.

When she finished, she held the garment up for inspection. It was beautiful! In fact, it was so lovely she didn't dare wear it while she herself was so grimy and her hair remained so tangled and stringy.

The men had forbidden her to go to the stream by herself, due to the danger of wild animals. But neither of them had taken an interest in going with her these last few days; they were too tired after working all day. So, she now thought it was time to take matters into her own hands. Anyway, the danger from animals wasn't at all bad during the daylight. She picked up her new dress and her comb of porcupine pelt and went down to the stream.

The water was crystal clear and making sounds like a babbling brook as it rushed by. The air was fresh and invigorating. Sabrina shucked off her dirty, coarse, gray fatigues, which it seemed she had been wearing forever, and flung them far out into the stream. She watched them float rapidly out of sight. Then she climbed down from the overhanging ledge of the bank and waded out into he water.

It felt wonderful! She couldn't remember ever enjoying a bath so much. She remained in the cool water for a long time, reveling in the joy of it. When she finally climbed out onto the bank, her body and hair were spotless and her skin could breathe again. She sat on a rock and brushed her hair with the porcupine-pelt comb. She curled her hair around segments of hollow reeds. Then she lay back happily and let her hair bake dry in the sun, thinking about what a good surprise this would be for Hunter and Michael.

She was waiting for them when they returned to the tree house that evening. She was sporting her new silk gown and her hair was radiantly, buoyantly curled. And she knew within seconds that this was one of the biggest mistakes she had ever in her life made.

They stood staring at her transfixed, their mouths agape. They couldn't believe their eyes. They had become used to seeing her dirty and smudged, wearing wrinkled gray fatigues, her hair stringy and soiled. Now she stood before them with her fair skin glistening, wearing a togalike gown that passed over one shoulder, leaving the other shoulder bare. The material was so silken it draped over every curve, clearly outlining the fullness of her figure.

The gown was gathered at her narrow waist with a belt of braided vines, and her curly, pinkish strawberry-blond hair was adorned with a tiara she had fashioned of white lilies.

Hunter and Michael continued to stare at her in tortured silence, their eyes greedily drinking in her total beauty. Their expressions turned to agonized torment, and all signs of goodnaturedness left them. The air became unbearably tense.

Sabrina had been standing somewhat shyly, waiting for their pleased reactions. Now the smile that was frozen on her face began souring as she saw the intense hunger in their eyes. She realized her mistake: she had thought innocently—foolishly!—that she would delight them by making herself pretty for them. Instead, she had rekindled the white-hot flames of passion. It was as if she had been so grubby before that they had forgotten how truly beautiful she really was. Now they were suddenly being brought back to the realization, with the impact of a slap in the face.

A lump came to Michael's throat and he swallowed hard. Sabrina couldn't bear the way they were looking at her; she lowered her eyes. This was a mistake. Now she could see the mightily straining bulges in both their pants.

Her skin became hot and prickly. To make matters worse, as she glanced at the bulges, she could not help but notice that her nipples were becoming hard and erect. And though there had been no problem with the filmy material of her gown before, there very definitely was one now. For the silken material draping over her breasts not only didn't hide her excited state, it clearly outlined it beyond any shadow of a doubt.

Sabrina didn't know what to do. The men stood looking at her, their faces tense and sweating, their heavy breathing filling the air. Finally she could not take it any longer. She jerked her hands up across her breasts and turned around, facing away from them. She shut her eyes tightly and said, "Leave me alone! Please! For a moment." When they climbed down to the ground from the tree, she quickly pulled on Hunter's dirty flight jacket, though it seemed a defilement of her pristine white gown.

During the next few days, the sexual tension between the three of them became so explosive that Sabrina expected a blowup at any moment. Hunter made it clear he was no longer willing to be refused in his overtures. He wanted to make love to Sabrina, and he had no intention of being put off.

Sabrina knew she could not let herself be seduced by Hunter, since this would be the spark that would set Michael off. Michael had sworn to protect her from Hunter's lust. He himself wanted to make love to her, she knew, but was too "proper" to do such a thing. His image of her was still that of an untarnished goddess, despite all that had happened in the mess hall. He was unaware of the fact that Sabrina had not only made love to Hunter many times, but had actually lived with him.

Though she had vowed to resist Hunter's advances, at least until they were out of here and back in civilization, deep down Sabrina doubted that she could really do so. Because the truth was she was weakening.

She couldn't help it! she thought to herself defensively, as she brushed vines out of her path now on the way down to the deep stream. How could she help but be excited and weakened by the constant presence of these two sun-bronzed, muscular men, who ran around half naked by day, and lay only inches from her body at night?

There were times when Hunter deliberately brushed against her. Sometimes he would shower from the water barrel they had constructed in full view of the tree house, knowing Sabrina was watching him, unable to force herself to turn her eyes away. He taunted her with his body every chance he had.

And Michael, though his stated aim was to protect her from any untoward advances, did not make it any easier for her by the way he wore his loose trousers very low on his hips, the beltline coming to well below his navel. Whenever he was looking away, Sabrina caught herself stealing glances at the portion of his flat, hard stomach that showed between the bottom of his shirt and the top of his pants.

She reached the bank of the stream now. She took off her white gown, then ran into the loud, rushing water, hoping the coldness of it would help quench the yearning deep in her loins. She had to get out of this jungle soon. How much longer could she take it? How much longer could she deny her body, which was responding the way that of any healthy young girl would react to being at such close quarters to rugged men like Hunter and Michael?

Fortunately, she knew, she would not have to suffer the situation much longer. Hunter had told her this morning that the plane would be ready for a test run by the end of the day. The skids had already been fitted on, and all that remained was to hook up the new stabilizer they had constructed; that would be finished within hours.

She was thinking about this with relief when suddenly she heard a rustling of bushes high up on the bank, then the sound of crashing, running feet sprinting through the jungle. Sabrina looked up, startled. Within an instant she saw Hunter and Michael both rush out through the underbrush, running toward her at full tilt. They leaped into the stream from the bank, still wearing trousers and boots.

Sabrina sank down in the water and her hands went to cup her breasts. "What are you—"

Hunter's hand went to her mouth and pressed roughly over it, stifling her protest. He and Michael dragged her backward to the edge of the bank, until they were in the shadow of the overhanging ledge. Sabrina was so surprised by the unexplained action that she began struggling, trying to scream. "Quiet!" Hunter commanded in a whisper.

Suddenly she saw why they were doing this. A group of fierce-looking, black-skinned natives came out from the jungle several yards downstream. They were dressed in loincloths front and back, leaving their flanks bare. Hoops of bone decorated their upper arms, and several wore necklaces made from the teeth and fangs of jungle animals. Their faces were painted around the eyes with red, yellow, and white lines, making them look truly frightening.

One of the natives who appeared to be the leader—an exceptionally tall, flat-nosed, barrel-chested hulk of a man—looked scrutinizingly up and down the bank. When he saw Sabrina's white silken gown, lying on the bank directly above where she, Michael, and Hunter lay hidden, he pointed at it with his spear. *"Uguba cha!"* he boomed.

The entire war party began rushing in their direction.

Chapter 15

The natives stood directly above them on the bank. Hunter pushed Sabrina against the wall of the overhanging ledge, and flattened himself over her, trying to hide the two of them from sight. Michael flattened himself against the side also, a few feet away.

The natives spoke in their tribal tongue. Their voices were fierce. They were obviously angry over something. The tall native whom Sabrina thought was the chief, and whose rumbling, booming voice was very distinctive, kept speaking an English phrase mixed in with his aboriginal tongue. "Winged chariot from sky," he persisted in saying.

Sabrina was terrified with fear that the natives would discover them. All it would take would be for them to lean forward and look down beneath the outcropping ledge they were standing on. That did not happen though. After several tense minutes, the natives left, their voices receding as they reentered the jungle.

Sabrina's mind came back to her immediate situation as she felt something hard prodding her in the area of her loins. She had felt it earlier, but had not thought about it; her attention had been focused on the immediate danger of the natives.

Now she instantly realized the source of the pleasant sensation: Hunter's maleness was pressing rigidly against her naked sex through the fabric of his fatigue pants. She was shocked back to reality now: the fact of her nakedness and of his powerful body pinning her to the side of the bank. Even the threat of the natives had failed to dampen his desire.

It was Michael who acted, before she had a chance to. He grasped Hunter's shoulder and pulled him away from Sabrina, pivoting the American around so that they faced. "All right, mate," he said in a hostile voice, "the danger's past."

Sabrina tried to cover herself with her hands and arms, knowing the effort was futile. "The least you can do is, one of you go get me my clothes!" she said, flustered.

Hunter just stood there looking at her. Michael scrambled up the bank and cautiously glanced around. "Gone," he said, sliding back down again. "They took it with them."

"Well get me something else then!" she persisted. Her nipples were hard again. Goose bumps rose all over her skin. "Find something for me to cover myself with."

Michael looked embarrassed by his inability to find anything nearby. He was about to say something apologetic, when Hunter cut him off. "Forget that. We've got to get back to the plane to camouflage it, before the natives get there first. They're obviously looking for it."

"One of us should stay here with Sabrina," Michael said. "In case they come back."

Hunter pulled a coin from his pocket, threw it

into the air, and caught it on the back of his wrist, his other hand covering it.

"Heads," Michael ventured warily.

Hunter looked, then showed the coin on his wrist to Michael. It had landed tails up.

"Uh, uh," said Michael, shaking his head resolutely. "I'm not leaving her with you. No sir."

"Neither of us will stay with her, then," said Hunter. "We'll take her with us. Now hurry up, damn it, we can't let them find that plane!" He grabbed Sabrina's wrist and pulled her forward with him, up onto the bank, despite her protests. Then he began running through the forest back toward the plane, still pulling her along with him.

She struggled as she was pulled forward, trying in vain to cover herself with her one free hand, looking ridiculous trying to do so. Michael was rushing after them, obviously distraught at the situation, but uncertain what to do about it. "Now hold it, Yank!" he called to Hunter.

"We've got to get to that plane and camouflage it!" Hunter called back, not slowing his pace. Sabrina was gasping and moaning as the vines and spring branches slashed across her naked skin as she was pulled forward through the jungle, stark naked. She felt horribly exposed. She knew Michael's eyes were burning into her from behind.

Finally Michael grasped Hunter's shoulder and stopped him. "All right then!" he said angrily. "You made your point. I'll go attend to the aircraft. In the meantime, *you* find something to cover Bree here with, and then if the coast is clear make it back to the tree house." He leaned forward now, his face belligerent. "But I warn you, Yank. You try anything with her, and I'll kill you. That's a rock-solid promise. You understand me?"

"Get moving," Hunter said. "If they find that air-craft we'll never get out of here."

Michael glared at him a second longer, then ran in the direction of the plane. Sabrina was leaning against a tree, trying to catch her breath. She turned her eyes to Hunter as Michael disappeared into the thick undergrowth. Hunter was staring at her with his one-eye-narrowed look, a hint of a tight grin on his lips. His eyes unabashedly traveled up and down her body.

"Well, what are you looking at?" she demanded, failing to make her voice sound as confident and righteous as she wished.

Hunter said nothing, just continued to stare.

"Oh, you're such a bastard," she said, trying to cower against the tree. "Pulling me through the jungle like that. Look at what you did to me!" She indicated the cuts and bruises where the vines brushed against her.

"Looks very nice," said Hunter, ogling her.

"And why don't you get me something to wear?" she demanded petulantly.

He stared at her, his eyes taking on a superior, mocking look. When he spoke, his voice was low and manly. "Come on, Sabrina, stop playing games. Your boy scout is gone. You don't have to keep up the charade." He started coming closer.

"I—I don't know what you mean," she said, cowering back.

He came forward and stood directly in front of her. "Don't you?"

He moved his hand toward her breasts. She slapped it away. He moved it down toward her

203

loins. She slapped it away once more. He was toying with her now, feinting with his hand, allowing it to be slapped away, then bringing it back. His grin was taunting. Sabrina felt the familiar yearning creeping over her. Her loins began to tingle and ache with the want of him.

"Please, Dallas," she said, "we can't . . . not now. When we get back, but not now."

He pulled her head forward suddenly, his hand at the back of her neck. He pressed his lips to hers tightly, silencing her. She felt her body responding, burning up with desire. Still she tried to resist him. Her mind told her no, reminded her of the horrible eruption of violence that would ensue if she let herself submit and Michael should discover it. But as Hunter's lips pressed down on hers, and his hand closed over her breast, kneading and rubbing, sparking her nipple into wild shocks of pleasure, she felt herself weakening. Her breathing became rapid.

Then suddenly he pulled back from her. She nearly stumbled forward from the weakness in her knees and the languor that spread all through her. She stood wide-eyed, with her hands out at her sides, fingers spread, knees slightly bent.

She watched him, a look of helpless pleading on her face. She knew she was too weak-willed to resist him now. Her body had become inflamed with the familiar desire. He knew all the tricks, all the ways of sparking her into unbearable pleasure. She was helpless against him now, and all she could do was look at him pleadingly, begging him to leave her alone until they returned to civilization and were away from Michael.

But Hunter had never been known for his mercy.

He grinned tautly in answer to her pleading look. Then, never taking his eyes off hers, he began to undress. He unbuttoned the trousers and pushed them down, threw off his sleeveless shirt. He hooked his thumbs into the waistband of his shorts, and smiled at the way Sabrina lowered her eyes to watch him, unable to keep her eyes away from the sight she felt irresistibly drawn to. She watched him remove his shorts, exposing his hard, thick maleness, straining angled upward.

He stood straight and tall now, his hands on his hips. She watched him, waiting in breath-bated suspense for him to come forward. Instead of moving toward her, though, he just stood there, looking at her commandingly.

She remained motionless, refusing to submit. She even crossed her arms over her breasts in a gesture of defiance. But resistance was hopeless, she knew, as her eyes locked onto his rigid, jutting maleness. The sight made her loins throb and ache with anticipation.

"You're mine," Hunter said in a deep, throaty voice. "You've always been mine, whether you knew it or not." He refused to come toward her. She knew that he was not bluffing. Either she would go to him, or she would not have him.

Sabrina threw back her head, whipping her hair in the air. She advanced several paces and stopped just in front of him. She could almost feel the heat of his body. Still he would not come forward, would not touch her. A sob broke from her throat. She came farther forward and pressed herself up against him, her hands circling his waist and clutching at his firm, tight buttocks. Her breasts pressed against his hairy chest.

He embraced her roughly then, lost to his passion. She could not breathe for a moment, due to the tightness of his embrace. She felt his manhood prodding against her naked stomach. Then his arms which were around her lifted her up off the ground, as he arched his back.

"Oooohhhh . . ." she gasped, as his shaft pressed up against her loins, and then its tip disappeared inside her. She exhaled sharply with the sensation. He lowered her slightly, onto the fullness of him and then he was in her completely, thrusting away.

The wild shocks of pleasure shot through her, making her loins burn with the frenzy of ecstatic passion. She was yelping and moaning with each thrust, unable to keep silent. Her hands clasped tightly around his neck, her fingers digging into his skin, scratching him in a mindless frenzy of pleasure, drawing blood.

Hunter put her down on the thick matted grass floor of the jungle, and came down on top of her. Now he began thrusting more frenziedly, driving her insane with the searing flashes of pleasure that forced her into sharper and sharper ecstatic release, until finally her lower body exploded with unbearable pleasure, making her cry out.

After a moment, Hunter's body tensed rigidly, and she heard a groan of unbearable pleasure escape from his throat. Then he rolled off her and lay beside her in the grass. He looked at her, grinning, panting for breath.

"Bastard," she said, with no conviction whatever.

He grinned at the folly of her having pretended she did not want it or did not need it. Then he rose and began dressing. Sabrina lay on her back watching him, realizing how much she had missed this and longed for it these past days. "And what am I to wear *now?*" she asked, looking down at her nakedness.

"This," said Michael, stepping forward into the clearing from between two trees, carrying a swath of white cloth he had just cut from the parachute walls.

"Michael!" she said in horrified surprise. "How long have . . . have you been there?"

"I just arrived," he said, handing her the material, which she grasped desperately. "But I can see enough to know what happened." His eyes were steely cold as he gazed at the still bleeding scratches on Hunter's body. "You raped her after all," he said, "even though I warned you."

"Michael!" Sabrina said, coming between him and Hunter, holding the material tightly against her. "It's not like you think! He didn't—" But it was too late. Michael swung on Hunter, smashing him in the jaw.

"Oh God, no!" Sabrina gasped, expecting Hunter to strike back viciously. But instead, Hunter just put his hand to his cut lip, touched it, looked at the blood on his fingers. His voice showed the effort of his restraint. It was low and tightly controlled: "I'm going to give you a second chance to live, Limey. I'm going to pretend that didn't happen. For two reasons. One, because you're too damn stupid to know what really happened here . . ."

"To hell with your bloody second chance!" exclaimed Michael furiously.

". . . and two, because I want to know what the hell you're doing here when I told you to go camouflage the plane before the natives got to it."

"The natives didn't go anywhere near it. They

changed direction and went off on a different course entirely. So I got this material for Sabrina, and ran back here as fast as I could, expecting you to try something sneaky and rotten like this, you low-life snake."

"Good," said Hunter, satisfied that the plane had not been discovered and that there was no immediate danger of discovery. "That's all I wanted to know."

"Excellent," said Michael sarcastically. "Now if we may continue?" He swung at Hunter violently.

"Michael, no!" screamed Sabrina.

Hunter ducked expertly under the arc of the swinging fist, and smashed Michael hard in the stomach. Michael grunted and doubled over, but his hands joined together as he did so, and he brought them down forcefully on the back of Hunter's neck, dropping the American to the ground.

"Stop it!" Sabrina shouted as the two men wrestled and slugged and fought ferociously, rolling around in the grassy undergrowth. Both their faces were bloodied within seconds, and they were beating at each other so furiously Sabrina thought that one of them might actually kill the other.

Hunter was the more rugged, street-wise fighter, but Michael—being an officer of the British commando forces—had learned a new type of fighting using the Oriental martial arts. He surprised Sabrina by matching Hunter blow for blow, using strange kicks and jabs, hitting with the heel of his hand, or with his elbows and knees.

The two of them seemed to be killing each other as Sabrina circled around them, almost hysterical, pleading for them to stop.

It took a long moment before she realized she

was not the only one watching the fight. She had a strange sensation of being watched herself, and when she raised her eyes sharply, she saw the war party of black natives staring at her from the edge of the clearing and at the two men who were locked in mortal combat. Only a few of the natives were staring at the rollicking, furious fight being waged on the grass. Most were staring fixedly at Sabrina herself. Their eyes held a blend of curiosity, awe, and menace. She jerked the swath of white cloth closer to herself, trying to hide her nakedness. "Dallas!" she screamed. "Michael! *Look!*"

The panic in her voice made the men pause in their battle and glance up. When they saw the natives, they scrambled to their feet, moving in front of Sabrina, standing between her and the warriors. They crouched forward in fighter's stances, their fists clenched. They were breathing heavily from their exertion.

"You take the ones on the right," Hunter panted to Michael, keeping his eyes on the natives. "I'll take the ones on the left."

"Right," gasped Michael, short of breath. "We'll see how long we can hold them off."

"Sabrina," Hunter said, still not taking his eyes off the fearsome natives who seemed on the verge of attacking, "when I tell you to, run like hell."

"But—"

"Do as he says!" commanded Michael.

Before she had a chance to protest, the natives charged.

"Now!" yelled Hunter. He and Michael rushed forward, to meet the attack, screaming fiercely. One of the natives threw a spear, which barely missed Michael's ear by an inch. He hunched low and hurtled himself at the spear-thrower, catching the man in the gut, knocking him down. Hunter dove into the midst of two approaching natives.

Sabrina did not know what to do. But one thing she knew for certain: she could not run away, could not desert Michael and Hunter. As she watched, they were both brought down by several of the natives, who jumped upon them all at once, beating them. They were struggling on the ground, trying to fight back.

Michael shouted to her from within the pile of squirming black bodies: "Get the hell out! Run, run for it!"

Sabrina looked around desperately. Her eyes lit upon a fallen spear. She went to it, grabbed it, and began beating upon the heads and backs of the natives who were piled on top of Michael and Hunter, beating them with all her might.

Several of the natives screamed as the hardwood pole smashed across their backs and heads. They scampered off Hunter and Michael, and then— furiously enraged—they began attacking Sabrina. Her white swath of parachute cloth lay on the ground at her feet. Her hair swirled around her face as she swung the spear furiously at her attackers, smashing and jabbing.

A hard blow from behind struck her on the head and she began sinking to her knees, stars dancing before her eyes. The last sight she saw before unconsciousness was of the powerful black arms that encircled her naked body from behind to prevent her from falling as she collapsed, sinking at last into a murky oblivion.

Chapter 16

There was the sound of many drums being beaten in a savage, pounding, jungle rhythm. Sabrina heard the sound, but she was in a dreamlike trance, and the reality of it did not penetrate the fog of her unconsciousness. Then, after an eternity, she slowly opened her eyes.

What she saw made her draw back with astonishment. It was awesome and unlike anything she had ever witnessed before. She was seated on an elaborately carved wooden throne, high above the ground. It was nighttime. In front of her, in the center of the encampment she found herself in, was an enormous bonfire, its bright yellow flames flickering up into the heavens.

Dancing around the fire were perhaps a hundred native warriors wearing leopard-skin loincloths and wrist and ankle bracelets of animal teeth. Their nearly naked black bodies glistened with sweat as they danced frenziedly around the fire, to the savage rhythm of twenty drums.

Farther back, ringing the fire and the dancers in a semicircle, were the women and children of the tribe. They were shaking their arms into the air, chanting loudly in their tribal tongue, while their bodies shimmied wildly.

Sabrina looked down at herself. She was almost naked. A grass skirt rode very low on her hips.

Breastplates of hammered copper, studded with diamonds, covered her bust line.

How had she gotten here? What was she doing dressed like this? She racked her brain, but could remember nothing. The back of her head ached painfully, as if she had been hit. She couldn't remember. The drumbeats became more throbbingly violent, the chanting louder. The brightness of the fire and the powerful scent of musk incense assailed her senses. How had she gotten here? she wondered again desperately. *And where was she?* She wanted to run, to escape. But there were no steps down from her high throne.

She stared out at the incredible scene before her, frightened, bewildered, her mind reeling. Two natives were approaching her. One of them looked vaguely familiar: He was toweringly tall and powerfully built. He had a flattened broad nose and long, shiny black hair. His skin was dark as the night; he looked like an ebony Hercules.

The man at his side was mean-looking and quite fat, with an enormous black belly that wobbled as he walked. He wore a headdress of white animal fangs and carried a staff of carved icons, studded with jewels, making it appear to Sabrina that he was the tribe's witch doctor. He was speaking to the taller man in native, angry tones as they approached.

They stopped in front of Sabrina's throne. The tall one bowed his head. He said to Sabrina, in a deep, rumbling voice, *"Oongala sho booku?"*

Sabrina stared at him uncomprehendingly, her eyes wide with fear and puzzlement.

"Mizmee suru," the fat witch doctor demanded of her angrily. When she did not respond, his expres-

sion became furious. "*Mizmee suru!*" he shouted. "*Suru! Suru!*"

"I don't under*stand*!" Sabrina cried out.

The men looked at each other. "English?" said the tall one, called Ulucong, who was evidently the chief of the tribe.

The witch doctor declared, "Did I not tell you, Ulucong? Did I not? She not sun goddess!"

Ulucong turned to Sabrina with a critical eye, not convinced of what the witch doctor was saying. "You speak the English," he said in halting but understandable English, looking up at her on the high throne. "But still, you are the sun goddess, yes?"

"Sun goddess?" she said bewilderedly. Her head throbbed from the painful bump on the back of it. She felt dizzy, lost, and disoriented. "I don't know who I am!" she cried. "Or where! Where am I? How did I get here? Who are you people?"

The witch doctor swiveled toward Ulucong. "She not sun goddess!" he shouted. "B-B Dada tell you she not," he shouted, pointing to his own chest. "But you no listen to B-B Dada!" He glared at Sabrina, then turned back to the chief. "She impostor! Send her to Death Cave to join the two other whites! Or better: slay her! We slay her now!" He raised his diamond-encrusted staff, which Sabrina saw had a jagged metal blade at the end. She cowered back in terror, throwing her hands up in front of her.

"*Sholo!*" shouted Ulucong, stopping the witch doctor from slashing at her. A heated exchange in their tribal language followed. Sabrina could tell that the Chief was asserting his authority over the witch doctor, who was insisting she be killed instantly. The warriors had stopped dancing around

213

the bonfire, and stood watching the argument. The drums continued to pound.

Finally, the witch doctor spat upon the ground and turned away angrily. He went over to the warriors around the fire and began addressing them in a murderous rage, shaking his staff and his fist in the air.

Ulucong turned to Sabrina, stern-faced, and spoke in an urgent tone. "Goddess, I believe in you still. I know you returned to us from the heavens—I spied your winged chariot falling from the sky! I have searched for you and your chariot ever since. And your hair, it is the color of the horizon sun, as our legends tell."

He glanced toward the witch doctor nervously. "But goddess, you must help prove this to my warriors! B-B Dada tells them now you are impostor. You must prove yourself, or I fear you will be denied your 'fulfillment' and your Ceremony of Leaving. You will be slain instead. Goddess," he said urgently, "give us some sign! Prove yourself to the doubters!"

"Sign?" she said dumbly. She looked at the warriors being incited to violence by the witch doctor. Many were glaring at her fiercely.

"Make the sun rise up!" suggested the chief. "Now! in the dark of night! That will surely convince B-B Dada and the disbelievers."

Sabrina's head hurt terribly. She could not make the sun rise up! Or could she, she wondered. She was not any sun goddess! Or was she? Her memory was completely blank. She certainly didn't *feel* like any sort of goddess. But in her lost, dazed state, anything seemed possible.

"Hurry, Goddess!" urged the chief plaintively,

seeing that some of the warriors had returned to their tribal dance—but that others had gathered behind the witch doctor, and armed themselves with clubs. They were glaring at her, the whites of their eyes very prominent.

As Sabrina looked at the few natives who had returned to their frenzied dance, she felt a flash of familiarity. Something about the intense gyrations struck a chord of memory. I've danced like that before, she thought; though she could not recall when or where. Maybe if she could dance that way again it would bring the memory back more clearly . . . ?

"Let me down from here," she said to the chief.

Ulucong clapped his hands firmly. Four strong boys rushed forward carrying a flat platform of boards and vines. They raised it above their heads to the level of Sabrina's throne. She hesitated to step onto it, thinking it would be unsteady. But to her surprise, it was as steady as the ground itself, even as the young natives lowered her down to the grass.

Everyone in the encampment stopped what they were doing and stared at her now. The dancers stopped dancing. The drummers stopped beating their drums. The women stopped chanting.

Sabrina nodded to the drummers. They stared back at her bewildered. The chief barked a fierce command to them, and they resumed pounding on their drums: a raw, animalistic, jungle beat. Sabrina spread her legs apart sharply, and flung her hands high up over her head, fingers spread. She brought her fingertips together. She flung her head back. Then she began dancing in the twirling, shimmying way that felt so familiar to her, though

215

much faster and fiercer now, in time to the pulsing jungle rhythms.

She soon felt the drumbeats deeply inside her, as if her heart were pounding to the rhythm. Her movements became frenzied and wild. A sudden feeling of joyousness swept through her. She was so happy at finding something familiar to her, some part of her unremembered past, that she gave herself up to it completely. The natives gaped at her in awe.

Soon she was like a wildly impassioned jungle beast, gyrating and shimmying as she danced about the bonfire, feeling the intense heat of it against her skin. The yellow glow made her skin appear golden and glistening. The women resumed their chanting, convinced that they were beholding something sacred. Sabrina's grass skirt swirled high around her as she danced, exposing her long, golden legs.

When she finally ceased, panting and breathless and covered with sweat, she looked out at the native warriors. They dropped to their knees before her, bowing, mumbling reverent tributes—guilt-ridden that they had ever doubted her, and fearing her retribution.

"You surely are the sun goddess!" claimed Ulucong, coming up to her. "How else could you know a dance so like our secret, sacred dance?" He turned to the witch doctor. "You see! You see! Do you doubt still?"

"Forgive me, goddess," said B-B Dada, very grudgingly. He hated to admit Sabrina was the sun goddess, for it meant he was no longer the spiritual leader of the tribe—she was.

"Now we can have the Ceremony of Leaving

after all!" declared the chief to Sabrina. "We begin preparations in the morning!"

The natives were chanting loudly in tribute to her, their faces animated. She let the chief lead her away to a thatched hut that would be hers for the night. She went inside and dropped to the grass mat, exhausted. The chief left without a word.

Sabrina lay on the mat feeling very confused, frowning in perplexity. She still could remember nothing about herself—except that she knew the natives' secret, sacred dance. *Was she really the sun goddess of these people*? The idea did not seem so ridiculous in her woozy, disoriented, headachy state. And why did she have no memory? Could it be that she had no past? That she had just descended from the heavens as the chief said?

She closed her eyes and tried to sleep. Suddenly she felt an overwhelming sense of aloneness. As if she were used to being with someone, or with more than one person, and now she felt a great lack, a great emptiness, because they were not here with her. But try as she might, she could not recall who these others might be.

The feeling nagged at her until finally she fell into a fitful, tossing-and-turning sleep.

In the semidarkness of the Death Cave, Hunter raised his pickax and smashed it down into the hard black coal of the cave wall. Next to him, Michael was swinging his ax too, but much more ferociously: raising it up, driving it into the wall, pulling it out, swinging it again.

"You keep up that pace," Hunter said, "and you'll drop from exhaustion in no time."

"I can't help it!" Michael declared, cleaving the

ax violently. "I'm so mad I could explode! It's either smash this into the wall or bury it into Mutt and Jeff's heads." He jerked his head over his shoulder to indicate the native guards who stood at the sun-lit mouth of the cave, far behind them.

"That wouldn't be such a good idea," Hunter said. The guards were both armed with spears. Behind them, ringing the entrance to the cave, were at least a dozen other natives, also well armed.

"To think we're in here," Michael thundered, swinging his ax furiously, "digging into this *bloody* bloomin' coal, while Bree is in their encampment somewhere, being subjected to *Lord* knows what!" He slammed his ax once more into the cave wall.

"Save your strength. You'll need it if we're ever going to fight out way out of here."

"Oh, right, right," Michael said sarcastically. "Fight our way out, will we? With Mutt and Jeff and the whole pack of 'em just waiting for us to try anything?"

Hunter leaned on his ax handle and futilely tried to wipe the rivulets of sweat from his sweating forehead with the back of his dripping arm. Getting free would not be easy, he knew. The natives outside the mouth of the cave were anxiously waiting for him and Michael to make a move. The only reason they didn't kill them outright was that the diamonds he and Michael were mining were important to their pagan religion. The natives couldn't go into the cave to mine them themselves because they were too superstitious. They believed the cave was haunted by the ghosts of all who had died in it.

And plenty had died in it, Hunter reflected, glancing around at the white-boned skeletons strewn about. They were the skeletons of missionaries who had come to the tribe to teach English and bring religion—and had ended up digging for diamonds until they died of exhaustion.

Exhaustion would not be far off for he and Michael, Hunter knew. It was sweltering hot in the cave, and the air was almost unbearably muggy. They had to force themselves to keep working because it was only their usefulness as diamond-diggers that kept them alive.

"White men!" came a shout from the mouth of the cave. Hunter and Michael turned to look. The silhouette of a very fat native was framed in the sunlight. "Come out, white men!" shouted the native.

The pair climbed back toward the mouth of the cave. They left the pickaxes inside, since it had been made clear that they would be killed if they brought them out. They then inched into the sunlight, which hurt their eyes and caused them to squint. The cooler air was incredibly pleasurable to their sweating skins and burning lungs, after the inferno of the cave.

The tribesmen stood in a semicircle flanking the mouth of the cave, their spears poised. The fat native who had just summoned Hunter and Michael stood staring at them moodily, rocking on his heels, making his fat, black belly quiver above his loincloth. They both recognized him. He was the witch doctor, the one who had condemned them to the Death Cave.

"In your winged chariot," he said to them, "you have machine that speaks thunder, yes maybe? You have 'gun'? B-B Dada know about 'gun.' Last missionary, he tell all about it."

219

"Where's Sabrina?" Michael asked furiously, now that he confronted someone who spoke English. "What have you done with her?"

B-B Dada looked appalled. "You no ask questions!" he declared. "B-B Dada ask questions! B-B Dada *kill* you if you no answer his questions!"

"Where is she?" Hunter parried. "You tell us about her, or you'll never find out if we've got that gun you want."

B-B Dada looked outraged at their insolence. But he wanted a gun badly enough to make him curb his anger and answer their questions.

"Tell us about Sabrina!" Michael demanded again, leaning forward menacingly, prompting the natives to raise their spears toward his face.

"Sabrina?" said B-B Dada quizzically. "Ah, you mean the sun goddess!"

"The bloody *what?*"

"The sun goddess. She be fine. She be very fine; your worry not needed. She about to be prepared for Ceremony of Leaving."

"She just got here," said Hunter. "Why hold a ceremony for her leaving?"

"Religion say to. She just come, yes, but only so she can be fulfilled. She be fulfilled here during ceremony, then must go back to heavens."

"What the bloody hell do you mean 'fulfilled'?" demanded Michael, his face reddening.

"Fulfilled," said B-B Dada irritably. His patience was wearing thin. "That what ceremony all about. First there be battle-to-the-death between all warriors who volunteer. To see who be bravest, strongest warrior. He who remains standing at end of battle-to-the-death has right to mate sun goddess. To fulfill her."

Michael lost his self-control and rushed murderously at the witch doctor. Hunter had to slap his arm across his chest to hold him back.

"Goddess is fulfilled by bravest, strongest warrior," B-B Dada continued, enjoying the fact that his words were taunting Michael. "Then, after, she is put upon sacrifical pyre and sacred fire is lit."

"Why, you bloody, heathen bastards!" Michael declared, blind with rage. *"You're going to burn her alive?"*

"That is what ceremony be all about, you crazy white man! Goddess's spirit must be released from mortal body it inhabits, for it to return to heavens! Now no more talk! Tell me about gun or I kill you!"

"We have guns," said Hunter. "Two of them. But they won't do you any good. They're both out of ammo." This was true. They had emptied the Luger and Colt pistols during their escape from the German base.

"What is this 'ammo'?" demanded B-B Dada suspiciously, thinking that he was being deceived.

"Ammo is what you put into the thunder machines to make the thunder. No ammo, no thunder." Hunter noticed the way B-B Dada looked very confused at this, and to confound him even further he added: "On the other hand, we've got plenty of ammo for the machine gun. But it won't do you any good, because the machine gun's stuck on its swivel-pivot." This was true too. He and Michael had tried half a day to dismount the machine gun from the aircraft, before deciding it was hopeless.

B-B Dada stared at Hunter a moment, bewildered and suspicious. Then he shouted "You lie!" and lashed out at Hunter's face with his knife-tipped jeweled staff. A long cut was sliced into Hunter's lantern jaw, spilling blood. Hunter grimaced tightly and clasped his hand to his jaw.

"B-B Dada need gun!" the witch doctor bellowed, shaking his staff in a wild rage. "B-B Dada need to send thunder at chief, but no be discovered. If B-B Dada not kill chief, then chief win battle-to-the-death, since he be strongest. *But chief be against burning goddess after fulfillment!*" His eyes filled with self-pity now, as well as rage. "If goddess not be burned, if she remain alive, she be religious leader! No one listen to B-B Dada! How B-B Dada compete with goddess?"

He shouted now, declaring firmly: "Sun goddess *will* be burned on altar, after her fulfillment! And chief . . . he must *lose* fight-to-the-death. He must die!"

Seeing B-B Dada's rage, and fearing he might kill them both instantly despite his need for their services as diamond-diggers, Michael began drawing Hunter back toward the cave. Hunter seemed dazed from the deep cut and the loss of blood.

The natives rattled their spears, but Michael managed to get the two of them into the mouth of the cave—and then deeper inside—without B-B Dada giving the order to kill them.

"They're going to 'fulfill' Sabrina," Michael said, almost in disbelief. "And then they're going to burn her alive."

"No," said Hunter, still dazed. "We'll stop them."

"Will we, Yank? Will we? *How?*"

Hunter said nothing. He grimaced against the pain from his cut jaw, and tried hard to think.

Chapter 17

Sabrina sensed, rather than heard, another presence in her hut. She opened her eyes and looked. There, standing straight and tall in the entranceway, was Ulucong. He was staring at her, his face hard and tense. His manhood was straining up excitedly beneath his leopard-skin loincloth.

"What do you want?" Sabrina asked in a panic, sitting up. "What are you doing here?"

"I have come to prepare you, goddess. For your Ceremony of Leaving."

"Prepare me? Just what in heaven's name does *that* mean?"

"During the ceremony, you will be fulfilled. Religion say it will be last fulfillment before you leave your mortal body to return to heavens. Because of this, your fulfillment must be most exciting, most wondrous ever. I am chief . . . the duty falls to me to prepare you to make it so."

"I don't understand," she said nervously, trying to keep her eyes away from his rigidly straining shaft. "Just how do you intend to do this 'preparing'?"

The chief didn't answer. Instead, his hand moved to the strap of his loincloth, and in a swift movement he ripped the scant garment off his body. He stood before her naked, his hard body looking more than ever like that of a black Hercules.

"You're not doing any preparing with *me*," Sabrina said fearfully, backing away from him in a crouch, her eyes fastened on his rigid member. "No sir, you're not!"

"It is written," said Ulucong in a throaty voice, coming forward. "It must be so."

She backed away until she was up against the thatched wall of the hut. Her eyes darted wildly around. He came directly up to her, his jutting maleness only an inch from her face. She looked at it, feeling wild panic. Her breath caught. She made a dash around his left side, toward the entranceway. Quickly his strong arm went out to bar her path, closing around her and folding her in toward him.

"Let me go!" she cried, struggling to pull away from him, feeling the touch of his naked skin against her like a searing, burning sensation. When his hand went to her copper breastplate and pushed in beneath it to grasp her naked breast, she slapped him stingingly across the face. He did not flinch. His hand closed over her breast and squeezed.

She tried to push away, but it was useless, the giant black Hercules was far too mighty for her. When his hand moved down her belly and pressed in between her thighs, she let out a sharp yelp and scratched him across the cheek. There was no satisfaction in scratching or beating him though, for he did not protect himself. He viewed his actions as his right and duty according to their religion—and he would not strike back at her because she was his goddess.

"Please," she moaned, as he touched her at her

womanhood, under her grass skirt, his big hand cupping and pressing upward. A tingling excitement surged through her lower body. The hand pressed harder against her. She began beating at his chest, but this only made matters worse; each time she touched his hairless, rock-hard chest, she felt an even greater sense of excitement.

Ulucong pinioned her arms behind her now, holding them with a single hand. Almost gently his other hand went to her breastplate and pressed under it. Again he began rubbing and fondling her naked breasts. His fingers found a nipple and pinched it into hard pertness. Sabrina moaned and tried to pull away.

He jerked at the jeweled copper breastplate and it came away in his hand. His hand roamed freely over her breasts now. Sabrina's head was forced forward by the way he held her arms pinned tightly back, and she could not escape looking down at what was taking place. The sight made her gasp as a tingling sensual thrill coursed through her body.

She saw his big black hand passing repeatedly over her creamy white breasts, slapping them gently from side to side, his fingers closing around her nipples, rubbing them between thumb and forefinger. His face lowered, and she saw his extremely thick lips close around her nipple. A shock of pleasure shot through her.

She tried to bring her knee up to hurt him and make him release her, but he quickly pulled her tightly against him to prevent this. Now she was forced to gaze down at the sight of her full breasts pressed against the hard planes of his ebony chest. He swayed from side to side, making her nipples

brush against him, sparking them into intense pleasure. She moaned loudly. "Please," she gasped,
"please don't . . ."

Ulucong jerked her head back to make her look
up at him. His thick lips came down on hers, pressing wetly, covering her whole mouth. He forced
her lips apart until it seemed her jaw might snap.
His thick wet lips undulated over her entire mouth,
enveloping it, his hand forcing her mouth open. He
sucked at her lower lip with his mouth, then her
upper lip. His mouth moved all over her face and
throat, licking and kissing wetly.

Then he laid her down on the grass mat as she
struggled wildly to break away. He forced her
hands over and behind her head as she lay on her
back, he held them there with one hand. His other
hand moved over her breasts, down over her flat
belly, which was moving in and out quickly with
her rapid breathing . . . down to her grass skirt.

"Don't touch me there," she begged him. "I
couldn't stand it if you . . ."

He ripped the grass skirt away in a single abrupt
jerk. She was completely naked before him now, on
her back, her arms over her head. His free hand
pressed down between her tightly closed thighs.
"Uhhh!" she gasped, her eyes going wide. His
mouth went down to her breast and closed over it.
He began sucking wetly at her nipple, his tongue
flicking at it mercilessly.

She shut her eyes tightly. Wild sensation surged
throughout her body, making her shudder with the
unbearable intensity of it. His finger pressed inside
her and began playing her up and down. Waves of
burning pleasure coursed hotly through her loins.

His mouth moved to her other breast and began torturing her straining pink nipple.

Sabrina was moaning continuously now, breathing in shallow gasps, unable to control herself. Her legs jerked about spastically trying to free her of the big black hand that cupped her womanhood. Waves of pleasure surged through her, becoming more intense, until finally, when she was only seconds from peaking, from reaching unbelievable heights of ecstasy—he stopped.

Ulucong withdrew his hand. He moved his face away from her breasts, and looked at her. She was shuddering and moaning on the ground on her back, almost berserk with passionate desire. Her hands went to her breasts and thighs to cover herself, out of modesty—but the feel of herself touching her sensitive loins and breasts almost drove her over the peak. Her body trembled with desire, tingled with the want of it, the *need* of it. She looked up at him helplessly, pleadingly. The question in her eyes was clear: why had he stopped?

"You are to be 'prepared' for fulfillment, goddess, so that on the night of the ceremony your fulfillment will be the most wondrous imaginable. But I have not the right to fulfill you now. Only he who wins the fight-to-the-death battle has that right." He paused, then added with a touch of conceit: "It will almost certainly be me that wins. I am the mightiest of warriors. But until then, you must not be fulfilled."

"You . . . you've brought me to this state," she groaned, rocking her head from side to side, the sensation still unbearable, "only to *leave* me like this?"

Ulucong said nothing.

227

"But this is torture!"

"It will make your fulfillment during the ceremony all the more intense."

"You have no right!" she said accusingly, sitting up, furious now that she had lowered herself to almost *asking* for it. How dare he bring her to this! Why, she had tried to fight him off to begin with! If he planned to do this to her all along, why, he should . . . he should never have started! How dare he!

She began beating on his chest furiously, her naked breasts shaking and jiggling as she did so. She noticed his eyes watching her breasts tormentedly, and she felt a stab of satisfaction at knowing *he* was suffering too due to his abrupt halt.

Ulucong moved away from her and put his loincloth back on, strapping it across his waist. Surprisingly, his eyes seemed sympathetic as they gazed at Sabrina. "I do not wish to torment you, goddess. Causing you to suffer distresses me greatly. But my duties are clear. The religion demands your preparation."

He turned and left the hut, leaving Sabrina teased almost to the point of insanity, a scorching-hot yearning blazing unquenched in her loins and breasts.

Ulucong came in again that night to repeat his sensual torture of her. He also came in the next morning, and the next night. When the day of the ceremony finally arrived, Sabrina was so sensually inflamed she could barely move without feeling the unfulfilled throbbing ache in her loins, the need to be driven over the peak of sensation . . .

The day dawned with the sun rising pinkly above the jungle treetops. Hunter and Michael had lain awake all night long, keenly alert, watching for the natives to lower their guard . . . to give them even the slightest chance to make an escape. There had been no lowering of the guard. The crudely hammered copper shackles had not been removed from their ankles. The two armed natives had watched them closely all night long, while the others slept.

Now, as the sun rose higher above the jungle, turning the misty moisture on the tree leaves into steaming dew, Michael turned on his side toward Hunter. "The instant they take off these bloody manacles," he whispered angrily, "I'm taking off. No matter what."

"Don't do it," Hunter whispered back. "That's when they'll be most on their guard. You'll only get yourself killed."

"Well damn it! You expect me to just sit here idly, while they're getting ready to rape Sabrina tonight in the village? And then burn her on a pyre?"

The natives who were awake, hearing Michael's fierce voice, turned to look at them. Hunter didn't answer Michael, now that the tribesmen were watching. Besides, what could he say? Michael was right. They *had* to get out of here. But how to do it? That was the question. The situation looked hopeless.

They were eating a breakfast of wild tomatoes, and cold meat from the boar that had been killed and roasted the night before, when B-B Dada came into the clearing. He bade greeting to the dozen natives near the mouth of the cave, and then came directly up to Hunter and Michael, his fat black belly quivering above his loincloth. "You ready to take B-B Dada to winged chariot now?" he said. "So B-B Dada can get gun? Or maybe you like go back in cave again, dig more diamond. Maybe you like die slowly this way."

"The gun doesn't have any ammo," said Hunter, "I told you that. And we can't take you to the winged chariot."

"Why cannot take B-B Dada," he asked, growing angry.

The real reason was that the plane had been repaired and was probably ready to fly again. Hunter couldn't be sure, since he and Michael were captured before they had a chance to test it. But if they led the witch doctor to it, it would surely never fly again. B-B Dada would smash it to pieces.

"Why not take B-B Dada to chariot?" he demanded again, his face showing growing rage at being refused.

"We don't have it anymore," Michael said.

"Where it be then?"

"Flew right up your arse when you weren't looking."

"Eh?" the witch doctor said, frowning in puzzlement. He saw Michael's sneering, amused grin, and said, "Ah! You joke with B-B Dada, yes? B-B Dada got good sense humor. B-B Dada like joke." Then he smashed Michael in the shoulder with his jeweled staff, nearly breaking his arm. A moment later, strangely, he smiled. "No matter, though," he said. "B-B Dada no need gun no more. B-B Dada very good witch doctor. He make . . . this."

He held up a small, leaf-wrapped parcel in his palm, and opened it up for them. Inside was a fine powder that looked like orange flour. "Tiny pinch, inhaled in nose, and . . ." He cocked his head to the side and shut his eyes, as if he had fallen into a deeply drugged sleep.

He looked at them again, smiling, showing his decaying yellow teeth. "My man, Oomlo, he send chief to dreamland, in middle of fight-to-death tonight. Then he kill him." He smiled more broadly. "Chief lose battle . . . sun goddess be burn at pyre . . . B-B Dada again be highest spiritual leader!"

Michael said nothing. Hunter took a bite from the wild tomato he was eating. B-B Dada, seeing that no one was applauding his brilliant plan, turned away angrily. "Oomlo!" he called. "Oomlo!"

A husky, mean-looking native stepped forward from the group, all of whom were supporters of the witch doctor in his power struggle against the chief. Oomlo had only one ear, the other possibly mauled by a wild animal.

B-B Dada handed him the leaf-wrapped parcel, and gave him instructions in the tribal dialect. Then he turned to Michael and Hunter. "You go back in Death Cave now," he commanded, his eyes red with evil fury. "You dig many diamond. You die slowly, from heat and small bit air. Soon you join ghosts of missionaries." He turned and stalked out of the clearing, Oomlo following close on his heels.

The shackles were removed from Hunter's and Michael's ankles. Hunter quietly put his tomato into his pocket, while all eyes were directed toward his ankles. Then the pair were prodded at spear-point into the mouth of the cave. It was already sweltering hot inside, and as they moved further away from the entrance, the air became so humid it was hard to breathe. It was like being inside an oven.

Michael grabbed up his pickax from the dirt and turned back toward the entrance, crouching as if about to sprint forward. "This is it, mate," he said. "Come what may, I'm making my move."

"Hold it," said Hunter, putting his hand on his arm.

"Get your damn hand off me, you blasted coward!" he shouted, slapping Hunter's arm away.

Hunter knew Michael was half crazed by the lack of oxygen and the baking heat that surrounded them, burning their lungs. Still, knowing this did not make it any easier controlling his temper. He too was suffering from the physical torment, and it took a mighty effort of will for him to resist knocking Michael's teeth out.

"Listen, Limey," he said through gritted teeth, trying, but failing, to keep the anger out of his voice. "This isn't the time for us to be fighting each other. Now, I've got a plan."

"What kind of plan?"

"A lousy one," Hunter said disgustedly. "It'll probably get us both killed." He wiped his damp forehead with his sweating arm. "You know how superstitious these natives are?"

"So?" Michael said irritably, impatiently.

"They believe in ghosts, right?"

Michael followed Hunter's eyes to the veins of white chalk that ran throughout the black coal of the cave wall, then to the nearby skeleton of the missionary, which was wearing the remnants of a tattered brown frock. Then he understood. "That's the worst plan I ever heard of," he said.

"I told you."

Michael wiped the sweat from his face. "You get the starring role, I suppose?"

"It's my plan," said Hunter, shrugging.

Michael looked at him and their stares locked. It was obvious to them both that their chances of succeeding in the escape were very slim. They would probably die trying. Hunter slapped Michael stingingly on the back, in the first gesture of friendship either had ever made toward the other. Michael's face remained hard and ungiving. After a moment, he held out his hand, making the sign of the flying corps. "Thumbs up, Yank," he said.

Outside the cave, most of the natives were busy chipping away at the rough diamonds that had been brought out the day before, scratching off the outer layer to reveal the shiny crystal surfaces within. Others were standing about near the mouth of the cave, spears in hand.

Suddenly a bloodcurdling scream came from within. The natives who were seated leaped to their feet, grabbed their spears, and cocked their arms, preparing to throw. They looked terrified, as did those ringing the mouth of the cave.

Another bloodcurdling scream came from within the cave. The natives' eyes bulged as they stared fearfully, trying to peer through the blackness inside. They began chattering nervously, their voices rising higher and higher in pitch. *What was going on in there*? they wondered. And more important: what would be coming *out*?

The scream shrilled forth again, sounding so agonized and tortured it did not seem earthly. "Wh—

wh—white ones?" the leader of the natives called into the cave. "Are you—"

"*Eeaaaauugghhhh!*" answered the howling scream, continuing without letup. The natives began quaking in fear. Soon a loud clattering sound began emanating from the cave. And suddenly they saw movement. Their spears jerked into hurling position.

Michael came rushing out of the cave. Instead of running forward, though, to try to escape, he was staggering backward, facing the cave. His hands were raised in front of him, as if to protect him from something horrible still within.

The tribesmen watched in terror as he backed away from the cave, and another figure emerged from the blackness, becoming more visible as it moved forward. Finally the apparition was at the very mouth of the cave, and the natives could see it clearly. They yelled in horror and began dancing about agitatedly. Half of the dozen present threw down their weapons and ran away screaming. The others held their ground, but were clearly panicky and terrified.

There was no doubt in their minds about what they were beholding: it was the ghost of one of the dead missionaries. Its face and hands were white as chalk, its eyes circled in rings black as coal. It wore the same brown smock and hood it had been wearing the day the missionary died.

The ghost walked forward slowly and stiffly, its arms rigidly at its sides. Suddenly, as the natives watched, the hands raised up to point at Michael's face. "*Ahhhhh!*" Michael screamed, as if in horrible pain, clutching his hands to his face. When he swiveled around to face the natives they saw pulpy redness oozing from between his fingers. It looked as though his face had magically exploded, oozing blood as red as the wild tomatoes.

The natives were screaming and babbling, hopping around in terror, shaking their spears. They were at a loss as to what to do. They could strike at the ghost with their spears, but how could anyone kill someone already dead? And by attempting it, wouldn't they be bringing a lifelong curse on themselves for despoiling the spirit of the dead?

Their indecision could not last more than a few seconds longer. Already their leader was emboldening himself to strike, ordering his men to hold their ground. He would show them there was nothing to fear.

Michael ran past two of the natives, clutching his face and screaming. No one tried to stop him. They jumped aside to avoid having him brush against them.

The leader shouted above the fearful cries of his men, ordering them to stand firm. The order was not followed. When the ghost raised his finger to point at two of the underlings, the men screamed in horror and ran away.

Four warriors remained. The leader shouted for them to attack. He hurled his own spear forward. It whistled through the air and struck the ghost in the arm, remaining there, its shaft bobbing up and down. The ghost staggered backward. Then it regained its footing, though, and came forward again.

The leader stared, realizing something was highly suspicious: the "ghost" was bleeding! He grabbed a second spear and crooked his arm to throw, his expression angry now rather than fearful. Suddenly he screamed, arching his shoulders and hips backward. The natives by his side looked and saw the spear sticking out of his back—and Michael holding the shaft.

Hunter reached behind himself and pulled out the pickax that was strapped behind his back, beneath the brown frock. He heaved it at one of the natives, catching him in the chest, dropping him to the ground. The remaining warriors screamed and fled into the jungle.

Michael rushed over to Hunter. He looked at him with concern. "That's going to have to come out," he said, nodding at the spear stuck in his arm.

"You think I need a damn blindfold or something?" Hunter declared, in pain. "Yank it out!"

Michael grasped it firmly and pulled. The spear came out, its metal blade bloody. He threw it down, tore off a strip of Hunter's brown frock, and wrapped it around the wounded arm. Then the two of them ran into the jungle, in the direction of the village. They ran wildly, darting in and out between trees, ducking under overhanging vines, leaping over knotty roots.

It took several grueling minutes before they realized an awful truth: neither of them knew precisely where the village was. Michael slammed his fist into a tree trunk in frustration.

They wandered aimlessly through the jungle for several hours, knowing they would not chance upon the village this way, but not knowing what else to do. Finally, just after sundown, they heard a sound. It was very faint, they had to listen hard to hear it. But when they did, they knew what it was: the steady beat of distant drums. They ran off in the direction of the drumbeats.

They passed the stream with the overhanging

bank. This gave them their bearing; they knew where they were now. Hunter wanted to detour to the plane to get something before continuing on, but Michael said, "Are you *mad*? They could be raping her, burning her, at this very second!"

They rushed on through the dark jungle, in the direction of the pounding, savage drumbeats.

Chapter 18

The ceremony had begun. Sabrina sat upon her high throne, awestruck, watching the spectacle of the Parade of Challengers. The parade consisted of a score of warriors who were the strongest and fiercest in the tribe . . . the ones who had volunteered to enter the fight-to-the-death battle that would decide who was the bravest and mightiest—and who would win the right to mate the sun goddess.

The purpose of the parade was to let the warriors flaunt their beautiful, muscular bodies. There had to be no doubt that they would be capable of satisfying the goddess, should they be the one so honored. They strutted before her now like peacocks, grandly showing off, each of them stark naked.

They danced in a circle around the enormous bonfire, their black bodies glistening with sweat. They shimmied and wriggled and thrust their hips out, flaunting their rigid male shafts. The air was thick with their scent.

Sabrina felt hot flashes all over as she watched the parade. Her loins ached and throbbed with sensuality and her nipples quivered with an electric tingling. She wished the parade would stop! She couldn't stand it much longer! Her body had been teased and tormented into such a sensual frenzy by

238

Ulucong that it seemed she might actually have a sexual peak right here, right now, as she sat on her high throne watching the excited native bodies strut flauntingly before her.

The drummers sat cross-legged on the outskirts of the clearing, pounding their drums in animalistic fervor. The relentless drumbeats penetrated deep into Sabrina's brain. Sparks of yellow flame shot up from the bonfire, streaking into the pitch-black night. The steamy fragrance of the jungle mingled with the musky scent of the warriors' sweat. Sabrina felt her head spinning from the way her senses were so greatly overstimulated.

The parade drew to an end as the warriors came together in a line facing Sabrina. They bowed low. The drumbeats ceased. The witch doctor came forward from the side and said to Sabrina, "Now fight begin. Warrior who still alive at end, he have honor to fulfill you. Then, after, comes the pyre."

"Pyre?" said Sabrina, not understanding. She had watched them build the elaborate tower of branches at the rear of the encampment, but no one had told her what it was for. She turned to the chief to find out, but he was dismounting his own throne now, and taking his place in front of the row of combatants. Because of his exalted position he had not been required to join the parade. Now that it was time for the battle, though, he stripped off his loincloth and flung it away. Then he too bowed his head to Sabrina.

"You are sun goddess," the witch doctor said to Sabrina, stating the ritual phrase. "And you will serve us truly."

Sabrina knew the ritual response; the witch doctor had drilled it into her earlier. She gazed out boldly at the warriors assembled before her, all but one of whom would die in the battle to win her favors. "I am your sun goddess," she said loudly. "I will serve you truly."

She meant every word of it. B-B Dada had indoctrinated her without letup during the last two days, making sure she believed she was the sun goddess—and that she would do whatever the religion demanded of her. In her disoriented, confused state, his words had been implanted deep in her mind. The strange golden liquid he gave her to drink had made her even more susceptible. She did not know all that was expected of her now, but one thing was certain: she would not let her people down. She was the sun goddess and would do whatever was expected of her.

"Bring forth the weapons!" B-B Dada shouted, off to the side.

Two young boys carried in a heavy wooden chest and set it in the center of the clearing. There was absolute silence now, except for the crackling of the fire, as the warriors went to the chest and chose their weapons. Knives were not permitted in the combat. Each warrior was allowed a single sturdy club and a rectangular wooden shield.

B-B Dada took a pouch from his belt and walked around the group of warriors, pouring a purple powder into the dirt as he walked, marking off the perimeter of the combat arena. Any warrior could leave the arena at any time by simply crossing over the perimeter border. To do so, however, would disgrace him for the rest of his days.

The warriors crouched low, eyeing one another. They held their clubs and shields poised aggressively, awaiting the signal from Sabrina that would start the battle. The air was so electric with tension, Sabrina did not hear the sounds of someone stealthily climbing up the rear of her throne.

Suddenly from the side of the clearing something startlingly unexpected happened: a white man came charging out of the jungle, ran to the bonfire, and grabbed up a burning stake. Holding it by its unlit end he swirled it wildly in a circle about him, screaming at the top of his lungs.

The villagers leaped out of the way of the blazing stake that swirled through the air. There was such stunned surprise, no one made a move toward the white man, Dallas Hunter. They jabbered in fearful astonishment, scrambling out of the way.

Taking advantage of the diversion, Michael leaned forward from the rear of Sabrina's high throne and grabbed her arm. "Here we go, pet!" he declared fiercely. "Jump down with me, we'll run for it!"

To his utter amazement, she tried to jerk her arm free. "Release me!" she shouted. "Who are you? How dare you defile the sun goddess!"

Michael stared at her, speechless. Then he tugged hard at her arm, trying to pull her with him. "Come on, damn it, Bree! We haven't time for this!"

It was too late already. Hunter's distraction had been intended to last only a few seconds, after which he would flee for his life. Sabrina's resistance forced him to continue the disturbance long after the natives had collected their wits. They tackled him at the waist and leaped upon him, burying him beneath an onslaught of bodies. Michael was dragged down from the rear of the throne and flung to the ground.

Soon the two of them were brought together in

front of the witch doctor. "You dare attack the goddess?" B-B Dada exclaimed in mock rage. "Slay them!" he yelled to the nearest warriors.

"No!" shouted Sabrina. Everyone looked at her, surprised that she would intervene. Sabrina herself was surprised. But somehow, though she did not recognize these two men, something deep inside her made her feel a strange bond of kinship.

"B-B Dada say they die!" declared the witch doctor, enraged at her interference.

"And the sun goddess says they do not!" Sabrina answered firmly. Their stares locked.

Ulucong stepped forward now and said to B-B Dada, "Sun goddess word final. These be white men escape from Death Cave. They be taken back now. Not be slain here. Sun goddess has spoken."

Hunter, overcoming his startlement now, shouted, "Sabrina, what the *hell* is going on?"

He was hit on the side of the face by one of the natives, and knocked to the ground. "*Sumbakalo!*" shouted the native, ordering him to be silent.

"Bree, now damn it!" yelled Michael, starting to move forward. "Why are you—" He too was hit hard and knocked to his knees. Then the two of them were pulled to their feet and prodded at spearpoint in the direction of the Death Cave.

Hunter and Michael both realized that once they left the clearing there would be no chance of saving Sabrina. She did not seem to even realize the danger she was in. Their only hope lay in somehow getting close to her and talking to her, trying to bring her back to her senses. They looked at each other, and realized there was only one way either of them would be able to talk to her, alone, in a hut somewhere.

242

Hunter turned back to Ulucong and opened his mouth to speak, to volunteer to join the fight-to-the-death battle. Michael shoved against him, knocking him off balance. Before he could say anything, Michael exclaimed to the village at large: "I demand to enter the competition!"

The natives who were prodding him forward stopped. The chief and the witch doctor looked at him in disbelief. Sabrina stared at him with such violently mixed emotions and deep feelings, it made her head throb painfully.

"I challenge the lot o' you buggers!" declared Michael, swiveling to face each of the naked warriors within the purple-bordered arena.

"It not be possible," said the witch doctor. "Return him to cave."

The natives prodded Michael with their spears, motioning for him to move. "What's the matter," he said, turning to Ulucong. "The big chief's afraid of me maybe?"

Ulucong looked at Michael levelly. "Hold," he ordered the natives who were shoving him and Hunter out of the clearing. He walked up to Michael and gazed down at him from his towering height. "Enter battle if you wish it, white man," he said. "You will only lose your life."

Michael glanced at Sabrina, who was frowning in puzzlement over the strange emotions she obviously felt toward him. He looked at the fierce warriors standing with shields and clubs. He turned back to the chief. "It's *my* life," he said firmly.

When it was indicated that he was to strip, he blanched slightly, looking embarrassed. But then he did as he was told. He handed his pants and boots to Hunter.

"You're a stupid son of a bitch, Limey," Hunter said without bitterness, taking the clothes. "Why didn't you let me do it?"

"It had to be me, Yank. You're the indispensable one. No one else can fly us out of here."

Michael chose a war club from the wooden chest, hefted it a few times to familiarize himself with the feel of it, then chose a rectangular shield. Then he stepped into the arena marked off by the purple powder.

The drums began to pound in a fast, pistonlike beat: *Boom boom boom boom*. The women and children of the tribe began chanting and wailing loudly. Michael crouched low and looked around him at the warriors who were his competition and at the chief. Each warrior was glaring fiercely at each of the others.

Sabrina raised her hands high above her head. All eyes turned to her now, awaiting the signal. Drawing in a deep breath, focusing her eyes on Michael and wondering why she felt such intense fear for his safety, she performed the irrevocable act: she clapped her hands together sharply.

They came together like ferocious animals, screaming, kicking, smashing wildly. Clubs and shields, arms and legs flashed so swiftly they blurred before Sabrina's eyes. The violent screams of attack shattered the night. Soon the ground was littered with the bodies of the dead and dying.

Sabrina turned her head away, unable to bear the sight of the mass carnage. But then she forced herself to look again at the battle. She had to see what was happening to the bold white man, and to Ulucong, who had tried as best he could to be a friend to her, despite his obligations to the religion.

The white man was still on his feet, moving with frenzied violence, striking in all directions at once. But Ulucong, Sabrina saw with a pang of alarm, was not doing so well. His towering height and strength gave him an enormous advantage, but as the battle wore on, it became clear that this was not really an "every-man-against-every-other-man" battle at all; many of the natives were ganging up on the chief.

Their strategy was clear: since he was the warrior no single native could conquer alone, they were allying themselves in their attack on him, to slay him quickly. Afterward they would begin fighting each other.

As Sabrina watched, Ulucong was fiercely driven backward until he was at the very edge of the purple border. There, he stopped his retreat and made his stand. A vicious animal roar erupted from his throat, and his club began swinging with devastating force.

The number of his attackers was too great, however, and their blows continued raining upon him. Sabrina stared in fearful apprehension at the spectacle of his valiant but seemingly doomed stand. He could not hold out much longer.

Then, from the rear of the group of attackers, came unexpected aid. Michael, finishing off the opponent he was fighting, saw the unified attack taking place against the chief. Though it was in his best interest to have Ulucong killed, he thought only of the fact that B-B Dada said it was the chief who refused to burn Sabrina on the pyre, who stood up for her right to live.

Michael bludgeoned his way through the mob of attacking warriors to the front. There he turned to face the attackers and took his place at the chief's side. Ulucong's face was drenched in sweat, as was Michael's, and there were bloody cuts all over it. His fierce glance acknowledged Michael's aid; there was a tinge of gratitude in it.

The two men let out a violent roar—"*Eeeyaahhhh!*"—and rushed forward into the midst of their attackers, kicking with their legs, smashing with their clubs, and swirling their shields.

Their opponents were unprepared for such reckless daring. One fled from the circle; the natives jeered and spat at him. Others began dropping to the ground, mortally wounded.

The odds were almost manageable now, when Michael saw the one-eared native to whom B-B Dada had given the sleeping powder. He was near the chief. He flung away his shield, and in his hand, the leaf-wrapped parcel was clearly visible. Michael saw him open it, exposing the orange powder within.

Michael dove in a flying tackle, hitting him at knee level, bringing him to the ground. He grasped the man's wrist. The native was powerful, and began forcing the wrist toward Michael's face, grinning maliciously, his white teeth bared in a snarl.

Michael ducked his head low, and smashed it into the native's jaw. There was a crackling sound, and a tortured scream. Michael's head hurt and he became woozy, on the verge of fainting. Once more, though, he butted his head forward, lower this time, into the native's Adam's apple. The man began choking, and quickly released Michael's arm.

Michael experienced a wooziness that was so intense he could do nothing but stagger to his feet and stumble backward. Another native saw the man helplessly choking on the ground, raised his club, and brought it down fiercely on the choking man's forehead, killing him instantly.

The native smiled at his good fortune in being able to dispatch an opponent so easily. But when he turned around with raised club to attack Michael, he saw Ulucong standing next to him, his expression fierce. The chief's fist smashed down on the back of the man's neck. There was a loud snapping sound, and the man dropped to the ground like a dead weight.

There was no movement now anywhere in the circle. The only sound was that of rasping breathing. Michael looked around him and realized that he and the chief were the only two left alive. At their feet lay the bodies of those who had been their enemies.

The two survivors looked at each other. Michael was unarmed now, but knew there was no hurry to pick up club and shield. He would not be attacked until he took a weapon. His chest heaved with his labored breathing, as did the chief's.

Sabrina watched the two men, who seemed to her like primeval warriors about to engage in a battle as ancient as mankind itself. There they stood, their skins glistening with sweat, stained with blood, bruised all over. The muscles of their naked chests, shoulders, and arms rippled mightily. Their stomachs were hard and flat, their masculine staffs long and thick, symbolizing the power of their maleness.

Their coming battle would be over an issue more basic than any other: who would win the right to mate the beautiful woman . . . whose hands would strip off her clothing and caress her body

. . . who would possess her and grant her the full-fillment she had been so long denied.

Michael bent down and picked up a sturdy club. He did not bother with a shield. Ulucong flung away his shield in response. With a mighty roar, the chief charged forward, his club high above his head. Michael charged too, his club held at both ends, to block Ulucong's blow. They came together, their clubs connecting with a smacking sound that shattered the air.

The chief's blow was so mighty it drove Michael to one knee, his club held horizontally above his head. He leaped to the side and regained his stance. The chief began a series of smashing, brutal blows, driving Michael continuously backward. Ulucong's strategy was clear: he did not want to kill Michael but force him backward out of the arena, past the purple border.

Michael understood what the chief was trying to do but refused to accept it. He could not let himself retreat from the circle, forfeiting the battle, abandoning Sabrina to this man. *He* had to be the one to take Sabrina into the mating hut, where he could prepare an escape for her.

As a mighty series of blows came raining down upon him, forcing him back to the edge of the circle, he stepped to the side, then smashed Ulucong in the stomach with all his might. The chief doubled over, grunting, wincing against the agony. But then he straightened up and turned to Michael with a new look on his face: a look of brutal fierceness.

He charged forward in such a wild frenzy, Michael barely managed to avoid having his head smashed. The attack was vicious and relentless.

One of Ulucong's blows splintered Michael's club in two. Michael dove out of the way and rolled over and over on the ground, passing over the bodies of the dead in his effort to escape the pursuing, pulverizing blows.

He came near another club and was about to grab it, when suddenly he had an idea. Instead of taking the club, he continued rolling. A blow smashed down an inch from his ear. He rolled over once more, then found what he was seeking: the burst packet of orange powder in the hand of the one-eared native. He snatched it, shot to his feet, and thrust it into the chief's nose.

Ulucong staggered backward. To the watching natives it looked as if Michael had hit him in the face with his fist. To complete the illusion, Michael did hit him in the face, twice, with all his might. The chief dropped to the ground, drugged into unconsciousness. Michael seized Ulucong's club, raised it high, and then—with the watching villagers gasping in unison—he smashed it into the dirt at the side of the chief's head. The blow came so close to the temple it appeared to everyone that it had actually struck the chief, killing him.

Michael dropped the club and staggered backward. His chest was heaving with his gasping breathing. He looked at the natives surrounding the purple circle. All eyes were on him. Everyone was stunned and amazed that he was the survivor, the victor.

Someone shouted *"Chinga saba lo!"* Others shouted the same phrase. Soon everyone in the village had picked up the chant. It echoed resoundingly through the clearing, shattering the night. *"Chinga saba lo!"* they shouted, their faces feverish, and Michael knew that they were applauding him as the victor.

He turned to Sabrina. Her eyes were wide as she watched him stagger toward her, his strong naked body covered with blood—mostly the blood of those he had killed. He stopped directly in front of her throne, looking up at her, his face demanding.

Sabrina stood up on the foot ledge, waiting for the bearers to rush forward with their platform. Michael grasped her about the legs and yanked her from the throne, refusing to wait. The natives gasped at this sacrilege.

He put a hand behind her knees, adjusted her roughly in his arms so he could carry her, and began stalking toward the distant hut that was decorated with multicolored flowers—the mating hut.

Sabrina looked at his face. It was the face of a crazed wild animal.

Chapter 19

He stopped before entering the hut to see what the commotion behind him was all about. Several natives were standing near the tree where Hunter had been held during the fight. Hunter was gone. He had escaped at the height of the battle, when all eyes were on the arena. The two natives who had been guarding him lay dead on the ground, one still clutching a bloody-tipped spear. A trail of blood led into the bushes.

Several natives rushed into the jungle after Hunter, following the trail of blood. There was nothing Michael could do to help the fleeing aviator; four guards ringed the mating hut. Michael brushed aside the hide that covered the entrance and went inside. He roughly half-dropped, half-lowered Sabrina to the grass mat.

She looked at him in the yellow glow of the wall-mounted torch, her eyes wide and uncertain. Her heart pounded fiercely in her breast as intense excitement swept over her. She stared at the hard, severe face of the man who had killed to possess her, and at the lean, well-muscled body that was covered with blood and dirt and sweat.

"I am the sun goddess," she said, throwing back

251

her head. "And you have won the right to take me for your pleasure."

"You're Sabrina St. Claire," Michael said, seething with anger, "and you bloody well better stop playing this stupid game. You nearly got me *killed* out there. Why did you fight me when we tried to rescue you?"

Sabrina frowned in puzzlement. She did not know what he was talking about. "I am the sun goddess," she said, repeating the phrase that had been drilled into her. "And you have won—"

"Oh, Christ! You really have lost your memory, haven't you. Now what'll we bloody well do?"

Sabrina looked at him uncomprehendingly. "I am the sun goddess," she repeated, not knowing what else to say. "You have—"

"Stow it, Bree, damn it!" He glared at her angrily. Then he put his hand to his forehead and said, "What am I yelling at you for? You can't help it." He stared down at her, at the way her grass skirt barely covered her womanhood. "Look, will you cover yourself or something," he said irritably. "It's damn hard trying to think with you like that."

Sabrina was completely disoriented. She had expected him to take her instantly, as was his right. She did not understand what he was talking about when he referred to her by that strange name—Sabrina—and when he talked about her memory. All she knew was what the witch doctor had told her: she knew what was expected of her now. "You must take me," she said. "It is written." She put her hands to her vine waistband and unfastened it. The grass skirt opened and fell away from her, baring her loins.

Michael stared down at her, amazed and surprised—and undeniably physically excited. "I don't want to take advantage of you," he said in a thick, throaty voice. "Not while you're like this, not knowing what you're doing . . ."

He gazed down at her lush, full body . . . at the way her hips flared out from her narrow waist . . . at the tuft of curly hairs covering the mound of her womanhood. Sharply, he turned half away from her. "Look, Bree, I'm not made of steel!" He pressed his hands to his eyes. She could see he was trying to resist her. His rigid maleness twitched upward, throbbing.

Then he turned back to her, his face hard and demanding. "I deserve this," he said in a hoarse whisper. "I killed for it, and now I'm bloody well going to take it."

He took her hands and raised her to her feet, pulling her tightly against him. She felt his hard shaft pressing against her, felt the heat of his body all up and down her. He put his hand to her breast-plate and jerked it away. Her firm, full breasts pressed against his sweating skin. It felt as if her breasts and nipples were being seared by the heat of the sensation.

He jerked her head back, his hand pulling her long hair. She watched as his mouth descended upon hers, his firm lips crushing hers with a strong pressure. She tasted the salty tang of blood and sweat. He forced her mouth wide open and his tongue darted in.

Sabrina moaned, unable to contain herself. His mouth moved all over her face, then down her throat. He pulled her head backward even harder, forcing her to arch her back. Her loins pressed tightly against his hips. His mouth moved down the swell of her breasts, over them. He found a nipple and sucked at it hotly, taking it between his teeth, inciting a wild flame of pleasure. His calloused hand squeezed her other breast tightly, rubbing the tip hard.

The sensation was so intense she had to push him away, gasping. She could not bear it. She stumbled backward a few paces and stood half hunched over, panting with her mouth wide open, her hands in front of her, fingers spread. She had not known pleasure could be so fierce!

He pulled her toward him, bending her backward. His free hand roamed over her breasts roughly, down her flat stomach, down between her legs. "Ahhhnnnn!" she moaned sharply. Her nerves seemed to be abraded raw, so that they flared up into burning ecstasy each time he touched her, rubbed her, probed inside her. She was being driven into a fit of wild, mindless rapture.

He put her upon the mattress clumps of long green grass and poised himself above her. His upper body was supported by his rigid arms, hands planted next to her shoulders. Sabrina looked down the lengths of their bodies and saw his shaft straining rigidly just above her loins.

Michael looked there too, and then glanced at her face. There was torment in his expression, but also a hint of gentleness. "When you become yourself again," he said, "and look back on this, you may think: That bastard took advantage of me, without any feeling for me at all, only for his own pleasure!" He shook his head. "The truth is, pet, I feel for you more than you know. You see . . . I . . . I . . ." He closed his mouth, unable to get the words out.

He pressed into her, filling her completely, sending her reeling into exquisite rapture until she thought she would faint. Warmth flowed languorously through her, making her body melt with pleasure. He remained deeply in her, not moving, watching her face. He seemed pleased with what he saw. Her eyelids were half closed, her mouth wide open in a silent scream of ecstasy.

His mouth wide open like her own, came down on hers. Only then, when his mouth covered hers completely, did he begin moving inside her, thrusting gently in and out. His tongue roamed about inside her mouth, picking up speed in time to his hips, which now thrust faster and faster into her loins. Suddenly, she felt it coming . . . she knew there would be no stopping it this time . . . she was over the brink and it was coming, it was coming, *it was catching up to her* . . .

She screamed uncontrollably as her loins exploded into a meteor of pleasure. She went wild beneath him, writhing, twisting, gyrating. The meteor that was her loins sent burst after burst of fiery pleasure shooting through her, reducing her to a mindless animal. The sensation would not end! And he—he would not stop! Finally, after an eternity of bliss, he lunged into her once more, and she heard the groan that escaped his lips. She felt the flow of him deep within her.

He collapsed on top of her, his body going slack. He lay like that, his face against the side of her head, both of them breathing in gasps, trying to catch their breath. Sabrina stroked his back gently, moving her other hand through his tousled brown hair.

After a moment he raised his head and gazed at

her, with a look of immense tenderness and affection. He took her hand and kissed it gently. "I love you, Bree," he said softly. "It seems strange saying this, with you not even knowing who I am. But the truth is . . . I love you."

She looked at him warmly, tears beginning to fill her eyes. "And I love *you*—Michael."

His face became alert with startlement. "You remember!" he whispered.

"Yes." Her memory had come back while they were making love. Feeling his naked body pressing against her, his manhood penetrating her, had triggered the flash of memory. She remembered the time she felt him inside her once before, in Wolfschmidt's headquarters. And she remembered everything else, too.

Michael looked intensely embarrassed. Here he was on top of her, both of them naked, with her knowing full well what he had done to her. "God, what you must think of me!" he said shamefacedly, starting to quickly rise and move away from her. "Taking advantage of you this way!"

She put her hands on the back of his neck and prevented him from rising. She pulled him down again, and looked into his face. Then she kissed him gently on the lips.

He lowered his head to the side of her face and put his arms around her, hugging her tightly. "Ah, Bree," he said, his voice filled with emotion. He rocked slowly from side to side. "Bree, Bree, Bree."

She kissed his ear and stroked his back, feeling warm and fulfilled.

After a while, they stood up and Sabrina dressed. Michael went to the entranceway, lifted the hide covering, and peered out. There were two guards visible a short distance away. He knew two others were standing on the other side of the hut, out of sight. He surveyed the scene carefully, dropped the hide back into place, and turned to Sabrina.

"There's only one way we may be able to bring this off," he said. "I'll slip out under the back flap of the hut. I'll be in the hut's shadow, since the bonfire is on the other side. I'll try to take out the two guards without being seen or heard. If I make it, you slip under the back of the hut too, and we'll be off into the jungle."

"All right," she said. Her eyes betrayed her fearfulness.

Michael took her hand and squeezed it, then went to the rear of the hut, knelt down, and raised up the thatched straw "wall." He was about to crawl under it when he heard a ripping sound. He jerked his head around to see B-B Dada standing in the entranceway, the hide flap he had torn down hanging from his hand. To his sides, slightly behind him, were two fierce natives, holding their spears ready for action.

"It is time," B-B Dada declared hatefully. He pointed at Sabrina. "To the pyre with her!"

Hunter raced through the jungle, the wound in his side burning with pain. He gasped for breath as he crashed through the undergrowth, tripping over vines and roots in the darkness, leaping back to his feet and continuing on.

The shouting voices of his pursuers were close behind. He had had a good head start originally, but the bleeding wound in his side slowed him down. He could hear the thrashing about as his pursuers crashed through the jungle after him. He did not want to lead them to the plane, but there was no choice any longer. He had to get to the plane; there was something he needed, something that offered the only chance of rescuing Sabrina—if it wasn't already too late.

He wondered how Michael had fared in the battle. He was probably dead by now, Hunter thought, as he leaped over a hedge of bushes, landing too hard on the other side, causing a searing bolt of pain to shoot up from his side. He bit his lip to stifle a scream of pain. Behind him he heard the sounds of the natives, not more than a few minutes away. He had to reach the plane, it was his only hope!

Finally he reached the tree house. He did not stop, but continued on past it, toward where the jungle came to an abrupt end in a wall of trees. He crashed on through the last line of trees, and found himself suddenly in the open clearing. The tall grass came up to his knees. The sky was brilliantly dotted with countless shiny stars. And there before him, only a few yards to the side, was the plane.

He raced to it and climbed on the bottom wing. He feverishly tried to pry the machine gun loose from its swivel socket, to disconnect it from the plane—but he had no more success now than when he and Michael had tried it the first time, the morning after they'd crashed.

Becoming almost delirious with pain and desperation, he began cursing the machine gun. "Come on, damn you! Disconnect! Get the hell out of that swivel socket!" He jumped down from the cockpit, grabbed a thick branch, and began beating on the gun where it was joined to the swivel socket. "Disconnect, damn you, disconnect!"

258

All the beating accomplished was to batter the socket even more than it already had been. Hunter realized the truth: there was no way in hell he'd be able to get the gun dismounted from the plane. It was an absolute impossibility.

But at least the gun could still fire and swivel, he thought, as the natives now broke through into the clearing, shouting and raising their spears.

A spear sang through the air and struck the fuselage of the plane, lodging itself firmly in the side. Hunter swiveled the gun and aimed it at one of the natives. Other spears whistled through the air toward him. The natives began charging, their knife blades flashing.

At least it would be an even fight, Hunter thought as his finger squeezed the trigger of the machine gun, making the gun jolt and sputter into life, spitting out its load of lethal metal. There were at least seven of the natives—but he had the machine gun.

"Come on, you bastards!" he raged, almost delirious with the pain and exhaustion. "Come on, I'll take you on, I'll take you all on!" The machine gun blazed and sputtered, the spears flew in on him from everywhere at once. Hunter's finger squeezed the trigger, sending out bursts of fiery metal as he screamed his curses into the starlit night.

Sabrina stood atop the high pyre with her wrists bound together over her head, tied to the pole behind her. The pyre was built in the shape of a pyramid, constructed of tiers of ascending logs. It was wide at its base, tapering to the small platform on which she stood, at the very top.

B-B Dada danced about the base of the pyramid,

chanting loudly, holding high the torch he would use to set the ceremonial pyre ablaze. Sabrina followed his every move with her desperate eyes as he danced about energetically, howling strange incantations into the night. The other natives all chanted along with him, their faces bright with excitement.

She turned her eyes to Michael. He was now dressed, being held across the clearing, near the bonfire. He saw the look of deathly fright on her face and made a violent effort to step forward. The native standing in front of him jerked his spear up to Michael's throat, stopping him. A second native was behind him, holding a raised spear against the back of his neck. There was nothing Michael could do to save her, Sabrina knew. She struggled against the leather straps that bit into her wrists, but it was useless.

The witch doctor completed his incantation, then stopped his chanting and dancing, standing very close to the pyramid. He turned to face the villagers, his back to Sabrina. He addressed them in their native tongue, his blazing torch raised high above his head. The villagers responded with loud shouts. Their faces were feverish with anticipation. The drums that had been beating wildly, now stopped, all at once.

There was suddenly a deadly silence and stillness. Sabrina's eyes and the eyes of everyone in the encampment were on the torch held above the witch doctor's head. Slowly he turned to face the pyre, glancing at Sabrina hatefully. Then he thrust the burning torch into the kindling at the base of the pyre.

Sabrina screamed and went wild. She struggled in such a fierce panic to free herself from her bonds that she gave herself leather burns from where the hide strips rubbed against her sensitive skin. Michael kicked wildly at the guard in front of him, and tried to rush forward to the pyre. The guard smashed the shaft of his spear against Michael's temple, dropping him to his knees, his forehead bleeding.

Sabrina felt the heat rising up toward her. Her skin broke out in beads of sweat. Tongues of flame licked from the base of the pyramid, spreading out at the base until three of the four sides were consumed in fire.

"No, no, nooooo!" Sabrina screamed hysterically. Then, when she was about to give up all hope, she saw a flash of movement at the side of the clearing. It was a running hunched-over figure. She squinted tightly to see through the river of sweat pouring from her forehead.

It was Hunter! Charging out of the jungle, bent low over the spear he held before him, he was rushing headlong toward the natives guarding Michael. He was bare-chested but had twin bandoliers of machine-gun ammunition crisscrossing over his chest. Several of the villagers saw him now, but before they could react, he reached the guards and jabbed with his spear, driving it into the stomach of the nearest one, driving it completely through the man. The guard screamed shrilly.

Michael took advantage of the surprise to kick at the knees of the guard behind him, then grab the man's spear from him. He pressed it over the guard's throat as he lay on the ground, smashing his windpipe. He turned and was about to try to rush through the mob of natives now coming at him, in an attempt to reach the pyre.

Hunter stopped him. It would be futile to do it that way. They could never fight off all the natives. Hunter had a different plan, and Michael understood what it was the instant Hunter unfastened his bandoliers of machine-gun bullets and handed one to him.

Instead of attacking toward the pyre, they both now ran in the other direction, toward the bonfire. A native loomed up in front of Hunter, blocking him. Hunter swirled his belt of ammunition, swiping the native along the side of his head, making him scream and stagger backward. Then he and Michael had a clear path to the bonfire. They ran to it and thrust the bandoliers into the center of the fiery inferno.

When they turned, the natives were upon them. Instead of resisting, the two white men quickly dropped to the ground. The natives looked stunned. Before they could react further, there erupted from the bonfire a barrage of thunderclap explosions that shattered the night, sending streaking bullets in all directions. The noise was earsplitting as the twin bandoliers of high-caliber ammunition exploded and flew about.

Not only was the sound of the exploding bullets terrifying to the natives, but the effects were even more devastating. Many of them dropped dead in their tracks, shot down by stray bullets that went zinging about in every direction. The superstitious natives did not understand what was happening. All they knew was that suddenly blood was sprouting from the faces and bodies of their tribesmen and themselves, accompanied by excruciating pain. The natives scattered in all directions, screaming in terror. Hunter and Michael were on their feet instantly, racing as fast as they could toward the pyre.

They circled the pyre, looking for an opening. They found a narrow section at the rear, not yet touched by the raging fire. Hunter and Michael both started for it at once, but Hunter grabbed Michael's arm, holding him back. "Stay here!" he shouted above the uproarious noise of the crackling fire, shooting bullets, and screaming natives. "Guard the base!"

Michael picked up a spear and readied himself to defend the unburned section of the pyramid from any natives who might try to block the way down. Hunter grabbed a knife from the sheath of a screaming native who had been shot in the stomach. Then he ran up the narrow section of the pyramid, feeling the heat of the flames on both sides of him, singeing his skin. He ascended the tiers of rising logs, holding his wounded side as he ran, until finally he reached the platform.

"Dallas!" Sabrina shouted at him joyously, deliriously. "Oh, Dallas!"

Tongues of flame leaped up at the front and sides of the platform, crackling noisily, casting a bright yellow glow over Sabrina's skin. Hunter slashed the leather straps binding her wrists. He grabbed her hand and pulled her after him as he started descending the rear of the pyre.

Coals and burning embers covered the logs, and Sabrina screamed as she stepped on them barefooted. Hunter turned, put his knifeblade between his teeth, and picked Sabrina up in his arms. He quickly swiveled around again and continued his descent, carrying her. His heavy-soled boots were impervious to the burning embers, crushing them underfoot.

On both sides of them, flames leaped up wildly. It was like rushing down a narrow alleyway with walls of fire on both sides. When they neared the base, Michael rushed to meet them and took Sabrina into his own arms, to lessen the burden on Hunter, whose side wound had started bleeding badly.

They rushed away from the pyre, out of the clearing, into the jungle. "Can you walk?" Michael shouted to Sabrina, above the din. When she nodded, he set her down. The three of them charged desperately through the thick, lush jungle, Hunter in the lead. The explosions had ceased by now, the bullets in the bonfire having all been spent. "They'll be organizing themselves to come after us," Michael said to Hunter. "We've stolen their sun goddess."

Hunter did not answer, just continued running, holding his side. Sabrina saw the way the blood streamed down his skin, and wondered how much longer he could go on without fainting.

They reached the tree house. Then a minute later they were charging through the last line of trees into the open, grass-covered field. The plane loomed in front of them. They ran toward it. Sabrina noticed the bodies of many natives all around the plane, along with a spear sticking shaft-up from the side where its point was imbedded. Dallas must have had one heck of a battle, she thought as she ran.

They reached the plane. Michael lifted her into the rear cockpit while Hunter climbed into the front one. "Rev the props!" Hunter yelled.

Michael went to the propellers and put his back into the effort, using all his strength to start them turning. The engine sputtered and coughed—and then sprang to life. The propellers began whirring powerfully, sending a strong breeze toward Michael. He rushed back to the cockpit and climbed in. The plane started forward. It moved slowly, tormentingly slowly, since the new skids on the tall grass were not in any way a match for wheels on a hard surface.

The natives burst into view now from the wall of trees. Spears were flung at the aircraft, several hitting it. Hunter was seated very low in the cockpit so that only the top of his head was visible above the fuselage. The plane gained speed.

Sabrina was swiveling her head, unable to decide which danger was worse: behind them were the natives, rushing at them, flinging spears; in front of them, though, lay another wall of trees at the opposite edge of the field. "Can we get up enough speed to get over the trees?" she asked Michael nervously. He didn't answer.

The natives were very close now, only a few yards behind them, running with all their might to catch the plane. The aircraft gained speed and rose into the air, pulling away from them. To the side, though, a second group of natives now appeared, very near the plane. B-B Dada was in the lead, urging the group forward with a rallying cry.

The plane was higher off the ground now, and climbing. Sabrina watched the thick wall of trees in front of them, wondering desperately if they could gain enough height to clear them . . . or if they would crash into their tops. Michael was not looking in that direction. He was watching the second group of natives, only slightly behind them now, his face set in hard determination.

He jerked out the spear that was imbedded in the side of the cockpit. Then he shocked Sabrina by standing up in the cockpit, exposing himself to the flying spears, risking falling out during the ascent into the air.

"What are you doing?" she screamed.

"Paying back a debt," he said, cocking his arm. B-B Dada saw him stand. His face showed his horror, but he was not quick enough to retreat. Michael's arm slashed forward, sending the spear hurling powerfully down. It slammed into the witch doctor's chest, knocking him backward. His dying screams could not be heard above the roar of the plane's engine.

"Get down!" shouted Sabrina, tugging at him to keep him from falling out of the plane. He sat down again in the compartment. Both of them turned their eyes to the front just in time to see the treetops looming up directly in front of them.

Oh, God!, thought Sabrina. We've come so far—only to lose it all now!

But fortune was with them. The engine continued to roar powerfully, carrying them to sufficient altitude so that they passed over the threatening treetops, clearing them by only inches.

"We made it, we made it!" she shouted joyously, hugging Michael. Michael was wild with joy too, returning her hug, grinning from ear to ear. Sabrina turned to the front to share her joy with Hunter, and was shocked to see him still slouched very low down in the cockpit. "Dallas?" she yelled above the roar of the engines and the whistling of the wind. "Dallas!" she screamed.

266

Michael leaned forward from the cockpit and tried to touch Hunter, to make him turn around. But he could not reach him. He looked at Sabrina with a worried, ominous expression. Then he turned back to the front, and climbed out of the cockpit.

Staying very low, he crawled along the fuselage top toward the forward cockpit. The wind pressure was incredibly strong, almost carrying him up and off the aircraft. He clung to the fuselage, staying very close. Then he lowered himself into the forward cockpit head first. He righted himself, and looked at Hunter.

Hunter's face was deathly pale, contorted in pain, sheathed in sweat. "Take the stick," he said to Michael in a low, hoarse whisper.

Michael grasped the control shaft.

"Just hold it up to keep us steady," Hunter said, his voice even weaker this time. "I think we're flying north, which is what we want. The sun'll be up soon, you can tell then." His head sank down on his chest.

The last words Michael heard from him were very faint: "Tell Sabrina that I . . ." Then he passed out cold.

PART III

The Impossible Decision

Chapter 20

Hunter opened his eyes. He saw Sabrina's worried, loving face bending over him. She did not look smudged and dirty as she had before, and her hair was no longer stringy and disheveled. Her face was clean and radiant, her coral hair draping down to her shoulders in soft lustrous waves.

Her green eyes lit up when she saw that he was awake. "Doctor!" she called off to the side. "Doctor, he's out of the coma!" She turned back to him, smiling lovingly, and took his hand. His hand, Hunter saw, was bandaged. In fact, his entire arm was bandaged. He looked around to get his bearings, feeling weak and groggy.

He was in a white hospital room. It was very clean, spacious, and airy. A large window let in a flood of pleasant, warming sunlight. He was lying in a comfortable bed with a white sheet covering him from the waist down. Bandages decorated his skin, dressing the various scars and wounds he had received during the past weeks. The wound in his side was hidden beneath a thick gauze bandage wrapped around his torso.

Michael was standing on the other side of the bed, looking down at him with concern. "How you doing, mate?" he said. He wore an English officer's coat, unbuttoned and open. Hunter could see that he too was bandaged in a variety of places.

"Where the hell am I?" Hunter asked groggily, starting to rise from the bed.

Sabrina put a hand to his chest, holding him back. "It's all right, Dallas," she said. "We're safe now. We're in Cairo, at the Ali-Raga Hospital. We've been here a week now."

"How did we get here? The last thing I remember is blacking out at about 2,000 feet."

"You flew us in, Yank," said Michael fondly. "You were out cold for a good while there, but when the petrol gauge showed that we'd about had it, I roused you up again. Just in time for you to make a hell of a cheeky landing in the desert near here."

"We were all in pretty bad shape," Sabrina said. "An Arab from Colonel Lawrence's command saw us come down and brought us to the colonel. He had us taken here."

Hunter remembered none of it. He had heard of Colonel Lawrence though—the mysterious Englishman known as Lawrence of Arabia. So I managed to fly us out of Africa after all, thought Hunter, slightly surprised, into Arabian North-Africa.

A short, quickly moving Arab doctor came into the room, followed by a slim, pretty Arab nurse. The doctor began speaking to Hunter in Arabic as he inspected his bandages. Hunter just looked at him, not understanding a word he was saying. The doctor continued his inspection, unperturbed, looking very busy and hurried.

Hunter turned to Sabrina. He reached up to the back of her neck, pulled her head down toward him, and kissed her full on the lips. At first, the surprise of the move prevented Sabrina from reacting. His lips pressed against hers, his mouth opening. But then she quickly pulled her head back away from him, looking very sheepish. She looked this way not because she was embarrassed, Hunter knew, but because Michael was watching with growing resentment. He obviously felt Hunter was taking advantage of the situation. Well, the hell with him, Hunter thought, reaching out to take Sabrina's hand.

She backed away from him skittishly. "I . . . I . . . how do you like my new dress?" she said nervously, trying to break the sudden tension between the two men by making small talk. She twirled around, showing off the light, frilly summer dress of lime-green voile. The long, lace-decorated skirt swirled about her legs as she turned, and her pink locks of hair touched her cheeks. Except for the deep tan on her skin from the weeks in the jungle, she looked very girlish and innocent.

"The English outpost here in Cairo gave it to me," she said. "They've been very good to us. They even got a billet for me to live in right near the hospital, so I can be near the two of you."

"Yorkshire here is staying in the hospital too?" he said.

"You're not the only one who got himself a bit mussed up saving Bree, mate," said Michael, resentment creeping into his voice.

Hunter had not meant to antagonize him. He only asked because of the uniform Michael was wearing. He thought maybe he had been returned to active duty, despite his wounds.

Sabrina was looking from man to man, frustrated, trying to find some way of lessening the tension between them. At the base of it all, she knew she was the cause of the tension. "Michael insisted on wearing the uniform," she said to Hunter, "even after they told him he'd have to stay here in the hospital until his wounds heal. After being out of uniform for so long, he wanted to—"

"You don't have to make excuses for me, pet," Michael said. "Least of all not to him." He looked at Hunter and at the same time started to put his arm around Sabrina's shoulders.

She moved away from him, not wanting to show any favoritism to either of them. Hunter reached out and took her hand when she came near, before she could pull away. She looked at the way Hunter and Michael were staring at each other stonily. "Oh will you two stop it, for God's sake!" Sabrina cried frustratedly. "Can't you be friendly to each other for just one minute? Why must you keep needling each other about who I care for most? I care about both of you, deeply, you must know that."

She saw that neither of them was paying any attention to her. Michael was staring sullenly at her hand now, which Hunter was holding. And Hunter was watching Michael's expression, grinning in a superior manner, as if to say: Go ahead and pretend she cares for both of us equally, kid—I'm the one holding her hand.

She pulled her hand away from his grasp angrily. "Oh, you two!" she cried. "Why must you *be* like this?" She hated the way they carried on toward each other. It surely couldn't go on like this. Each time she showed any affection toward one, the other became hurt and angry. She felt very nervous, wondering how the situation would finally resolve itself.

The doctor said something in Arabic to Sabrina and Michael. The pretty, black-haired nurse, who up till now had remained silent, translated: "Doctor say you must go now. Major *Hoonter*," she said, mispronouncing the name, "he must rest."

"Is he going to be . . . uh . . . all right?" Michael asked, looking embarrassed at showing concern for Hunter.

"Be very fine. But now he need rest."

Sabrina looked at Michael, glad he had asked the question. It showed there really was some hope of friendship developing between the two men, replacing their antagonism. She felt even more hopeful after she kissed Hunter good-bye, and saw Michael reaching out to shake Hunter's hand before leaving, instead of getting angry.

"Better take care of yourself, Limey," Hunter said with a hint of warmth, shaking his hand. "You've got enough bandages under that coat to make you look like an Egyptian mummy."

Sabrina smiled, and felt relieved and optimistic. The situation between the three of them really *would* get better! She knew it would! The rivalry over her would become less and less tense, and soon they would all be friends. She thought of this as she left the hospital to return to her billet, feeling very happy inside.

Her happiness was shattered the very next day, when she went back to the hospital to visit Hunter and Michael.

As soon as she entered the long hospital corridor, she heard the loud ruckus and commotion. The corridor was filled with white-garbed attendants shouting angrily, and several eagerly curious patients jockeying back and forth for position—outside Hunter's door.

"Oh, damn!" Sabrina cried in a small voice. She rushed through the crowd toward the front. She finally made her way to the open door of Hunter's room, but before she could enter, a body came flying out, forcing her to jump back. The body slammed against the corridor wall. "Michael!" she called, seeing who it was, rushing to him.

"Out of my way, Bree," he said, leaping back to his feet, charging back into the room.

An instant later it was Hunter who came careening backward out of the room. Michael came out after him, swinging with his fists. The crowd backed away in panic, afraid of getting hit. They roared their approval, though, of this fine break in the monotony of hospital life. The attendants shouted for order, in Arabic. No one paid any attention to them.

Hunter smashed Michael in the stomach. The Englishman went down, but he grabbed Hunter's knees as he did so, jerking him down with him. The two began wrestling ferociously on the faded linoleum floor, panting and cursing and swinging wildly with their fists.

"Stop it!" Sabrina yelled at them, filled with a sudden fury at the way they were hurting each other—at their stupidity! "Stop it, you hear me! Stop it, you two, you're going to kill each other!" The sight overwhelmed her with such unthinking rage that, without knowing what she was doing, she leaped into the midst of the fray, beating on them both with her small fists.

The spectators went wild with delight. They had never witnessed such an incredible scene: two bruised, injured men, bandages wrapped all over their bodies, smashing at each other fiercely. And on top of this, a beautiful young girl leaping into the battle, trying to beat the daylights out of both of the men while screaming—of all things—"Stop it, you're hurting each other, you're hurting each other!"

It took six attendants to finally break up the fight, holding the three of them away from each other. Sabrina was breathing heavily, her blood racing through her, her heart pounding. The men were glaring at each other like caged animals, struggling to return to the attack. The bandages covering their wounds were loose and torn, speckled with blood.

The short Arab doctor was between the three of them now, and he wasn't taking any chances with any of them. Sabrina saw him angrily order forward the attendants carrying the syringes. She felt the sting as a needle was poked into her arm. Then: blackness.

She awakened several hours later on a white-sheeted bed, in a white-walled room. A cold compress pressed wetly against her cheek. The black-haired Arab nurse was sitting beside her, holding the compress in place. "You wish some coffee?" asked the nurse, smiling, showing the prettiness of her features. "To awaken you fully?"

Sabrina shook her head. "How are—oooooh!" She had risen up too quickly, and now felt the stab of aches and pains all over her body. She sat still for a moment, not wanting to move. "How are Michael and Dallas?" she asked. "Are they hurt?"

"Hurt, yes," said the nurse in a soft voice. "But not so badly they will not heal."

"I have to see them," Sabrina said, standing up slowly. "Who is hurt the worst? I'll go to him first."

"They are together."

"Together?" She couldn't believe it. After the way they had just tried to kill each other, who in his right mind would put them both together?

"It be all right," the nurse said, smiling. "They come out from sedation more soon than yourself. They come together then. They talk."

She still could not believe it. She walked out of the room and looked around. She was only a few doors from Hunter's room, across the hall. She went to it, and saw it was empty. She continued on down the hall to Michael's room. There they were, both of them, sitting on the edge of adjacent beds, facing each other.

Neither seemed violent or angry anymore. In fact, as Sabrina entered the room, she was surprised at how well they seemed to control their emotions. It was as if they had finally realized that fighting would not solve the problem of their rivalry . . . as if they had come to a decision about some other way to solve the problem, and had resigned themselves to it.

She was glad they had found a new way of solving the predicament other than fighting—until she found out what this new way was.

"We've come to a decision," Hunter said, looking at her seriously.

"You're going to have to choose between the two of us," said Michael. "Whoever you choose, you marry."

"The other gets out of your life for good," said Hunter.

"Right," said Michael. The two of them stared at

her with intense, searching, expectant eyes. "Now then, pet . . . who'll it be?"

"You're mad, both of you!" She stared at them, flabbergasted.

Michael stood up and came over to her. "It's the only way," he said softly, his expression sincere and almost apologetic.

"None of us can keep going on like this," Hunter said, "you know that. Both of us love you. Both of us want you. We fought about it once already. It'll happen again if we don't get it settled."

"Triangles never work, pet. There's always that one extra person. The one who doesn't belong."

Sabrina said nothing. She felt almost paralyzed.

"So instead of fighting about it, to decide which one of us you love, we're doing the only other thing that makes any sense. We're asking you." He grinned bitterly. "It saves a lot of wear and tear on the body that way."

Sabrina still said nothing. She just stood there, looking at them. She felt stunned and unable to cope.

"So tell us," Hunter said. "Which of us do you love?"

"It's a foolish question," she said, her voice low and surprisingly childlike. "I love you both. And you both know it, too, so don't pretend you don't."

"Then you'll have to tell us whom you love the most," said Michael.

She looked at him accusingly, silently asking: How could you do this to me, forcing me to choose this way? She could see in his expression the great regret he felt at putting her in this painful situation. His jaw, though, was firmly set, and he refused to waver in his demand. Hunter's expression showed that he too would not give a single inch on the issue. They both watched her, awaiting her decision with the solemnity of men engaged in a game of Russian roulette. There could be only one winner, they knew, and the loser might as well be dead.

Sabrina sat down on the nearest bed, averting her eyes. She could not look at either of them, fearful her eyes might betray an answer she was not prepared to give in words. Many strong emotions swept over her now, but the strongest were confusion and indecision—and sorrow. She did not want to make this choice.

"You must be able to see why we're doing this, pet," said Michael. "It can't go on like this. You do see that, don't you?"

"No."

She did not know what to do, what to say. She felt horrible. How could they *do* this to her? How could they put her in such a situation? She remained seated on the bed, refusing to move or speak, thinking that she might just sit there forever, not looking at either of them, not responding to their demand. Just sit there, quietly, until the storm blew over . . .

But strong arms gripped her shoulders and raised her up to her feet. Hunter put his hand under her chin and forced her to raise her head and look at him. "Sabrina, there's only one reason you won't choose now. It's because you're a coward."

"I say!" declared Michael. "Ease off there, mate!"

"She knows what I'm saying is true," said Hunter, looking at her. "So let's stop playing games." He looked at Sabrina with his deep, dark eyes. "I may be turning you against me by forcing the issue like this. But I'll take that chance. We're going to get this settled, and we're going to do it right now. There's no point in any of us living in a fantasy world any longer. Life is hard; no one said it was easy. And the hardest part of all is making choices."

She raised her eyebrows and looked at him defiantly now, rebelling against being treated like a child.

"There are some things I want to tell you," said Hunter, "and I want you to listen well. First: If you don't make a decision about which of us you want to be with, we're going to keep fighting about it . . . getting more and more violent all the time. Do you see that?"

"Yes," she said, forced to admit the obvious truth. "I see it."

"And do you also see that sooner or later you're going to want to be married to one of us. Probably sooner."

"How presumptuous you are!" she declared. "Why, just because—"

"Be honest now, pet," said Michael.

She lowered her eyes. "All right," she said. "I'll want to . . . to marry one of you."

"Next point," said Hunter. "When you make your choice, it's better for the other one—whoever ends up as the odd man out—not to be around afterward. It'll only cause pain for him. And it'll be a constant agony for you to have to see him, knowing how he feels."

She took a deep breath. "I won't answer that," she said. She added quickly, out of desperation, "Can't we be friends? Can't we all just be friends?"

"No!" said both men in unison.

"Not a chance," added Hunter. "And you know it."

Sabrina looked away from him.

"And the last point," he said. "I've got a right to know your answer. Yorkshire has that right too. We've been through a lot so far, and we'll both go through a lot more during this war. Life is too short for you to draw this out, keep putting the decision off, just because you don't want to hurt one of us."

"It's not because of that!" she protested. "It's because . . . because . . ." But there was nothing else to say. It was just as Hunter said. She did not want to choose one over the other because it would be agony for the one she rejected. And it would be agony for her too, terrible agony, to have to reject one of them.

Michael and Hunter stood together now, facing her. "It's all right," Michael said. "Neither of us is a schoolboy. We can take it. Now out with it. Which of us will it be?"

She looked at the two of them as they stood side by side, stood straight and tall . . . Hunter looking at her with his narrow-eyed gaze, arrogant and commanding even now . . . Michael watching her with his jaw unconsciously pushed forward, unable to hide the sensitivity in his face though he was clearly trying.

She looked at them for a long moment, and then she burst into tears, and turned her head away. "I can't!" she cried. "I can't, I can't, I can't!"

Michael came up to her and put his arms around her, hugged her to him gently. "There, there, pet," he said, stroking her hair, letting her cry against his chest. "It'll all work out for the best. Truly it will. No matter which of us you choose."

She could not stop crying. "Please don't make me choose," she begged. *"Please!"* How could she choose between the two? It was impossible! She loved them both, she could not bear sending one away, possibly never to see him again. No! She wouldn't do it! Nothing could make her do it!

But deep inside her she knew they were right. A choice had to be made. It wasn't fair to either of them to let the triangle continue. She looked up at Michael, tears in her eyes, as he held her in his arms, stroking her hair.

"You've made your decision?" he asked in a quiet voice.

She nodded.

He took his hands away from her and moved back to join Hunter. The two men stood side by side, watching her tensely. "All right," said Hunter in an unusually gruff voice. "Who is it?"

She cast her eyes down, unable to look at either of them. When she spoke the name, it was so low that neither of them could hear it. The name caught in her throat and would not come out. She had to say it a second time, and the waiting was sheer agony for all of them.

But she did say it a second time, and all three of them heard it. "Dallas," she said.

She did not look up. No one said anything. She felt a whisper of movement going past her side. When after a moment she finally did look up, Michael was gone. She began crying softly. Hunter came to her and held her in his arms tightly. When he spoke, his words were meant to be reassuring, but they only made her feel worse. "It had to be done," he said.

Suddenly she had a wild impulse to run to Michael, to tell him that it wasn't that she didn't love him—she did love him!—but that . . . that . . . No, she didn't know what she would say to him. But she knew she had to go to him. She couldn't let this remain the way they would part, this cold, cowardly way she had taken, without even showing him her eyes and letting him see the love for him that was clearly in them.

"I have to go to him," she said to Hunter, breaking away from his embrace. "I'll be back."

He did not release her wrist, though. His expression was grim. "It's better to just leave it," he said. "Better for him, as well as you. Don't make him suffer having the pain dragged out."

"I have to go to him!" she declared, pulling her arm free. Nothing seemed as important as trying to ease his pain, to explain, to make him understand. She fled from the room.

Michael was not in the corridor. She rushed out the exit into the bright sunlight and saw him in the rear of a stretcher-carrier truck as it disappeared down the dirt road in a thick cloud of dust. She went back inside and hurried over to the dark-haired Arab nurse at the duty station.

"He go to English base-camp hospital," the nurse said, answering Sabrina's question. "He say no reason stay here this place no longer."

Sabrina left for the base-camp as soon as she found someone willing to take her. When she reached the base hospital, the starched English nurse at the admissions desk looked at her very cattily. "There's no Leftenant Yorkshire here, missy," she said. "No one by that name at all."

"Please," she said. "I know he came here. Maybe

he used a different name. He's tall and slim and blond, with a black eyepatch and—"

The nurse cut her off. "No one here by that description," she said, turning her back.

Sabrina stared at her back angrily. It was obvious she knew Michael had entered the hospital, but refused to admit this—probably on Michael's orders. Her anger quickly turned to sadness now as she remembered the words Michael had spoken earlier: "Whoever loses will get out of your life for good. You'll never see or hear from him again. That's the only way to make it bearable."

The reality of it hit her at last, making her feel weak and hollow. She would never see Michael again. He had stepped out of her life—forever.

Chapter 21

Sabrina stood before the mirror in her bungalow, in her wedding gown, smiling softly at the sight she beheld. The gown was of embroidered Arabian silk, white as snow, long and flowing. It was trimmed in pleated lace, and modestly tailored in front, exposing only the uppermost swell of her ample breasts. Her naturally wavy hair was brushed back from her forehead, radiantly pink, covered by a white bonnet and long sheer veil. The gown had been provided by an English colonel who had bought it for his niece back home. It was too tight in the bustline, but fit fine otherwise.

Sabrina could not really believe this was happening; she was really getting married. The truth was that deep in her heart she had never believed this would happen. All her life she had felt that the fates were somehow conspiring to deprive her of this happiness. But now she realized this was untrue. At this very moment, she knew, Dallas was getting ready for the ceremony too, in the hospital. He was dressing in the tuxedo that had been secured for him at great effort by the scavenger quartermaster of the English garrison.

He had not wanted to wear what he referred to as the "monkey suit," but Sabrina had insisted. A girl only gets married once, she told him. The marriage to Von Himmel, of course, didn't count. Even the English minister who would perform the ceremony agreed with that. And besides, the marriage was considered legally null and void, since Von Himmel was a citizen of a nation they were at war with.

Sabrina adjusted her bonnet, then checked the clock on the wall. She would have to leave soon for the hospital, where the ceremony was to take place. Then afterward she and Hunter would sail back to France. Their bags were already packed.

As a finishing touch, she began fastening the pearl and white-gold necklace the minister had lent her. As she did so, she saw in the mirror that she was scowling. She knew why: she kept thinking about Michael. It was too bad he wasn't here to join them in the ceremony, she thought. To give them his blessing so she could know he understood and forgave her. It pained her terribly to have to live with the knowledge that she had hurt him so deeply.

Oh, why couldn't he have understood? Why couldn't he have said, "Yes, Bree, I love you and wish you'd chosen me, but still I give you two my blessing and wish you the very best." But no, instead of saying that, he had simply remained in the British base-camp hospital, refusing to come out.

She had gone there several times in the two weeks since he had become a patient. Each time she had been told that no one by that name was staying there. She knew better, though. One of the nurses had confided to her that Michael was indeed present, but had threatened to raise absolute hell with anyone who admitted so to Sabrina. He spent his days sulking and brooding, the nurse said. He refused to accept any of the notes she left for him, and continued the charade of pretending he wasn't there when she came to visit.

Oh, damn him and his childlike sensitivity! she thought now. Why did he have to be so "vulnerable"? It was because of this trait in him that she had chosen Hunter. Michael didn't seem to have the strength of character, hardness and manly maturity she needed in a man. Hunter had these traits in abundance.

She had just finished adjusting the pearl necklace when there was a knock at the door. She answered it and was surprised to find Michael standing there in his uniform, looking very handsome, gazing at her with a resolute and purposeful expression.

"Michael, you came!" she declared joyously, flinging her arms around him. She assumed that his presence here meant he accepted her decision and harbored no ill feelings—that he was prepared to give his blessing.

"That's right, luv. I did indeed." His tone was quiet and controlled.

"Oh Michael, I hoped you'd come, but I didn't really think you— But you couldn't stay away, could you?"

He shook his head, smiling a very slight, mysterious smile. "No," he said. "I thought about it, and I came to a decision. There was no way I could stay away. I came to a realization, pet. Coming here now was something I just had to do. And when a man has something he has to do, well . . . if he's a man, he does it."

"That's right," she said, not really knowing what

he was talking about, but feeling that his showing up in time for the wedding spoke for itself. "So you've come to give us your blessing, right?" she said happily.

"Hell, no!" he declared. "I've come to get you the hell out of here. You're not marrying any two-bit, adventure-addict flyboy. You're marrying me!"

"*What!*"

He swept her up into his strong arms and carried her, struggling, out the door.

They were halfway to the ambulance he had stolen from the English base camp's motor pool before Sabrina overcame her shock and realized he was serious. "Michael, you can't do this!", she exclaimed. "Put me down! Put me down, I say!"

He lowered his face to hers quickly, catching her by surprise, and kissed her passionately. When he raised his head, he was smiling. Sabrina's mind was reeling with disbelief. Finally, as he lowered her to the front seat of the ambulance, it occurred to her that he really did intend to go through with this.

"Michael, you can't—This isn't fair!" she screamed at him, struggling. "I've made my choice!" she shouted as he tied her arms behind her, slammed her door, and then rushed around to the driver's side and climbed in behind the wheel. "It's Dallas I chose! You can't just pick me up and take me away!"

"That's just exactly what I can do, pet. And what I'm doing."

"But you have no right!"

"I love you. What more right is there than that?" He gunned the engine. The rickety ambulance shot forward in a spray of loose gravel and dust. People were beginning to filter out of the hospital across the field now, to see what the shouting was about. They stood watching the abduction, not knowing what to do.

Sabrina saw Hunter come out in his black long-tailed coat and gray pants, looking completely out of character. "Dallas!" she screamed to him through the open window. "Stop him!" But there was nothing he could do. The ambulance was roaring and jolting down the craggy dirt road. It crested a knoll and the hospital and people vanished from view.

She looked at Michael, seeing red now, blinded by indignant rage. Who was he to dictate her life for her? To impose his wishes on her despite what she might want and think best for herself? How dare he do this to her! After she had finally gotten over the agony of the choice she made between the two of them! After she finally decided she would marry Hunter!

"I hate you!" she cried, almost hysterical at the disruption of her plans.

"Do you really, pet?"

"You don't care about me at all," she said, shouting above the noise of the engine and the creaking of the ambulance as it jolted along the ravine-lined road. "You don't care about my happiness!"

"That's all I care about," he said, looking at her. "Which is why I'm not going to let you ruin your life by marrying that bloody son-of-a-bitch flier. He's not right for you, no matter what you think."

"Oooooooh," she cried, in helpless frustration.

The ship was already weighing anchor when they came to a screeching halt at the dock. Michael had obviously arranged in advance for the ship to await his arrival and be ready to depart at an instant's notice.

Sabrina kicked and thrashed about as he tried to guide her up the ramp onto the ship. Finally he gave up trying to prod her, and slung her unceremoniously over his shoulder instead. He carried her up the ramp to the raucous laughter of the French crew. "Sorry, luv," he said to her, "but you leave me no choice."

The ship pulled in its towlines and ramps and set out under steam into the Nile. It was a large merchant vessel and moved rapidly out of the harbor. Michael set her down on deck and the two of them watched the harbor disappear in the distance. They both saw the cloud of dust rise up on the dirt road off in the distance, as two military cars raced along it toward the harbor. The ship was so far out at sea by now, though, that the vehicles presented no threat at all.

The French ship captain came up to Michael and Sabrina. He was a stodgy, weather-beaten man with a bristling beard and the smell of fish about him. He wore a dirty, nautical cap. "Ze money you pay me for ze hasty retreat from ze harbor," he said to Michael. "I thought surely zat you had much contraband you weesh to smuggle out. But instead of contraband you bring *thees*? A young girl? A *bride* no less?"

"You got your money," said Michael. "What's it matter to you what I bring?"

"No matter," said the captain good-naturedly. He looked at Sabrina and grinned a happy, lecherous grin. "I am *français*, I understand zeez things. You weesh to bring your bride, zat is very *français* thing to do."

"I'm not *his* bride!" Sabrina declared.

The captain's eyebrows arched. He lowered his

head thoughtfully and scratched behind his ear. "You bring someone else's bride?" He looked at Michael carefully. "You *must* be *français!*"

Michael shook his head. "Sorry, chum, not a bit of it. British to the core." Now that they were out at sea, Michael untied Sabrina's wrists. The captain's eyebrows went up even further; he hadn't noticed that her wrists were bound, having been standing in front of her.

The instant she was free, Sabrina slapped Michael stingingly. She glared at him with fiery eyes, and breathing angrily through flared nostrils. Michael didn't respond, except to return her stare. "Well, if you'll show me to my cabin now, *kidnapper*," she said scornfully, "I'd like to be alone."

"Our cabin," he corrected. "And you can 'like to be' whatever you damn well please. But alone is one thing you're not going to be. I'm going to stick to you like glue, Bree. Night and day. That's the plan. This is a very slow boat back to Europe, and I'm going to make you love me no matter what it takes."

He started down the deck toward the cabin he had reserved. She just watched him, her arms folded across her chest, her nose high in the air. She'd be damned if she'd follow him like some docile lamb. After a moment, though, she noticed the happy, hungry, leering eyes of the crew members staring her up and down. She became nervous and frightened. She turned and rushed after the Englishman.

In the following days, Sabrina found that she was a captive, but in a very strange way. She was not bound by ropes or chains, or confined behind iron bars. Instead, she was held captive by the intensity of Michael's love for her.

It surrounded her. It suffused her. It was relentless and touched her in every part of her body and soul. She could see it in the loving way he gazed at her, and feel it in the tenderness of his touch. She could hear it in his voice each time he spoke her name.

Whenever the ship stopped at a trading port on its way across the Mediterranean, he returned from shore with small gifts for her: flowers from Palermo, carved figurines from Naples, nougat bonbons from Barcelona. He took her out on deck at night, and stood gazing with her at the star-speckled black sky and the moonlit sea, his arms clasped lovingly around her from behind.

Though he was tender with her, he was not at all shy about using gentle force if she resisted him. At first she had tried to resist his physical advances. She was still angry with him over the way he had high-handedly taken her fate into his own hands. Resisting him physically was useless, though, since he was too strong for her. So she then made up her mind to resist him in the only other way possible: she would refuse to let her body respond to his caresses; she would fight down the sensations, and act physically cold toward him.

But as the days wore on, she realized she could not do this. There was so much tenderness and affection in the way he took her, she found herself becoming strongly emotional—and responding to him.

He made love to her like no one ever had before. He began by kissing her—everywhere. His lips traveled over her mouth and cheeks and eyelids . . .

her forehead and ears . . . down to her throat, across her breasts. He kissed her arms, her wrists, her thighs, her rounded belly. When he began touching her with his hands, he did not stop until minutes turned into hours, and every inch of her skin was aflame with wild rapture. And when he came into her, he quenched the burning fires he had lighted, satisfying her totally.

After their lovemaking, he cradled her in his arms and rocked her gently. He would kiss her shoulders or her fingertips. And he would say to her in a soft voice, "Bree, I love you more than I ever thought I could love anyone. I love you so much I'm burning up inside. You're everything to me, pet. And I'll never let you go."

Sabrina found herself returning his caresses, and the wall she had planned to put up around her emotions crumbled under the intensity of his affection. Her feelings toward him changed completely. The reason she had chosen Hunter over Michael was her feeling that the Englishman lacked strength and hardness; that he was too sensitive. He was still sensitive, there was no doubt of that. But the bold, audacious way he had kidnapped her showed a side of him she had never seen before. How could she doubt his strength and hardness? He had shown himself to be a man who ruthlessly took what he wanted, and refused to give it up.

By the time they reached the port of Marseilles, Sabrina was more in love with him than she had ever been. And if she had to make her choice between him and Hunter all over again, she doubted it would be Hunter that she'd choose. But one thing was certain: she could not go back on her promise to marry Hunter. That would not be honorable at all.

Michael insisted this was ridiculous. "What rot, Bree!" he exclaimed, slamming the door of their hotel room, which he had taken the day of their arrival. "You deserve better than that man. The bloke isn't *nearly* good enough for you. Honor's got nothing to do with it!"

"Michael," she protested, "I told him I'd marry him. I accepted his proposal. That's not something a girl like me takes frivolously."

"You don't know what he's like," he said, shaking his head. "You're blinded by his charisma. I'll say this for the man, he knows how to turn the ladies' heads, that's quite clear enough."

"You're not being fair, Michael. You just don't want me to—"

"No, no," he said, waving off her protests. "I know what he's like, I've got a sixth sense for his sort. And I'll tell you this. I'll find a way to prove it to you. Then you won't feel any silly notions about being honorable to him. Once you see how honorable he is to you."

She turned away from him, folding her arms across her chest. "I won't listen to you maligning his character. You're only doing it for your own selfish ends."

He came to her and turned her toward him. He took her hands in his and looked at her with a completely sincere expression. "Now listen, pet," he said earnestly. "I know I've carried on as though I despise the bloke. But I'll level with you now. The truth is, I think he's really not a bad sort at all.

"I don't think he'd do anything to hurt you, not on purpose. But the thing is, Bree—and you've got to understand this—he's not the sort that's made for settling down with a woman. Men can tell this about other men. It's just something that's clear as the day. Oh, he loves you, sure, and he wouldn't want to hurt you. But in the end he would. You see? He couldn't help it, it's the kind of man he is. The philandering kind, the adventure-seeking kind."

"I don't believe you," she said firmly, raising her chin. "You're saying this just to sway me in your favor."

Michael threw up his hands in frustration. The next evening he disappeared from the hotel, and when she asked him where he'd gone, all he said was "out searching." He was absent the next night too, and again offered the cryptic reply in answer to her question. The third evening he returned only an hour after he'd left, and told her to hurry and get dressed.

"Why?" she asked. "Where are we going?"

"Out," he said. "For a night on the town."

She put on the off-the-shoulder evening gown of crimson satin that he'd bought for her in Barcelona. It was inset with silver bands of guipure lace. There was no time to do anything with her hair other than brush it out, since Michael kept rushing her. He gave no reason for his impatience.

He himself dressed in his officer's uniform, for the first time since leaving Cairo. He had avoided wearing it in France for fear of being picked up by British authorities. When he had left the British base in Cairo to kidnap Sabrina, he had not bothered to ask anyone's permission first. He planned to report back to his unit of his own free will, to face

AWOL charges—but not until he had solved what he referred to as the "Hunter problem."

Michael hailed a cab and gave an address on the Rue St-Charles. When they arrived, Sabrina saw that their destination was an allied officer's club. It was raucous and crowded inside. Uniformed bodies jostled them as they walked through the bar toward the dining room. The atmosphere was good-natured if desperate. Many of these men were on temporary leave from the front and did not expect to come out of the war alive.

As they passed beyond the bar, Sabrina noticed a Frenchman wearing a black beret and black turtleneck sweater who stared at her disbelievingly. The intensity of his look was enough to make her glance down at her dress to make sure her buttons were all properly fastened. When she looked up again, the man was rushing off through the crowd toward the telephones. Strange man, Sabrina thought.

When they entered the dining room, the maître d' tried to seat them at a table near the front. Michael waved him away, though, and continued forward, making a beeline toward a table he had picked out in a different part of the dining room. Sabrina thought his behavior was strange. Since this was a dinner club rather than a cabaret, no table was any better or worse.

Once they were seated at their table, though, facing the main part of the dining room, Sabrina understood why he had insisted on this particular location.

Seated across the crowded room, directly in her line of vision, she saw what Michael had obviously brought her here to see. Dallas Hunter sat in a booth against the wall. At his side, in the booth, was a beautiful young chestnut-haired girl who had very French features: small, upturned nose, round face, pouting lips. Hunter was leaning close to her, flashing his suave seductive grin as he spoke to her. His arm was around the girl's shoulders at the back of their seat.

The girl sipped some wine from her glass, and then smiled coquettishly at a remark Hunter had just made, wrinkling her nose in a flirtatious way. As Sabrina watched, Hunter moved his face closer to the girl's, and kissed her on the lips. Her hand went to the back of his head and began playing with his hair.

Sabrina turned to Michael, aghast. He returned her look, his expression hard and unemotional. The sternness of his look and his tight-lipped refusal to make any comment underscored the fact that none was necessary.

Sabrina looked back at Hunter. He was gazing intently at the girl now, pouring on the full force of his rugged, masculine charm. He was out for the kill, closing in on his prey. Sabrina knew the look. God, did she know it! The girl stared back at him, enthralled. Her eyes showed her longing.

When Hunter finally glanced to the side, he saw Sabrina glaring at him across the room, pain in her eyes. He blinked in startlement. Then he became aware of Michael at her side, and Hunter's expression made it clear he understood exactly what had happened.

He stood up from the booth and started forward. The French girl looked at him bewilderedly and began to rise. He put his hand to her shoulder, none too gently, and motioned her to stay seated. Then he strode across to Sabrina and Michael. He stopped in front of their table and stood staring down at Sabrina, saying nothing. He looked apologetic—but also defiant. I'm sorry you had to see this and be hurt by it, his expression seemed to say; but you'd best get used to it.

Sabrina held his stare. She tried to make her green eyes show nothing but scorn and anger, but she knew they were showing her agony too. She could not keep the hurt to herself. It welled up inside her and made her eyes mist as she looked at him. "How could you?" she said, her voice choking. "Here you are with . . . that one (she could not even bring herself to say 'that girl'), as if I never existed."

Now she noticed the pain that was hidden in Hunter's eyes, and she knew it was hurting him to have her see him like this. Still there was another emotion in his eyes too, and this, relieved her: it was one of relief. He seemed to actually be relieved she had seen him in this situation; contented that the marriage would no longer take place.

Sabrina stood up and slapped him hard across the face. She hadn't intended to do it. It just happened, her pain was so great. "I hate you!" she cried in a girlish voice, tears now welling up in her eyes, streaming down her cheeks. "I never want to see you again! Stay out of my life!" Then she said something she had not wanted to say. A sob broke from her throat, and she moaned in agony: "Oh Dallas, how *could* you?" She turned and ran from the room, the diners' startled eyes all following her.

She rushed through the bar, then out the doorway into the chilly, fog-filled night. She leaned against the cold brick wall, sobbing. Michael had not followed her yet. He was talking to Hunter, or fighting with him. Sabrina did not care which. He would come out soon enough. They would go back to the hotel, then sometime tomorrow or the next day they would be married. It was what she wanted. She loved him and wanted to marry him, and now there was nothing standing in the way any longer.

Her body shuddered violently as she cried. She turned to face the brick wall, to hide her eyes, when someone came up to her and put a hand on her shoulder. She looked around.

It was the Frenchman in the black beret and turtleneck sweater from the bar. Next to him were two French soldiers. "Sabrina St. Claire?" he asked her in a businesslike voice.

"Y—Yes?"

"Alias Princess Breena?"

She wiped the tears from her eyes and looked at him apprehensively. "Who are you?"

He took a leather billfold from his pocket and snapped it open, holding an identification badge out to her. "Inspector Moreau. Counterintelligence. You weel come weeth us, Mademoiselle St. Claire."

She looked at him, baffled, dumbfounded. She started to back away, but he grabbed her. "You're under arrest," he said. "Ze charge eez espionage and high treason." He turned to the soldiers: "Take her away."

Chapter 22

They took her to French Intelligence Headquarters, to the same building she had been in only a few months earlier when she went to ask the French to rescue Michael. The building was almost deserted now. Sabrina was taken to a small, windowless, green-walled room; the same one she'd been in the last time.

Inspector Moreau motioned her to the single chair in the room. He sat down on the table facing her, his legs dangling over the side. "Go fetch Culp," he said to his sergeant. He dismissed the second soldier, then lit a cigarette and sat smoking in silence. He kept gazing at Sabrina with a contemptuous look.

Sabrina felt horribly uncomfortable seated in the straight-backed chair, in the stuffy room, under the man's withering stare. A naked bulb dangled from the ceiling, covered by a conical tin shade. It cast a circle of brightness down on her, leaving the rest of the room in shadows. She had tried speaking during the trip to the place and had been told to shut up. Now she glanced at the pitcher of water on a side table and said, "May I have a drink?"

Inspector Moreau looked at her hatefully. "You

know how many Frenchmen died at Verdun, slaughtered by your heinie masters?"

Before she could protest, the door opened and the sergeant came back into the room, followed by the man called Culp. The latter was clearly an Englishman, with a jowly English face. He wore an unpressed white shirt, the sleeves rolled to his elbows. A dark tie hung loosely from his open shirt collar. He wore suspenders. "I say, so this is the famous German spy, Princess Breena. Or X-79, as you're known to us."

"I'm not a spy!" she protested.

"Oh, jolly good show!" he declared, turning to Inspector Moreau. "She's not a spy. Did you hear that, Moreau? Jolly good sense of humor."

"But it's true!" she exclaimed.

"Of course it is, darling. All you did was milk a few bits and pieces of vital information from allied sources, then pass them on to our dear friend Wolfy."

"But it was garbled! The information I gave him was almost all false!"

"Wonderful!" declared Culp, clapping his hands together merrily. "What a joker, eh what, Moreau?"

Sabrina's face was reddening with the frustration she felt. She made an effort to stand, and it was then that Culp's cheery face turned vicious, and he slapped her hard. She gasped in shock. "Sit down, bitch," he ordered.

She backed herself into the chair, her eyes wide. Then she heard a strange sound behind her and glanced around to see the French sergeant playing with a blackjack he had taken from his pocket, slapping it absently against the palm of his hand.

"This has gone far enough," Sabrina said, trying

to keep the fear out of her voice. "I demand to see the American ambassador. I'm an American citizen."

"You're a German spy," said Culp murderously.

"We are all professionals here," Moreau said to her, taking a let's-not-kid-ourselves tone. "You know ze espionage business eez dirty, zair are no rules of fair play. Your heinie masters have ravaged my country, killed my countrymen. Do not expect mercy, spy."

She looked at their brutal, ruthless faces, and felt a growing sense of terror. They *hate* me, she realized. And there's nothing to stop them from doing whatever they want to me!

"You don't understand!" she cried out, desperate to make them see the truth. "I did what I did only because the Germans were holding an English officer." She turned to Culp. "One of your own countrymen! They were going to kill him unless I did as they asked. But even so, I never—"

She was interrupted by Culp's smirking, cynical laugh. "That's a good one, eh Moreau? Next thing you know, she'll be telling us this 'captive' Englishman was her cohort Leftenant Yorkshire."

She was stunned. "But it was Michael Yorkshire! Then you know about him already?"

"*Oui*," said Moreau, "of zat traitor we know plenty. We know he was in Wolfschmidt's headquarters, betraying English military secrets for most of ze past half year. He too eez a spy."

"That's not true! He was being held prisoner! That's why I was forced to do as I did, because they'd have killed him if I hadn't!"

"Quite so, quite so," said Culp. "By the way," he added with false casualness, gazing down at his shoes, "where is the bugger now anyway? We'd like to have a chat with him, clear this thing up a bit, eh what?"

Sabrina looked at his overly casual expression and said nothing. So they didn't realize it was Michael who had escorted her into the officer's club, she thought. Well, she certainly wasn't going to tell them so. Not with them thinking he was some sort of spy! In fact, she had to get out of here so she could warn him. Otherwise he'd report back to his unit tomorrow, now that the situation with Dallas had been solved. He had no idea what was waiting for him.

"She knows," Moreau said to Culp snidely. "I think she knows where ze English traitor eez. We beat it out of her, *oui?*"

"My God," said Sabrina in a terrified low voice, realizing they really *could* do anything they wanted to her. Now for the first time she began to feel stark terror, knowing she might not get out of the room alive.

"Listen," she said to them desperately, "I can prove I'm not what you think, and Michael isn't either. I came here once before, right here to this headquarters, to—"

"Stow it, X-79," said Culp sharply. "You're not going to talk your way out of this." He reached into the folder he had brought with him and withdrew a sheaf of yellow legal-size pages. He held it out to her. "Your cover's been blown," he said. "Wolfy outsmarted himself this time. Sent his instructions to you and Yorkshire in a code we'd broken."

Wolfschmidt! Sabrina thought. He was behind this!

"Don't you see?" she pleaded, "he did it deliberately! To get even with us for escaping! It's a frame-up!"

Moreau took a drag on his cigarette and exhaled the smoke through his nose, looking impatient. Culp folded his arms across his chest, his face closed. Sabrina glanced at the newsprint she had been handed. The first page held a jumble of nonsensical, seemingly random, large block letters. She turned to the second sheet and read the handwritten notation at the top: DECODED MESSAGE. REFERENCE QE-311, CRYPTOGRAPH. The message below it was typed in blue ink on the yellow paper:

"Instructions for X-79 and T-17. X-79 to seduce the visiting English Minister of the Admiralty. Ascertain info re Gallipoli campaign. T-17 to transmit data. Explain absence during past months as being due to captivity in our HQ against will."

There was more. The message contained information that clearly pointed the finger at Michael and Sabrina as being the two agents in question. Wolfschmidt had arranged this perfectly. The decoded message was like a noose tightening around their necks.

Culp ripped the sheaf of papers from her hands. "All right," he said, his expression ruthless, "let's get on with it. You know why we brought you here."

Sabrina looked frightened. "Why?" she breathed.

He bent over her, his angry, rough face very close to hers. "We want information. To start with: where's Yorkshire?"

The sound of the sergeant slapping the blackjack

sharply into his palm made Sabrina jerk in her seat. She glanced from face to face, her eyes wide with fear. The cone of light emitted from the single bulb dangling from the ceiling chiseled the men's faces into sharp shadows. There was absolute silence except for the sound of heavy breathing and the slapping of the blackjack. The air was muggy and hot, and now thick with cigarette smoke.

"Where is he?" demanded Culp, grasping her hair and pulling her head forward.

"I can prove I'm not a spy," she cried. "And Michael isn't either! An American major knows the truth! He rescued us from—"

Culp slapped her stingingly, leaving her cheek flushed with red. "Stow it! Forget your cover-story lies! Where's Yorkshire?"

"They're not lies!" she persisted, tears welling in her eyes from the sharp slap. "He rescued us from Wolfschmidt's island base. He can prove that we escaped and—"

Culp jerked her to her feet and flung her at Moreau, who caught her. "Maybe you feel too comfortable, yes? Zair are ways to make you less comfortable, so you do not resist so much." He bent down, grabbed the hem of her scarlet gown, and jerked it up to her waist.

"Please!" pleaded Sabrina, fighting him. "Listen to me!"

The sergeant came over and aided Moreau, pulling Sabrina's skirt all the way up to her breasts, then over her head and upraised arms. At that point she could not see; the dress was covering her face. She felt horribly exposed, knowing all the eyes in the room were staring at her practically naked body. But she had to go on. There was no hope

305

except to continue trying to convince them, no matter how violently they tried to stop her. "Dallas Hunter is the American's name," she declared. "He can vouch for what I'm saying!"

"Zat proves nothing," said Moreau. She felt him rip away her slip, and suddenly she was naked except for her underpants. His rough hands pinched her breasts. "Zis 'escape' you speak of could have been arranged as a deception, so zat we believe you are not a spy." He squeezed her breasts suddenly, making her scream. She still could not see, due to the bunched-up dress. "Now where eez ze traitor Yorkshire?"

"Please," she cried, "you have to believe me. I can prove it, I tell you. I came here before, right here to your headquarters, to tell you that I'd been forced to work with Wolfschmidt, and to offer to spy for you as a double agent."

Someone's hand pressed into her underpants and grasped her between the legs. She cried out and arched her back, struggling fiercely to escape the clutching hand. Still she forced herself to go on: "The man I talked to, here in your headquarters, he was—uhhh, stop that!—he was a German agent! He—"

"Where eez Yorkshire!" shouted Moreau, jamming his hand inside her underpants from behind, so that now there were two hands down beneath her waist, front and back, linking up and pressing into her.

"*Uhh . . . uhh . . . uhh!*" she moaned, as the hands began bouncing her up and down.

Then when she was about to give up all hope, she heard Culp's English voice say in a quiet tone, "Stop it, Moreau."

306

"What! *Pourquoi?*"

"Let go of her."

The hands stopped pressing her. They withdrew from her underpants. The hands that were holding her arms above her head released her. Sabrina was breathing in sobbing gasps now, pierced with fear and humiliation. She stumbled backward, trying to remain steady while pulling her dress back into place. Someone jerked the dress over her head and arms again, though, pulling it away. She could see again. She was trembling, her eyes were wide and frantic, her hair falling down into her face. She cupped her naked breasts in her hands.

"Look at me," said Culp. When she turned to face him, he said, "You say one of the men here at Counterintelligence is a spy?"

She nodded. She could hardly speak. She kept stealing fearful, nervous glances at Moreau and the sergeant.

"Tell me about him," said Culp.

"He—he was the one who told me to go to Wolfschmidt's headquarters. I came here offering to spy for the French, if they'd rescue Michael. And he said yes, they'd rescue him, if I—"

"Thees eez absurd!" declared Moreau disgustedly. "She's lying. Let me continue."

Culp held out a steady hand, motioning him to stay back. His eyes were on Sabrina, intense and probing. "What did he look like, this German spy in French headquarters?"

"He had a thin mustache. That's what I remember most. And . . . and his tobacco! It had this strange, pine-scented fragrance."

"Giscard," said Culp, naming the man. He looked at Moreau with a pointed glance that said: there's more here than meets the eye. Even Moreau was gazing at Sabrina with a look of alert interest now.

"Did anyone else see you ze day you say you came here?" Moreau asked. "To verify your story?"

Sabrina racked her brain trying to remember. The tortures her two interrogators and the sergeant had put her though to make her weakened and confused had worked. She could barely think straight. And standing here almost naked didn't help. Think, she ordered herself, squinting her eyes in concentration, desperately trying to bring forth the memory of that day.

"She's lying," sneered Moreau. "See how she cannot answer even a simple question."

"I can!" she exclaimed. "There was . . . there was . . ." She fought to drag the memory up into her mind. "I remember!" she declared exultantly. "There was someone else, yes! I saw him when I first entered the building. I told him I wanted to spy for the French, and asked him where I should go, whom I should talk to. He looked astounded and said for me to wait against the wall, in the lobby. Yes, I remember! And then, when he left, this Giscard came up to me."

"What was his name?" asked Culp. "The one you talked to."

"I don't know!"

"What did the bloke look like? Describe him to me."

She thought hard for a minute, frowning in concentration. Then she cried out in anguish, "I can't!" She knew how false this all must seem. But there was no way she could recall the image of the man. She had seen him for only a second, and her mind now was so cloudy and frightened and confused.

She began to cry. She couldn't help it. The torture they had put her through had left her in a traumatized state. And now they were probably going to begin abusing her again.

Instead of ordering the other two to return to their assault, though, Culp said to Moreau, "Put her in the detention room. I want to look into this." He turned to Sabrina with a sharp, warning look in his eyes. The look promised that if this interruption proved to be for a false reason, she would pay for it dearly.

The sergeant started Sabrina toward the door. When she reached for her dress, which was on the floor, he pushed her forward, preventing her from grabbing it. Then he marched her half naked through the corridors, to a detention room. He let her in, then shut and locked the door from outside.

She sat on the bed, hugging herself, huddled against the corner, her legs folded under her. She was cold, but there were no blankets or sheets on the lumpy mattress. She tried to relax, to ease some of the frightful tension surging through her body. It was impossible. She remained that way until morning, when the sergeant came back into the room.

She tried to huddle still further into the corner as he came up to her. "Keep still," he ordered. He had a white neck-scarf in his hand. He put it over her eyes and tied it behind her head, blindfolding her. "Keep ze head raised," he said when she lowered her chin and turned her head to the side. His hand roughly returned her head.

A moment later, Sabrina heard footsteps passing the door, which the sergeant had left open. She heard muttered words spoken in French. Many people were being moved past her doorway, she knew; they stopped long enough to look in at her, then moved on. She pressed her hands more tightly over her breasts, wishing she had something to cover herself with.

Finally, one man said something in French, in a voice that sounded excited. She heard Moreau's voice answer him. The man said something else.

From the way the sergeant's hands went to remove her blindfold, Sabrina guessed what was taking place: the headquarters staff had been parading past her, to see if anyone recognized her and could verify her story. She was kept blindfolded because they still believed her to be a German spy. The man who had just spoken so excitedly probably thought he did recognize her, but needed to see her entire face, without the blindfold, to be sure.

The blindfold was removed. Sabrina's eyes lit up at the sight she beheld. "It's him, it's him!" she declared. "He's the one from the lobby!" She remembered him clearly, now that she could see him again.

"Quiet," said Culp, who was standing at the side of the doorway, next to Moreau. He was staring expectantly at the stoop-shouldered, timid-looking man who stood in the doorway, gazing at Sabrina. The man's eyes—unlike Sabrina's—did not light up with instant recognition. Sabrina's heart pounded with anticipation as she watched him observe her. Please God, she prayed, let him remember. *Let him remember!*

The man's expression remained blank, though. His eyes were not even on Sabrina's face, but were wandering down over her breasts.

"Cover her up, you blithering idiot!" Culp shouted to the sergeant. The sergeant looked around the room in panic. He found nothing, so he took off his own jacket and put it over Sabrina's upper body. Culp continued staring at the timid-looking man. After a moment of silence, he said to him, "Well? Do you recognize her?"

Very slowly, the man nodded. "*Oui*," he said.

Sabrina's face showed the flood of relief and gratitude that overwhelmed her.

"You're certain?" said Culp.

"Most certain," responded the man. "Ze mademoiselle, she came into ze lobby zat day, and she wanders around like a lost lamb. When I ask what she wants, she says she has been forced to work for ze Boche, and now she wishes to spy for France. I tell her to wait right zair; I say do not go away. But she was gone when I came back weeth my superior."

From that moment on, Sabrina's situation changed drastically—for the better.

She was taken to a large room on the next floor up, where she was allowed to shower and then dress in her crimson gown. A hot meal of scrambled eggs and grilled kipper was served to her, with steaming coffee and a decanter of potent red wine. Through the window she could see the early morning sun sending rays of sunlight out from the pink horizon.

Culp and Moreau came into the room and sat down across from her at the table. Culp looked apolgetic, but only slightly so. Moreau did not look apolgetic at all. "Sorry for the way we treated you," Culp said. "But it's a dirty business. The evidence against you was quite strong. It was only your mentioning about Giscard being a spy that made me think you might be on the level."

311

"You see," said Moreau, "we ourselves discovered zat he was a spy, only last week. Heez code name was 'Deep Mole.'"

"What did you do to him?" Sabrina asked.

Culp shrugged. "He was cleaning his rifle when the bloomin' thing went off. Shot himself right in the back—accidentally, of course," he added sarcastically.

"But enough of Herr Deep Mole," said Moreau impatiently. "Now we speak of you. Since you were duped and were not a willing spy, we weel not harm you. But before you leave, please to tell us thees: do you know ze whereabouts of zeez spy Michael Yorkshire?"

"He's not a spy I tell you! He was captured by the Germans while helping me escape from a group of them that were chasing me. He was a prisoner!"

"No," said Culp, shaking his head. "He's a spy all right. We're sure of it."

"But I know him," Sabrina pleaded. "Why won't you believe me? I know him well, and the last thing in the world he'd do is work for the Germans. He detests them!"

Moreau snorted cynically. "Tell me thees," he said. "Do you love thees man?"

"What business is that of yours?" she said defensively.

"You see?" he said, spreading his palms in a very French gesture. "You cannot be ze judge of thees. You are a young girl blinded by love."

Sabrina felt like crying out in frustration. How narrow-minded these men were! They had been wrong in accusing her of being a willing spy. But did that make them pause to doubt themselves?

312

Not in the least! Here they were again, just as certain that Michael was a spy—and just as wrong.

"No, no," said Moreau, raising a finger to make a point, "we have evidence against heem. Ze coded message, for instance."

"But you know now that that was false!"

"Eet was not false, mademoiselle. Though you were working for ze Germans under duress, and giving them false information, zay steel were giving you instructions. Thees message clearly contains instructions to you and Yorkshire."

"Oh, you're so *wrong!*"

"There's other evidence, too," Culp said. "Certain secret information Yorkshire had access to has fallen into the hands of Wolfy and his bunch."

"But . . . but couldn't this man Giscard be responsible for that?"

Moreau raised an eyebrow. "Very unlikely. Possible, *oui* . . . but very unlikely."

"But—"

"Besides," said Culp, "if he was innocent, why did he desert from Colonel Lawrence's command in Cairo, just as orders were being issued to arrest him for questioning?"

Sabrina winced in anguish. She didn't want to have to tell them about how Michael had gone AWOL from the military hospital in order to kidnap her and make her love him more. But she had to tell them. His life was at stake. Feeling very awkward and embarrassed, she related the story to them, keeping her eyes lowered as she did so.

When she finished, Moreau laughed openly. Sabrina glared at him. God, she hated this man!

"Very romantic," Moreau laughed cynically. "*Très charmant*. But does eet not seem ze least bit coincidental zat he decides to woo and win you at ze precise moment he eez about to be arrested? No, no, ze evidence against heem eez too strong. I must insist zat you tell me his whereabouts eef you know it."

"Isn't there any way I can convince you he's not a spy?" Sabrina cried out in frustration.

"Impossible," said Culp, brushing a hand back through his hair. "The only way to show for sure if a man's a spy or not is to get the roster of active agents from Wolfy himself . . . to jolly well steal it right out of his safe. And since that's obviously out of the question—"

"Out of a black, steel safe?" Sabrina interrupted.

Culp stopped short and stared at her. Moreau stared too. "How do you know about that?" Culp said suspiciously.

"I was in his office three times, and each time I saw that safe—open and unlocked."

"We know about his keeping it unlocked," said Culp. "He does it whenever he's in the office, figuring there's no danger of anyone messing with the safe while he's right there." He looked at Sabrina sternly, probingly. "Are you suggesting what I think you're suggesting?"

She swallowed hard. She felt she must be crazy for what she was offering to do. But there seemed no other way to save Michael. "I could get back to see Wolfschmidt," she said, "by saying I want to spy for him again. I can lie that I heard Hunter was shot down over German territory and captured . . . and I'll offer to spy for Wolfschmidt again if he promises not to kill him. I'll be able to get into his headquarters that way. Once I'm there

I might find some way to steal the roster of agents you mentioned."

Moreau and Culp exchanged interested glances. "You wouldn't actually have to steal it," said Culp. "Moreau's Q-Section can outfit you with a special miniature camera hidden in a hair clip. All you'd have to do is photograph the roster."

"*Oui*," said Moreau, becoming excited at the idea. To get the enemy's list of active agents would be a major coup. "Zair eez also a contact drug we can give you, on ze tip of a needle. You can put Herr Wolfy to sleep instantly—eef you can get near him with it. When he awakens, he weel think he just fainted for only a second or two, eef at all."

"There's a lot we can do to help you," said Culp. "We can make sure Wolfy never finds out we arrested you last night. We can arrange to meet you at the border after you cross back into France from Germany."

"Germany?" said Sabrina. "I thought Wolfschmidt was on an island off North Africa?"

"He moved his headquarters back to Germany," said Culp. "His North African base was destroyed by aerial bombardment. We know the route across no-man's-land the Germans use to cross into France and back. We can arrange to meet you on the French side after you photograph the roster." He paused and looked at her seriously. "We'll do everything we can to help you. But the question is: do you really intend to try this? You know your chances of success are awfully slim."

"If I do it," Sabrina said, "will you believe Michael is innocent?"

"If you somehow manage to bring this off and get us that roster . . . and if Yorkshire's name isn't on it . . . then there's no question about it. We'll know he's not one of them."

No one said anything for a long moment. The men stared at her intently. Moreau especially had a greedy look in his eyes. He wanted with all his heart to get his hands on that roster. "Well?" he said finally. "Will you do thees thing?"

Sabrina lowered her eyes. She remembered all the agonies and humiliations she had endured at the hands of General Wolfschmidt. She thought she was through with him for good. But now, here she was considering going back, walking right into his clutches all over again.

But what else could she do? She knew something Moreau and Culp didn't: Michael was probably in their hands at this very moment, even though they didn't realize it. He had probably reported back to his unit the first thing this morning. At this very instant he was most likely in the brig, awaiting transport to Intelligence Headquarters. If she didn't do this to save him, she knew what the outcome would be. He would "accidentally" shoot himself while cleaning a rifle. Neither Culp nor Moreau would feel any obligation to give a fair trial to a man they considered to be a ruthless enemy agent.

"If I do this," Sabrina said cautiously, "you'll have to promise to leave Michael alone while I'm getting you that roster. Don't arrest him. Don't hurt him. Don't do anything to him. And you mustn't tell him about my doing this."

"That's fine," Culp said. "We'll agree to that."

Moreau nodded. "But of course, mademoiselle, zair eez something you must realize. Eef you fail to get ze roster and prove heem innocent, we will proceed with our original plans. With what we call ze 'critical elimination.'"

"Meaning you'll *kill* him," Sabrina accused sharply, her eyes flashing.

"That's right," said Culp combatively, fixing her stare. "You think this is some kind of game we're playing here? We'll kill him. That's what we do to enemy spies during wartime."

Chapter 23

Getting to Wolfschmidt's headquarters would not be as easy as she hoped, Sabrina soon realized. In fact, it began to look as though she might not be able to do it at all.

As soon as the French released her she went to the waterfront cafe that had always been her rendezvous for meeting her contact, Gunther. She waited in the cafe all afternoon and into the evening, not knowing if he would show up. When finally he did arrive, he looked astounded to see her. He obviously thought the French had made short work of her, and never expected to see her again.

"What are you doing here?" he demanded in a low, urgent voice as he sat down at her patio table. His eyes darted from side to side in paranoid nervousness.

"I want to see Wolfschmidt," Sabrina said.

"Out of der question!" His eyes darted around some more before coming to rest on her. "Why aren't you in ja—" He cut himself off, looking as if he had almost betrayed a secret. "Hafn't you had trouble mit der . . . authorities?" he asked instead.

"I only just returned to the country," she said. She leaned over the table slightly to get closer to him. "I *have* to see Wolfschmidt," she said. "I know he has Major Hunter. I know he captured him after he was shot down over German territory. I want to make a deal. If he doesn't harm him, if he spares his life, I'll spy for him again."

Gunther squinted his eyes in a cunning look. "Dot is right," he lied. "Ve haf Major Hunter. But you think Herr General vill vant to see you again? After you tried to betray us to der French last time? Impossible!"

"I won't do anything like that again," she pleaded. "Please, talk to him. Ask him. I have to see him!"

He stared at her probingly for a moment, thinking. Then he said, "Meet me at der statue in der park, at midnight tonight." He stood up quickly and left.

Sabrina waited until he was out of sight, then she too left the cafe. She hurried back to the hotel room she and Michael had been living in since their return to France. Michael wasn't there. She paced the room nervously, wondering if he would come. Had he been imprisoned when he reported back to his unit, as she suspected? And if so, had the French let him go, as they had agreed to do? Or did they intend to hold him after all and execute him as a spy?

Several hours later, a key turned in the lock. Sabrina jerked the door ajar before it could be opened from the outside. Michael stood there in his uniform, looking at her with a reserved, somewhat distant expression. "Michael!" she exclaimed, flinging her arms about him. "You had me so worried!"

He hesitated a moment before putting his arms around her waist and hugging her. They came into the room. He shut the door and looked at her with

319

a shade too much seriousness. "Bree, are you all right?" he asked.

"Me? Yes. It's you I was worried about. When you didn't show up all evening, I thought—"

"Where were you last night?" he said suddenly.

The question caught her by surprise. She hadn't expected it, and now she didn't know how to respond. She couldn't tell him the truth, that was for sure. One thing that was crucial, Sabrina knew, was that Michael not find out about her plan to go back to Wolfschmidt's headquarters, to get the roster that would save his life. If he found out, he would forbid her from doing it.

"I was . . . I was upset after seeing Dallas with that girl," Sabrina said, lowering her eyes. "I wandered around for most of the night."

She thought she detected a suspiciousness in the way he looked at her. But then his glance softened, and he said "Poor pet. My poor darling Bree." He hugged her in his arms and rocked softly from side to side, his hand gently on the back of her hair, holding her head against his chest. "It was a horrible trauma for you, wasn't it? I'm sorry. I'd never have taken you to see it, pet, but . . . truly, it was something you had to see."

"I know," she said, feeling sorrow and pain even now, at the remembrance of it.

"I wish I could have consoled you, given a bit of a shoulder to cry on. But when I came outside, you were gone. And the doorman said something about how you'd left with a very handsome bloke in a black beret."

She pulled her head back and looked at him with wide eyes. "You thought I was . . . spending time with another man, Michael?"

"Oh, I know, you'd never do anything like that," he said defensively. "You don't think I believed it for even a minute? It's just that, well the way you didn't call me or didn't come back to the room . . ." He shook his head. "I should have known you'd be in a tizzy. After what that bastard did to you."

"Oh, Michael," she said, "he's not a bastard. Not really. He's just not the kind that's made for marriage. You said so yourself." She looked a bit wistful and regretful now, as she sighed, "I just wish I hadn't slapped him like that, and said I hated him and never wanted to see him again."

"You're too understanding," Michael said with an edge of bitterness. "When you're in love with someone, and you catch him in a situation like that— well, the situation speaks for itself. Only a bloody fool would stay in a relationship after seeing something like that. I certainly wouldn't if I ever caught you with another ma—" He bit off his words and frowned in anguish.

"Michael!" she breathed, shocked that he could even think such a thing about her.

He turned away and slapped his palm hard against his forehead. "Damn!" he cursed, angry at himself. He turned back to her and took her hands. "Forgive me, pet. It's just—it's been one hell of a day. You know where I was? You know why I wasn't here all day? I was in the blooming brig, that's why! Listening to the crazy stories of the blokes in the lock-up, about how there was some famous dancer with a name that sounded something like yours, and how she was the most promiscuous whore in France." He frowned in agony. "God, why do I even repeat trash like that!"

She cast her eyes down, unable to look at him.

321

He raised her head and gazed at her with deep affection. "It's because I love you so much, pet. And I can't bear to think that you'd ever love anyone but me."

"I'd never be unfaithful to you, Michael," she said softly. "All my love, it's all for you now. And only you."

"I'm crazy about you, you know that?" He picked her up in his arms and carried her into the bedroom.

"Why were you in jail?" she asked as he put her down on the bed. She tried to make her voice indicate surprise.

"Some crazy thing. I don't know. They even said they were going to turn me over to the French for some damn fool reason. They came to their senses and let me go, though, the buggers. I still don't know why."

He had been undressing her as he talked, and now she lay before him naked. "One thing though, pet," he said as he took off his clothes. "I'm back on active duty now. Tomorrow morning I process in, then in the afternoon I ship out to an artillery brigade near the Somme."

"Oh, Michael," she said in an emotion-filled voice, sitting up on her knees in bed and putting her arms around him. She buried her face against his hard, hairless chest. The thought of him going off to fight in this bloodbath of a war filled her with sorrow and dread.

"I'll come back to you, pet. I promise I will." He raised her head and looked at her with such loving affection it made Sabrina feel as if she were melting inside. He kissed her gently, but the gentleness soon turned into passion as their bodies became inflamed with the intensity of their love for each other.

When he lowered himself on her and entered her, Sabrina gasped at the sensation. Their lovemaking became violent and desperate, and she felt she would burst from the sweetness of the rapture.

As he drove deep into her, her eyes filled with tears, and she thought: God, how I love him! She ran her fingers through his hair, feeling the searing waves of wicked pleasure flashing through her, thinking: I won't let him go. I won't let them take him away from me. I'll succeed, I'll get that roster from Wolfschmidt, no matter what it takes! And we'll be together then, we'll be together always.

The tingling fire in her loins exploded into a meteor of pleasure, overwhelming her, sending streaks of wild ecstasy shooting through her body and soul and mind. She cried out and clasped her legs tightly around his hips, her arms around his muscular back. She clutched herself to him, wanting to never let go, to never have it end . . .

An hour later, when Michael finally fell asleep, Sabrina dressed quickly, left very quietly, and hurried over to the park. It was freezing cold out, and nearly pitch-dark. Gunther was there, in his gray trench coat.

"Herr General refuses to see you," he said. He raised a hand against her objections, and said, "He does not trust you. There is a vay you can prove yourself, however." He handed her an instruction envelope and a bundle of clothing. "Complete this mission successfully, und you vill show you can be trusted. Then you vill be transported to Berlin, to speak to him about safety for your captured friend."

He refused to listen to Sabrina's protests. He pivoted on his heel and rushed away into the night. When Sabrina returned to the dark, warm bedroom, Michael was raised up on his elbows looking at her. "I . . . went for a walk," she said guiltily. "To get some air."

He didn't answer. He motioned her over with a nod of his head, and took her onto the bed with him. He held her against him as they lay on their sides. She could feel the warmth of his naked body. She thought there had been suspicion in his gaze, but there was no sign of it now. He held her against him. She could feel his heartbeat against her breast and his breath on the side of her face. "I love you," he said, his voice filled with emotion.

When she awakened in the morning, Michael was already gone. A scrawled note lay on the bureau top: *I'll write care of General Delivery, pet. The instant I can get leave, I'll be back and we'll be married. Love always. Michael.*

Sabrina looked at the note for a long time, and then did something that surprised her. She touched it to her lips and kissed it. After she put it in her purse, she fished out the instruction envelope Gunther had given her the night before. She slit it open along the fold, pulled out the piece of flimsy white paper, and while standing up, read it.

ASSIGNMENT: K. C. (Casey) Donnelly; multi-millionaire American industrialist and major armaments manufacturer.

MISSION: Learn arrival date of next shipment of arms to the Western Front.

MEANS OF APPROACH: Herr Donnelly has reputation of being attracted to beautiful women who dress vulgarly.

LOCATION: Arrives central railway station noon today, track eleven.

The instructions went on to describe what the American industrialist looked like. Sabrina put the missive down and went to the bundle of clothing, which she had hidden under the sofa last night. She tore it open. She frowned as she held up each article. She flung the pieces of clothing angrily down on the sofa. She stared at them, breathing through flared nostrils, seething with anger. Then, slowly, she picked them up again and began dressing.

Casey Donnelly was a tall, apple-cheeked man, with a country-bumpkin look to him that he deliberately exaggerated. He was from Texas, and in addition to his well-tailored business suit, he wore a big, white, stetson cowboy hat, and a string tie with a bull's-head clasp. He had a shiny silver belt buckle, and wore hand-tooled leather boots with shiny spurs. He walked with a loose-limbed lankiness and spoke with a down-home cowboy drawl.

When Sabrina first saw him, she couldn't believe that anyone who looked like such a hick could actually be a multimillionaire. She was at the station when he arrived and saw him disembark from a private car with an entourage of American men who looked like government security agents. They were deadly-serious-looking and businesslike. Donnelly himself, though, was smiling, laughing, cracking jokes in his cowboy drawl.

Sabrina was dressed in the clothing she had been supplied. Her blouse was orange and quite sheer, with large gawdy ruffles running down the front and around the low-cut neckline. Beneath it she wore a black brassiere, which showed through the thin material in a vulgar way, revealing too much cleavage. Her multicolored peasant's skirt came down to her ankles, covering most of her high-heeled, laced-up black boots.

As Casey Donnelly came down the ramp toward the main concourse, Sabrina made a point of walking directly into him, while looking off to the side as if she were searching for someone. She fell down, making sure her legs rose up in the air for a brief second, showing her black hose and garters. A hot flush of shamefulness came over her at her brazen display of herself. But she had to do it. If she did not entice him now, there would be no other opportunity. A second "chance encounter" would make his security agents suspicious.

"What the *hayull*—?" said Donnelly as Sabrina bounced off his chest and fell to the concrete, on her behind. Donnelly stared at her thighs as the hem of her dress flew up in the air.

Quickly he bent over and reached out a strong hand to help pull her back to her feet. "I *do* beg yore pardon, young lady, I shorely am sorry for— But what the hayull, you can't understand me anyway."

"I'm American," she said, brushing herself off, acting embarrassed. "I understand you."

"My, you shore are one fine-looking filly, if you don't mind my sayin' so. What's your name, honeybun?"

"Mr. Donnelly," said one of the serious-faced

men in his entourage, glancing around the terminal nervously. "We'd better be going. The security risk in here is enormous."

"Oh, cool your heels a minute, Erwin, cain't ya see I'm addressin' a lady?"

The other men in the entourage crowded close around Donnelly, making a circle to protect him in the crowded station. Since Sabrina was standing very near him, she was encircled too.

"My name's Sabrina," she said. She stood on her tiptoes and looked to the left and right, pretending disappointment. "I was supposed to meet my boyfriend, Freddie, here, but I guess he decided to jilt me. It's been over an hour."

"Aw, you poor, sweet young thing," Donnelly said.

"Sir," said another of his men, "for security reasons we really better—"

"Now, Harry, cain't you see this young lady here is in distress? And she's a countryman, too." He stared at Sabrina, taking in her full figure from head to toe before looking her in the eyes and smiling at her. "You must be hungry as a colt, honeybun, it bein' close to lunchtime and all."

"Yes," Sabrina said, lowering her eyes, "I could use some food."

"Then come on along, honey, you just come on along." He put his arm around her waist and began walking her forward with him down the ramp. The security men followed, glancing suspiciously from side to side at everyone who passed.

Outside the terminal, a black limousine pulled to the curb. The driver got out and bowed respectfully to Donnelly, who winked back. Then the driver opened the trunk for the porters who would soon be arriving with the baggage.

One of the security men held open the rear passenger door for Donnelly. The Texan motioned Sabrina inside. Then, instead of entering himself, he went around to the driver's side, whistling casually. Suddenly, with a fake look of alarm, he pointed off to the side, exclaiming to his guards: "Wayull I'll be, ain't that Kaiser Bill hisself, standing there with the gun?"

When the security men swiveled abruptly, two of them pulling out guns from shoulder holsters, Donnelly jumped into the driver's seat, gunned the engine, and screeched out into the street away from the terminal.

"Wheee-ooo!" he wailed happily, pointing with his finger at the surprised, frustrated guards who were rushing after the car. "Ain't they surprised? Wayull, little lady," he said to Sabrina, "looks like we'll be alone for a spell after all. Wouldn't have been no fun atall with them govmint people cramping my style." Looking over his shoulder, he smiled a fiercely charming smile at Sabrina. Sabrina smiled back. The limousine streaked down the street, the driver's door and trunk flapping wide open.

They took several turns to avoid being followed by Donnelly's security men, then doubled back and stopped at the main restaurant near the train station. It was crowded, loud, and smoky, and they took a booth near the rear. Donnelly was delighted with their surroundings, as jubilant at having temporarily escaped his entourage as a child would be playing hooky from school. He smiled a lot and was clearly taken with Sabrina.

328

Sabrina thought it might prove easier than she had figured to get the information from him. He seemed completely guileless and naive, as if it seemed impossible to him that anyone could have an ulterior motive for acting friendly toward him. He talked freely and easily, answering many of Sabrina's questions.

She found that the more she smiled at him and allowed him liberties, such as putting his arm around her and touching her knee, the more liberal he became with his answers to her questions. If she acted in any way standoffish, such as when she made the mistake of pulling her head back to avoid a kiss, he acted hurt and sullen, and stopped talking.

Sabrina was acting like an eager young girl who was asking so many questions only because she found Donnelly "so fascinating," as she put it.

He had responded so well that Sabrina was about to spring the major question on him right there in the middle of the meal. Maybe she might actually be able to avoid having to go back to his reserved room with him, she thought hopefully. But the instant she was about to ask the key question, something went wrong.

They were sitting very close together in the rear booth, Donnelly's arm around Sabrina's shoulders, his hand on her knee. She was smiling flirtatiously at him, and he had been smiling back, seeming to her like putty in her hands. Then he turned his head away to reach for a piece of cheese, and instead of turning back, he continued looking out toward the front. Sabrina looked to see what he was watching, and gasped at the sight, jolting upright.

Standing before their booth, his hands on his

hips, a piercingly hurt look on his face, was Michael. He stared directly at her. He seemed to not want to believe what he was seeing. Then, after an electrifying moment of tense silence, he said in a voice that tried to hide his deep pain: "Maybe Hunter was the better choice for you after all. You both seem to have the same idea of faithfulness."

She was about to speak, not knowing what she could possibly say, when Donnelly stood up from the table, smiled at Michael, and held out his hand. "Say there, feller, you must be Freddie, huh, the boyfriend she was going to meet at the train station?"

Michael's expression became dumbfounded for an instant, and when he looked back at Sabrina, the pain and the anger were even more intense. This cowboy isn't bad enough, his expression said. There's a "Freddie" too?

"Michael," Sabrina said, "it's not what it seems. Please . . ." What could she *say* to him?

"Oh, it's Michael is it?" said Donnelly pleasantly, still holding his hand out. "How d'ya do, pard, happy to—"

Michael slapped the hand away viciously, his lips breaking into a snarl, the blood rushing to his face. Sabrina had never seen him so enraged. "Keep your *blasted* hand to yourself, you bloody hillbilly, or I'll kill you."

"Michael!" she exclaimed, leaping to her feet. She went to him and took his arm and looked him right in the face. He stared back expectantly, woundedly. But what could she say to him? With Donnelly standing right there, eyeing her with growing disfavor? If she asked to be excused for a moment to talk to Michael, Donnelly would clearly take it as an insult and leave.

"Please, Michael," she said to him quietly, "you have to trust me." She said even more quietly, hoping Donnelly would not hear: "If you love me . . . you'll trust me."

From the way Michael looked at her, Sabrina could see he wanted to believe in her, to trust her— he wanted to desperately.

At this moment, Donnelly moved closer to Sabrina and put his arm around her shoulders in a possessive way, his hand touching the upper swell of her bosom. His jaw jutted forward competitively. It was a challenge. He felt bitter that his friendliness had been rebuked. With a sinking feeling, Sabrina realized the challenge was not mainly to Michael—it was mainly to her. Donnelly was looking at her severely, and his ultimatum was clear: you're either with me or you're with him. If you're with me, you'd damn well better show it.

Both men stared at her. She closed her eyes tightly against the torment she felt, and lowered her head. She put her hand on the back of Donnelly's hand, which was around her shoulder. She had to do it. If she failed to get the information from Donnelly, she wouldn't be allowed to visit Wolfschmidt—and Michael would be killed as a result.

Michael said nothing, just stared at her hand on Donnelly's hand. After a moment, two young British soldiers entered the restaurant. They looked around, saw Michael, and went up to him. "Sir, the train's arrived," one of them said urgently. "If we don't leave now, we'll miss it."

Michael looked at Sabrina, his face racked with

pain. He turned and stalked out of the restaurant, followed by the two young soldiers.

Donnelly reached into his wallet, pulled out a wad of folded American bills and left a few on the checkered tablecloth of their booth. "Let's get the hayull outa here," he said.

They went back to his limousine, which by now was surrounded by a crowd of gawkers. Donnelly drove Sabrina to the Hotel Ritz, where he left the limousine with the doorman. He was besieged by his security men as he went through the lobby with Sabrina, but he waved them away angrily. "Not now, boys," he said, "just leave us alone. I want to get this damn thing over with."

Sabrina was puzzled by his attitude. He seemed hurried, efficient, and businesslike. As soon as they arrived at the luxurious suite that had been reserved for him, he went over to the large veranda windows that fronted the street and drew the curtains open. Then he stepped out onto the balcony, and motioned for Sabrina to join him with a curt nod of his head.

"All right, honey," he said to her without any preliminaries, "take off your clothes."

"What . . . ? But—"

"Let's get this over with, huh? I'm beginning not to like this assignment at all."

Sabrina frowned in deep puzzlement. When his hands went to the buttons of her blouse, she did not resist. He removed her blouse and then her black brassiere, right there on the windy balcony. Anyone from the street below could see them if they looked up.

"Come closer to ole Casey Don," he said to her. Sabrina did as he asked without protest, her head lowered, shoulders sagging forward. Donnelly put his arms around her and drew her close, kissing her on the lips. He held the kiss for a long time, but it was a dry, passionless kiss. It seemed as if he were doing this because he had to, rather than wanted to.

When he released her, he motioned her back inside. He followed her in and drew the shades. Instead of beginning to take off his own clothes now, he surprised Sabrina by saying: "Honey, it's time to get down to brass tacks. You get dressed while we're talking. Now, about this here arms shipment you've been hinting at with your questions. The fact is—"

Before he could continue, the door burst open with a splintering of wood, as if kicked. Michael came into the room, his expression fierce. He glared at Sabrina as she tried to cover her naked breasts with the orange blouse that was in her hands. Sabrina shook her head pleadingly, her mouth open in a silent scream.

Michael went straight to Donnelly and slugged him with all his might, sending him crashing back against the wall. He advanced on him again and started to pummel him. By this time, though, Donnelly's security men were in the room. They rushed at Michael and pulled him off Donnelly, holding him back. Michael was looking at Sabrina now. "Trust you," he sneered, shaking his head cynically. The look on his face was one of intense pain.

"Oh, Michael!" she moaned in soul-deep pain.

"Sorry, sir," the security men were saying to Donnelly, who was picking himself up off the floor. "He ran right by us before we could stop him. We'll take him to the police."

"Naw, boys, don't bother," said Donnelly, massaging his hurt jaw. "He's with her. Her beau, I think. Must have followed us here from the restaurant. Just let him go."

The security men looked at him in amazement.

"I said let him go!" commanded Donnelly.

The security men released him. Michael was still looking at Sabrina.

"Michael, please," she said, going up to him, taking his hand in hers. "Please, Michael, just . . . you have to . . ."

"Trust you?" he said. He shook his head. He began backing away from her toward the door, looking at her with bitterness. "Don't worry, pet, you won't have me around to ruin your 'romances' anymore. You won't see me again."

"No!" she screamed, going down on her knees.

He stopped at the door before leaving and said to her in a soft, wounded voice: "The pain of it is, pet . . . I loved you. I truly did love you." Then he turned and was gone.

Sabrina began crying, her face in her hands. Donnelly tried to help her up to her feet, but she resisted him fiercely. He motioned the security men out of the room. Then he went to the veranda window and peered out through the drawn curtains, parting them with his hand.

"All right, honey," he said, "this crazy damn-fool assignment is getting out of hand. Let's get it over with. Here's what you want to know: the next shipment of armaments bound for the Western Front is due to arrive in the middle of June."

She stopped crying and looked up at him in astonishment. "You *know* I'm trying to get that information from you?"

"Hayull yes!"

"But . . . *how?*"

"You know ole Casey Don heads up a big munitions plant back home in Texas. But what you didn't know is I also happen to be an Intelligence agent for Uncle Sam."

She stared at him in shock and confusion. He came up to her and took her by the shoulders, helping her to her feet. She did not resist this time. She was too bewildered to do anything but stare at him.

"It's not as confusin' as you think, honeybun. We knew you had to get this information, and that you planned to give a false, garbled version of it to our old friend Wolfschmidt, the son of a bitch. Instead of lettin' you garble it any old way you please, we figured we'd give you the *exact* wrong information we want them to believe." He picked up his white stetson cowboy hat from the floor and dusted it off. "It'll do Uncle Sam a whole lot of good, honey, to have Wolfy believin' mid-June is the date the arms arrive."

Suddenly Sabrina understood, and her blood began boiling with rage. "Why didn't you just *tell* me! Why did you make me go *through* all of this?"

"I started to tell you—remember?—when that plumb loco two-fisted sweetheart of yours come bustin' in, smashin' up things."

"But you . . . you took off my clothes, and you made me stand there like that out on the balcony!" She was shaking her hands in the air.

"C'mere." He motioned her over to the window and parted the curtains slightly. She looked out and saw what he was pointing at. Down on the street below, hiding in the shadow under the awning of a

335

butcher shop, was Gunther. He was wearing his gray trench coat and had his hat pulled down low.

"That's one of Wolfy's boys. We leaked it out that I was registering at this here hotel. He planted himself down there to see what he could see."

He shut the curtain. "And what he saw made him think that X-79—you, honey—managed to seduce ole Casey Don. Since our Intelligence people worked hard to give the impression I always loosen up after some good lovin', that Kraut down there is goin' to have a lot of respect for the information you give him. If he didn't think you and me made it together, he wouldn't believe I gave you the information."

"You *used* me!" she cried, lunging at him, beating at his chest and shoulders with her small fists. "And now I've lost Michael!"

"Hey now," he said gently, "come on, darlin'." He held her wrists, trying not to hurt her.

"He thinks I'm unfaithful to him," she cried, trying to beat at him. "I may never see him again."

"I'm sorry, honey. Really I am. But—there's a war on. Look, I'll tell you what. After the mission's completed, I'll track him down and tell him the truth. I promise you that."

After the mission's completed, she thought. So much depended on getting that roster from Wolfschmidt! Michael's life . . . her own life . . . their life together.

"Moreau over in French Counterintelligence, he says for a long time he thought of you as a German spy. And near as I can tell, he's still not one hundred percent convinced otherwise. Ole Casey Don, though, I'd never think a thing like that about a filly like you." His eyes were sincere and warm.

336

Sabrina began to feel that basically he was a good man.

"I've got intuition strong as any woman's," he said, "and my intuition tells me you could never be a spy for those Krauts. I know what you're like. You're a good, brave, scared little girl, honey, that's what you are. And I swear, I'll do anything I can to help you."

She saw the earnestness in his eyes. "Thank you," she said in a small voice. She finished buttoning up her blouse, then started for the door. By the end of the night, she thought, she would be on her way to Berlin. "Good-bye," she said, looking back at him.

"*Auf wiedersehen*," he grinned, winking at her. "Give my regards to Wolfy."

Chapter 24

The train rumbled eastward, jolting Sabrina about in her seat. She could hear the sound of the rails rushing by beneath the floor of her compartment, and the creaking of the railroad coach walls. It was pitch-black outside. She looked out the window but saw only her own reflection because of the lighted interior.

Gunther, seated across from her, was looking glum and angry. She had refused to give him the information he wanted, insisting on delivering it to Wolfschmidt personally. He had had no choice but to give in to her demand. The information was too valuable to risk not having.

They disembarked at a small station very near the front, then took horses supplied by a local agent to get even closer to the border. The next stretch of their journey was to walk across the open no-man's-land that separated the French and German forces. Gunther walked ahead of her, moving quickly, but very carefully. The field was mined, he told her. She was to step directly into the imprints made in the dirt by his boots. Sabrina felt terribly frightened. There was only a quarter moon, and the night was so dark she could barely see his steps. It was freezing, and her breath turned into mist before her eyes.

Finally they were across the mine field and into the German lines. An infantry captain was waiting to escort them to Wolfschmidt's headquarters. He took them for a long ride in a staff car, along a bumpy road, which brought them to the building where the general now resided.

It was a cavernous, fortified, reinforced-concrete bunker. It was built entirely underground, covered by several yards of dirt and rocks above. So he learned his lesson, Sabrina thought, after having his last headquarters destroyed by bombs.

She and Gunther were taken down mazelike concrete corridors, dimly lit by lights built into the walls. She could hear her footsteps echoing sharply against the walls and low ceiling. Finally they turned another corner and found themselves in an office area where two armed guards wearing combat uniforms stood at attention on either side of a floor-to-ceiling steel door.

The guards snapped their heels together and saluted the captain, who said something in German. Then the steel door was pulled open and Sabrina and Gunther were motioned in. The door boomed shut behind them. There would be no escape from this underground fortress, Sabrina thought nervously. Either they would *allow* her to leave, or she would not leave at all.

The room was long and seemed empty and austere. There was a table, a file cabinet and desk, some chairs—and the black safe. Sabrina felt a pinprick of excitement on seeing that the door was partially open. Wolfschmidt was nowhere in sight. Then Sabrina noticed that the long room was actually L-shaped, and continued around the far right corner. She and Gunther went forward to peer around the corner.

Gunther snapped to attention and saluted. General Wolfschmidt, bent over a large, multicolored map on a table, looked up casually and returned his salute. He turned his eyes back to the study of his map. "So you insisted on seeing me personally again, Fräulein?" he said to Sabrina in his clipped, staccato voice. "Perhaps you do not remember the circumstances of our last meeting."

"I remember," she said quietly. Her words echoed slightly within the concrete walls. There was also a *sh-sh-sh-sh* sound from the air being blown into the room through the ventilator ducts.

"You were my prisoner," he said venomously, "being punished for attempting to shoot me. Then you managed to escape." He looked up at her now, the light glinting off the monocle in his eye. "What makes you think your punishment will not be continued, now that we have you back as a guest of our hospitality?"

"I have information you need," Sabrina said, looking him directly in the eye.

"There are ways to get that information from you *without* your cooperation. And I tell you frankly, I would enjoy employing these ways. Your rescuers obliterated my headquarters! Can you imagine how that made me *look*?"

Sabrina felt her heart filling with fear.

"Is there some other reason I should not choose to continue your punishment?" Wolfschmidt asked.

"I . . . I can get you more information," she said, trying to sound confident and unintimidated.

"If you'll promise not to hurt Major Hunter, I'll become your spy again."

"Tell me the results of your mission," he said sharply. "When is the first shipment of arms due to arrive?"

"First you have to promise not to hurt Major Hunter. Otherwise—"

Wolfschmidt grasped her by the chin and pulled her close to him. "The date of the arms shipment!" he demanded, shouting directly into her face.

Her eyes went wide. "The middle of June," she said.

He squeezed her chin in his bony hand, hurting her. He stared into her eyes with a cold, searching gaze, trying to decide whether to believe her. After a moment, he released her with a slight shove, making her step backward. "It is lucky for you that you succeeded in your mission," he said. "If you had not, you would be a welcome addition to our prison." He returned to his map, losing all interest in her. "All right," he said, "now get out. Gunther, escort her back across the lines. Her next assignment will be delivered by the usual means."

"*Jawohl!*" said Gunther, saluting once more and clicking his heels. He turned to leave. When Sabrina did not follow him, but instead kept looking at Wolfschmidt, Gunther grabbed her arm and began pulling her with him.

"No!" said Sabrina. "Wait!"

Wolfschmidt did not look up from his map. Gunther shook a fist at her threateningly, showing that she had better come with him.

But she could not leave now. She had to photograph that roster! "Wait," she said again. "What about . . . the agreement? Do you agree not to

341

harm Major Hunter? I . . . I want to see him! To make sure he's all right!" She was trying to buy time for herself. She had to find some way to stay in the office longer. Some way in which she could be alone with Wolfschmidt, without Gunther at her side.

"You can't see him," Wolfschmidt said irritably. "He's being held in Düsseldorf, not here." He lied very convincingly, saying this as if he actually had Hunter in captivity.

"But—"

"*Kommen Sie!*" shouted Gunther angrily, tugging at her arm.

"There's another reason I came to see you," Sabrina declared desperately to Wolfschmidt, wildly resisting Gunther's efforts to pull her out of the room.

This made Wolfschmidt look up from his map finally. "What reason?" he asked.

"I . . . it's because I . . ." Think! she ordered herself. What reason could she possibly give him? "It's because the missions you sent me on, forcing me to make love to those men . . . it . . . it *did* something to me."

"Yes?" said Wolfschmidt, his interest perking up. He motioned for Gunther to stop pulling her away. "And what precisely did it do to you, Fräulein?"

"It made me . . . need it." She saw the hard, searching look in his eyes again, as he debated whether to believe her or not. "And the way you made love to me that one time," she continued. "It was . . . the best I've had." She lowered her eyes. She could not look at him and say these words. "I want you to do it to me again," she said in almost a whisper.

Wolfschmidt did not answer. When she glanced up, though, she saw him looking at her with a smug smile. She knew then that she had won. She had penetrated to his male ego. He could not let himself believe she was lying. What she said only confirmed what he knew all along—what *every* man knew all along, no matter how untrue it usually was: that he was an irresistible lover.

He sat down on the edge of his map table and lit a cigarette with a gold lighter, holding the cigarette in the crook of two straight fingers. "You will show me that you want me," Wolfschmidt ordered, staring her up and down with an insolent look. "Take off your clothes."

Sabrina glanced at Gunther. "Make him leave?" she pleaded.

Wolfschmidt did not answer, but his fierce look made his feelings clear. Do not dare to give me orders, his expression said; I give the orders, you obey them.

Slowly, Sabrina's hands went to her heavy pullover. But then she hesitated. The drug-tipped needle was hidden in the side seam. She had to keep the sweater on until she was alone with him. Her hands moved to the side buttons of her dark-brown wool skirt. She unfastened them slowly. Then, with Wolfschmidt's eyes staring at her with burning fixation, she lowered the skirt and stepped out of it. She pulled down her slip and stepped out of that too.

She stood straight again, her shoulders thrown back. Wolfschmidt was gazing at her white underpants, at the "V" between her thighs. She wore no garters or hose, having worn socks and boots instead. She stood with her long legs exposed, feeling a slight draft from the ventilator duct nearby.

She glanced briefly at Gunther, hoping to indicate to Wolfschmidt that the man should be ordered to leave. Gunther was staring down at her underwear with absorption, his face sweating, his eyes bulging.

Wolfschmidt did not take Sabrina's hint. Instead, he said, "A skirt and a slip is all? That is supposed to show me your great desire?"

She could not take off the sweater. She knew what she had to do. There was no choice. She hooked her thumbs into the hem of her underwear and pulled it down. The underwear was at her ankles. She was about to step out of the garment when Wolfschmidt came forward suddenly and pushed her in the shoulder.

She yelped, falling backward, her naked buttocks hitting the cold concrete floor. She quickly drew her knees together and looked up at Wolfschmidt. He was sneering at her in amusement. He had pushed her down only to heighten her embarrassment. "Do not stop," he said, his voice thicker. "Go on, take it off."

Sabrina jerked the underwear over her ankles, then covered herself with it. Wolfschmidt reached down and grabbed it away from her. She lay on the floor, naked from her waist to her knees, feeling the coldness of the concrete against her skin.

Gunther was breathing heavily, his eyes bugging out even more as he stared at her nakedness. There was a noticeable bulge in his pants. Only now did Wolfschmidt become disturbed by the man's presence. "*Achtung!*" he ordered. Gunther snapped to attention, the bulge in his pants protruding bizarrely. *"Verlassen Sie!"* ordered Wolfschmidt. "Out!"

Gunther executed a sharp about-face and disappeared around the corner. A moment later Sabrina heard the *wooshing* sound of the steel door being pulled open, then slammed shut.

She looked at Wolfschmidt now as he sat on the edge of the table, his arms folded across his chest, grinning at her in a closemouth, smug way. She stood up from the floor and started forward, parting her lips as if she were coming to kiss him. Her hand slowly went down to the hem of her sweater where the needle was concealed.

"Halt," Wolfschmidt commanded while she was still several feet from him. She stopped moving forward, and looked at him in bewilderment. "Continue your undressing," he said in a throaty voice. "It pleases me."

"But I want to . . . touch you."

"I said continue." His face hardened menacingly.

Sabrina dared not defy him. He might call the whole thing off if she did not do it exactly as he wanted. Reluctantly she raised the maroon sweater over her head and took it off. She thought for a second of removing the pin before putting the sweater down, but realized how fatally stupid this would be. She could not hold the pin in her hand without Wolfschmidt seeing it.

Regretfully, she dropped the sweater to the ground near a chair, to join the skirt, slip, and underpants. The she removed her camisole and dropped this to the floor also. She stood before him stark naked, feeling the chill breeze from the ventilator over her entire body. A feeling of self-loathing crept over her as she realized she was about to give this despicable man the pleasure of her body.

"Come to me," he said.

She advanced toward him. He took her hand and placed it at his crotch. She felt the hard swell behind the rough trousers. She hesitated, then she squeezed it, and watched his eyes close in response to the pleasure he felt. Sabrina looked back at the pile of clothing on the floor. She had to get to that needle! Wolfschmidt stood up from the map table and shoved her hard, back against the wall. Now she was farther away from her sweater than ever. He undressed slowly, sneering at the way her eyes went wide at the sight of his thick, jutting maleness.

He dropped his uniform to the floor carelessly, put his monocle on the map table, then came up to her. He put his hand to her hair and touched the hair clip containing the miniature camera the French had given her. He snatched it from her hair and threw it across the room onto a cushioned chair. Then he grasped her hair and pulled her face toward him, kissing her hard on the lips. Since Sabrina had to continue the charade of wanting him, she returned his kiss, feeling the tenseness of his hard, stony face.

His body ground against hers, pressing her back and buttocks up against the rough concrete wall. His chest and male shaft pressed against her breasts and loins, hard, as if he wanted to crush her between his body and the wall. His hands went under her arms and he raised her up so that her feet were inches above the floor. Then, looking her in the eye, he penetrated her. "Unnnhhh!" she moaned, feeling him thrusting in and out of her, pressed to the wall as she was.

Even as she felt the wretchedness of having this horrible man inside her, her mind was still racing, desperately thinking: she had to get that needle! If she could not get it soon it would be too late. This was the way he had taken her last time. It was not a prelude, she knew; it was all there was! If she could not somehow get to her needle within the next few seconds, he would be finished with her and it would be too late. She would not have a chance to get close to him afterward. She would be ordered to leave.

A desperate idea came to her, and she acted instantly. She began moaning and writhing as if in wild pleasure, then *slashed* her long fingernails down the back of his neck, scratching him deeply.

"Ow, damn it, you bitch!" he screamed, pulling away from her. He stared at her in violent, questioning fury.

"I couldn't help it!" she pleaded. "The feeling overwhelmed me; you're so good, I went crazy with it."

"You'll learn what it means to have the feeling overwhelm you!" he said angrily.

"Yes," she begged, "yes, do it to me more, please more!" She moved quickly along the floor toward her clothing. Then she went down onto her back and spread her thighs open to receive him as if she had moved along the floor for this very purpose.

"Bitch," sneered Wolfschmidt. "You think *pleasure* is what I wish to give you!" He came down on top of her and entered her roughly. Then he began thrusting brutally, tearing her apart, while his hands cupped her breasts and squeezed them tightly, his nails digging into her flesh.

Sabrina reached behind her head with her hands and felt around blindly on the concrete for her clothes. She found them, and after a moment managed to pick out her sweater. She was panting heavily now, hurting under Wolfschmidt's sexual abuse—but also feeling wild flashes of pleasure, in response to his intense, relentless stimulation of her breasts and her sex. She struggled to keep her mind focused on what she was doing with her hands. searching along the seam of the sweater for the hidden needle.

Finally she found it, just as Wolfschmidt groaned deep in his throat, his body going rigid. She yanked off the protective plastic cap and pricked the needle point into Wolfschmidt's shoulder. The drug took effect instantly. His body went completely slack, his head dropped down to her shoulder.

Sabrina took a moment to catch her breath, breathing rapidly in gasps. She felt dizzy from the exertion and from his vicious abuse. After a moment, she struggled to push the lean, sweat-soaked body off her, finally managing to slide out from under him rather than push him off. She stared down at him. She wanted to spit on him, to kick him, to release the violent fury that threatened to explode from her. She forced herself to turn away.

She put the cap back on the needle and dropped it through the slats of the ventilator grille in the wall. Then she fetched her hair clip camera and rushed over to the black safe at the corner of the L-shaped room. She glanced nervously at the closed steel door of the office. Anyone could walk in at anytime. She knelt down and began sifting through the files in the top pullout drawer.

There wasn't much time. French Intelligence had warned her that the effects of the drug lasted only a few minutes; it had to be this way to maintain the effect of having the victim think he had merely blanked out for a brief second or two.

She found the folder bearing the label Moreau had told her to look for: *SPÄHEREN IN FRANK-REICH*. She removed it from the safe and took out the three sheets of paper inside it. She was spreading the pages out on top of the safe when suddenly a knock came to the steel door. Sabrina froze.

"Herr General?" called a voice through the door. *"Ein minute, bitte?"*

The door didn't open—yet. Sabrina cocked the hairclip the way the French had shown her, and began hurriedly taking pictures of the pages. The knock came to the door once more, making her jerk in panic. She took the last picture, then returned the clip to her hair.

Eyeing the door nervously, she put the papers back into the folder. She started to put the folder back into the safe in the place where she had found it, when she heard a click at the door. She jammed the file in without looking at it, half closed the front of the safe, then rushed around the corner just as the door began to open.

Wolfschmidt was still on the floor on his stomach, out cold. She struggled wildly to get fully under him, succeeded only partially, then pulled him over her to finish the task. The sound of footsteps on the concrete floor was coming closer and closer.

She raised Wolfschmidt's head and pinched his cheek, trying to wake him. He didn't stir. The steps were almost upon them. They couldn't find him like this, out cold, or all would be lost! As a last resort she slapped him hard on the cheek.

"Uh . . . wha?" he sputtered, coming back to consciousness. He raised his head and chest and stared down at Sabrina in angry puzzlement. She was breathing heavily, just as she had been doing when he passed out, her expression one of mingled pain and pleasure. There was no indication that more than a second had elapsed.

One of the guards came around the corner, holding his rifle diagonally across his chest. When he first appeared, his expression was hardened into suspicion. Now that he saw what was happening, he looked embarrassed and fearful at having interrupted. He said something to Wolfschmidt in German.

"Of course I'm all right, you *Dummkopf!*" roared Wolfschmidt. "Get the hell out of here!" He was incensed to wild fury by this intrusion, his skin becoming red with anger.

The guard ran out of the room. The general rose up from Sabrina and began dressing hurriedly. Sabrina forced herself to remain on her back, as if too weak to move after their just-this-instant-concluded tryst. She let Wolfschmidt see her face, so he could notice the faked expression which showed that he had given her pleasure.

"You animal," he said to her with disgust in his voice. "You take pleasure from my abuse. Have you no shame?" He did not seem at all aware of having been unconscious for several minutes.

Sabrina began dressing. Wolfschmidt clearly felt that he had not degraded her enough to suit him. He had not achieved the satisfaction he wanted, and now she was continuing to deny it to him by refusing to cringe and act humbled before him. He grabbed her arm and marched her toward the door before she had a chance to put on anything but her underpants. Then he pulled open the steel door and shoved her through it, her hand still clutching her clothing.

The guards and Gunther, ringing the doorway, stared at her with wide-eyed surprise and lust as she was flung to the ground in front of them. Wolfschmidt slammed the door. Sabrina stood up and finished dressing under the burning stares of the three men. Then she said to Gunther in a quiet voice, looking down at the floor, "Can we go now?"

He snorted his disgust. Then he started down the corridor, Sabrina following quickly after him. Outside, they entered the waiting staff car and began the drive back toward the checkpoint unit at the border of no-man's-land. Sabrina felt the chill wind on her face and arms in the open car. Her body ached from the brutal way Wolfschmidt had taken her, but surprisingly she felt good.

I did it! she exulted, as the car raced through the night, carrying them toward the border checkpoint. She touched the hair clip on the back of her head. It's almost over, she thought with grateful relief. Soon she and Michael would be together again, no longer in danger. His suspicions would all be put to rest.

She slouched low in the seat and rested her head against the top of it as the car jolted and rattled along the shell-hole-pocked road. The fresh smell of the green trees bordering the roadside wafted into her nostrils, and the cold night air stung her skin refreshingly. She touched her hair clip once more, and smiled a small, secret smile.

General Wolfschmidt sipped the hot coffee, trying to concentrate on the map he was studying. He frowned in annoyance at his inability to keep his mind focused on the terrain and troop dispositions highlighted on the map. Something was bothering him, preventing him from concentrating.

What was it? he wondered irritably. But try as he might, he could not figure it out. It was something minor, he knew; something probably very inconsequential. But still, no matter how insignificant this thing might be, the fact remained that *something was definitely wrong*. He sensed it deep in his soul. And he knew himself well enough to realize that he would not be able to get any more productive work done tonight until he figured out the minor thing that was troubling him.

He walked away from the map and sat at his desk, frowning. As he puzzled out the problem, he scratched absently at his shoulder, which had been itching for the past hour. He sipped his bitter black coffee and turned his thoughts back to this feeling of something being wrong, out of place . . .

Suddenly he had it. He leaped up from his desk, realization and puzzlement mingling in his mind. Here's what's bothering me, he thought: I threw that damned hair clip halfway across the room, yet when I got up from the girl to dress, *it was back on her head*! Now how the *hell*? . . .

Is it possible I'm remembering incorrectly? he asked himself, pacing back and forth. Maybe I'm working too hard? But no, he decided firmly, slamming a fist into a palm, he knew what he'd seen.

His eyes had not lied to him. And though he *had* been working very hard lately, on very little sleep, he hadn't gotten to the rank he now held by being low on endurance. He trusted his memory. He wasn't going mad. Something unusual was definitely happening, and he'd find out what it was—and *fast*.

As he stomped about the room, he found himself scratching his shoulder fiercely. Damn! he thought. How was he supposed to concentrate while this itch kept bothering him, refusing to go away. He went to the door and said to the ranking guard, "Get a doctor in here. *Schnell!*"

He was kneeling at his safe, searching through his files and drawers, when the doctor came into the room. "Give me some salve for my shoulder," he said to the pudgy man. "It won't stop itching."

"You'll have to remove your shirt."

Wolfschmidt took off his coat and shirt, knelt back down and continued looking through his files. Nothing seemed to be missing. But here was something odd: the roster of agents in the French sector was in front of the folder containing the roster for the Belgian sector. Could he have put it back in the wrong place accidentally? He had never done so before. But certainly no one else could have touched the folders without his knowing about it.

"This is interesting," said the doctor, holding up a white strip of paper with a blue blot near the top.

"What is?" said Wolfschmidt irritably, not wanting to waste his time on a frivolous medical matter.

"Well," said the doctor, looking intrigued by an unusual discovery, "I took a specimen from that tiny red mark on your shoulder, and I tested it against my dilithium hydroxide strip. Then to isolate the recombinant, I—"

"Stop this gibberish!" declared Wolfschmidt angrily. "You medicine men and your damn foreign language. Just tell me about my shoulder."

"You've evidently been pinpricked with a sleep-inducing drug of the 3-milo type. Though I certainly didn't prescribe it. Who could have—"

"Guards!" screamed Wolfschmidt, rushing out of the room, his face turning beet red with fury. "Get me the security officer! Get me finance! Get me a wireless line to Hegel! *We've got to stop her!*"

Chapter 25

Sabrina and Gunther reached the border checkpoint on the German side of no-man's-land and left their staff car. Gunther wanted to waste no time in crossing the field. It was almost daybreak. Any hint of daylight would make their crossing more perilous, since French patrols sometimes set up border outposts during the day.

The lieutenant in charge of the German checkpoint nodded him through without incident. He and Sabrina went to the edge of the field and were about to begin their trek across, when suddenly the field telephone rang several yards behind them. The German lieutenant answered it, and an instant later came running out of the command post tent shouting urgently to Gunther.

"Vat do you vant?" Gunther asked irritably. "Don't bother me. Ve have to get across der field before daylight."

"The call is for you," the lieutenant said urgently. He glanced at Sabrina for the briefest second, then turned his eyes away. "You must answer it before you cross. It's imperative you do so!"

"What could be so important?" Gunther asked obstinately, not wanting to delay his crossing. Already the horizon was beginning to blush with a faint pinkness. "No one even knows I'm here except . . ." He broke off his sentence, as if in realization of something important. "Wait here," he said to Sabrina. Then he hurried off toward the command post.

Sabrina watched Gunther go to the tent and raise the heavy field telephone to his ear. She watched his expression become grim and foreboding as he listened to the voice on the other end. He glanced over at her furtively, then turned his eyes away quickly.

Something's gone wrong, Sabrina thought fearfully. But then, when he did not look back at her again, she thought maybe she was just being jumpy over nothing. She hoped this was the case. Because if something really had gone wrong, there was nothing she could do about it—except make a desperate run through the mined field that was no-man's-land.

She watched Gunther's eyes, hoping he would not look at her again with that same ominous expression. "*Ja,*" he said into the phone. "*Jawohl, mein General.*" He glanced at her sharply, and she could see his look of angry regret—regret that he had left her at the edge of the field rather than bringing her with him back to the post.

He waved Sabrina forward, trying to make the gesture look casual. She didn't move. He waved her forward again, more urgently. Still she didn't move. He put down the telephone and said a word to the lieutenant. They both turned to her and began moving forward slowly, cautiously, trying not to spook her until they were close enough to grab her.

Sabrina began backing away into the field.

"*Nein, Fräulein!*" called Gunther. "Vait! I wish to

speak to you, it is over a simple matter." He tried to force a smile, to reassure her. The grotesque expression fell far short of a smile. Sabrina inched further into the field.

The lieutenant at Gunther's side was not taking any chances now. He unfastened the flap of his holster and reached for his Luger. Sabrina turned and ran into the field. "Stop her!" shouted Gunther, behind her. "She carries top-secret data!" A series of shots rang out. Dirt churned at her side, spraying her with pebbles. She was rushing through the darkness, though, and did not present a clear target.

She ran across the forbidding stretch of no-man's-land, dodging the jagged, burnt-out tree trunks and stumps. She was terrified of stepping on a land mine, but there was nothing she could do. She had to run as fast as she could from her pursuers, and trust her safety to prayer and luck.

More shots rang out behind her, zinging past her ears. She looked over her shoulder and saw that both men were rushing after her through the field. Gunther was moving less quickly, stepping gingerly in an effort to avoid the mines. The lieutenant in charge of the checkpoint, though, was charging across the field heedlessly. He was obviously more fearful of Wolfschmidt's wrath should Sabrina escape than he was of the land mines.

She turned her head forward again and continued running. She was panting now and out of breath. The line of trees at the far end of no-man's-land was approaching rapidly. If she could just hold out another moment or two.

Suddenly she heard a fearsome blast and found herself flying forward onto her face, scraping her cheek and chin in the dirt. Her eyes went wide in horror, for she thought she had stepped on a land mine. She heard a moaning behind her, though, and realized the truth. It was not she who had stepped on the mine; it was the lieutenant. The concussive force of the blast had knocked her off her feet and flung her forward. The lieutenant's moan was shrill with pain.

A bullet zinged into the earth near Sabrina's head. She looked behind her and in the faint light of the dawn saw Gunther only a few yards back, aiming his pistol at her. She got to her feet and sprinted forward. She ran toward the line of trees with all her might now, heedless of the land mines. Would there be any French patrols there to greet her, she wondered, if she made it across?

She was only a few yards from the trees now. Gunther was firing at her with increased desperateness. Suddenly she saw a figure rise up in the bushes, aiming a rifle at her. She gasped, thinking she was finished now, there was no escape. But then she noticed with wild relief that the figure was Culp, the Englishman attached to French Intelligence, and that the rifle was actually being aimed at Gunther close behind her.

He came! thought Sabrina, remembering his statement that he was aware of the German crossover point and his promise to meet her there. There were two French soldiers on either side of him. Culp fired the rifle. Evidently he missed, for another pistol shot rang out behind her, and suddenly she felt a searing pain in her left hip.

She screamed and fell down. Ahead of her, she saw Culp still standing in the clump of bushes, aiming the rifle-with-fixed-bayonet he'd taken from one of the soldiers, and firing again. Sabrina saw the muzzle flash with flame, then heard Gunther scream in agony behind her. She turned and saw him writhing about on the ground, holding his bloody chest. Culp fired once more, and Gunther lay still, his eyes lifeless and bulging.

Culp ran forward and knelt beside Sabrina. Though she was half traumatized and in pain from the wound in her hip, she had the presence of mind to notice wryly that Culp's first question was not, Are you all right? The first thing he said, with desperate concern, was: "I say, do you have the pictures?"

"Yes," she said, half in a moan. She took the clip from her hair and handed it to him. He clutched it and looked as if he were about to kiss it. Only as an afterthought did he disguise his joy at having the pictures and show a look of concern for her. He inspected the bloody line that ran along her hip. "Oh, you'll be all right," he said shortly. "It's only a crease. Could have jolly well been a great deal worse, I daresay." He stood up and shouted over to the bushes. "Will somebody get a blasted medic down here, for Godsake!"

Several hours later she and Culp were riding the train back to Marseilles. Her flesh wound had been cleaned and bandaged. It still stung, but she knew it was not serious, though she knew also that there would be a scar, and this bothered her. Culp was sitting across from her in the compartment, smiling cheerfully. He wore a handcuff on one wrist, and the other end of it was attached to the handle of a foliocase. Inside the case was the hair clip.

When they finally arrived at the St. Charles terminal in Marseilles, after a long journey, Moreau was on the platform waiting to meet them. Sabrina knew instantly that something was wrong. Moreau's expression was too smug and self-satisfied.

"We've got it!" Culp said exultantly to him when they reached him, holding up the foliocase triumphantly.

"Excellent," said Moreau. He removed his hands from his pockets, brought forth the pair of handcuffs he was carrying, and clasped them on Sabrina's wrists. "And now we have ze German spy, too."

Culp looked as surprised as Sabrina. "What are you talking about?" he said. "She's not one of theirs. How can you even suggest such a thing after what she's just done for us?"

With a gesture of his head, Moreau motioned forward two French soldiers who were standing inconspicuously a few yards behind him. One of them held a brown rectangular courier pouch, which he handed over to Moreau. Moreau fished about inside it and withdrew a letter. He gave it to Culp, who opened it and read it, frowning as he did so.

"What is it?" Sabrina cried in panic, seeing the way Culp's frown deepened as he continued reading.

No one answered her. Culp finished the letter, looked up at Moreau, and said, "Damn! She's a spy after all, then."

"I'm not!" she said desperately. "What's in that letter?"

Culp held up the foliocase attached to his wrist. "So the photos she got, they're completely useless!"

Moreau brightened and looked even more pleased with himself than before. "Zat eez where you are wrong, my friend. Even though she eez a

360

spy, I believe she really *did* photograph ze roster, ze genuine roster. She did so to save ze man she loves." He smiled in a cocksure way. "I knew she was a spy all along. I told you so. But still I figured we could manipulate her for our own ends, knowing how great her love eez for zis Englishman Michael Yorkshire."

"Will somebody please tell me what's going on?" Sabrina pleaded. "I'm not a spy! Why won't you believe me? Look, look what they did to me to stop me from bringing that to you!" She pointed at the bloodstained tear in her skirt where the bullet had creased her.

A small crowd had gathered around them by now, attracted by the commotion. Moreau and Culp looked at the crowd uncomfortably. Then, without a further word, they started Sabrina forward and marched her between them out of the terminal, to a waiting car.

She was terrified during the ride to Counterintelligence Headquarters. She knew from experience what could happen to those they thought of as spies. Neither of them answered her questions about why they now suspected her; they sat in stony-faced silence. Even so, Sabrina knew one thing for certain: whatever the reason was, Wolfschmidt was behind it.

The last thing Counterintelligence wanted was to hold a public trial. One of the people who had seen Sabrina being arrested at the train station, though—and who had recognized her—was a reporter for *Le Figaro*. The story hit the front-page headlines of the evening edition, and was soon picked up by major newspapers all across Europe.

PRINCESS BREENA ACCUSED
OF ESPIONAGE

FAMED EXOTIC DANCER NAMED
AS GERMAN SPY

HIGH OFFICIALS IMPLICATED—
PARAMOURS LEAKED INFORMATION

It was impossible now for the matter to be swept under the rug or handled as an internal "critical elimination." Sabrina was too famous a celebrity. The incident turned into an international scandal, making a trial unavoidable.

It was during the first day of the trial that Sabrina found out why she had been arrested. The most damning piece of evidence was brought forth and presented to the court: the letter Moreau had shown Culp at the train station. It had been "captured" from a German espionage courier named Hegel.

The letter contained information relayed by wireless from Wolfschmidt's headquarters. It stated that agent X-79 told Wolfschmidt the Allies wanted him to believe the shipment of arms for the Western Front would arrive in mid-June—but that this was a deception. X-79 informed him, according to the letter, that the information was intended to trick him, and that under no circumstances should he believe the mid-June date.

"This information *was* intended to trick General Wolfschmidt," the prosecutor said to the judge, gesturing with one hand, holding the lapel of his coat with the other. "And other than two Allied Intelligence officers, only the defendant knew this. She deliberately informed Wolfschmidt of this deception, in order to warn him."

"That's not true!" Sabrina protested from the witness stand. "I gave him the mid-June date, just as I was supposed to!"

"Then how did he know the mid-June date was a deception?" asked the long-faced prosecutor harshly.

"Why he . . . he probably figured it out as soon as he saw the spy roster had been tampered with. He knew then that I was working for the French and wouldn't give him accurate information."

"I submit that this is conjecture," said the prosecutor. The judge grunted his assent.

The second day of the trial, evidence was brought forth showing Sabrina's supposed motivation for betraying the information. "We've discovered a bank account in Mademoiselle St. Claire's name," said the prosecutor, "at the Bank of Marseilles, where 50,000 francs were recently deposited in her account. The source of the deposit has been traced." He looked at the judge pointedly. "The deposit was made, secretly, by the German Finance Ministry."

"But they're doing this to make you believe I'm guilty!" protested Sabrina. "I have nothing to do with that account. I never even knew it existed until just this minute."

"Did you also not know about the 85,000 German marks," the prosecutor asked cynically, "which were discovered yesterday hidden inside the mattress of your hotel room?"

She looked at him stunned. "No," she said. "I didn't know about that. But don't you see? That's just another way they're trying to make you think I'm guilty!"

The prosecutor lost patience with her. "And just *why*, mademoiselle, do you believe the kaiser's government would go to all this effort and expense to make a young girl such as you appear guilty?"

"So you won't believe the roster is authentic! If you think I'm a German spy, you'll think the roster is a fake one, made up to fool you. And you won't trust the list."

"Aha!" declared the prosecutor, pouncing upon her argument. "That is where your deceit crumbles. For the fact is," he said, addressing the judge, gesturing animatedly, "this roster has been proven to be true! To be authentic!" He turned to Sabrina. "Your argument, therefore, that the Huns would wish to discredit you in order to discredit the roster is a false one. Since you *are* discredited, Mademoiselle "Princess Breena," but the roster is not!"

The judge bent forward over his high platform and asked, "How do you know ze roster eez authentic?"

"The agents listed on it were investigated, Your Honor. Inspector Moreau informs me that conclusive proof was found in all cases. Half the agents on the list have fled. Four were apprehended trying to cross into Germany." He looked at Sabrina, while still addressing the judge. "Also, the desperateness with which the Huns tried to stop the mademoiselle from delivering the roster attests to its genuineness."

Sabrina shouted at the man in frustration. "And doesn't their desperation in trying to stop me, also show that I can't *possibly* be one of their agents? They tried to kill me!" How could these members of the court not see the truth? she wondered, appalled. It was right before their eyes!

"Mademoiselle," said the prosecutor snidely, "that shows only that they realized what we now realize too: that you have no loyalty to *any* nation. You would betray your Hun masters just as quickly as you have betrayed *la belle France*—if it suited your private ends."

"No!" she screamed in torment and anguish. "It's not true!" But they wouldn't listen to her. No one believed in her innocence. The atmosphere in the courtroom was the same as it was throughout the country: highly emotionally charged against her.

The facts of the case, distorted as they were, did not really seem to matter. The thing that weighed most heavily against her was her beauty and her fame. Women hated her because she was young and lovely, and had dared to flaunt convention by dancing nude in public. Men hated her out of envy at not having been among those chosen to receive her supposedly notoriously promiscuous favors. The entire country was frantic for her to receive her just comeuppance—regardless of her innocence or guilt.

As Sabrina watched the trial progress, becoming more damning with each passing day, the thing that bothered her most was not the outpouring of public fury against her. It was the horrible *aloneness* she felt. It was the fact that each day she scanned the spectator gallery for sight of Hunter or Michael . . . and each day she was heartsick with disappointment to see neither of them.

Michael was free to visit her, she knew. The roster had proved him innocent of being a spy; Moreau had said so in open court. So why didn't he come to see her? she wondered tormentedly. She wanted to see him more than anything else in the world. She could accept what was happening to her, no matter how unjust, if only she could see Michael one more time . . . to have him smile at her gently . . . to show that he still loved her.

Day after day she prayed he would come to visit her—and day after day she grew more forlorn and disappointed. By the final day of the trial her pain at his avoiding her was so great, she could barely restrain herself from breaking down in shuddering tears right in open court. She knew the truth. She had to admit it to herself: he had meant it that time he said he never wanted to see her again, or have anything to do with her . . . that time he had caught her half-naked with Casey Donnelly.

He would never learn the truth about her, she realized with a stab of pain. He would think of her forever after as being a wanton, unfaithful woman.

God, it hurt to think of this! And to think that Hunter, too, would carry with him the wrong image of her. He would remember the last time he had seen her: the time she had slapped him and screamed "I hate you, I never want to see you again!" But I don't hate you, Dallas, she thought now, as she scanned the courtroom, praying for sight of him. And oh, how I wish I could see you now! But you must have taken me at my word . . . and now you're staying away.

Tears came to her eyes and streamed hotly down her cheeks. God, what a mess I've made of my life, she thought. The two men I love most dearly . . . I love so much it hurts . . . neither of them knows it, or will ever know it.

"Ze defendant will rise," said the judge, snapping

her back to reality. She stood up in the dock. "Sabrina St. Claire, alias Princess Breena, alias agent X-79 . . . ze court finds you guilty of espionage and high treason. You are sentenced to execution by firing squad, at dawn tomorrow." He banged his gavel sharply, signifying the end of the trial. "May ze Lord have mercy on your soul."

Chapter 26

She stood at the far end of the dusty courtyard, her back to the mortar wall. Behind her was a shallow ditch. Many yards in front of her stood the soldiers of the firing squad. The quartermaster was moving down the line of soldiers with his rifle-laden dolly-cart, finishing the task of handing out the weapons.

The drumroll became louder and more insistent. The gates at the other end of the courtyard were opened and a black hearse drove in. It waited patiently across the field from Sabrina, its engine running.

Sabrina turned her eyes up for a last look at the cloudless blue sky. It was already hot and sunny. It would be a scorcher of a day, she thought. Too bad she wouldn't be around to see it . . .

Suddenly a strong sense of rebellious pride swept over her, and she said to herself commandingly: Oh, stop it! Stop this self-pity. I did what I had to do. So it didn't work out the way I wanted. At least I did what was right. If I hadn't stolen that roster from Wolfschmidt, it would be Michael standing here now, facing the firing squad. I'm sad it had to work out this way . . . but I'd do it again! Yes, I would! Because I love him more dearly than life itself.

She looked out at the firing squad now and thrust her shoulders back defiantly. She didn't want to die. But she was woman enough to take what Providence had in store for her. And if she must die for her love, then so be it.

Thinking this now, she raised her head proudly and glared at the men of the firing squad, defiance in her eyes. She glared at each of them, and when the quartermaster finished handing out the rifles and turned around, facing her for the first time, she glared at him too—and was shocked at the sight of the black eyepatch. "Michael," she gasped in a soundless whisper.

She saw a faint grin cross his lips before he quickly turned and left the field, rolling the empty rifle-cart in front of him.

"Readyyyyy," the commander of the firing squad yelled, drawing his ceremonial sword and raising it high. The drumroll became thunderous.

"Aim!"

Sabrina closed her eyes, her brows arching. She felt the summer breeze swirling the skirt of her light, pale-blue dress.

"*Fire!*"

The roar of a dozen rifles firing all at once blasted through the courtyard, a thunderous, resounding volley. Sabrina flung herself backward, falling into the shallow ditch and remaining motionless, as if she had been hit by the volley . . . as if the rifles had contained real bullets instead of the blanks Michael had loaded them with.

She heard the engine of the hearse as the vehicle drove forward across the field, stopping next to the ditch. She heard the door swing open and the attendant climb out, then his footsteps as he went around to the rear of the hearse and opened the double door. Then the attendant came over to her. She felt the coarse, heavy blanket that descended over her body covering her from head to toe. She felt herself being raised up in strong arms.

"*La criminelle est morte,*" the attendant called out, making the official declaration of execution. The voice was familiar to Sabrina, even though it spoke in French. When she was placed in the open back of the hearse, the voice became even more familiar, as it spoke to her, very quietly, in English. "You're going to have to lose weight, babe," said Dallas Hunter. "If I have to carry you off any more execution fields, I want to make sure I don't rupture anything."

She heard the doors slam shut. Cautiously she pulled the blanket away from her head and looked out. She was inside the darkened interior of the hearse. Next to her, tied and gagged and lying unconscious, was a man in his under-wear—obviously the real attendant/driver of the hearse. Hunter climbed into the driver's seat from outside, put the hearse in gear, and began driving back across the field toward the front gates.

"Oh, Dallas!" she said emotionally, the words sticking in her throat.

"Not so loud," he said, keeping his eyes straight ahead. "Corpses are very quiet people."

"How did you *do* it?" she asked in a hushed voice. "How did you arrange such a thing?"

"Not me, babe. It's that Limey loverboy of yours. He's quite a guy. I didn't give him enough credit. Tracked me down all the way to Gibraltar, to tell me you were in trouble and that he wanted my help in this rescue he'd set up. We just got back last night." Sabrina saw through the front windows that they were approaching the guard post at the exit gate. "Keep quiet now," Hunter said.

Sabrina pulled the blanket back over herself and the unconscious attendant, even though it was so dark in the back that the guards couldn't possibly see anything. The guard said something to Hunter in French. Hunter mumbled *"Oui, oui,"* obviously not understanding anything the man said. Then they were outside, driving away from the gates, along the outside wall.

Sabrina uncovered herself and sat up. "Dallas, the way I slapped you that time, and said what I said . . ."

"I had it coming. You were right to do it. And listen," he said, grinning his old familiar grin, "it was the best thing that ever happened to me. I mean, can you imagine me married? Me? Hell, my airplane is all the wife I'll ever need." He looked back at her and winked. "I love you and I always will, Sabrina. You know that. But as for whose the best man for you to be *married* to . . . we both know the answer to that."

They pulled around the corner of the mortar walls, and Hunter brought the hearse to a screeching halt. The back double door swung open and then, suddenly, Michael was there in the back with Sabrina. Hunter gunned the engine, and the hearse sped forward with a roar and a jolt.

Michael and Sabrina sat looking at each other for a frozen moment, at opposite ends of the back of the hearse. She saw the deep love for her that was in his gaze, and a hint of sensitivity. She felt a flood of emotion well up inside her as she watched him watching her. She felt paralyzed. She remembered the way he had last seen her, when he had found her with Casey Donnelly.

"My love," he said softly. He opened his arms.

"Oh Michael!" she cried, bursting into tears, rushing to him. His arms closed about her and he held her tightly, as she cried against his chest.

"I'm sorry I ever doubted you," he said. "That American cowboy, that Donnelly chap, he came to me and told me the truth."

"I love you, I love you, I love you," she cried, sobbing against his chest, squeezing her arms around his lean torso. She could not stop crying, she was so filled with love and joy.

"There now, pet," he said softly, stroking her hair, holding her. "It's all right. Everything is all right. And it'll be all right from now on. I promise you."

"But . . . where will we go?"

"You're going to neutral Switzerland," Hunter said loudly from the front seat, speaking above the roar of the engine as he raced the hearse down the city streets, causing puzzled, shocked looks from the pedestrians they passed. "It's my honeymoon gift to the two of you. My plane is gassed and waiting out beyond the aerodrome. I'll fly you down, let you off near Zurich, then fly back here."

"Then we'll somehow make our way to America, pet. But not till after the war."

"Everyone thinks I'm dead," said Sabrina, marveling at the curious thought. "The whole world thinks I'm dead."

"Yeah," said Hunter, grinning happily, "but your legend lives on. The legend of Princess Breena."

Sabrina turned to Michael and, looking up at his face, she saw an expression of such deep, tender love it made her breath catch in her throat. "Come here, legend," Michael said to her in a low, throaty voice. She bent her head back and his lips fell upon hers, pressing down burningly, unyieldingly.

She began crying again, practically sobbing into his open mouth. Tears of joy cascaded down her cheeks, wetting her whole face. He crushed her against him, and Sabrina knew he would never let her go.

SPECIAL PREVIEW!

PASSION'S PROUD CAPTIVE

by Melissa Hepburne

The following pages are excerpts from the author's recent best-selling novel, also published by Pinnacle Books, now available at bookstores and newsstands everywhere.*

Jennifer struggled wildly to break free from the grip of the two sweating, smelly sailors as they dragged her down the ship's narrow passageway toward the ladder to the upper deck. She did manage for a moment to break away, after kicking the bearded one in the shin. But there was nowhere to escape to. Desperately, she ran back down the passageway a few paces, but then they had her again and the bearded one twisted her arm viciously behind her back.

*Copyright © 1978 by Melissa Hepburne.

"You filthy Colonial slut," he sneered, as he marched her forward.

He would have beaten her mercilessly, Jennifer thought through her agony and despair, but for the fact that the ship's captain was still standing at the far end of the passageway, stern-faced, hands at his hips, supervising her transport to the upper deck. The punishment she would suffer, she knew, would be at the Captain's pleasure, not that of a lowly seaman.

She had gone too far this time, she was sure. She should never have slapped the Captain. But what else could she have done? The long-faced, rough-skinned mariner had come into her tiny cabin and, this time, had not stopped at the lewd overtures he made toward her, but had become physical. He had come up to her and without any warning put his cupped hands to her breasts, over her clothes, and squeezed them gently.

She had slapped him stingingly, instinctively, without thinking, and that was when he had yelled for the two sailors to come into the room. "To the deck with her!" he ordered in a rage. "Bind her to the mast!"

Captain Trevor stopped directly in front of Jennifer, who had to crane her neck back painfully against the mast to see him. A tense hush fell over the ship as the Captain reached down with a crop he was carrying in his hand to the hem of her frilly, high-necked brown dress. Slowly he raised the hem of her dress, and the petticoats beneath, up to above her knees. A sharp exhaling of breath and an appreciative murmur emanated from the crowd, along with several low whistles. The seamen's eyes were wide, their attention rapt.

The Captain, looking at his audience, grinned sardonically. He struck his hand in under the hem of the dress and then let it fall back down into place, so that his hand was inside her dress, hidden from view.

For a long moment there was no movement, no sound, no change in Jennifer's expression. Then suddenly she let out all her breath and yelped in horrified surprise, her mouth remaining wide open. The Captain's hand was still invisible. With his other hand, he raised the skirt high.

The sight lasted but a fraction of a second, and then the hem of the dress was quickly dropped and his hand removed. Jennifer was panting for breath and sobbing unrestrainedly, in burning shame and humiliation. She had never been touched by any man before. She had never been exposed to a man's eyes. And now, to be laid bare and abused like *this,* before a horde of filthy, drooling beasts.

Jennifer felt strips of leather against her skin, as the First Mate placed his cat-o'-nine tails above her naked white backside, letting the strips of raw leather dangle down so that they touched her in intimate places.

The Captain came around in front of her and moved forward quickly, so that the crotch of his britches brushed against Jennifer's lips before she could jerk her head away. There was a hard, roll-shaped swelling behind the britches. He squatted down to face her at eye level and said with sneering superiority, "Does the representative of the Colonies care to submit now . . . or later?"

Jennifer looked at the mob of lusting seamen, staring feverishly at her degradation and nakedness. No, she thought through her terror and agony and humiliation, she could have done nothing differently. She had done what she had to do. And now she would take what Providence had in store for her. She hawked up all the saliva in her parched throat and spit it into the Captain's face.

"Aaarrr!" he roared, reeling backward, jerking his sleeve up to wipe his face. "Flail the bitch!" he shrieked. "Whip her skinless!"

A shout of approval rose from the seamen. The First Mate raised his whip high, the leather straps swishing up in the air, and then, laughing maniacally, he jerked it violently downward.

But the whip leathers did not slash forward. They seemed caught on something. The First Mate turned in startled puzzlement and saw that a strong-featured, blond-haired man had come up behind him and grasped hold of the whiplashes. A look of utter disbelief registered on the First Mate's face as the blond man smashed the heel of the drawn sword he was holding in his other hand into the center of the Mate's forehead, knocking him down unconscious.

An angry roar went up from the surprised seamen and they surged forward. But instantly a black-haired man with a scar on his cheek sprang forward with a dagger that he jerked against the Captain's throat. "Have them hold!" he ordered.

"You'll be hanged for this, you pirate!" the Captain yelled at the black-haired man.

At this, the blond man, who was just finishing cutting the lashes from Jennifer and helping her to her feet, said in a heavy French accent, "Excuse me, *mon Captain,* but if you please, thees eez no pirate. He eez Lancelot Savage, a captain in ze Americain Navy."

* * *

Jennifer had never known anyone like Savage. His brooding, intense manner . . . the flashes of charming boyishness that sometimes surfaced through his ruthless masculinity . . . the dashing heroic way he had rescued her . . . all these things struck an emotional chord in her. She felt a powerful feeling of deep affection for him. But she felt anger, too, at the way he refused to give any sign of feeling similarly toward her.

Did he have any deeper feelings for her at all, she wondered. Yesterday she had caught him in an unguarded moment, gazing at her with a look of strong affection and caring. Then when she casually asked what plans he had for his future now that his wound was almost healed, he answered in an unexpectedly harsh, stern voice, "My future involves my men and my ship, and a war, and a *damn* good chance of getting killed. Let's not pretend it's otherwise. It wouldn't be fair to y——" He broke off the sentence, unfinished.

As she was remembering this now, Jennifer suddenly heard a loud crashing sound. She jerked upright in the bed, her body tense. Something heavy had been thrown against the wall in Silas's room, as if in frustration. She heard footsteps upon the wooden floor. She saw a hint of movement at her doorway, and looking there, she gasped and jerked the blanket up to her chin.

Savage stood in the doorway, illuminated by the yellow glow from the fireplace. His lean, powerful body was stark naked. He stood rigidly with his legs braced apart, hands down at his sides closed into fists. His handsome face, which at times could look so boyish, now looked gauntly masculine and menacing, his cheeks sunken, lips pressed together in a hard, unyielding line. It was the face of a

377

jungle animal that knew only one law: the urgency of its own need.

Jennifer was crying uncontrollably, trying to curse him through hr tears and sobs. She clutched the rumpled blanket from the base of the bed and pulled it over her, her legs curled up to her chin as she lay on her side. "You bastard," she sobbed. "Oh, you bastard!"

He said nothing. His expression was that of a man who has done what he set out to do, but was not at all happy about it. He turned and left the room.

She lay awake all the rest of the night, huddled in her bed with the blanket wrapped tightly around her, still trembling from the violent sensations that had wracked her body. The sensations had been unlike anything she had ever experienced. She had not known such feelings were possible.

Her mind wanted to dwell on the feelings, to recall in intimate detail the things that lean, muscular animal had done to her body to make her feel this way . . . but she forced herself to turn away from such thoughts. At the back of her mind she knew there was grave danger in admitting to herself the way she felt. It went against all she had been raised to think of as right and proper.

She must fight the memory of what tonight's brutal, degrading rape had made her feel. Even so, she knew that the true way she felt about it would always be with her, at the back of her mind, threatening to come out. Something powerful had been awakened within her and she would always have to be on guard against it. She would resist the feelings with all her might, hold them down in the deep recesses of her soul, no matter what it took!

* * *

Without warning the Governor went behind her, bent down, and stuck his hands under the hem of her pink dress and petticoats. He rose quickly and grasped her buttocks tightly through the thin cloth of her underdrawers. Jennifer yelped in shock and tried to turn, but he was clutching her too tightly. Finally, she managed to jerk around and step away from him, her eyes wide in horrified outrage, her mouth open. She raised her hand to slap him—but then hesitated in midmotion, her hand just inches from his face.

The Governor smiled maliciously at her hesitation. "You do have an idea what this is all about, don't you?"

She slapped him. Then she rushed for the giant double doors, only to find them locked. She turned back to face him, breathless and fearful, her palms and back pressed against the doors. "You can't do this," she said under her breath. "Even a Governor can't rape a citizen—"

He laughed an evil, sneering laugh. "Rape?" he scoffed. "That will hardly be necessary." He went over to the windows overlooking the courtyard and drew aside the brown velvet curtains. Jennifer looked out and now saw the source of the thumping sounds emanating from the courtyard. Lancelot Savage was down on the ground, his hands manacled, being beaten by two large, burly guards. His expression as each new blow landed on his body was one of pure agony.

Jennifer screamed in shock and revulsion, then covered her mouth with her fist. "Make them stop!" she cried. The Governor did not budge. She said it again, this time with pleading in her voice. "Make them stop!"

The Governor smiled. He came forward and put his hands on her breasts, over the thin bodice of her dress. Jennifer started to pull away from him, but the sight of Savage being beaten to death in the courtyard below made her stop. She forced herself to remain motionless, her face wincing in torment.

The Governor smiled even more maliciously. As Jennifer stood there, he pushed her shawl off onto the floor, then unlaced the front of her dress slowly, as if time meant nothing to him. Then he jerked down the bodice and the white chemise beneath it. He pulled the bodice and chemise down to just below her breasts. Her full young bosom stood nakedly exposed, rising and falling with her quickened, fearful breathing. The Governor looked her right in the eye, smiling as he put his hands to her breasts and began squeezing and kneading them. He pinched her nipples, hard. She tried, but could not stifle the groan that came to her lips. Still she did not pull away from him.

In keeping with his end of the unstated agreement, the Governor now went over to the window, opened it, and yelled down to the guards below. "Cease that barbarism, you heathen scum! This is a civilized age. Prisoners are not beaten . . ." he closed the window and pulled the drapes

379

shut again, then turned back to Jennifer. ". . . Only hanged," he concluded.

Jennifer now stood with her arms crossed in front of her, a hand on each shoulder. The Governor slowly walked around her, looking at her appreciatively. "You will be my mistress," he said, "for a period of one year. In return, I will pardon your pirate from the gallows. And when the year you spend with me is over, I will let him go free."

Jennifer said nothing. Tears welled up in her eyes and streamed down her cheeks. She pressed her arms tighter against her breasts, as if that somehow protected them.

"Come, come," demanded the Governor harshly. "I haven't all day. Do you accept my conditions or do you not? I'd really as soon hang the bugger anyway."

Jennifer's eyes showed her agony. She could not make herself speak. Slowly, with deep anguish, she nodded her head.

"Excellent," said the Governor. He grasped her dress and chemise and jerked them down past her hips to her knees. His hands went to her petticoats and pulled them down also to around her knees.

She could not just stand still and take it! It was impossible! When his hands reached for her underdrawers, she lost control and shoved them away. She tried to scratch his face. He grasped her wrist. She swung at him with her other hand, nails bared, and he grasped that, too, then pushed her backward until her buttocks and shoulder blades slammed up against the wall.

"A spirited one, eh?" he said, grinning cruelly, his face almost touching hers. "Fine, fight me if you can. It'll only make your degradation all the sweeter when I finally break you. And break you I will! I'll have you cringing and broken long before your year is through!"

*   *   *

At the mercy of a man she despises, Jennifer makes a supreme sacrifice and becomes a prisoner of lust. It was but the beginning of unspeakable humiliations that she would endure. Her beautiful, voluptuous body would excite many others, driving them to acts of unbridled passion . . . shattering her very innocence . . . igniting fires she would struggle desperately to control . . . reducing her to a hopeless captive of her own unquenchable hungers—until love set her soul free!

380